CALAMITY JENA

INVERTARY BOOK 4

JANET ELIZABETH HENDERSON

In memory of my mum,
who passed away while I was finishing this book.

CHAPTER 1

The New Jersey mob arrived in the Scottish Highlands four months after Jena Morgan. The three men strutted down Invertary high street, looking for something—or someone. Dressed like cast members of *The Sopranos*, the men fit in about as much as a shark would blend at a pool party.

Jena didn't spot them straight away. The famous go-go dancer was too busy haggling with the owner of the local hardware store.

"Please." She wasn't above pleading. Or flirting. She batted her eyelashes at the old man. He laughed. "I'm desperate and I can't afford your quote. It's going to rain and I need to patch the holes in the roof before I end up swimming around the house."

"This is Scotland, Jena, it's always going to rain. Rain does *not* constitute a desperate need." Gordon Stewart folded his arms over grey, paint-splattered overalls and grinned. The sparkle in his eye told her he was eager for her next argument. It was a dance they did every time she came into his store.

Brenda, Gordon's wife, came in from the back of the store

1

sipping a mug of tea. "Stop messing with the girl; give her what she needs. She's got enough on her plate sorting out the wreck she lives in without dealing with your dodgy sense of humour as well."

Brenda winked at Jena, who beamed back. Part of her wished Brenda would adopt her. If she'd had parents like the Stewarts she might have developed the ability to make smart decisions. Instead she'd grown up with a missing father and a mother obsessed with becoming the next Mariah Carey.

"Look," Jena said to Gordon. "We both know I can't afford the full price. What about a payment plan?"

He shook his head, earning an elbow in his ribs from his wife. He grunted at her before stroking his grey beard. It was his thinking pose. Jena crossed her fingers behind her back.

"Fine," he said. "How about you give me what you can afford and then work here two mornings a week to make up the difference?"

Brenda nodded her encouragement.

Jena's jaw dropped. "You can't be serious. I don't know what half this stuff is."

"I know." Gordon laughed so hard he had to wipe tears from his eyes. "It's the funniest thing I've ever seen. I read somewhere that laughing can add years to your life. Having you around will make me immortal."

"Gordon!" Brenda scowled at him. It had no effect.

Jena took a deep breath. "Okay." Like she had a choice. She pointed at him. "But you're delivering the materials for free."

"Done. You start in the morning."

"And you supply lunch."

"Only if you don't eat that rabbit crap."

"I eat anything." She couldn't afford to be fussy. "I'll see you in the morning." She pulled the heavy door open and cool October air made her skin tingle. "You evil old black-mailer," she muttered, and heard him laugh.

Waving at Brenda, Jena stepped out into the high street and was stunned anew at the picturesque quality of her new home. Streets lined with crooked whitewashed buildings, quaint little shops and a cobble-stoned road. All surrounded by emerald-green hills and reflected in a gentle blue loch. She took a deep breath and felt something settle within her. Her whole life she'd wanted a proper home, a place to belong, and she'd finally found it.

And that was when she saw them. The three men who were looking for her.

She almost fell on her backside scrambling to get back into the hardware store. "Going out the back way," she shouted, sounding more than a little hysterical.

She passed the stunned faces of the store owners as she ran straight through the shop and out the back door.

"Oh no, oh no, oh no..." She stumbled her way up the back alley in three-inch neon pink wedges, grateful she'd worn her lowest heels to town.

Her heart almost burst from her chest when she spotted her destination—the ancient grey Presbyterian church. Someone called her name. She didn't turn to see who. Instead, she picked up her pace, flying up the street on legs toned by years of dancing.

"Oh no, oh no, oh no..."

It took all her upper body strength to pull open the heavy church door.

"Coming through," she shouted at the vicar as she ran past him into the ladies' toilet.

"Jena?" His voice carried after her.

She slammed the old wooden door, bolted it and wedged a chair under the handle. Then she sank to the floor, curled her knees to her chest and rested her cheek on them. This was not happening. It was a hallucination brought on by too much DIY and not enough Pop-Tarts.

There was a thump at the door. She squealed before smacking her hands over her mouth.

"Jena, what do you think you're doing? Is this some weird American thing I don't know about?" It was the vicar, sounding grumpy—as usual.

She let out a shaky breath. Her hands fell to her knees.

"I'm claiming asylum," she shouted.

There was a pause. "You're claiming what?" the minister boomed.

Jena pulled her iPod out of her handbag, inserted her earbuds and pumped up the volume. She needed some Taylor Swift. Life was always better with Taylor.

There was more thumping. Jena closed her eyes and pretended that she hadn't seen her ex-boyfriend walking up Invertary high street.

And he definitely wasn't flanked by two goons.

With that thought, she closed her eyes and let Taylor work her magic.

MATT DONALDSON, Invertary's entire police force, was already fed up with his day and he'd only been working for twenty minutes.

After dealing with yet another missing cat report, he'd been called out to the Presbyterian church. He found the ancient vicar blocking the main door, glaring up at three huge strangers. It didn't take a genius to spot that two of the men were muscle-for-hire. Although the fact one of them wore a T-shirt with the word "goon" on it helped clear things up. The third guy was obviously the boss. He looked like he'd walked straight off the set of an American mob movie. His black suit screamed custom made. The black silk shirt beneath it was open at the neck, where it flashed the obligatory gold chain. As Matt approached, Mr Suit grinned unnaturally white teeth and splayed his hands in a conciliatory gesture. The afternoon sun glinted off his pinkie ring.

Matt cocked an eyebrow at the guy, before dismissing him as he turned to the aging vicar. "What's going on?"

"The new American girl has locked herself in the toilet. She's claiming asylum." Reverend Morrison pointed to the men. "These three want to have a word with her. They were chasing her up the street when she barrelled in here."

"Frank Di Marco." The guy in the suit held out his hand. Matt didn't take it. Frank shrugged like it meant nothing. "Jena is my fiancée. We had a disagreement and she moved country. We're reconciling."

Matt didn't buy his harmless buddy routine. "Aye, I can tell by the way she's hiding in the toilet that she's eager to reconcile." He nodded to the goons. "You brought a couple of bodyguards with you to talk to your fiancée?"

Another wide smile, just as fake as the first. "These are friends of mine." He pointed at the guy wearing the goon T-shirt. "That's Joe; the big guy is Grunt."

"Grunt?" Matt looked at the big guy. He grunted. Matt nodded. That answered that.

Joe folded his arms over his joke T-shirt. His eyes betrayed an intelligence that wasn't obvious in his boss.

"So." Matt rubbed his chin. "If this is a misunderstanding, why didn't you visit Jena at her home instead of chasing her into a church? Better yet, why not call her and set up a meeting?" He hardened his eyes. "Preferably somewhere public."

A muscle ticked at the edge of Frank's jaw. "I don't have her number; she changed phones when she moved. Get her to call me, will ya? Tell her I'm real eager to see her." He put on his black sunglasses, even though the day was overcast. "Good meeting you, officer."

Frank nodded to his men, turned and sauntered back down the high street. Matt could have sworn that Joe smothered a grin as he passed.

"What the hell was that?" Matt muttered.

"Although I don't appreciate the language, I'm with you on sentiment. Looks like our newest resident is in it up to her eyeballs."

Matt allowed a small smile. "In what exactly, vicar?"

"Why, manure, boy—thick, smelly manure."

Matt let out a sigh. Jena Morgan was currently number one on the list of reasons he'd compiled for why he needed a proper police job. One far away. In a city where real crime happened. Where he wasn't called out to talk strange American women out of toilets.

"Did you ask her why she's claiming asylum? Maybe tell her that her actions aren't legal? That the church doesn't offer any more protection than she'd find in the pub?"

"Are you comparing the house of God to the local pub, son?"

Matt grinned. "I've heard better sermons in the pub."

The vicar smacked him on the back of the head. Matt rubbed it, but chuckled at the same time. "Have you talked to Jena or not?"

Reverend Morrison threw up his hands in disgust. "I tried. It's impossible. She's singing at the top of her lungs. Something about shaking herself all night long. I can't get through the door. You're going to have to deal with this."

Matt smothered a groan. "Do you have a spare key for the toilet?"

"Son, that door is about a million years old. I didn't even know it locked."

"Brilliant." He pinched the bridge of his nose. "Will it bother you if I kick it in?"

The vicar laughed. "No, but it might bother you when you

break your toes. The door is several inches thick." He beamed with pride. "They don't make them like that anymore."

"Window?" Matt was quickly losing what little patience he had left.

The vicar pointed to the side of the church. "You'll know you have the right one when you hear the toneless wailing."

The vicar was right. It didn't take long to zero in on the right window. He could hear singing, or wailing, coming from inside the room. The window was level with Matt's shoulders and it wasn't locked. He peered into the darkened room, but couldn't see Jena. The ladies' toilet was the old-fashioned type, combining a room for women to wait and fix their makeup with a room for them to do their business. Matt could only see a portion of the waiting room. With a sigh, he heaved himself up and launched his body into the room.

He turned the corner and found Jena sitting on the floor beside the main door. His breath stuttered in his chest, as it usually did when he saw the woman. It was easy to understand why the men of Invertary were falling over themselves to date her. Unfortunately, after about ten minutes in her company, you also realised why none of those first dates led to a second—the woman was chaos personified. He'd never met anyone so easily distracted and accident-prone. She was a one-woman weapon of mass destruction.

But she was stunning. Waist-length honey-brown hair that fell in waves over golden skin. Curves, voluptuous but toned, that made a man itch to touch her. Her lips were the colour of a ripe peach and just as lush. But it was her eyes that undid him. Wide eyes the colour of warm honey. Eyes a man could melt into. He shook himself from the daze she induced.

Matt crouched down in front of Jena and tapped her knee.

Her shriek had him covering his ears.

"Stop that right now!" Matt watched as comprehension dawned in those sinful eyes. It was followed closely by relief.

"Matt." Her shoulders sagged. "I'm sorry, I thought…" She looked around nervously. "You startled me."

"Yeah, I got that from the screaming." Matt stood. "Come on, we need to get out of here." He turned towards the door.

"No." Jena scrambled to her feet. She pulled the earbuds from her ears and stuffed them into her massive canvas bag. "I claimed asylum. I'm staying here. I have water. A toilet. I can order pizza and they'll deliver through the window. I'm all set."

Matt took a deep breath and looked down at her. In her platform shoes, the top of her head made it just past his shoulders. She blinked up at him, wide-eyed and earnest. It took him a minute to figure out who she reminded him of, and then it hit him—the cat from Shrek. He closed his eyes for a second to regroup.

"Number one." Matt held up a finger. "This is Invertary. There is no pizza delivery. Number two. You can't claim asylum. There's no such thing."

"Of course there is. I saw it on TV."

"Those are political asylum seekers. Generally they register with the government, who then reviews their case. They live in houses the councils provide. They don't hole up in church toilets."

She seemed confused. The cutest little lines appeared between her brows. "I didn't see that show. I was talking about the movies. Clint Eastwood. That sort of thing."

He stared at her as his brain rebooted. "You mean cowboy movies. Westerns?"

She smiled widely. "Exactly. But if you need me to register, hand the paperwork through the window and I'll sign it."

For a minute he was tempted to give up on the conversation and leave her in the bathroom. "Jena, those movies aren't real. They're fiction."

"Those movies are based on historical fact. They have to research them and stuff."

"They're also based in America. You're in Scotland. Even if they were real, we don't let you claim asylum in churches over here. Come on, it's time to leave. The Weight Watchers group meet in half an hour and they like to use the toilet before the weigh-in. They won't be happy to find the door locked."

She eyed him suspiciously. "How would you know something like that?"

"I have a mother and two younger sisters. I know everything there is to know about needless weight loss and insane diets. Now, let's get out of here."

She grabbed his arm. "I can't leave. I..." She looked around, maybe hoping that an excuse would present itself. At last her shoulders slumped and she seemed resigned. "There's someone in town looking for me and I need to hide. Or run." A thought occurred to her. Her eyes went wide. "Wait a minute. Are you going to arrest me? Did he send you in here to take me to the big house?" Her brow scrunched. "No, that can't be it. He wouldn't send in the cops." Her face went white. "Those have to be Rizzoni's men he's got with him. There can only be one reason he brought mob lackeys to Scotland." She took a deep breath. "He's going to kill me. I claim asylum."

With a screech, she ran into a toilet stall and locked the door.

. . .

9

JENA SLAMMED the toilet lid down and sat on it. She was going to die. She knew it. Why else would Frank come all the way to Scotland? It wasn't as though he loved to travel. He thought New York was too far to visit, and that was only a two-hour drive from Atlantic City.

"Jena." Matt sounded like he was gritting his teeth.

Jena felt instantly guilty. It wasn't his fault she'd brought all this trouble to town. He was doing the best he could, but a small-town cop in the Scottish Highlands wasn't equipped to deal with the Atlantic City mob.

"Tell me what's going on right now." His commanding tone sent shivers down her spine. Still, she didn't answer.

"Jena? Why did you think I was going to arrest you? Why do you think Frank wants to kill you?"

Jena chewed down on her thumbnail before stopping when she remembered she would never be able to afford another manicure.

Matt sucked in an irritated breath. "I'm ten seconds away from ripping that door off its hinges, dragging you to the station and putting you and Frank Di Marco in a room until someone tells me what's going on."

Nausea assaulted her at his words. At least she was in the right place if she wanted to vomit.

"Jena. Talk. Now. Why do you think your fiancé is going to harm you?"

She sat up straight. "Fiancé? What fiancé?"

He let out an exasperated sigh. "Frank Di Marco."

Jena shot to her feet and pointed at the door. "He is not my fiancé. He's a cheating man-whore, that's what he is. He's never even proposed. Not that I would have accepted. But there has to be a proposal for there to be a fiancé."

"Okay, so he isn't your fiancé. Why would he say he is?"

"Insanity?" She was pretty sure that was the underlying reason for everything Frank did.

"Tell me what's going on or I can't help you." A vision of Officer Donaldson's deep blue eyes looking all earnest and stern flashed in her mind. She wavered.

"Can you have him kicked out of town? Maybe deported?" She tried not to sound too hopeful.

"Possibly. If I know the truth."

Jena bit her bottom lip as she shuffled foot to foot.

"It will be okay." The cop's soothing brogue almost undid her. "Tell me what the problem is. Trust me, Jena."

Jena felt herself cave. She took a shaky breath, grateful she was telling her stupid story from behind a door where she couldn't see the judgment in his eyes. "Frank and I lived together for a while. He cheated on me with a series of strippers. I'm pretty sure they were all called Candy." She couldn't keep the snide tone out of her words, which made her feel ashamed. She was better than that. She was better than Frank Di Marco. "Anyway, when I found out about the strippers, I lost the plot a little. I kicked Frank out of the house, sold everything we owned and used the money to move here."

She took a deep breath while waiting for his reaction.

"Okay, so far I'm not hearing anything that has me worried. I don't see why the man would come all this way to get revenge over you selling his stuff."

She bit her bottom lip. "I also sold his perfectly restored 1966 Chevrolet Chevelle. He loved that car more than anything. Definitely more than me."

There was a pause. "You sold the man's classic car?"

Jena frowned at the door. "Should I have hit it with a baseball bat and set fire to the seats instead?"

"Point made. Carry on."

Jena rolled her eyes. Men and their cars. "That's all there is to tell. Once everything was gone, I surfed the net looking for a new place to live. I remembered my mom talking about Invertary—she's a huge Josh McInnes fan and gives me updates on what he's doing. Next thing I knew, I was looking at the town website. Then the town's real estate site. After drowning my sorrow in a bottle of tequila, I bought a house." She paused. "And here I am."

There was silence for a minute. If it wasn't for the sound of his breathing, she would have thought he'd left her.

"Let me get this right. You sold everything the guy owned, without his knowledge, and bought a house in Scotland with the proceeds?"

She felt her cheeks burn. "I had a holiday in Paris too. But bear in mind that he isn't really a guy. He's a scum-sucking man-whore."

For a moment she heard nothing, and then deep laughter echoed throughout the room.

"Remind me never to piss you off," the cop said between gasps.

Jena frowned at the closed door, wondering what the correct response was to that statement.

"Am I going to be arrested for selling his stuff?" It had been worrying her.

"You didn't do it in Scotland, Jena."

"Will they extradite me?"

The cop started laughing again. "I only talked to Frank for a couple of minutes, but I figure the cops in Atlantic City will give you a standing ovation rather than charge you with theft. I don't know much about American law, but in Scotland if you live with someone for a couple of years you're considered to be in a common-law marriage and your property is shared. Over here the stuff you sold would have legally belonged to you too."

"I did put a lot of money into our relationship. I kept us afloat for years while Frank tried to make it big."

"Well, there you go, then. Can you come out of the toilet now?"

"I can't leave here, Matt. Frank must be here for revenge. He'll want his money back. Along with his car. And I don't have either."

"Come out of the toilet, Jena. I'll deal with Frank."

She cracked the door open and peered up at him. Instead of the usual disapproval, his eyes were sparkling with amusement. It wasn't an improvement.

"Let's get you home," he said.

She shook her head. "He has to know where I live. I can't go back there."

"Are you afraid he'll hurt you?" His features turned to stone. "Has he ever hurt you?"

"No." He didn't look convinced. "No, he's never lifted his hand to me."

"Then why are you afraid? Why not just talk to the man?"

"Didn't you hear me in there?" She gestured to the toilet stall where she'd spilled her guts to him. "He's here with Vince Rizzoni's boys."

Matt held up his hands in exasperation. "So?"

"They're the mob. Frank got into bed with the guy about a year ago—along with every other skanky woman in stilettos on the East Coast."

His huge hands clasped her shoulders. "Focus, Jena."

For a few seconds she was too mesmerised by his perfectly squared jaw and deep-set eyes to focus on anything other than the man in front of her.

"You were telling me about Frank and the mob," he prompted.

Jena felt herself blush. "Yeah, he started hanging with Vince's men. He changed. Became harder, more cagey. He kept secrets, other than the women. I didn't like the men who started to visit. Some of them scared me."

"Those guys here today, were they the ones visiting?"

She shook her head. "Other guys. Rougher. I felt like I

didn't know Frank anymore. I was worried and he wouldn't listen to me. He'd get angry. Real angry. I would like to think he isn't capable of harming me, but he changed, and I don't know for sure what he's capable of now."

Matt let out a heavy sigh. "Okay. There's no need to worry. You aren't in America anymore. The mob doesn't have a lot of pull here. I'll deal with Frank and find out what he wants."

"I think it's best if I stay here until you have a chat with him."

"You can't hide in here."

Jena disagreed. She wasn't proud. She could definitely hide. Hiding was exactly what she needed to do. She took a step back into the toilet stall and slammed the door shut.

"Thank you for helping me. I really appreciate it, and I hate being rude like this, but I think it's best if I stay here until you sort out Frank."

"Jena." Matt's tone was a threat.

Jena swallowed hard as she put her earbuds back in place. She'd do something nice for the cop later as a thank you. Something that didn't involve money, as she had none. She'd bake him cookies but she couldn't cook. Maybe she'd teach him to dance? Everybody could use some dancing skills. Yeah, that was a great idea.

She sat on the toilet lid, tuned out Matt's shouting and let Taylor Swift's voice calm her racing heart.

CHAPTER 2

After informing a disgruntled vicar that he had a temporary resident in the ladies' loo, Matt headed down the high street towards the town's only pub and hotel. If the wannabe Sopranos weren't staying there, he'd eat his hat.

"Hey," Josh McInnes called as Matt entered the restaurant area. "We thought you weren't going to make it. We already ordered."

"I'm not here for breakfast, guys. I'm dealing with another Jena Morgan mess."

The men grinned.

"Who did she date this time? Is the poor guy still alive?" Josh said. "Dougal, get the board. Jena's at it again."

There was a murmur of delight amongst the breakfast crowd as a grinning Dougal flipped the smaller of the two chalk menu boards over. The pub owner rubbed out the name of the last guy Jena dated and poised ready with his chalk for the next.

"Who's the latest victim?" he said.

"I don't care who it is," one of the old guys at the bar said.

"I'll take ten to one on a concussion. We haven't had one of those for a while. We're about due."

"Concussion it is." Dougal marked the board.

Matt took off his hat, ran his fingers through his hair and frowned. "You do realise you're running an illegal betting pool right in front of a cop?"

Dougal grinned, making him look even more like Father Christmas than usual. "You'll be wanting to place your usual bet on a broken leg, then?"

"Not this time." Matt let out a sigh. "This latest mess isn't about her love life. I'm looking for some American guys. They're in town asking after Jena. She ran away from them and claimed sanctuary in the church."

There was a disbelieving pause before the room was filled with laughter. Dougal flipped the board back over after promising the old guy he could still bet on the next of Jena's victims getting concussion.

"You look stressed. Tell Uncle Joshy all about it." Josh patted the empty bench beside him. "You might as well eat now you're here."

Matt shrugged. Jena wasn't going anywhere. In fact, she didn't want to go anywhere. Suddenly, he didn't feel such an urgent need to sort out her latest mess. He plopped into the seat beside Josh.

"For the record," he told the American singer, "that whole Uncle Joshy thing is seriously creepy."

"Told you." Mitch pointed at his friend.

Lake Benson, the retired English soldier, poured a mug of coffee and handed it to Matt. That was what Matt appreciated most about Lake—he was a man of action, not chit-chat.

"So, what's the story?" Josh was bouncing around on the seat beside him, reminding Matt of an overgrown puppy. A really annoying puppy. "Is Jena on the run from the law? She killed someone she was dating in the States, didn't she? But then, that would only be manslaughter. Do they extradite for manslaughter?"

The men gaped at the hyper singer for a minute before Mitch confiscated Josh's coffee mug. "That's it. We're cutting off your caffeine."

"Hey, not fair. I'm sleep deprived."

Mitch rolled his eyes. "Last I heard it was Caroline getting up through the night to deal with the baby, not you."

"Yeah, but she disturbs my sleep when she gets up."

Lake laughed. "I'm telling her you said that."

Josh grimaced. "Don't even think about it. What happens in the breakfast club stays in the breakfast club."

They all groaned.

"We keep telling you," Mitch said, "this isn't a club. It's food."

"It could be a club. I got us matching T-shirts. If we all wear the shirts it will feel more like a club."

"You can wear your T-shirt if you want. We can't stop you. But we aren't a club."

"We could be." Josh stroked his hand down the front of his vintage *Breakfast Club* T-shirt. "This is a great shirt. It was a great movie. Iconic."

The men ignored him.

"There they are." Matt pointed to the Americans coming through the door that led to the upstairs hotel.

Before he could get up and approach the men, Mr Suit spotted the group. He grinned widely and headed straight for them.

Frank Di Marco stopped in front of their booth, flanked by his bodyguards. "If it isn't Atlantic City's favourite crooner. How you doing, Josh?"

"Good, Frank, good." Josh and Mitch both stood to shake hands with Frank.

"It's been what?" Frank spread his hands. "Twenty years? You were just a kid, working the clubs."

"If I remember rightly"—Mitch sat back down with a grin —"you were working the clubs too."

Frank laughed. "True. Too true." He shrugged. "Talents lie in different areas, eh, boys? You did what you were good at and I did what I was good at. Such is life. And here we are, in our prime, men of influence."

"I don't know about that," Josh mumbled.

"Did you move up in the world, Frank?" Mitch arched an eyebrow at the man.

Frank shrugged. Matt assumed it was supposed to look humble. It just looked fake.

"Got myself a club. Remember Legs? Acquired it a year ago. I'm turning it around. Also got myself a partner. You mighta heard of him." He paused for effect. "Vince Rizzoni."

Mitch let out a low whistle. "I hope you know what you're doing, man."

"I told you when we were kids," Frank said, "we were destined for greatness. Now look at you two—Josh here is setting underwear on fire all over the globe and you're watching his back, making sure that talent of his earns the money and respect it deserves. Now I have someone watching my back too. It's taken a lot of work, but now I have the capital and the backing I need to implement my plans. Legs is just the beginning. I'm aiming for world domination, boys."

Matt watched as Joe, the guy wearing the goon T-shirt, turned a laugh into a cough.

"Tell me, officer," Frank said. "Did you manage to get Jena out of the church? We have a lot of catching up to do."

Matt studied the guy before speaking. "No. She's still in there. She doesn't want to talk to you. Or see you. She's wondering why you're calling her your fiancée. I'm kind of wondering the same thing."

Frank chuckled, like the whole conversation was deeply amusing. "What can I tell you? We lived together for four years. She's been here a while; you know what she's like. Kooky. Isn't that right, Grunt?"

Grunt grunted. Helpful guy.

Matt felt his jaw clench. "She's worried you might be here for payback."

Another fake laugh. Matt was getting seriously sick of Frank's we're-all-guys-together routine.

"Now why would she think that?"

"Maybe because she cleared out your house, sold everything that wasn't nailed down and when she was done there found a buyer for your car."

Frank wasn't smiling now. Matt stood. Pleased to see he had a couple of inches on the guy. "A 1966 Chevelle, wasn't it? Perfectly restored, I hear."

Josh let out a low whistle.

"Ouch," Mitch said with a wince.

Frank's fists clenched. "A misunderstanding. That's all, officer. This is a domestic issue. Nothing for you to concern yourself with." He tugged at his cuffs, flashing gold cufflinks that would have cost Matt more than a month's salary. "I'm here to take Jena home. She belongs to me."

"Don't you mean *with* you?"

Frank shrugged. "Tomato, tomahto—isn't that how the song goes? Jena and me, we got history. She's the girl for me and I'm taking her home. Where she belongs."

"I think it's best if you leave Jena alone. You two have nothing to talk about. Your relationship is over. The fact she moved country without telling you should have clued you in." Matt took a step towards Frank, invading his space.

"There's nothing for you here. I suggest, strongly, that you go home."

Frank's eyes hardened. "It's a free world. No law against me visiting with my woman. No law against me persuading her to come home with me. No law against seeing the sights while we're here. Last time I checked, this town welcomed tourists." His smile was cold. "I'll be seeing you around, officer."

Matt clenched his teeth as he watched him go. Apart from warning him off, there was nothing he could do. Once the door closed on the men, he sat back down and glared at Mitch and Josh.

"Talk," he ordered.

A plate loaded with a cooked breakfast appeared in front of him. The smell of sausages, black pudding, baked beans and potato scones made Matt's mouth water. There were even locally grown mushrooms and home-baked soda bread. It was heart attack heaven. Dougal, the pub owner and the town's unofficial mayor, clasped his shoulder. "Thought you could use that, son."

Matt half expected the man to hang around and insinuate himself into the conversation, but he left as quickly as he'd arrived. Matt suspected it was the murderous look he knew was in his eyes that deterred Dougal.

Josh and Mitch shared a look. Matt read it loud and clear: trepidation.

"Looks like Frank got what he wanted," Josh said.

Mitch rubbed his chin. "No kidding, if he's in bed with Rizzoni, he's on his way to being a made man."

Matt held up his hand. "Explain. From the beginning."

Mitch sighed. "We were teenagers when we knew Frank Di Marco. He was a hustler back then. A guy trying to make a buck and a name for himself. He talked big, but was harmless. He was decent enough, funny, entertaining. He had a code. You could trust him."

"That doesn't sound like the guy we just had a chat with," Matt said.

"No." Mitch glanced towards the door Frank had disappeared through. "He's changed. He's managed to get into bed with the big boys." He looked back at Matt. "Vince Rizzoni is well connected; he's high up in the Rizzoni family. We're talking Jersey mob. I don't know where Vince sits in the structure of things; we're out of touch. But he's definitely mob."

Matt felt a throbbing start in his temple. "What's this club he's talking about?"

"Legs? It's a strip club. Used to be *the* strip club. Sounds like Frank's got plans to take it to the top again."

Matt relaxed slightly and forked some baked beans into his mouth. It took a lot more stress than this current fiasco to ruin his appetite. "So, he's not mob, only connected to the mob. American mob, which is far, far away." He looked at Mitch. "I don't have to worry about him, then?"

Mitch was grim. He shook his head. "No, it means you have to worry more. Sounds like he's trying to impress the Rizzonis to get in deep with them. It doesn't look good if his woman ran out on him."

"Especially if she cleaned him out beforehand," Josh added.

Mitch nodded. "Something like that will make a man lose face. Trust me. If you want to impress the mob, you sort that crap out pretty damn quick. I saw this a lot when I was studying law. Mob guys up on charges over something that started out as a loss of respect and ended with violence, and bodies with cement shoes."

Everything within Matt stilled. "Is Jena in danger?"

"I honestly don't know," Mitch said. "With the Frank I

used to know I'd say no, but that Frank didn't make deals with the mob. I don't know what this Frank is capable of."

Matt didn't like that answer one bit.

"I wouldn't trust him," Josh said. "His image has taken a hit. For a guy like that, image is everything. A good image promotes respect. I would guess that's why he hooked Jena— she's gorgeous. That kind of woman gives a man status. It's also probably why he's pissed about his car as well. A pristine Chevelle is nothing to sneeze at. They sell for what? A hundred grand?" He looked at Mitch, who nodded.

"They can go for that much, but around about the fifty-k mark is more common."

Matt buttered his toast. "Why the hell would Jena hook up with a guy like that?" He wasn't sure why any woman would date Frank.

Josh shrugged. "Money? Lifestyle?"

No. No way. Matt shook his head. "Does she strike you as the gold-digging type? She's out there fixing a house that's beyond repair. Doing it all by herself. If she was into money and lifestyle, she'd have hit on a wealthy single guy or cosied up to someone willing to do the work for her."

"You're forgetting about the dates—she's had a lot of them since coming to town." Josh pointed his fork at Matt. "Men are falling over themselves to get at her. Maybe she's looking for a sugar daddy."

Lake laughed. He'd been so quiet that Matt almost forgot he was there. "If she was looking for a sugar daddy she wouldn't have gone out with half those guys. She went fishing with George the mailman last week. He isn't exactly rolling in it."

Matt sighed heavily. "I don't like this." He went to eat his black pudding, and his plate was empty. What the hell? Did he eat it without noticing? He looked up and found Josh trying to appear innocent.

"I'm telling Caroline," Matt told him. "Didn't she put you on a diet? I remember her lecture on how you need to be fit for your new tour. She won't be pleased you're eating a fat-filled Scottish breakfast. And she definitely won't be impressed that yours wasn't enough for you and you had to steal mine."

"Have a heart, man. That's plain evil." Josh paled, and the men laughed.

Matt pulled out his phone and dialled his computer genius cousin, Harry. "Can you run a background check for me?"

"Sure thing. Let me get a pen. Who's the lucky victim whose privacy gets invaded this time?"

"Three guys, new in town. Joe something. Grunt, that's a nickname, I don't have a real name for him. And Frank Di Marco."

There was a pause. "Tell me you mean 'something' is Joe's last name, otherwise this is a needle in a haystack scenario. I mean, seriously, Joe? It's right up there with John Smith. And you want me to run a search on somebody called Grunt? Are you running a fever? Do I need to call your mum and get her to check on you?"

"I thought you were the genius? You have computer superpowers. Nothing is too hard for you. Isn't that what you keep telling me? That you're king of the cyber world?"

Josh and Mitch laughed, while Lake's top lip twitched.

"You're an annoying pain in my backside, you know that, right?" Harry said in resignation. "Do you know anything else? Or is this all I'm getting?"

"They all come from Atlantic City. They have mob connections. And Frank was Jena Morgan's boyfriend. Emphasis on was. He owns a club called Legs."

Harry let out a heavy sigh. "You owe me for this."

"I'll offer my services to check under your bed for rats. I

know you still have nightmares about them. Don't worry. Your big cousin will protect you and we'll call it even." Matt grinned as he hung up on Harry's blustering threats. He sobered as he turned to Lake. "I know your security business is busy right now, but we need to keep an eye on Jena. Can you spare anyone?" He winced. "There's no money in it."

"I'll cover the costs," Mitch and Josh said at the same time. They laughed and high-fived each other.

Josh saw Matt's querying look. "Caroline would kill me if I didn't help out."

"Damsel in distress," Mitch said by way of an explanation.

Matt looked at Lake. "So we're good?"

Lake nodded. "We'll work out a rota. I've got a couple of guys I can spare until we know what's going on, but they won't be free before the weekend. You okay to pitch in?"

"Aye," Matt said. "I probably should, seeing as this is my idea."

Lake's lip twitched in an approximation of a smile, and he cocked an eyebrow at Matt. "Still planning on leaving town for a more exciting job in the city?"

Matt made his thoughts on that comment clear with a gesture.

The men laughed and Mitch signalled for more coffee.

JENA WAS BORED. For some reason she thought claiming sanctuary would be more exciting than the reality. Since she was no longer sitting in the main restroom area, but locked in one of the toilet cubicles, the Weight Watchers group were able to use the toilets. For a while she was kept busy answering questions as to why she'd moved into the ladies' loo, then the meeting started and she was alone again. Alone and hungry. Yet the thought of snacking while sitting in a toilet cubicle was less than appealing.

"Aunty Jena? Are you doing a poopy?"

Jena grinned widely at the sound of her young neighbour. "No, honey."

"Good, they're stinky and I don't want to come in if it's stinky."

The next thing Jena knew, a brunette head appeared under the door and a little body shimmied in. The four-year-old was dressed head to toe in pink, with a headband that looked like Minnie Mouse ears. Without blinking, she climbed up on Jena's lap and kissed her cheek. Jena's heart melted, as it usually did any time she was around Katy.

"Muma says you're stuck in here. Why don't you go under the door?"

Jena hugged her close. "I'm a little bigger than you, honey. I can't fit under the door. But I'm not stuck. I'm hiding."

The little girl frowned. "This isn't a very good spot, Aunty Jena, I found you really fast."

"Good point." Jena snuggled her. "Where's your mum?"

"Right here, you dingbat. What crazy mess are you mixed up in now?"

At the sound of her friend Abby's voice, Jena felt her eyes tear up. Stupid. She blinked them away. She was so grateful for her neighbour. They'd hit it off the minute Jena had arrived in town. Abby was the sister Jena had always wanted.

"If you lock the main door, I'll come out and tell you," Jena said.

"Already done."

Jena put Katy on her feet and unlocked the door. Katy held her hand tightly.

"Look, muma, I found her."

Abby's face melted as she smiled at her daughter. "Yes, you did. You're super clever. Now let's go next door and eat." She held up a large bag and shook it at Jena. "Figured you'd be hungry by now."

"You're a saint." Jena hugged her friend.

"Yeah, so I hear. Come on, let's go have a picnic in the waiting area."

"Picnic!" Katy rushed off into the other room.

The women followed, although with a lot less enthusiasm. Abby reached into her bag and produced a red tartan shawl. She spread it flat on the floor before emptying the contents of the bag onto it. It mainly contained pies and cakes from Morag's bakery.

Abby winced as she looked at the spread. "We'll have to live on vegetables for the rest of the week to make up for the lack of vitamins in this meal."

Jena grinned at her before reaching for a meat pie and a can of Pepsi. She plonked into one of the old armchairs and sighed with contentment. Food made all things better. Just like Taylor.

"Are you going to tell me what's going on?" Abby made sitting in a church restroom look elegant.

Her friend's ability to ooze class and refinement no matter the situation made Jena smile. She cast a glance at Katy to make sure she was occupied before she spoke. Katy had emptied her Minnie Mouse handbag of soft toys. The Disney characters were arranged in a semicircle and were "eating" some of Morag's cake. With a deep breath, Jena turned to her friend.

"Frank is in town and he brought a couple of the Rizzoni boys with him."

Abby stopped eating, the pie halfway to her mouth. "You need to stay with us until he leaves."

Jena's heart melted. She reached over and gave Abby's hand a squeeze. "I can't, honey. You have the kiddo to think about. It's best if I keep away from you two. It's safer."

"I don't like this. Not one bit. You don't owe that guy anything."

"I did sell everything he owns and ran with the money," Jena pointed out.

Abby's eyes lit with fire. "You spent years helping to fund every cockamamie scheme that man came up with. You bailed him out of trouble time and again. He owes you."

Jena actually managed a laugh. She grabbed her friend's hand. "See? This is why I love you."

Abby squeezed her back. "I don't understand why he's here. Surely he's figured out by now that you've spent the money. He can't think you're going to return with him. That's insane."

"Frank isn't known for his sharp mind. I should probably talk to him and find out what he wants, but I don't like arguments. I have a tendency to cave when people shout at me. I think I'd rather stay here in the toilet until he goes back to the States. I mean, he can't hang out in Scotland forever."

Abby's lips pursed and her eyes hardened with determination. "You can't stay here. You'll be all alone in a big building. There are too many ways to get into this place. It's easy access. It isn't safe."

"I couldn't agree more," a deep voice said from the window.

The women's heads snapped in the direction of the words. Jena's heart calmed slightly when she found Matt staring in at her. As they watched, the local cop pulled himself up and effortlessly climbed into the room. Jena felt a little bit of drool escape at the sight of all that flexing muscle. She wiped her lip and hoped no one noticed.

"Mattie!" Katy launched herself at the cop, wrapping her arms around his legs. He chuckled, picking her up to give her a cuddle.

Jena felt a pang of envy that she wasn't the one in Matt's arms. It made her question her sanity. Obviously she was feeling insecure and needed a hug. Any strong arms would do. It wasn't just because it was the grumpy control-freak cop who was doing the cuddling.

Matt put Katy back on the floor and ruffled her hair, making her scowl at him. He nabbed a meat pie. "I spoke to Frank," he said between mouthfuls. "I don't like this situation. He won't tell me why he's here and I don't trust him. I don't think it's a good idea for you to be alone while these guys are in town."

Jena chewed her bottom lip. She couldn't stay with Abby, not with Katy around. If anything happened to that baby, Jena would curl up and will herself to die. She couldn't stay at the pub—even if she could afford it, Frank was probably staying there. She didn't know anyone else well enough to impose on them. And even if she did, she wouldn't want to for fear it would put them in danger. She was out of options. It was the church or nothing. At least the church was in the centre of town, surrounded by people. Her house was on the outskirts by the hills—no one ever came there, not unless they meant to. No. The church was her best option. She looked up at the cop.

"I'm staying here. I can't go home alone."

His smile unnerved her. "Who said anything about going home alone? Say hello to your new roommate, princess." He gave her a finger wave.

Jena's jaw dropped as Abby choked on her soda.

CHAPTER 3

For some reason, Matt thought being in Jena's house would be more comfortable than bunking down in the church. He was wrong. As he looked around her kitchen, he felt the hairs on his arms stand in protest. Even a night on the vicar's old couch was better than this.

"We can't stay here." Just standing in the house was giving him hives. He'd never be able to sleep in it.

"Sure we can." Jena threw her huge bag on the rickety old dining table, making it wobble. "I stay here every day."

"In this?" Matt looked around in disgust.

Jena's cheeks flushed slightly. "It's a work in progress."

"Is that what you call it?" Matt would call it a disaster zone. Then he'd cordon off the area and call in a demolition crew.

The state of the overgrown garden—complete with the burned out shell of a car—should have been a hint at the horrors to be found inside the house. Unfortunately, Matt missed the hint. And now he was standing in the aftermath of a war zone. Wallpaper, turned brown with age, peeled from the walls. Cracked linoleum curled up under his feet.

Cabinet doors were missing. The counter was chipped and warped, making it look more like a rollercoaster track than a place where you prepared food. The ancient electric cooker had lost the oven door. Three mismatched metal bistro chairs sat beside the table, and two of the seats had been mended with duct tape. A pane of glass in the window was covered with card. The fridge was about a million years old, the white stained yellow with age, and it made the same noise as an airplane engine.

Matt shook his head in wonder. "You've been living here?"

Jena opened the fridge. It took two hands and a hefty yank. "Where else would I live? This is my house. I bought it."

Matt noticed that every surface, no matter what state it was in, was scrubbed clean. There wasn't a cobweb or a smidgen of dust anywhere. The knowledge that she'd cleaned the place made him relax—slightly. "Even after you saw a picture of this?" He motioned around the room.

Instead of handing him a can of Coke, Jena slammed it into his stomach. Her face an irritated scowl. "They didn't post photos of this room on the real estate site. And the exterior photos they did post turned out to be years old. I talked to a lawyer about suing, but the sellers had covered their asses in the fine print and I don't have the money to fight the case."

"I can see how you'd need every penny you have to fix this place." He popped the can and took a long drink. It was icy cold. At least the fridge worked. He eyed it suspiciously. If it wasn't so solid, it could possibly fly too. "Why don't you pay someone to renovate for you?"

She let out an exasperated sigh. "Because, Einstein, I don't have the money to pay someone. I didn't know the house needed this much work, so I went on holiday on my way to

Scotland. If I'd known what I was coming to, I'd have skipped Paris."

She motioned at a chair for him to sit. Matt tested its strength before trusting it with his weight. Jena rolled her eyes at him.

"Do you think I'd give you a chair you couldn't sit on?"

"Hey." He held up his hands. "Men have a tendency to get injured around you. Better safe than sorry."

She pursed her pretty lips before turning her attention to the cupboards behind her. "Are you hungry? Have you had dinner? Do you like Pop-Tarts?"

"What's a Pop-Tart?"

She beamed at him, back to being perky and bubbly. "Only the best snack food in the universe. You're in for a treat."

It was amazing to watch her sunny personality bounce back into place. An evil part of him wondered what it would take to keep Jena in a bad mood for any length of time. Then he remembered Frank and decided all it took was cheating on her. For some reason he had a sudden urge to break the man's nose.

IF JENA HAD to pick a movie role for the hunky cop sitting in her kitchen, it would be Wolverine—without all the hair and the claws. He definitely had the same bulk as Wolverine and, unfortunately, the same surly, sarcastic attitude.

"Okay, so I have strawberry, chocolate and s'mores Pop-Tarts. What do you want?" Matt looked at her blankly. "Chocolate it is." She tried to keep her voice light and cheery. Normally it didn't take this much effort.

She opened one of the last few boxes of Pop-Tarts she'd had shipped from the States and put four in the toaster. While they were heating, she grabbed another couple of cans of Coke from the fridge. A minute later, the little pockets of sugary goodness were sitting on plates in front of them. Jena grinned with delight as she pulled her chair closer to the table.

Matt stared at the food. He poked it with a fingertip. Suspicion oozed from him when he turned to her. "What is this?"

"Dinner." She lifted one of the brown rectangles. "Be careful, the filling is hot." She took a bite from the corner. Her eyes shut in delight. Delicious.

When she looked back at him, Matt was holding a Pop-Tart in front of his nose. He sniffed. "Are you sure this is food?"

"Take a bite, you big coward. It won't hurt you."

He frowned at her before biting into the tart. It was as though she'd asked him chow down on live worms.

"Good, right?" She reached for the second tart.

He chewed laboriously, swallowed hard, reached for his can of Coke and gulped until it was empty.

"That"—he pointed at the tart—"is the most foul thing I've had in my mouth since my cousin Flynn dared me to eat mud when I was a kid." He gave her a look of utter horror. "It's like sugar-coated cardboard." He pushed the plate away. "It doesn't taste anything like chocolate. I'm not sure it even qualifies as food."

Several thoughts fought for prominence in Jena's head. One—he'd dissed her all-time favourite food. Two—he was being rude in her home. Three—she'd tried Scottish food, and he had a damn cheek calling Pop-Tarts cardboard. Four —she'd just wasted two of them on the jerk. She felt her fragile grasp on a good mood snap. She pointed a finger at him.

"That criticism is hard to take when it's coming from a guy

whose country thinks deep-fried Mars bars are a gourmet treat. The same country that gave us haggis-flavoured chips. The people who claim that blood-soaked oats fried in fat is breakfast. You wouldn't know decent food if it bit you on the ass. Give me that." She reached for his rejected Pop-Tart and took a bite out of it. "Mm, mm, delicious."

"There's nothing wrong with haggis or black pudding."

She shuddered before cramming her mouth with more rejected tart.

"Mature." His censure was ruined by his grin. "Do you have any proper food in here?"

She waved at the fridge. "Be my guest. Make yourself some proper food." She had no idea what constituted proper food for the surly Scot, but she was pretty sure she didn't have it. Since money was tight, she'd been living on Pop-Tarts, and the mushrooms and eggs Abby gave her.

He opened the fridge, peered inside then turned to her in disgust. "One egg and a handful of mushrooms?" He stretched up to his full height, which had to be way past six foot, because, at five foot four, Jena felt dwarfed in his presence.

He folded his arms over his black T-shirt, making his muscles bulge, and for the first time in memory, Jena was distracted from her Pop-Tarts. Her mouth watered. There was actually something out there that was more enticing than a warm chocolate tart.

"What do you normally eat?" he demanded, breaking the spell his muscles had cast on her.

Jena pointed to the empty plate in front of her, while wondering if there was an IQ test to become a cop. Had he passed?

"I don't understand how you manage to look the way you do," he said. "The problems must be hidden under the skin.

You're probably a walking time bomb for diabetes and heart disease."

"Well, thanks for that cheery thought." She stuffed the last of the Pop-Tart into her mouth.

"While I'm here, I'll take care of the food. There's no way I'm living on those." He pointed at the empty plate in disgust.

"Nobody put a gun to your head and forced you to eat it."

Matt frowned, reached into the back of his jeans and came out with his phone. Still glaring at Jena, he dialled.

"Dougal, can you find someone to bring a couple of meals to Jena's place?" A pause. "That would be great. There's nothing to eat here." Another pause. "Oh, you heard. Yeah, we'll be needing breakfast as well. I'll go shopping tomorrow and stock up. Thanks Dougal." With a swipe of his thumb, he ended the call.

Jena noted that he didn't even identify himself or say goodbye. Typical macho-man phone etiquette. Emily Post would turn in her grave.

CHAPTER 4

Matt hated being idle, so he killed time waiting for food to arrive by stripping paper off the kitchen wall. Jena had disappeared into her bedroom to do who knew what, and Matt was stuck in the kitchen alone. He hadn't seen the rest of the house and was too afraid to look. Who knew what he'd discover? Plus he wanted to put off finding out where he'd be sleeping. He feared he'd find a bare mattress in a room with holes in the walls. Memories of policing derelict houses full of druggies in Glasgow filled his mind. He never thought he'd be sleeping in the same conditions.

He didn't know how Jena lived in this mess. Part of him wanted to pick her up and carry her off to his house. He might live in the ugliest house in Invertary, but at least it was in one piece.

"What do you think you're doing?"

Matt turned to find Jena behind him, hands on hips, tapping the toe of her ridiculous shoe on the old linoleum. "I'm sorry, did you want to keep this on the walls?" He couldn't have stopped the sarcasm even if he'd tried—which he didn't.

She speared him with a cute little glare. "No, but this isn't the room I'm working on next. You're messing with my plan. This room isn't a priority."

Matt felt his brain go momentarily fuzzy. "How can the kitchen not be a priority? You cook here. You spend most of your time in here. You store your food here. It should have been the first room you worked on."

"I don't need the kitchen. I toast Pop-Tarts or bake an egg. I don't live in here. I live in my bedroom. Or now that the living room's finished, I spend time in there."

"You did your bedroom first. That's insane. Everybody knows you renovate the kitchen and bathroom first."

She stomped over to him and poked his chest. "Excuse me, but last time I checked this wasn't your house. I can start wherever I like. And I wanted a bedroom I could sleep in."

"Women." He threw up his hands in disgust.

"You did not just say that." Jena's jaw dropped in horror.

"Trust me," Matt said before turning back to stripping the wall, "I have two sisters. I know all about the fickle workings of the female mind."

"Are you for real?" As she opened her mouth, to no doubt berate him, there was banging at the front door.

"Food. Great." Matt strode past her and down the hall to the front door. As soon as he opened it, he regretted it. "Oh, hell no."

"Hey, Don Don. Where's your girlfriend? We want to meet her." His younger sister Claire thrust a bag full of hot food at him before pushing past into the house.

"Does Mum know you're shacking up with someone?" Megan, Claire's twin, asked as she followed her sister.

"Get out," Matt ordered them. "Couldn't Dougal find anyone else to deliver the food?"

They gave him identical grins, each equally wicked. "We volunteered. Where is she?"

"What were you doing in the pub anyway?" He stomped down the hall after them.

They turned to him in unison. "We're twenty-two, Don Don, not kids anymore. Don't you just hate it?"

Aye, he bloody well did. He growled at them and they laughed.

Jena chose that moment to appear in the kitchen door-way. She was obviously still fuming. Her eyes went wide when she spotted his sisters. Most people had the same reaction. They were tall, blonde and beautiful. Unfortunately they were also evil. When they were six, they'd declared that their mission in life was to drive him mad. So far they were right on target.

"You must be Jena." Claire held out her hand. Jena took it, looking a little bewildered. "We've seen you around now and then, but haven't managed to say hello. Sorry about that. I'm Claire, Matt's sister. That's Megan. We came to rescue you. We figured that seeing you'd been alone with Don Don for an hour now, you'd probably need rescuing. Am I right? I am. I know. You don't need to confirm it."

Jena looked a little stunned before laughing loudly. The sound did strange things to Matt's stomach, which he immediately attributed to hunger. With a grumble, he barrelled past the women and into the kitchen.

"Jena, come eat. You can't live on cardboard."

"Oh my sainted aunt, what crawled up his bum?" he heard Megan say.

"I think it was a Pop-Tart," Jena said, and the three women laughed.

With a frown, Matt dug out the meal Dougal had sent over. Beef, gravy, mashed potatoes and baby veg. Nothing fancy, but beautifully cooked and no doubt delicious. The chef at The Scottie Dog knew what he was doing. Matt had checked him out the minute he'd arrived in town. It took a lot to impress Matt where food was concerned. He took his stomach very seriously, and the guy at the pub could be trusted.

"Jena," he shouted. "The food is getting cold."

He heard more laughter and knew his sisters were filling Jena's head with rubbish. It was their gift. One of them. Along with driving him insane, getting into trouble and attracting unsuitable men.

The moment the three women walked into the room, Matt knew Jena had sided with the twins. It was to be expected. Women always stuck together.

He dished out food for Jena and pointed at the table. He was actually surprised when she did as she was told. Matt sat at his spot and dug in. Experience told him that the best reaction to his sisters' interference was to ignore it. Sometimes it even worked.

"What's the story with you and Don Don?" Claire asked with an evil glint in her eye.

"Why do you call him Don Don?" Jena at least was eating. For some reason, Matt felt relieved that she was getting some decent food in her. A person could not live on sugar-coated card.

Claire gave him a mischievous smile. "Didn't big brother tell you?"

Matt knew better than to rise to the bait.

"It's his name," Megan said. "Donald Matthew Donaldson. Don Don."

Jena started to laugh and covered her mouth with her hand. Her look was pure pity. "Oh, you poor soul. Your parents must have hated you."

He frowned. "It's a family name."

"We called him ding don when we were kids. He didn't like it," Claire said helpfully.

"He didn't like being called ding-a-ling either, but we thought it was hilarious," Megan added.

From their laughter, they still thought it was pretty funny.

Claire wiped her eyes. "You were going to tell us how long you've been dating Matt. We didn't even know he was seeing someone, let alone living with them." She looked around. "I don't know how he can stay here without having a breakdown."

"Yep, this place is his worst nightmare," Megan added. "He's totally OCD. The mess must be driving him nuts."

"Sitting right here," Matt reminded them, but was ignored.

"He must like you a *lot*," Claire said. "So spill. Details."

Jena seemed caught between amusement and fear. He saw that look a lot where his sisters were concerned. She opened her mouth to answer, but Matt decided to save her before she got in deeper with his crazy siblings.

"She's not a girlfriend. She's work."

The women gasped. "That's a horrible thing to say." Claire smacked him on the back of the head.

He rubbed the spot. "I mean I'm here to protect her. I'm not dating her. I'm her bodyguard."

"Is that what you kids are calling it these days?" Megan waggled her eyebrows at him.

Matt pointed his knife at her. "Knock it off."

Her eyes narrowed. "Or what? You'll lock us up again? Been there, done that. Your threats don't impress."

Jena's eyes went wide. "Your brother locked you up?"

"They deserved it," Matt said.

"It was terrible." Megan laid it on a bit thick, even for her. "I was traumatised. I'm still seeing a counsellor about the whole experience. I doubt I'll ever get over it." She lowered her voice. "Especially my time getting to know Big Bertha, if you know what I mean."

Jena started to giggle. Matt looked to heaven for the strength not to throw his sisters back into Invertary station's tiny jail.

"They spent one night in a single cell, here in town. They broke into my house and filled it with rats," Matt said. "The other night they spent in the same solitary cell was for dying Kitty Baxter's sheep pink."

His sisters grinned at each other—no remorse there. Jena looked bewildered.

"There was no Big Bertha," Matt said. "And the only member of this family getting therapy is me—for dealing with them."

Claire smacked him on the back of the head again. "That's just mean."

He pointed his fork at her. "Do that one more time and I'm locking you up for assaulting an officer."

"Killjoy," Claire grumbled.

"So, is it true? Is he guarding your body? Does that involve getting naked?" Megan said.

"Gross," Claire said. "You're talking about Don Don. Remember, we have a deal. We *never* use the words naked and Don Don together in the same sentence."

"Technically, I didn't," Megan said.

Jena held up her hands. "Nobody is getting naked. My ex is in town and I don't want to deal with him." She lowered her voice. "He's connected to the mob. Matt is watching out for me." She smiled at him. "It's very sweet of him, even if he has been rude about my food and taken it upon himself to peel off my kitchen wallpaper."

The twins glanced around the room. "That might be a good thing," Claire muttered.

Matt wanted to add an amen, but kept his mouth shut.

"The mob?" It worried Matt that Megan sounded more intrigued than afraid. "What on earth were you doing with a mobster?"

For the first time in this ludicrous conversation, Matt was actually interested in what they had to say.

Jena let out a heavy sigh. She seemed to be searching for the right words. "When I met Frank, he wasn't involved with the mob. He was a bit of a hustler, sure, but he was charming and kind." She got a dreamy look in her eyes. "He treated me well. Was really attentive, know what I mean?"

The twins nodded and Matt frowned. Jena's love-struck look made him want to beat Frank Di Marco to a bloody pulp.

"After a while," Jena said, "his constant get-rich-quick schemes began to grate. I was forever bailing him out of trouble. He was forever promising that his big break was around the corner. He was obsessed with 'keeping me in the kind of lifestyle I deserved'. His words. Not mine. I don't care about that stuff. I think it was an excuse. He had a lifestyle in mind that he wanted. Badly. I didn't realise how much until it was too late. One day he came home, said he was now the proud owner of a strip club. He was real cagey about where he got the money to buy it. Next thing I knew, he was dressing like a pimp and spending time with Vince Rizzoni."

"Who?" Megan said.

"Bad news, honey, bad, bad news." Jena shook her head sadly, and Matt had an overwhelming urge to pull her into his lap and comfort her. He told himself to snap out of it. She was a job. That was all. He didn't need the hassle that followed Jena Morgan like a cloud wherever she went. Nope, he had plans that involved a proper police job, far away from Invertary.

"Over the last year we were together, Frank changed. He became arrogant. Entitled. Kept talking about his reputation.

Had whispered conversations with guys with no necks, if you know what I mean."

Claire nodded. "Bodybuilders."

Matt looked at the ceiling and bit his tongue to stop from laughing. Jena stared at his sister for a beat.

"No, honey, mob enforcers. Goons. Hard men. Criminals."

"Oh." Claire turned pink, and Matt wanted to ruffle her hair. He was glad his sisters didn't know about men like that. Damn glad.

"What happened?" Megan said. "What made you leave?" She lowered her voice. "Did he turn into a hard man too?"

"Worse," Jena said. "He started auditioning the women in his club."

The girls shared a confused look.

"On their backs," Jena clarified. "He was having sex with the strippers. I caught him with one of them. And that was it. I sold our gear to make up for the years I'd poured money into him, and his schemes, and I bought this place." She grinned. "Bad story over. New beginning in Scotland."

"Is he here to get his money back?" Claire said.

"I don't know why he's here." Jena looked at Matt. "If he's looking for money, there's none to get."

"Do you think he's come to rub you out?" Claire said. "That's the right way to put it, isn't it?"

Matt rolled his eyes. "Okay, enough of this. Thanks for bringing the food over. Time for you two to go home."

They made the same disgruntled whines they'd made as kids when he was left babysitting them and had to put them to bed. It made him grin.

"We'll talk tomorrow," Megan promised Jena.

Matt herded the women out of the house.

"Leave Jena alone," he told them when they were outside the door. "She's got enough on her plate."

"Don't worry, we won't be any trouble at all." Megan batted her eyelashes at him in an attempt to look innocent. Yeah, like that would work.

"If I believe that, then I also believe in Santa."

"You mean he's not real?" Claire held her cheeks in shock.

"Get out of here." Matt shooed them away. "And don't forget to visit Dad this week. Mum says he's having some better days."

A sad look passed over them. "We're going tomorrow," Claire said.

"Good."

They turned to face their car. "Love you, Mattie," they both sang at the same time.

He found himself grinning when he went back into Jena's house.

CHAPTER 5

Jena was washing dishes when Matt came back into the kitchen. She knew he was there because the air tingled, sending shivers up her spine. She glanced at him, wondering for the millionth time what she'd gotten herself into.

His black shirt was pulled tight over muscle. His jeans sat low on his hips and clung to thick thighs. Black hair, usually short and neat, looked like he'd ran his fingers through it. He had one of those square jaws you usually only found chiselled on marble sculptures—or on underwear models. Deep-set blue eyes made him appear continuously broody. Even if the guy had been a total airhead, the eyes would have made it look like he was thinking hard.

"Where am I sleeping?" That deep brogue of his made her mouth water.

"I'll show you." She dried her hands on a purple dishtowel.

She manoeuvred past him and into the hall, aware that he was close behind her. She pushed open the heavy wooden door to the living room. She'd stripped about twenty layers of paint off it by hand—and felt every single minute of the work. It'd cost her a manicure, but it was worth it every time she ran her hand over the warm surface.

"The couch pulls out into a bed. It's not very big, but you'll be fine for the night."

Abby had given her the couch. It had originally been grey, but Jena had made a cover for it from a vibrant blue chunky cord material she'd found on sale at Kirsty's mum's shop. There was also an oversized beanbag made from a paisley patterned material in pinks, blues and purples. Apart from that, the only other furniture in the room was a tiny end table she'd found in a skip and sanded to perfection, before painting it the same shade of pink that was in the beanbag. There was a silver standing lamp beside the couch and a small silver TV fixed to the wall above the fireplace. Jena had like the simple lines of the fireplace, but had painted it white to freshen it up. The part that would house a fire had long since been boarded up, so she'd placed a vase of flowers in the space. Pink and purple ones Abby had let her pick from her garden. She'd made the floor-length curtains out of the same material as the beanbag and painted the walls a lovely shade of lavender, and the trim white. Overall the feeling was one of warmth and comfort.

When she turned towards Matt, his eyes were wide with shock. "Who did this?" He motioned to the room.

It took Jena a few seconds to realise he meant the décor. "I did."

He slowly walked around the room, his steps echoing over her polished wooden floors. He ran a hand over the stripped and stained window ledge, before examining the lavender-coloured walls.

"You did a good job, Jena."

She couldn't help it—she felt her heart swell at the praise. "You sound surprised."

He grinned at her. It was panty melting. "Yeah, I am. You don't strike me as the DIY type."

"I can learn. I had to." She shrugged. Why did people always look at her and see a bimbo who was incapable of reading a book? "Besides, this room wasn't too difficult. I just stripped everything in it. And years of making dance costumes means I'm a dab hand with a sewing machine."

He frowned at her. "Don't put yourself down. This is a lot of work. You didn't *just* strip everything. You gave it a new lease of life. And you did a great job."

Jena felt her cheeks burn. It was hard to look him in the eye. "Glad you appreciate it. This room happened before I ran out of money. You won't see this again, so soak it up while you can." She gave him a wide grin as he stared at her, as though assessing. "I'll get the bedding."

She turned, heading for the stairs and the only other room in the house that was finished—her bedroom. When she returned, Matt stood in front of the wide bay windows texting someone. A muscle in his jaw clenched and unclenched, piquing Jena's curiosity.

"Trouble?" she asked.

There was a pause, as though he was unsure whether to answer or not. "My dad. He's having a few good days. I need to make time to go see him."

"Good days?"

His gaze turned to the darkened windows. "Alzheimer's. Late stage."

"Oh, I'm sorry."

He didn't say anything else. Eventually Jena felt uncomfortable waiting for him. "I'm going to head to bed. I need to get up early tomorrow. First day of work." She flashed a nervous smile at his back, aware he could see her reflection in the window.

"I didn't know you'd gotten a job."

"It isn't a proper job or anything. It's at the hardware store, Gordon says I can work for supplies."

"Sounds like a proper job to me."

"Not really." She shrugged. "I'm the in-house entertainment. He thinks my ignorance is funny."

"That's small-town living—you take your fun where you find it."

For a minute Jena's libido sabotaged her brain and she imagined having all sorts of fun with the sexy cop. She took a step back.

"Okay, I'm off to bed. Bathroom's at the top of the stairs." She gave him an apologetic look. "There's no hot water. If you fancy a cold shower then be my guest. I'm saving for a new boiler." She chewed her lip. "Or I would be saving for a new boiler if I had any money."

His gaze zoomed in on her, reminding her that he wasn't only a houseguest, he was a cop.

"If you're working in exchange for building materials, what are you doing for money to live?"

Jena forced a smile. "Don't worry, officer. I'm not doing anything illegal."

Before he could ask any more questions, Jena ran for the stairs and headed to the sanctuary of her bedroom. The truth was that she wasn't doing anything to earn money. She was living off what little savings she had left and selling the few bits and pieces of jewellery she'd brought with her. By her estimation she was about two weeks away from living without electricity and eating raw mushrooms from Abby's farm three times a day. She hadn't had any time to look for work, and her marketable skills were seriously limited. As far as she was aware, Invertary wasn't in the market for a go-go girl.

For a second the stress of her life stole her breath. She lay on her bed and stared at the pristine white ceiling. Problems

JANET ELIZABETH HENDERSON

were stacking up and she had to fight not to drown in them. Her money was running out. Her house was falling down around her ears. Her ex was in town looking for payback. And there was a cop sleeping on her couch.

A very sexy cop.

She pulled the pillow over her face and screamed into it.

"If you're going to kill yourself there are easier ways to do it," came the droll voice from her doorway.

Jena shot up straight to find Matt grinning—she'd forgotten to shut her door. With a wink, he headed into the bathroom. As soon as she heard the door click behind him, Jena tiptoed over to her bedroom door and shut it quietly.

As she climbed back into bed, she wondered if it was possible to die from embarrassment.

"Night, Jena," Matt called as he passed. "Hope you don't talk in your sleep. Every little noise in this house echoes. Wouldn't want to overhear any X-rated dreams you might have."

Yep, Jena decided—you *could* die of embarrassment.

CHAPTER 6

The twins were still laughing when they climbed into the ancient lime-green Mini Cooper they shared.

"I don't know who to feel sorry for more." Megan angled the car out into the dark country road. "Matt for having to suffer Jena's pit of a house, or Jena for having to suffer Matt."

"Jena, definitely."

Megan took her eyes off the road long enough to turn to her sister and share a grin. When they turned back to the road, it was just in time to spot the horrified look on the face of a man running towards them. Megan yanked the wheel. The guy made a dive for the bushes. They felt, rather than heard, a loud thud. The two women screamed. The car screeched to a halt at the side of the road.

"Did we hit him?" Megan's voice was barely audible.

"I don't think so." Claire's hands shook as she opened the car door. The front corner of the car was wedged against a tree stump. She let out a shaky breath. "We hit a tree."

"I can't see the guy," Megan called.

"There!" Claire ran towards the black-clad body, which was lying on the grass verge against the hedge.

The twins fell to their knees beside the man. "Who is it?" Megan demanded. "What happened? I didn't hit him. Why isn't he moving?"

"I don't recognise him." Claire reached over and put a trembling hand on his wide chest. Relief made her giddy. "He's breathing. I think he hit his head when he dove out of the way."

That news jerked Megan out of her daze. "Good. That's good. Not good he hit his head. Good we didn't hit him and he's still breathing. What do we do?"

"I don't know."

He made a little groaning sound. Claire patted his chest, hoping her gentle touch would reassure him. Hard, corded muscles met her fingertips, making her suddenly aware that she was petting a very large, strange man.

"Can you hear me?" she said. "You've been in an accident."

With a gentle groan, his head turned towards Claire, and the air was sucked out of her. Masculine. He was the definition of the word. His dark hair was cropped military short, and an old scar ran from his hairline over his temple to the curve of his cheek. His nose had been broken at some point and had healed slightly crooked. For a second Claire had the urge to trace the bump on the ridge. Full lips were the only soft feature in a harsh face. She stared at them and wondered briefly if they were as soft as they looked.

"What's your name?" Megan's voice snapped Claire's attention away from her inappropriate thoughts.

His eyes didn't open, but he mumbled a word: "Grunt."

"No, honey, she asked your name." Claire patted his chest. "Tell us your name."

There was silence as the guy slid back into unconsciousness.

"Did he say Grunt?" Megan said.

"He's totally out of it." Claire studied the man in front of her. "We need an ambulance."

"It could take an hour for the ambulance to get here from Fort William, maybe longer."

Megan had a point.

"We could take him to Doctor Murray," they said at the same time.

"Should we move him?" Megan said. "What if he's broken his neck?"

The man groaned softly. His eyes flickered open, unfocused and dark. He blinked, searching for something to rest on. His gaze hit Claire. His eyes softened.

"Angel." His voice rough as gravel. He lifted a beefy arm. Slowly and awkwardly reaching for Claire. She gasped as he cupped her cheek. His huge palm felt rough against her skin and her body hummed with awareness. "Mine," he growled.

The word came out strong, like a vow. His eyes rolled back in his head and his hand fell to the ground. Claire forced herself to breathe again.

"Well, that was weird," Megan whispered.

"At least we know he isn't paralysed. We need to get him into the car."

"Shouldn't you check him for injuries first? Make sure nothing is broken. Do some first aid."

"Why me?" Claire said. "You check him."

"You're a teacher; you have first-aid experience."

"I'm a kindy teacher. We fix everything with Mickey Mouse Band-Aids and lollipops."

"Just check the man. He could be bleeding to death while we argue."

"Fine." Gritting her teeth, Claire tentatively ran her fingers down his arms and legs, checking for breaks and blood. She found nothing except solid muscle and biceps that would make Dwayne Johnson weep with envy. "Go grab the flashlight so I can see if he's bleeding anywhere."

Her sister jumped up, and a minute later she was back with the flashlight in hand.

"Shine the light at his head."

Claire was painfully aware of every movement, and sound, his body made. Her fingers felt something wet at the back of his head. She held up her hand. Blood. He groaned but didn't gain consciousness. "Help me roll him onto his side. We need to stop the bleeding."

"Yeah, we don't want blood all over the car," Megan said.

"I was thinking more along the lines of the guy bleeding out and dying on us."

"That too."

"Do we have anything we can use to stop the bleeding? Do we have a first-aid kit in the car? We need to dress this wound. He's bleeding a lot."

"I think I have something. Be right back." Megan ran for the car.

Claire caressed the man's face. "It's going to be okay. You hit your head. I don't think anything else is damaged. Don't worry, we'll take good care of you."

"Got something," Megan called out breathlessly. She collapsed in the dirt beside them. "Here." She thrust a box of tampons and a pair of red tartan tights at Claire.

Claire stared at them for a minute. "What the heck am I supposed to do with this?"

"They're absorbent. Tie them to the wound with the tights, then voila, no more bleeding."

Claire rubbed her temples.

"Have you got a better idea?" Megan demanded.

Unfortunately Claire didn't, and the guy was still bleeding out in front of them. "Okay, hold them in place while I fix these to his head." She pressed a row of tampons to the wound, then Megan held them to his head as Claire fixed them in place with the tartan tights. The tights wound around his head several times before she secured them by tying a bow on his forehead.

They leaned over him.

"Is he still bleeding?" Megan said.

"Shine the light here and I'll check." To her relief, there was no fresh blood. "We're good. It's stopped."

She gently placed him back on the ground and stood. The women stared at him. From the neck down the guy was a badass wrestler for WWE. From the neck up he looked like a five-year-old had played doctor with him.

"The bow's kind of cute," Megan said. "Makes him look less intimidating. I'll get the car."

Megan reversed the car up beside Claire.

Claire looked at the huge man, then back to the tiny car. "I think he may be bigger than our car. We'll never squeeze him in the back. We'll have to put him in the passenger seat. His knees will be up around about his ears, but he won't notice. Guess there's an upside to being unconscious."

Megan nodded, then pushed the passenger seat back as far as it would go. They looked down at the unconscious man.

"We should probably have kept up those yoga classes," Claire said. "This is going to take muscle that I just don't have. You grab the feet; I'll take the arms."

Megan held his feet, which were clad in black running shoes. Claire grabbed hold of his hands, noticing how massive they were compared to hers. She looked at her sister. "On the count of three, we lift him and get him to the door. From there we can lever him up into the seat."

"Got it."

"One, two, three."

They strained. They grunted. They pulled. He barely

moved an inch. Red-faced and panting, they stared at each other.

"Is he made of frigging rock?" Megan said.

"Solid muscle. Trust me. I felt it." Claire rubbed the back of her neck while she tried to think. "Come over here—we'll take an arm each and drag him to the car."

Megan rushed to her sister's side.

"Ready? Go."

They grunted and yanked him backwards, relieved when he moved. "Lift upwards," Claire said. "We don't want to bang his head again."

"I am lifting up. He isn't a man, he's a frigging mountain."

The guy's head lolled but it didn't hit the ground. Thankfully. About forty years later, they'd dragged him to the car door. Claire's shoulder muscles were aching and she was trying not to pant. She definitely needed to spend more time getting fit and less time eating chocolate in front of the TV.

"Uh, Claire, should be do something about that?" Megan pointed down his body.

His shorts had been dragged down to his ankles—and he wasn't wearing any underwear. Claire's mind went blank.

"I think it's best if we pretend we don't notice," she croaked.

"How can you miss it?" Megan pointed. "He's perfectly proportioned for his huge, huge size."

"Megan!" Claire elbowed her sister hard.

"Stop it." Megan rubbed her side. "It's not like I'm deliberately being a pervert. I didn't take his shorts off."

Claire chewed her lip. "We should probably pull them back up." She elbowed her sister again. "You do it."

"Nuh-uh. What if he wakes up and finds me messing with his clothes? What if he thinks I'm molesting him? You do it."

"You're the one who's impressed by his package, you can be the one who gets a closer look at it."

"Ha! I'm not the one who's still staring at it."

Claire snapped her gaze away, and her cheeks flushed. "There's something glinting on it. I think we may have damaged him dragging him along like that."

"We can't have. His penis didn't touch the ground."

"There's definitely something stuck to it. Go check it out."

"You do it. I'm not studying his penis."

"What if he's injured?"

"He can stay injured. Let the doc check him out."

"Bloody coward." With a grumble, Claire walked to the guy's middle. Her eyes popped. "He isn't injured." She pointed at him. "He's pierced."

"No way, let me see." Megan rushed to stand beside her sister.

Claire rolled her eyes. "What happened to you not wanting to get up close and personal with his privates?"

"He's pierced. I've never seen that before."

The women stared at him. "That had to hurt," Claire said. They winced.

The guy let out a moan. The women screamed, shot back from him and fell on their backsides. They froze, scared to move in case he woke up. He didn't.

With a shaky sigh of relief, they scrambled to their feet.

"Maybe we should pull his shorts up now?" Megan said. She pointed at Claire. "You do it."

Muttering about her cowardly sister, Claire headed for the shorts. After she'd struggled for what felt like hours to get his shorts past his ankles, it became clear it wasn't going to happen.

"What's more important?" she asked her sister. "Making sure he's decent, or getting him medical help?"

"We've seen it all now anyway."

"Good point. I'll take them off. That's easier."

Claire tried to get the shorts off over his shoes, but his

huge freaking feet made it impossible. In the end, she took off his shoes too. As she lifted his legs, she couldn't help but notice that his backside had been scraped to hell from being dragged along the ground.

As she yanked his shorts off, there was a flash. She snapped her head up to find Megan holding her phone.

"Tell me you didn't take a picture."

Megan grinned. "Trust me. You'll appreciate it later." She put the phone back in her pocket.

They worked together to get him sitting upright at the open door.

Claire scrambled onto the driver's seat. "I'll put my arms under his and you wrap yours around his waist."

"I'm not sure I like that idea. That's leaving me a little too close to his penis."

"Will you stop saying penis? It's freaking me out. I don't want to talk about his privates."

"But it's okay to stare at it?"

Claire clenched her jaw and counted to ten. "Just get on with it. We need to get him to the doctor. Now isn't the time to freak out about his privates."

"Fine," Megan grumbled. "But I'm not happy about this." She wrapped her arms around his waist.

Claire put her head on his shoulder as she wrapped her arms around his body. The heat coming from him was distracting, and even through the heavy smell of wet grass he still had a musky scent that was all man.

"On three," Megan said. "One, two, three."

They yanked hard. He flew upwards. His head crashed into the top of the doorframe.

"Oh no, did we kill him this time?" Megan wailed.

With a shaky hand, Claire checked his pulse. "No. He's okay." *I hope.*

Claire climbed into the back to hold his head, while

Megan folded his legs into the tiny car. Megan snapped the belt into place. She went to shut the door, but changed her mind at the last minute. She pulled out her camera and snapped another picture. With a grin, she slammed the door shut, ran around the car and climbed into the driver's seat. "All things considered, I thought that went quite well," she said. She reached into her pocket and pulled out a crumpled tissue. With care, she smoothed it out and threw it into the stranger's lap. "I can't drive with his penis winking at me." With that, she put the car in gear.

It didn't take long to get to the doctor's house, which also doubled as his practice rooms. Doc Murray was in his forties, fit and in possession of a wheelchair—so they didn't have to drag their victim to the door. He took one look at the patch-up job the twins had done on the stranger's head and burst out laughing.

"Priceless." He wiped his eyes. "Is that tampons under the tights? I've got to wake up Janice and show her this."

"How about you fix his head first?" Claire snapped.

Five minutes later the guy was in the examination room while the sisters paced outside the door.

"Okay," Doctor Murray said as he came into the room. "He's going to be fine. Blood loss and mild concussion. I'll keep him here overnight to make sure he's okay. I'll call when he's up and around. There was no ID so I don't know who to contact about him, but I'll call the pub. If he's visiting town, he might be staying there. Dougal will know if he is. The guy is pretty distinctive—his description should be enough."

"Can we see him?" Claire asked. "Is there anything we can do?"

He shook his head. "He's still out cold. It happens that way with some people." He gave them a sly grin. "If you know where his underwear and shoes are, that'd be handy."

Claire felt her cheeks burn. "I'll get them from the car."

"Mm." The doc eyed them. "An explanation would be good too. I can't figure out why you took off his trousers when it was his head that was injured."

"I can do better than explain," Megan said. "I have pictures." She dug out her phone.

With a groan, Claire went to fetch the big guy's clothes.

CHAPTER 7

Surprisingly, Matt slept well on Jena's pull-out bed. In fact, when he opened his eyes to find the beautifully restored room, soft early morning light coming through the huge bay windows and thick green foliage outside, he almost didn't want to get up. It was a strange feeling. One he never had at his own house.

He silently climbed the stairs to use the bathroom, noted that Jena's bedroom door was firmly shut and grinned. Twenty minutes later, he was dressed in a crisp uniform and accepting delivery of breakfast from the pub. This time it was Lake who was the bearer of cooked goods.

"Can get a man to cover here on Saturday," he said by way of hello.

Matt nodded, but was mainly interested in the flask of coffee Lake still held. He reached for the food and coffee. "You coming in?"

"Too busy." Lake pointed in the direction of Matt's feet. "You going to take those inside?"

Matt looked down and his heart stilled. There was a large bunch of red roses in a crystal vase. He frowned, wondering which one of Jena's many admirers was dropping off flowers now.

"My hands are full." He nodded to the vase. "Can you read the card?"

Lake picked it up, opened the tiny envelope and pursed his lips. "Jena, baby, all is forgiven. Love you, Frank."

Matt glared at the card, hoping it would burst into flames.

"Who's at the door?" Jena's sleepy voice broke through the rage that clenched Matt's stomach.

"Just Lake delivering breakfast."

He was hoping she'd go through to the kitchen, but she had to be polite. She pushed up beside him. Her face breaking out into a wide smile.

"Hi, Lake. Thanks for bringing food. Matt doesn't want to eat my Pop-Tarts and I don't want to waste them on him."

"Pop-Tarts?" Lake cocked an eyebrow at him.

"Think flavoured cardboard with a sugary syrup filling that's hot enough to burn the taste buds off your tongue."

Lake's lips twitched. One of these days the guy would have to give in and join the rest of humanity by actually smiling when the feeling hit.

"Oh, flowers!" Jena pushed past Matt to scoop up the vase. She inhaled deeply. Her eyes sparkled and she grinned at him. "Where's the card?"

Matt nodded at Lake, who solemnly handed it over. Then he watched as the joy melted from Jena's face when she read it.

"He forgives me?" She looked up at him. "He forgives me?"

She thrust the vase at Matt. Making him drop the bag of food in order to catch the flowers. Jena fisted her hands on her hips. Her eyes were blazing. She tossed her wild, uncombed hair.

"He forgives me. How freaking gracious of him. I wasn't

the one who slept with every stripper in Atlantic City. I wasn't the one who threw away a four-year relationship by being a man-whore. I wasn't the one who was caught balls deep in a stripper called Candy." She pointed at Matt. "A woman with a bad boob job and bleached hair." She looked like she wanted to punch someone. Lake must have seen it too, because both men stepped back at the same time. "I'm going to kill him."

She stormed into the house, her cute behind swaying in her purple cotton shorts, her matching tank slipping off her shoulder. At the bottom of the stairs, she spun back towards them.

"Forget I said that about killing him. If anything should happen to him, I'm sure it would have nothing to do with me and would in no way be premeditated." With that, she stomped up the stairs. "Give the flowers to your mother, Matt," she shouted. "I don't want them wasted, but I don't want them in this house." Then her door slammed shut.

The men waited in silence for a minute to see if she had anything to add.

"Want me to drop those off at your mum's house? I'm passing." Lake reached for the flowers, and Matt didn't hesitate to hand them over.

"Best she doesn't see them again."

"That's what I was thinking." Lake took the flowers. His jaw hardened. "I'll check in with Harry, see if he's come up with anything yet. You want me to have a word with Frank's boys?"

"Not yet. Let's talk to Harry first."

He cast a glance into the house when he heard banging coming from upstairs. "I need to deal with this."

Lake gave him a rare grin. "Yeah, have fun with that."

With a grunt, Matt grabbed the food, kicked the door closed and headed for the rickety kitchen table.

"Come eat, Jena," he shouted as he passed the stairs. "You need energy to kill a man."

With a grin of his own, he poured a mug of coffee and sighed. This was not a day he could face without being fortified by caffeine.

It took almost an hour of listening to Jena rant before she wound down. When she did, Matt gently explained that he had everything under control, and until they were better informed the best course of action would be to ignore the flowers.

It took another ten minutes to get her to promise to do as she was told. He then dropped her off at work and had a chat with Gordon. The old man was grim, but promised to take good care of his charge. Lake's security business was two doors down from the hardware store, and Matt knew without asking that Lake would be on the lookout. With Jena as secure as he could make her for the morning, Matt decided to visit his dad.

THE DRIVE to Fort William took him through the ominous scenery of Glencoe, with its barren hills and narrow valley road. It wasn't hard to imagine it as the scene of a massacre. There would be nowhere for people to hide. Nowhere to run. The place always made him feel melancholy. Especially when the piper was at the top of one of the hills blasting out bagpipe music for the tourists. Matt hated the bagpipes. It sounded like someone was abusing a bag of cats.

His mood hadn't improved any when he pulled into the car park of the nursing home—his father's residence for the past two years. He spotted his mother's car. He wasn't surprised she was already there. She visited every single day, ill or well, no matter the weather, and she never complained when he didn't recognise her or called her someone else's name.

He swept through the corridors, nodding hello to the nurses until he made it to his dad's olive-green door. It was open and his mother was sitting beside the hospital bed telling his father all about her day.

"You should have seen Morag's face when the big tourist complained about her pies. He said that there was too much fat in his. I thought Morag was going to burst a blood vessel. I swear I saw her head swell, and she pursed her lips so hard they disappeared into a tight wee line. You know how proud she is of her pies. They won one award twenty-two years ago and she's never stopped telling people since." She mimicked the local bakery owner: "My award-winning pies are the best pies in Scotland." She grinned before her voice returned to normal. "The man said, 'I don't care if they've won awards, I want my money back. I'm not eating fat-filled pastry.' It was brilliant. Best thing I've seen in ages. It's about time someone took Morag down a peg or two."

She leaned over and brushed his father's hair off his forehead with her fingers. "You used to love those pies," she said softly. "I'll bring you some tomorrow."

His father stared into space, oblivious to her words. Matt felt his chest tighten. He cleared his throat as he strode into the room.

"Hey, Mum." He bent to kiss her cheek. "How's it going? How is he today?"

She gave Matt a tight hug. "He's doing great." She looked back at her husband of thirty-five years. "Aren't you, Bruce?" The room may as well have been empty. She turned back to Matt. "He's thinking hard today." She smiled sadly.

"Good to hear." He settled into the chair beside the bed, noticing the dark circles under his mum's eyes. She wasn't sleeping. Instead she was grieving the husband who slipped through her fingers a little more each day, and there was nothing her son could do to make it better for her. "Why don't you go get a cup of tea and a bite to eat while I sit with him? He needs a little man talk, don't you, Dad?"

Matt's chest hurt looking at the man who'd once taken up so much space in his life. The man who'd taught him how to be a man. He owed everything he was to his dad.

"Thanks, love," his mum said. "I am a bit hungry. I won't be long."

"Take your time," Matt said. "But bring me back a coffee. I can't shake that dozy feeling today."

"No problem." She winked at him, smoothed her hand over her short blonde hair and glanced at her husband with such brutal longing it made Matt hold his breath. "I'll be back soon," she said as she left the room.

Matt rubbed his chest as he turned back to his dad. "I've got to tell you about this crazy woman I'm looking out for," he said. "You'd get a kick out her."

His dad's eyes fought to focus on Matt's face. "Donald?" His voice was a raw croak, brittle from lack of use.

Matt swallowed hard. His dad never called him Donald. That was the name of the uncle he'd been named after. Matt didn't mind; he was used to playing the part of his long-dead uncle. "That's right," Matt told him as he reached for his hand. "It's Donald. How's the family doing, Bruce?"

"Good, good." He looked confused. "I thought you were at sea."

"I was. Came back to see you, you old codger."

The smile his father gave him was worth every moment of the pain Matt felt. "Who you calling an old codger? I'm two years younger than you."

"That you are, that you are." Matt squeezed his father's brittle hand. Holding on to more than his skin, trying to hold on to the man who was fading away. He fought to get words past his tight throat. "Tell me about that lovely wife of yours."

He watched as his dad's whole face lit up so much it was blinding. "Heather," he said on a sigh. "She takes my breath away. You know what I'm talking about?"

"Aye," Matt said. "Aye, I do."

And an image of a crazy American woman flashed into his mind.

He watched as the effort of talking proved too much for his dad and his eyes became heavy with sleep. Matt didn't move, he just sat there, holding his hand.

The way his father had always done for him when he was a boy.

JENA WAS close to the end of her first shift at the hardware store and she couldn't have been more ready to go home. Gordon and Brenda had hovered over her all day, like a couple of grey-haired bodyguards. She was fine with the hovering—the hovering was kind of sweet. What she didn't enjoy was Gordon's constant laughter. The man, along with his sick sense of humour, was beginning to get on her nerves. It was time to deal with him—after she'd dealt with her latest customer. She gave the man a beaming smile.

"Welcome to Stewart hardware, how can I help you?"

"Do you have any size-six washers?" the timid little man asked.

Jena frowned. "I think you have the wrong shop. We only sell DIY stuff. If you want a washer you need to go along the road to the furniture place. They've got a selection of washing machines and dishwashers. I don't know if they have size six, but I'm sure they'll order one if they don't have it in stock."

The guy stared at her, open-mouthed. Gordon's laughter

told her she'd screwed up again. That was it. She'd had enough. She held a finger up to the guy in front of her, giving him a strained smile. "Give me one minute."

She stomped over to stand in front of Gordon. She put her hands on her hips. "That's it. I've had enough. This isn't funny. Nothing about this is funny. How am I supposed to know this stuff? It isn't like it's genetically programmed into you at birth." She pointed a finger at him. "Somebody taught you, Gordon Stewart. Now stop laughing, get up off your lazy backside and teach me what I need to know."

She stomped back to the customer, who looked like he was going to hyperventilate and pass out. She gave him her winning smile. It had no impact. She felt Gordon come up beside her.

"All you had to do was ask," he grumbled. "There was no need for the histrionics."

Oh, she could feel her blood boil now. It must have come across in her face, because Gordon paled slightly. "Is that even a word?"

He swallowed hard. "Let's get back to dealing with the customer. We do sell washers."

Jena looked around. "Where? I haven't seen any, and I think I would have noticed something that size."

Gordon pulled a drawer open in the wall of drawers behind the counter. "Size six, you said?"

The customer nodded, his relief clear.

"Here you go." Gordon passed a small, flat metal disc with a hole in the middle to the guy.

"That's a washer?" Jena pointed at it. Her eyes narrowed. "Are you pulling my leg?" She turned to the customer. "Did he put you up to this?" She jerked her thumb at her boss.

"No." The guy went wide-eyed. "That really is a washer and I really do need one."

"Mm." She folded her arms and tapped the toe of her

Mexican wedge sandal on the tile-covered floor. "Pay the man," she ordered the customer.

The guy rushed to do as he was told, grabbed the tiny metal disc and ran from the shop.

"There's no need to be rude to the customers," Gordon said gruffly.

Jena growled, the noise startling even her. "I'll get something to take notes with. You"—she poked a finger into his burly chest—"are going to open each of those drawers and tell me what's in them. I want to know what it is and what it's used for. Got it?"

"Got it." Gordon looked suitably cowed. Good.

"Here you go, love." Brenda passed her a notebook and pen. "I wondered how long it would take you to snap. You're far too nice. Most people wouldn't have lasted an hour, and you made it through the whole morning." She turned to her husband. "I hope you had your fun this morning, because it's the only fun you're getting all month." Her raised eyebrow and Gordon's suddenly red cheeks made Brenda's meaning clear.

It was Jena's turn to laugh.

THE FIRST THING Matt did when he returned from Fort William was check up on Jena. Much to his disgust, he found her being asked out on yet another date. The sight made Matt bristle, pushing aside the melancholy feeling a visit with his dad usually caused. Her latest suitor was Bob the butcher. The guy was a sleaze. Matt knew for a fact he'd only broken up with his girlfriend the day before.

"Shouldn't you be mourning, or something?" Matt plonked the sandwiches he'd picked up for lunch on the polished wooden counter.

Bob gave him a wide grin. His teeth practically sparkled.

There was no way they were that white naturally. Now that Matt noticed, he was pretty sure Bob's hair had never been that blonde either.

"Lisa and I were over for a long time before we called it a day," Bob said. "There's no mourning to be had." He shrugged muscled shoulders. "These things happen." He gave Jena another dazzling smile. "I'll pick you up at eight tomorrow, then?"

She nodded, smiled, blushed. Matt wanted to roll his eyes. With the amount of dates she got asked out on, surely this routine was old hat by now. Matt folded his arms over his black sports shirt, a part of his uniform that could pass as civilian wear when he didn't have his stab vest over it. He felt gleeful when he noticed his upper body bulk put Bob's to shame. Bob straightened his shoulders, puffed out his chest and winked at Jena. Now Matt was really irritated. It was time to wipe that smug smile off the guy's face.

"Jena is indisposed for the next wee while," Matt said. "She'll not be going out on any dates."

"Matt!" Jena glared at him. "You don't make those decisions for me."

"Aye, I do." Matt fought the urge to grin. Take that, Bob the bloody butcher.

Bob's eyes narrowed briefly before he flashed a poor imitation of a movie-star smile. "Are you and Jena dating, then?"

"No!"

Jena's answer was a bit fast in coming for Matt's liking. She dated anyone who asked her, yet was offended at the suggestion he might be in the running? Yeah, Matt didn't like that one bit. There was nothing wrong with him. Women loved dating him. They were falling over themselves to get his attention. He was a much better catch than Bob the bloody butcher. For a start, he was taller, he had more muscle mass and he didn't need a bottle of bleach to fix his hair. He frowned at Jena. He'd deal with her outrage later. Right now he had to get rid of Bob.

"This has nothing to do with romance. Jena has a situation going on right now. Her activities are restricted. It's too dangerous for her to wander around in public. That means no dates. With anyone."

Bob eyed him thoughtfully. "You're playing her bodyguard, then?"

"I'm looking out for her until this situation is resolved. She's keeping a low profile. She isn't dating." Matt felt the need to repeat himself. He was pretty sure his words weren't getting through the cloud of hairspray that surrounded Bob's head.

Bob nodded and Matt felt smug.

Then the butcher ruined it by turning to Jena. "You can come to my house for dinner. I'll cook. My place is far from public, so I'm sure Officer Donaldson won't have a problem with it. Will you, Matt?"

Matt smothered the need to wipe the smile off Bob's face —with his fist.

"Thank you, that's real kind of you, Bob." Jena gave Matt a pointed look. "I should be fine at Bob's house, right? It isn't a public place."

Matt didn't like this one bit, but couldn't see a way around it. He nodded once, sharply. It was Bob's turn to look smug.

"I'll pick you up at eight, then," Bob said.

"I'll drop her off," Matt told him. "Make sure she isn't followed."

The butcher cocked an eyebrow at him. "You do that."

With one last smouldering smile, Bob sauntered out of the shop giving Matt his back. The butcher's jeans were a shade too tight around his rear end. Another thing Matt didn't understand. Or like.

"That was rude." Jena pointed a finger at him. She had that little line between her eyebrows that always seemed to be present whenever he was around. He sighed. Well, sue him for doing his job.

"I was being honest. It isn't safe for you to date right now. You need to curtail your activities until these guys are back in the States."

She pointed at the door. "You hurt his feelings."

Matt laughed. Bob was about as sensitive as a brick wall. "No, I didn't. He could have waited a couple of weeks until this whole thing blew over. He's just being an arse pushing to see you right now."

Jena put her hands on her hips and started lecturing him. Matt noticed, yet again, that the cute cut-off dungarees she wore were designed to flatter every inch of the curves beneath them. Not to mention showcase those luscious legs of hers. She might not be the tallest woman on the planet, but her legs were perfectly formed.

"You aren't even listening to me." She threw up her hands in disgust.

Damn. Had she been talking? He'd totally missed whatever she was ranting on about.

Instead of admitting his mind had wandered, he decided to bluff his way out of trouble. "I don't need to listen to you, Jena. I don't need to acknowledge your complaints. They make no difference to me. I'm only here to make sure you're safe. To make sure the baggage that followed you over the ocean doesn't cause any trouble in my town."

Jena muttered something that sounded like "annoying, pig-headed, rude men". Matt ignored her.

"Come on. Work's over. I'm hungry. I brought you a sandwich. We can eat at the station while I go over some paperwork."

Her eyes went wide, distracting him for a moment from the food he was desperate to get at. "I don't want to go to the station. I want to go home. I have a lot to do."

"We'll go back to your place after I finish the paperwork. You need to eat. You might as well do it at the station."

"Your bossy attitude sucks. I don't like this one bit."

For some reason Matt heard that as *I don't like you*. His stomach spasmed sharply. He rubbed it. Had to be hunger pains.

"You don't have to like it. You just have to do what you're told."

With a growl, Jena picked up the huge bag she carted everywhere, called to Gordon that she was done for the day and stomped behind Matt to his car.

Women. They should come with a manual.

CHAPTER 8

"Wake up, sleeping beauty."

Grunt felt something prod his shoulder and struggled to open his eyes. It felt like he'd been beaten over the head with a baseball bat. He groaned loudly and the noise hurt his ears.

"Are you sure he's okay?" That sounded like Joe. Where the hell was he? Why were his eyelids so heavy?

"Aye, he's fine. Some people are like this when they have a head injury. They conk out and wake up when they feel a lot better. It's not exactly normal, but it's within parameters. I'm not worried." The Scottish voice sounded more amused than worried.

"Okay, big guy, you need to get up and put some pants on."

What the hell? Grunt forced his eyes open. Bright light bit at them. Joe's grinning mug appeared in front of him.

"You're in the doc's office. You've got a concussion. Nothing serious. You'd need a brain for it to be serious."

Grunt grunted, making Joe laugh. Pain in his ass. Grunt struggled to sit. It felt like his head was going to fall off.

"Pain," said the Scottish guy. "I'll give you a shot for that."

Grunt wanted to lie back down and wake up after his day had improved. Instead he let Joe pull him to sitting. He looked down to find he was on a hospital bed, in a fully equipped examination room. He still wore his workout shirt. His shoes were gone and there was a sheet over his lap. He peeked under it.

"Where are my shorts?" His voice sounded like gravel under heavy boots.

Joe's grin got wider. He folded his arms over a T-shirt that said "Mob Minder". The guy's sense of humour was going to get them killed.

"I don't know how much you remember, buddy," Joe said. "You went out for a run. Two chicks almost ran into you on a road at the edge of town. You hit your head jumping out of the way of their car. They bandaged you up." Joe started to laugh. He held up a hand, signalling he was getting it under control. Grunt frowned, but it hurt his head, so he stopped. "They got you into their car and brought you here. Doc fixed you up and watched you overnight."

"Why didn't he call you?" His tongue felt furry. Did he eat dirt when he avoided the car?

"Here you go," said a cheery voice.

Grunt turned towards it and found the red-headed doctor holding a large syringe.

"Hell no," he croaked.

"Don't be a big baby," the guy said.

Before Grunt could stop him, the doc whipped down the back of the sheet and jabbed him in the ass. Grunt yelped and rubbed the spot. It hurt more than it should have. He strained to look over his shoulder to see why. It felt like there were bumps on his skin, cuts maybe. The doc followed his actions.

"Ah, about that. You have a scraped backside from the girls dragging you to their car."

What the? He looked at Joe, who was trying hard not to laugh and failing miserably.

"Spill," Grunt ordered.

Joe pinched the bridge of his nose as a grin escaped. "Your shorts slid off when they dragged you. They couldn't get them up, so they took them off. Along with your shoes."

Okay. Not great news. A little mortifying, sure, but he could deal. Why was Joe still grinning? Grunt narrowed his eyes. At least that didn't hurt.

"What else?"

"We didn't know who you were," the doc said. "You didn't have any ID on you."

Grunt just stared at him. Who carries ID out running? Answer: no one.

"I called the pub to see if you were staying there, but Dougal wasn't working. The girl covering the bar was new and didn't know who'd booked in." The doc paused and looked at Joe.

"The chicks who hit you posted a picture in the bar to see if anyone knew you."

Grunt waited. There had to be more to it than a mugshot if Joe was straining to keep a lid on his hysterics.

"Show me," Grunt said.

Joe pulled a folded piece of paper from his back pocket. The doc shuffled away from him. Not a good sign. Grunt prepared himself for the worst. Had they taken a picture of him with his junk hanging out? Nah. Nobody would do that.

Joe unfolded the paper and held it up for Grunt to see. He sucked in a breath, his eyes shooting between Joe and the doc.

The doc held up his hands. "I had nothing to do with it."

Joe was laughing too hard to talk. Grunt felt his cheeks heat for the first time in memory. There he was in full colour. Out cold. Drooling. A big-assed tartan bow in the middle of his forehead. Women's products stuck to his head. His knees up to his chest, folded into the car like an oversized pretzel. And someone had used a black marker pen to censor his junk.

There were words printed under the photo: "Do you know this man? He's currently unconscious at the doctor's office. If you know him, go get him."

Joe was wiping tears from his eyes. He was useless.

Grunt turned to the doc. "Who brought me in?"

An image of a blonde angel flashed into his mind. Had he died when he hit his head?

"It was the Donaldson twins." The doc spoke in the direction of his feet before looking up at Grunt. The bastard was trying not to laugh. "You should know before you look them up that their elder brother is the town police officer. You should also keep in mind that they were trying to help."

Great. This day just got better. "Where are my shorts?"

The doctor rushed to get them while Joe plopped into a chair, trying to catch his breath.

"I'm framing this," Joe said.

Grunt frowned at his friend and wondered whom he'd kill first. So many options, so little time.

It was a hard decision.

CHAPTER 9

Friday didn't start well. For one, Jena found another bouquet of flowers on her doorstep. The card with this one said, "Please forgive me, I can't live without you, love Frank." She clenched her teeth, ripped up the card and handed the flowers to Matt.

A few minutes later, Lake turned up to watch her while Matt ran some errands, taking the flowers with him. Lake was better company than Matt. He sat at the kitchen table reading the newspaper. He didn't talk, he didn't criticise and he didn't take over renovating her house. At the changing of her guard, Lake smiled, nodded and disappeared quietly. It was perfect. She decided that she wanted Lake to watch her all the time. Surely Matt would be thankful?

Matt arrived back at her house after lunch. He brought in bag after bag of groceries, lecturing about the need for healthy food as he did so. Jena ignored him, went into her living room, pushed the sofa back against the wall. Plonked her iPod into the speaker dock. And danced.

For one long, glorious hour, she didn't think about Matt, Frank or the fact her money was running out. Nope, instead she let the music take over as she swayed and pirouetted and stretched in time to the beat. When she finally wound down, she actually felt relaxed for the first time in days.

And that was when it hit her—she could teach dance lessons to earn some cash.

Before she could think twice about it, she ran into the kitchen.

"I'm going to teach dancing," she announced.

Matt looked up from where he was stripping the paper from the wall beside the door. Jena had given up on telling him not to take over her renovation. Instead, she started viewing him as cheap labour. He'd even brought tools from home to help with the job. Including a steamer thingy that she wished she'd had when she'd stripped the living room walls. She'd gotten the paper off by soaking it with a sponge full of warm, soapy water. By the time she'd finished, the room looked like a big bubble bath. But it smelled great. She'd used a juniper bubble bath mixture in the water.

"Did you hear me, Matt? I'm going to run dance classes." She bounced on the spot.

"Great?" He seemed confused.

"It just came to me," Jena told him. "It's the perfect way to make money fast. It can be a cash business. I won't need to worry about tax and stuff." She beamed at him.

Matt muttered something under his breath. Was he counting to ten? That made no sense at all.

"Jena, are you telling me—a cop—that you're planning to rip off the government by avoiding tax?"

"No, silly, I'm telling you I'm going to run casual classes." She bit her lip. "If I get all the junk out of the garage I can hold them there. The floor is concrete and the ceiling doesn't leak."

He blinked a couple of times. "You want to run classes here?"

"No, Matt, in the garage." Was he being deliberately thick? "Can you help me clear it out? I could use some muscle."

"You can't hold classes in the garage. Or anywhere near this house. It's a health and safety hazard. You need a permit to do something like that. You'll never get one."

She narrowed her eyes at him. She was so getting him a T-shirt emblazoned with the word "Killjoy"—in pink. "Who hands out these permits?"

"The council." He folded his arms over his grey muscle shirt, making her momentarily lose her place in the conversation. "Over here that's Caroline McInnes. She's a stickler for rules. There's no way she'll let you run a class. Not unless the garage is in pristine condition before you apply for a permit."

Jena's shoulders slumped, then jerked straight back up to their happy position as soon as another idea hit her brain. "You don't need a permit if you're just having some friends over for an evening of dancing, do you? And if they decided to give me gifts, of, say, money, what could I do to stop them? Refusing to accept would be rude." She beamed at him.

Matt let out a heavy sigh as he rubbed a hand over his face. "Jena, you're telling me you plan to run illegal classes in a derelict building and take money you have no intention of paying tax on. Seriously, princess, is it that hard to remember I'm a cop?"

She threw up her hands in frustration. "So I can't even talk to you now?"

"Sure, you can talk to me. Just not about any illegal plans you might have."

Damn, that ruled out quite a chunk of what she had in her head. She put a hand on his arm. "Why don't you pretend you didn't hear anything?" She batted her lashes at him. "I'll give you free dance lessons to turn a blind eye." She smiled hopefully.

Matt's loud groan wasn't encouraging. "That's bribing an officer. Stop now. Don't say another word. We'll pretend this conversation never happened."

"Exactly." Jena winked at him as she grinned. "This never happened. You know nothing." She gave him a quick hug, shivering at the feeling of his firm body under her hands. "Thanks, Matt."

MATT FOUND his arms wrapping around her without his brain telling them to. There was something about crazy Jena Morgan that was irresistible. Man, but she smelled good. Flowery. Spicy. He wasn't sure how it was possible to smell both. Or how the smell managed to make him feel hungry and horny at the same time. A thought he quickly tried to tamp down.

The doorbell rang. He frowned in the direction of the front door, hoping that whoever was there would leave. Then he remembered Dougal was sending food to save Matt from trying to cook in Jena's derelict kitchen. Not that his reprieve would last for long. There was still breakfast to make in the morning. He eyed the cooker. He really hoped the damn thing didn't blow up on him.

Jena stepped away from him, which felt strangely wrong. "I'll start clearing out the garage. You never know when all that space might come in handy." She winked at him again.

Matt fought the urge to roll his eyes. Subtle was not a word he'd use with Jena. And after this conversation, neither were the words "law-abiding citizen".

"Uh-uh, princess." He reached around her waist and pulled her to him. "No wandering off until we talk this through properly. There will be no illegal classes."

"I thought we had an understanding," she wailed.

"I know you did."

She wriggled to get out of his hold and he tightened it. The doorbell rang again. There was no way he was letting Jena out of his sight until he'd knocked her latest plan on the head. Who knew what she'd get up to if he left her unsupervised?

He shifted Jena around so she was balanced under one arm, dangling against his hip. Holding her like a rugby ball, he headed to the front door.

"Let me go, Matt, this isn't funny."

Yeah, that wasn't happening.

"Matt. Put me down. I'm not a toy you can cart around and do what you want with."

Now that was an interesting idea. He looked down at Jena's flushed face as she glared up at him. Her long hair glistened as it swung around her. Her breasts were pushed up tight against him. She was a tempting bundle. One that would make the perfect toy.

"I'll put you down when we're eating. We can talk then too."

"Has anyone ever told you that you're an unreasonable bully?"

"All the time." He opened the door.

"Help," Jena shouted as she struggled to get free. "The cop has lost it, he's gone nuts. Get me out of here."

Matt rolled his eyes at his mother, who stood with her mouth hanging open. "Hey, Mum, ignore Jena. She's having issues."

"Yeah, with you, dumbass," Jena snapped.

He grinned down at her. "Now, Jena, is that polite behaviour around my mother?"

His mum opened and shut her mouth several times.

"Mrs Donaldson, can you please do something about your son? This is not normal behaviour."

"Call me Heather, dear," his mum said helpfully.

Jena growled at him. "I'm getting a sore stomach. You're squeezing too tight. Put me down right now, Matt Donaldson."

He relaxed his hold immediately. As he placed her on her feet, she made a fist. He held up a hand. "You hit me, I'm picking you up again until you learn some manners."

Jena tried to incinerate him with her glare. She was so cute he wanted to pat her on the head, but didn't think that would go over well at all. He turned back to his mum.

"Did Dougal ask you to bring food? Is that it?" He reached for the bag in his mother's hand. It was a safe bet it held food. There was steam coming out of it. He stuck his nose in the bag and breathed deeply. "Excellent." He turned towards the kitchen. "Come on, Jena, you need to eat some real food."

"I'm not eating. I have a dinner date, remember?" Jena shouted at him. "Does he have any mental health issues that I need to be aware of while he's living here?" he heard Jena ask his mother, and let out a sigh.

Compared to Jena, everyone in town was sane. A minute later the women came into the kitchen after him. He felt a sense of déjà vu—didn't he play this scene with his sisters the day before? He shrugged. He didn't care how many members of his family came visiting, just as long as they brought food with them.

"I love what you've done with the place," his mother said with a cheeky grin.

Jena smiled back. "I'm calling it derelict chic."

His mum laughed.

Matt dished out the food and his mouth watered. He bet this was better than whatever Bob served up. Jena was missing out by insisting she go on this date. He shrugged. More for him, then.

"I'm surprised Matt is staying here with this mess," his mum said.

"That's what the twins said too."

"Matt could never stand being around chaos." His mum pulled up a chair. "His bedroom at home was as neat as a pin and organised to the last inch. His sisters used to go in and move things when he was out to see if he noticed. The slightest shift and he could tell. The girls thought it was a great game, until he put a lock on his door." His mother gave him an indulgent smile. "It's the same with the house he has now. Everything in its place. Not a speck of dust anywhere. I swear half the time you can't even tell he lives there."

Jena sat back in her chair and considered him. "That sounds awfully repressed, Matt. Maybe you should get some counselling."

"There's nothing wrong with this brain." Matt tapped his temple.

"I can think of at least half a dozen issues off the top of my head that would have you in therapy for decades."

"Aye, like you would recognise normal," he scoffed. "Most women would be ecstatic if a guy helped renovate their house. You spend your time complaining."

"Most women would like to be asked first before the guy rips off her wallpaper and declares he's in charge of the kitchen. I keep telling you. This is my house. Go rip off the wallpaper in your own house."

"My house doesn't need it. This one does. This kitchen is a biohazard. While I'm here I'm going to help you sort it. If we left it to you it'd be the last room you looked at. I want to be able to cook in a kitchen that won't give me salmonella."

"Well, go home and cook in your own kitchen."

"Children." His mother held up her hands, a look of absolute delight on her face. "This is very entertaining, but I came by to invite you both over to lunch on Sunday and to thank Jena for all the lovely flowers she's been passing on to me."

"Don't mention it," Jena said to his mum while glaring at Matt.

"We'll be there Sunday," Matt said at the same time.

Jena frowned at him. "What happened to it not being safe for me to socialise?"

"That didn't stop you from accepting a date with Bob the butcher, now did it?" He gave her a smug smile. "Don't worry, Jena, you'll be safe at my mum's house, because I'll be there." He grinned widely. "Exactly the same way I'll be right by your side this evening at Bob's house."

Jena sputtered. "You can't come with me on a date."

Matt leaned towards her, pleased when her cheeks flushed. "Watch me." He bit off a huge chunk of steak and chewed hard.

Jena glared at him before looking around the room. No doubt for something to lob at his head. It was a relief to see there was nothing close to hand. Matt suspected Jena Morgan had a bloodthirsty side when she let loose. He grinned. He'd quite like to see that.

"I can see you have everything in hand." His mum stood, hung her handbag over her shoulder and smiled a little too brightly for Matt's liking. "I'll see you both for Sunday lunch."

With a spring in her step, his mother let herself out of the house. Leaving him in a stare off with a very grumpy American.

CHAPTER 10

Friday evening arrived too fast for Matt's liking. Jena was in her bedroom getting ready for her date. Matt shook his head in disgust. *Bob the bloody butcher*. He was nothing more than a shallow pretty boy who knew how to charm the pants off the ladies. Matt shook his head as he cleaned up the paper strips from the kitchen floor. He'd better stay away from Jena's pants. She had enough to deal with without fending off Bob the butcher. He stilled. She would fend him off, wouldn't she? He shuddered. The thought that she might actually want Bob's hands on her didn't bear thinking about. He'd just have to remind Bob that if anyone in Invertary could get away with murder, it would be the only cop.

Matt stood back, hands on hips, and surveyed the result of all his hard work. He'd gotten most of the old paper off the walls now. All they needed was a good wash, then he could plaster and sand them ready to paint. He was thinking they'd look good painted a nice pale blue colour when he caught himself. This was Jena's house. He should probably let her pick the colour of her kitchen.

"Okay." Jena came into the room. "How do I look?"

Matt turned towards her and felt his heart skip a beat. Maybe two. He rubbed his hand over his chest. Yeah. Definitely irregular. He'd need to see the doc about that. Thirty-two had to be too young to suffer from heart disease. Didn't it?

"Matt, pay attention. How do I look?" She twirled, her arms held away from her sides.

Matt's mouth went dry. His eyes narrowed. Hell no. "You can't wear that."

Her smile disappeared as she looked down at herself. She had on a bronze-coloured dress, made of some silky material. There were bat-like sleeves. The neckline slid off a shoulder. He felt his anger build—was she even wearing a bra? The skirt section was a tight band across her thighs, stopping mere inches below her backside. Her skin was shimmering, her eyes were painted dark and sexy and her hair fell in soft waves over her shoulders and around her breasts. Cupping them like gentle hands. Matt forced his eyes to move on. Unfortunately, it didn't help. Her perfect legs made him want to groan with need. He swallowed it down as he eyed her shoes. They were basically stilts. This time shimmering bronze stilts with straps that criss-crossed up her calf, tying in a bow at her knee. Her toenails were painted to match the shoes.

One look at that mini dress, and those shoes, and Bob's focus wouldn't be on food. No, it would be on untying the shoes, then running his hand up those shimmering legs to get to the hemline of that tight little skirt. *Not happening. Not on his watch.* Matt's job was to protect Jena. And he'd damn well do it. Whether she liked it or not. He'd start by protecting her from Bob's lecherous attention.

He pointed to the door. "Go get changed. Put on jeans and a T-shirt." He thought about it. "A high-necked T-shirt. A loose-fitting one. And put a bloody bra on too."

Jena gaped at him. "Are you serious?"

He folded his arms. "You can't wear that. You're giving out the wrong signals. You're inviting Bob to come get you. Go get changed."

Jena folded her arms too. She held a tiny bronze clutch bag in one hand. Her arms pulled the top of the dress tight across her breasts, and Matt felt the blood rush away from his brain. *She was so not wearing that dress.* Jena tapped a toe on the old linoleum floor, drawing his attention back to her legs, when it had taken a great deal of effort to get his attention off her legs.

"This is a date," she said. "You dress up for a date. There is nothing wrong with my clothes. And for your information, I am wearing a bra."

Matt's eyes shot back to her chest. "I don't see a bra."

"You're not supposed to see it, you lunatic. Now stop whatever you're doing to my kitchen. You're my lift and we need to go."

"Uh-nuh, you're not going anywhere until you change. You can't go out like that. Do you want him all over you?" He held up a hand. "Don't answer that. Just get something else on."

"Donald Matthew Donaldson. Do I look like one of your sisters?" She didn't let him reply. "No, I don't. We are not related. You are not my big brother. You don't get to tell me what to wear on a date. After meeting your sisters, I'm sure you don't get to tell them either. If I want Bob's hands all over me, then that's my business. This is my date. Not yours. If you're not going to take me to Bob's house, I'll go on my own. Or better yet, I'll call Bob to come pick me up."

Matt glared at her for a minute. She seemed serious. It took all of his self-control to stop from throwing her over his shoulder, stomping up to her bedroom and demanding she wear something else—even if he had to dress her himself.

Instead he took a deep breath, snatched his keys off the table and stomped to the front door. "Fine. I'll take you."

He stopped inside the front door frame, spinning so fast that Jena fell against him.

"For the record, princess. I'm more than aware you're not my sister." He slowly ran his gaze down her body. "For a start, if you were my sister, I wouldn't be thinking about what kind of underwear you have on under that dress. Or if your legs feel as silky as they look." Matt put a hand on the small of her back and leaned in to her ear. "I definitely wouldn't be wondering how long it would take to get you out of your dress and into my bed." He stared down at her. "Still sure this is what you want to wear for Bob?"

He watched her eyes widen and her throat roll as she swallowed. She nodded.

He clenched his jaw at her stubbornness. "Don't say I didn't warn you. Let's get this over with." He released the warm woman in his arms and stalked to the driver's side of his car.

"I CAN'T BELIEVE you dragged me out tonight," Claire whined. "I don't want to be out. I want to go home and read my new book. In bed. In my fleecy onesie. With a mug of hot chocolate and Adele playing. I don't want to hang out at the local pub. I don't want to socialise. I don't want to be here. Full stop."

"When did you get to be so boring?" Megan frowned at her. "It's like I blinked and missed it. One minute you were my fun-loving sister. The next you want to stay in on a Friday night. Last time I checked, we were still twenty-two. Women our age don't curl up with a book on a Friday night."

"The smart ones do! It's not like I'm making you suffer by staying home all the time. When was the last Friday I stayed home? Huh? Tell me that?" Claire stomped her red suede boots as Megan pulled the heavy pub door open. "You can't answer because it was never. That's when."

"I see your lips move, but all I hear is blah, blah, blah." Megan stuck her nose in the air. "Fantastic. It's karaoke."

Claire's mood plummeted even further. "Great. A bunch of old people taking turns to sing 'Stand By Your Man'."

"Tammy Wynette. Can't beat a classic." Megan grinned widely. "But you can murder it when you're tone deaf and have downed several whiskeys. Not to mention the Scottish accent lends its own unique appeal." She scanned the room. "Ooo, front-row seats." She grabbed an armful of Claire's red cowl-neck sweater and dragged her towards a round table over in the corner near the toilets and, unfortunately, the makeshift stage.

"Kill me now." Claire let out a groan.

"What do you want to drink? Kopparberg?" Megan was already heading towards the bar. Reaching into the front pocket of her tight jeans for her tiny wallet.

"Just a Coke. Diet."

Five minutes later they had their drinks and were being tortured by the dulcet tones of eighty-seven-year-old Betty. The tartan-clad cube of a woman was singing the song she always sung on nights like this, "Boogie Woogie Bugle Boy". Unfortunately for everyone watching, she had a dance routine to go with it.

"I need to film this one week and put it on YouTube," Megan said in Claire's ear.

"Yeah, why should we be the only ones who suffer? Let's spread it around."

"Oh, you're a delight tonight." Megan reached for her raspberry-flavoured cider and took a large gulp. The bottle stopped at her lips. Her eyes went wide. Claire could feel the panic coming off her as though it was her own.

"What?" Claire turned towards the door to see what had ratcheted up Megan's anxiety level.

A second later, she was just as frozen as her twin. Standing in the pub entrance, his attention currently fixed on the stage, where Betty was gearing up for her big finale, was the man they'd almost run over.

"What do we do?" Megan whispered. "Run? Talk to him? What?"

Claire felt the bottom of her stomach plummet. "Maybe he won't remember us."

Before they could make a decision, the guy's eyes swept over the room. They snapped back to zoom in on them. He jerked in place. His friend was still talking to him, but he didn't seem to notice. His lips thinned in clear determination as he stalked towards the twins. His eyes never left their faces, making them act like deer caught in headlights.

"I say we run," Megan whispered.

Claire felt her sister grab her arm and take a step back towards the toilets, and the corridor that led to the hotel entrance. From the look on the guy's face, Claire agreed it might be wise to run. Unfortunately, her feet hadn't received the memo from her brain and were stuck to the floor.

He came to a stop in front of them. His eyes ran over Megan, before turning to Claire. "Two of you," he muttered. He studied both of them for a few seconds more before focusing in on Claire. Recognition flared in his eyes. Claire felt her world tilt. "Angel." He growled as he reached for her. "Mine," he said.

Claire took a deep breath. "Run," she screeched.

The twins spun in their matching boots and darted along the corridor to the hotel reception. A minute later they were out in the cool night air.

"How the hell did he recognise you?" Megan demanded as they sprinted away from the pub. "We're identical. We're wearing the same freaking clothes tonight. Only three other people can tell us apart."

"Less talking. More running," Claire shouted back.

"I don't think so," a voice said behind her as an arm swept around her waist, and Claire found her feet dangling above the ground. Her back pressed against a firm chest. An arm made of solid muscle held her tightly.

"Mine," the voice said again.

"As entertaining as this caveman crap is," said another male voice, "I think you should probably put the nice girl down so we can talk this through."

Claire spun around as the man holding her turned to his friend. "Mine."

"Down, boy." The other guy grinned. He, at least, looked approachable. Possibly even friendly. Also, he wasn't growling "mine" every few seconds, which was a plus.

"Let go of my sister," Megan snapped. "This isn't the Ice Age. You can't come along and claim ownership of a person. Put her down right now. Or so help me, you'll regret it."

Megan was furious. Her cheeks were flushed, her eyes were sparkling and her hair was flying. She looked ready to do some damage. The less terrifying guy laughed. "Hold it together, Tinker Bell. The big guy here only wants to have a chat. Right?"

Claire felt the muscle behind her tense before his breath warmed her ear. "I'm going to put you down. You will not run. You get me?"

She nodded. She wasn't capable of speech. Slowly, he lowered her down his body and placed her on her feet beside him. He kept his arm wrapped around her waist. His large palm was flat against her stomach above the waistband of her jeans. Claire swallowed hard and looked up over her shoulder at him. And up. He had to be about seven foot tall.

He'd been a whole lot less intimidating when he was lying down. Being unconscious helped too.

"Come over here, honey." Megan used the same tone people adopted with skittish animals and terrified children.

"Stay," the mountain rumbled.

Claire stayed.

She cast a glance at Megan out of the corner of her eye and saw her own confusion and fear mirrored there. Neither of them knew what to do.

"This is going well," the cheery guy said. "I'm Joe Barone. The big guy is Grunt. We didn't mean to freak you out. Grunt here would like to have a chat about his head injury. He's missing some information." He chuckled. "Although the poster you made cleared up some of his questions." He spread his hands wide. "How about we find somewhere quiet and have a chat? Friendly like. Nothing to worry about."

Megan hitched a thumb towards Grunt. "Can you keep a leash on the gorilla? Because if you can't, I'm calling my brother to come get us." She turned to Grunt. "My brother, the cop."

Grunt stepped closer into Claire's side. She could feel his body heat overwhelm her. "Mine," he said again. He took her hand in his. It swallowed hers whole. His grip was firm, but not threatening.

Claire couldn't move. Couldn't talk. Couldn't do anything.

"He has to stop saying that," Megan said to Joe. "Make him stop saying that. Claire does not belong to him."

"Claire." The reverent way that Grunt said her name went right through her, making her shiver. His free hand gently stroked her cheek as his eyes softened. Then heated. Claire gulped, but still she couldn't move her feet. Was this how a kitten felt when a rambunctious toddler claimed it? If that was the case, she'd taken her last animal to kindy for the kids to pet.

"Is he mentally disturbed?" Megan said. "Is he capable of speech? Should he be out without supervision? Please, tell me there aren't a bunch of guys wearing white coats running around Invertary trying to return him to his own special institution." She turned to Grunt. "Mountain man, do you normally wear a jacket that buckles in the back? Think hard. Are you usually in a white room? Alone? With padded walls?"

Grunt frowned at her, while Joe laughed hard. "No, he isn't insane. He's just Grunt. Come on, let's go get a coffee, and some food. I need to eat and we all need to talk."

Megan linked her arm through Claire's and firmly yanked her away from Grunt. His hand held fast and Claire felt like the rope in a tug-of-war. It wasn't a pleasant sensation.

Grunt growled at Megan, who backed up a step. His eyes softened when he looked down at Claire.

"I won't hurt you." His words and manner were so earnest that Claire found herself believing him. She relaxed slightly, casting a nervous glance at her sister.

"Glad we've got that sorted," Joe said. "Let's go back to the pub and get some food."

Warily, they turned back towards the big white building. The tortured sound of more locals killing popular songs wafted on the cool night air. As Claire stepped back into the restaurant area of the hotel pub, Grunt leaned over to whisper in her ear.

"I would never hurt you." He paused as she shivered. "But I am keeping you," he vowed.

Claire tripped at the words. Instead of curling up with a good book, she'd become the unwilling pet of a Neanderthal wannabe.

CHAPTER 11

For the first time in his police career, Matt was pleased that Scotland didn't issue its officers with firearms. He was pleased, because if he'd had a gun on him, he would have shot Bob the butcher. Not somewhere life threatening. Just in a place he didn't use much. Like his brain.

"How about you go watch Jena from outside the house," Bob said. "Sit in your car. I've got the inside of the house covered. Nothing will happen to her while I'm with her." He leered at Jena. "Nothing she doesn't want to happen, anyway."

Matt folded his arms and leaned on the edge of the desk he'd commandeered in the living room area of Bob's house. The whole bottom floor of the house was open plan, making it easy for Matt to keep an eye on the kitchen and dining area from the spot he'd picked. Jena was currently sitting on a high stool at the breakfast bar, her legs crossed, sipping a margarita. It was in the biggest glass Matt had ever seen. No, not a glass, a freaking goldfish bowl. There had to be a whole bottle of tequila in that one glass. From the looks of it, Bob had gone easy on the lime and heavy on the alcohol. Talk about an obvious attempt to get his date drunk.

"I'm fine here." He used his official voice. The one that brooked no argument. "Just doing my job. Pretend I'm not here." Yeah, he really hoped Bob wasn't able to pull that off.

The guy looked ready to spit fireballs. "Give me a break here. Would you like a chaperone on your date?"

"I'm not a chaperone. Do what you like." He pointed to his laptop. "I brought paperwork to keep me busy."

Bob clenched his fists before making a clear effort to relax his shoulders. He flashed a wide, fake smile. "Whatever you want, Matt. You want to play the voyeur, then sit back and enjoy the show." He winked. "You might learn something."

He sauntered back to Jena, leaving Matt to mentally go through a list of offences to see if there was one he could charge the guy with. He came up empty.

Matt focused on the report on the screen in front of him. It was busywork. Irrelevant. Not that it mattered what he was working on. His complete attention was on the other side of the room. He heard Jena give a high-pitched, girly giggle that was obviously fake, and frowned at her. She made bug eyes in his direction. He almost smiled, and then Bob trailed a finger over Jena's bare shoulder and Matt's humour evaporated.

"Best steak in Scotland," the moron was saying, "probably in the world."

Jena seemed to cast around for something to say. "Did you, ah, cut it yourself?"

Bob puffed up his chest, acting like he'd invented the bloody wheel. "Sure did, sweetheart. The key to a great steak is in the cut. It isn't the amount of meat, it's the marbling that gives it the flavour..." Matt tuned Bob out as he waxed lyrical about the perfect steak.

He allowed himself a smug smile. Bob definitely wasn't going to get a second date. Not if the glazed look on Jena's face was anything to go by.

"You made the place really pretty, Bob," Jena said, interrupting his lecture on the best ways to tenderise meat. "I love the candles."

Bob stroked a hand down Jena's hair, making Matt clench his jaw so hard it almost locked in place.

"Got to make an effort for a beautiful girl," Bob said.

Pass the bucket—it was time to vomit.

Jena tittered again. Why couldn't Bob tell her laugh was fake? And candles? Big deal. Anyone could light a few candles. Plus, what guy in his right mind bought chubby pink ones? Matt felt a little growl escape him. Jena cast him an angry glance. He scoffed at her. She glared at him before flashing a wide smile at Bob and picking up her bucket of tequila.

"Why don't we sit outside for a little bit? It's such a nice night."

The smarmy smile Bob shot Matt made his fists clench. "Great idea, sweetheart."

Matt stood, ready to follow.

"Stay," Bob ordered.

Matt cocked an eyebrow. "Do I look like a poodle? I don't think so." Matt folded his arms. "Where she goes, I go."

Jena stared at the ceiling. "For heaven's sake..." She stomped towards him as best she could on her killer heels. The tub of tequila-heavy margarita sloshed around in her hand.

"You don't need to follow us," she whispered through another fake smile.

Her eyes were blazing. She was seriously cute when she was pissed, kind of like a hissing kitten.

"Yes, I do. I'm here to protect you."

"Not from Bob!" She kept her voice low. "How am I supposed to get to know him if you're hanging over us all the time?"

"What's to know? He's full of himself. That's it. Whole story. Move on."

She pursed her lips. He thought she might hit him, but instead she swivelled on her heels and strode away from him. Flashing those luscious legs and reminding him again that she shouldn't have worn that dress.

"Come on, Bob, we can't get rid of him, so let's pretend he's invisible." Jena cast an irritated look over her shoulder at Matt.

And that was when it happened.

Her heel caught in the 1970s faux-shag rug and she lurched forward. Bob reached for her. The margarita flew through the air, soaking Bob. He cursed loudly. Jena reached for the breakfast bar to break her fall. Two candles went flying. One hit Bob.

And the butcher went up in flames.

Matt had been rushing to catch Jena when Bob screamed. He changed direction. He lunged at Bob, tackling him down onto the ugly rug. A second later he had the guy rolled up like a sausage in pastry. The flames were out. The rug smouldered around Bob, who was sobbing hysterically.

Jena fell to her knees beside the butcher, patting his face gently. His head and feet were the only parts of him not rolled in rug.

"I am so sorry."

Jena's voice trembled. She was clearly in shock. Matt eyed her with worry. He'd seen her during the aftermath of many a disastrous date. She'd never been this upset before. But then, she'd never set a guy on fire before either. As he dialled for an ambulance and the local doctor, he watched Jena. Did she actually feel something for Bob the butcher?

The thought left him with cement in his stomach.

"Get away from me," Bob shouted. "You're the kiss of death. Every guy who comes near you gets hurt. What is wrong with you, woman?"

Jena jerked backwards as though she'd been slapped. She climbed to her feet and placed a hand on the breakfast bar to steady herself. Matt didn't like how pale she looked.

"You're a menace," Bob shouted. "No wonder they call you Calamity Jena."

Jena sucked in a shocked breath. Her whole body shook.

Bob spat his words at her. "I thought the stories were lies. No one as hot as you could be that accident-prone. I was wrong. You're a freaking mess. No guy should get anywhere near you. Not if they value their life."

Jena's eyes turned glassy, but she didn't say anything. Her bottom lip trembled, and what little sympathy Matt felt for the butcher evaporated. He nudged the Bob-filled rug with his toe. Okay, maybe kicked would be more accurate. Whatever. "Cut it out. It was an accident. No need to be more of a dick than usual."

Bob's mouth fell open. "You kicked me. I'm dying of third-degree burns and you kicked me. What kind of cop are you? You're as crazy as she is."

At that point there was a thump at the door. Matt looked at Jena's ashen face. "Not one word," he threatened an irate Bob.

Matt went to let the doc in.

"What we got?" The doc rushed past Matt, clasping his medical bag.

"Jena accidentally set Bob on fire. He's in the rug. He's fine. Jena's in shock. You need to check her out. I'm worried about her."

"Check Jena? I'm the one who was on fire!"

"Can you give him something to put him to sleep?" Matt

gave the Bob-filled rug a look of disgust. "I'm fed up listening to the guy."

"That's it. I'm lodging a complaint. Your superiors are going to hear about this…"

Matt tuned out Bob's rant. Instead he pulled Jena into his arms, surprised when she curled into him. "It's okay, princess," he murmured against her hair. "Don't let him get to you. It was an accident. His fault. He's the one with the bad décor. Anyone could have tripped on that huge, hairy rug. You were bound to hit a candle when you fell. There are about a million of them in here. Don't worry about it." He rubbed her arms as she shivered.

Doc unwrapped Bob. The guy was still ranting. Doc let out a sigh. "Mild burns. You got him fast enough. Nothing to worry about. The clothes and the rug are trashed, but he's fine."

"See," Matt told Jena, "he's just being a big baby. He's fine."

Jena hiccupped against his chest as her shoulders shook. Matt held her tighter. He glared at Bob the bloody butcher and couldn't resist giving him another *nudge* with the toe of his boot.

"Man up," he told the pathetically wailing guy. "You're upsetting her."

Ignoring Bob's outrage, Matt led Jena to his car.

CHAPTER 12

"Here's what we're going to do." Joe led the twins, and Grunt, to a table in the corner of the pub's restaurant. "We're gonna talk about this calm like. Nobody is gonna freak out. We're all friends here."

Megan barked a harsh laugh. "No we're not." She spun on Grunt as he pulled out a chair for Claire. "King Kong, stop manhandling my sister."

He growled at Megan. Megan growled right back. It was like a Chihuahua taking on a Doberman.

"He isn't manhandling me." Claire found her voice at last. For a minute there she'd worried she might have become permanently mute. "He's only holding my arm. He's stopping now. Aren't you, Grunt?"

What the hell kind of name was Grunt?

"No," he said.

Great, that was helpful. Claire frowned at him before attempting a smile for her sister. They all needed to calm down. This was crazy enough as it was without hysterics coming into play. She felt a tug on the seat of her chair. It jerked closer to Grunt, and the next thing she knew she was wedged against him. His arm slid around her waist. His thumb traced tiny circles on her hip.

Claire tried to shrug him off. His hold tightened. Her reaction to his behaviour confused her. Part of her wanted to run screaming in panic. The other part wanted to melt into him. He was huge, solid and smelled like a Highland forest on a warm summer's day. He was also a strange American man who thought he owned her. Okay, it was official: she was losing her mind.

"Hands off my sister, King Kong." Megan pointed at Grunt. "Or I'm calling my brother in."

Claire turned in time to see her captor's reaction to Megan's threat. A slow smile curved his lips, turning his face from terrifyingly masculine into sexy as hell. Claire's mouth went dry at the sight. The only thing that ruined the transformation was that the smile didn't reach his eyes. They were hard. Calculating.

"Call him." His voice rumbled through her. "I've been wondering why he hasn't been to see me. Figured he'd want a statement. Seeing as I was run off the road by a negligent driver."

Megan paled. Joe looked astonished. "Shit, man, that's the most I've heard you say at one time in about five years."

"Don't faint yet," Grunt told his friend. "I ain't done." He leaned across the table towards Megan. "You want to keep this whole business from your brother, and that fits in with my plans, so I'm gonna to give you that. I'll keep things to myself. But I want something in return for helping you out."

Claire had trouble swallowing. She didn't need to be clairvoyant to know what he wanted.

"What?" Megan demanded.

"Claire."

Yep, and she was right.

Megan slapped the table. "You can't have her, King Kong. She's a person. Not a card you trade."

"Done dealing with you." Grunt cut off her sister by turning in his seat towards Claire. His eyes softened. "Gonna be straight with you, baby. I like what I see and I want more of it. Never had a reaction like this before." He gently cupped her cheek, and, to her disgust, a tiny sigh escaped her lips. He smiled, soft and delicious. "Want more of this. Want more of you. You give me a chance to get to know you and I don't talk to your brother. What do you say, baby? I'll treat you right. You got my word on that."

"I don't even know you," she whispered.

"Gonna fix that for you, babe."

"Claire. Resist the insanity." Megan's voice cut through the little world she'd fallen into. The one where only Grunt existed. She blinked at her sister as though coming out of a daze. Megan's mouth hardened. "You're suffering from Stockholm syndrome. Fight it. Don't get sucked in by his blue eyes and Dwayne Johnson shoulder muscles."

Joe laughed. "I like you, sugar, but to suffer from Stockholm syndrome you have to be kidnapped for a while. My buddy here has only been holding your sister for ten minutes."

"Feels longer," Megan snapped at him.

"This is between you and me," Grunt said softly to Claire. "Give me a chance."

"No," Megan wailed.

"Yes," Claire whispered.

She felt every muscle in his huge body vibrate against her. "Not gonna regret that, babe."

Claire bit her bottom lip as she eyed her sister. Her very furious sister. She smiled weakly. Megan wasn't impressed.

"Listen up, King Kong," Megan said. "I'm watching you. You hurt her—you die. You make her cry—you die. You pressure her into anything—you die. Why you couldn't have asked her out on a date like a normal person, I don't know. I do know that you're walking a fine line with me. One where you die if you cross it." She leaned over the table. "Don't be fooled. We might look like members of Charlie's Angels, but we're capable of a whole lot more than roller-skating and flipping our hair. You hurt her and you hurt me too. You don't want to hurt both of us. Am I clear?"

Grunt nodded solemnly. Although the only thing clear about Megan's threats was that they were empty ones. If Grunt wanted to, he could snap the twins like a couple of twigs.

Megan picked up her menu. "Let's eat. Consider this your first date. Impress me with your behaviour."

Claire smothered a grin—Megan should have been the one to study kindergarten teaching. She watched Megan stiffen as Joe trailed a finger over her shoulder.

"Just so you know. I don't need to kidnap a woman to get a date."

"Good for you." Megan flicked his hand away. "Just so *you* know. Nothing will happen between you and me. Ever."

"Gotcha." Joe looked more amused than rejected.

Claire's attention was torn away from the entertainment on the other side of the table when Grunt held her tight and leaned down to whisper in her ear. "Samuel Dayton," he said. "People call me Grunt. You don't. You call me Samuel, or Sam." He smiled against her cheek, sending shivers through her body. "Nice to meet you, Claire."

"We are in so much trouble," Megan muttered.

Claire blinked up at Grunt and felt her brain freeze. Oh yeah, they were in trouble all right.

With a slow smile, Grunt lifted the menu and opened it in front of both of them.

"Got to feed my baby," he said.

"Does anybody else find his behaviour really creepy?" Megan asked loudly.

Grunt ignored her sister and smiled at Claire. "What do you fancy?" he said.

And yet again, Claire felt like the monster's pet. Only in her head he'd morphed into one of those cute, cuddly monsters that you found on *Sesame Street*.

Yep, she was in serious trouble.

CHAPTER 13

Jena was uncharacteristically silent during the short drive to her house. The light that normally shone from her had dimmed. It made Matt want to go back to Bob's house and kick him some more.

She climbed out of the car before he could help her and picked her way up the broken and overgrown path to her door. The stiff set of her shoulders gave out the clear message that she didn't want him near, so he stayed close behind in case there were any more accidents. But he didn't touch. Even though his fingers were burning with the need to comfort her.

The door swung open and the light came on. A bare bulb casting the hallway in sharp, unforgiving light. Jena turned to him. Her eyes didn't make it to his face; they focused somewhere in the middle of his chest.

"I'm off to bed." If she was aiming for a light-hearted tone, she was nowhere near it. "See you in the morning."

Before he could stop her, she turned to the bare wooden staircase and started the climb to her room. Hurt radiated from her. He hated it.

"It's still early," he said. "How about a warm drink in the kitchen? Or on the sofa? I make a mean hot chocolate."

She turned and smiled. It was a shadow of her normal smiles. The ones that lit up a room. The ones that made people smile in return—whether they wanted to or not.

"Maybe tomorrow. It's been a long day. I'm tired."

Matt clenched his fists as she continued her slow ascent. This was wrong. She shouldn't be alone. She'd had a shock. And she'd had to deal with Bob. He ran his fingers through his hair. His feet wanted to follow her. His arms wanted to hold her. Hell, even his lips wanted to whisper words of comfort.

With a growl of frustration, he turned and strode into the living room. She didn't want his comfort. He was just there to protect her. A job. She was a job.

Not an official job, the small voice whispered in the back of his mind. *You're here because you want to be here. No one is making you.* He looked back at the open doorway. *She needs you.*

Matt shook his head to clear it.

She didn't need him right now. She'd made that clear. As he made up the sofa bed, he came up with a plan. He'd leave the living room door open, and if he heard anything that worried him he'd go up and check on her.

He stripped to his boxers, climbed into bed and stared at the ceiling. Straight up to the spot where Jena slept. Alone. Hurting. His ears strained for the slightest noise. One whimper was all it would take, and he'd allow himself to take care of her.

JENA STRIPPED off the clothes she'd taken so much time to choose. The shoes thunked as they hit the floor. The dress pooled at her feet. She stepped out of it and left it there. She didn't have the heart to pick it up. She just wanted to leave it where it fell and let it rot away. The wonderful lingerie she bought at Kirsty's shop, before she'd run out of money, followed the dress and landed in a heap at her feet.

She tugged open the drawer to the old dresser she'd sanded and painted pale pink and pulled out her favourite pyjamas. They were years old, the cotton bottoms faded to the point where you couldn't make out the pattern anymore. The matching vest top had thinned over time, becoming so soft she barely felt it against her skin. Once she was dressed, she headed to the bathroom, where she painstakingly removed every hint of makeup still left on her face.

A few minutes later, she was tucked under her thick duvet, staring into the darkness, wishing she could run away. But where would she go? Even if she had the money. She had nowhere to go. And running was stupid. Coming to Invertary proved that. It didn't matter where she went; the same problem would always be there—her.

Suddenly the last thing Jena wanted was to be alone with her thoughts. Her eyes went to the door as she thought of Matt downstairs. He'd offered her comfort. She hoped the offer was still open.

Before she could second-guess herself, she slipped out of bed and tiptoed downstairs. The lights were out, but the living room glowed with moonlight that filtered through the curtains. Matt was stretched out on the small pull-out couch, the bedding pulled up over him, one hand slung above his head, the other on his stomach. His very bare stomach. Jena chewed her lip as she hesitated on the threshold. Torn between longing and unworthiness. In the end, it was his scent that made the choice for her. The room smelled like Matt. Fresh, musky and solid. And tonight she needed solid.

Her steps towards him were silent.

She stopped beside the bed. Was he asleep? "Matt?" she whispered.

"Come here." His deep voice startled her.

A solid arm wrapped around her and jerked her down into the bed and to his side. Her cheek was singed by the heat of his chest as her head rested against him. Her hand was a fist on his stomach.

"I just want to cuddle," Jena whispered.

"I know." He kissed the top of her head.

Jena slowly relaxed against him. He engulfed her senses. A cocoon of muscle, strength and warmth. They lay in silence for the longest time. Aware that neither of them had given in to sleep. Jena soaked up his comfort. The sound of his heartbeat soothed her. His steady breathing gently rocked her cares away.

"I've never set anyone on fire before."

Matt gave her a reassuring squeeze. "It couldn't have happened to a nicer person."

She pinched his side. "Behave."

"Menace," he grumbled.

"So I've been told." She took a shaky breath and blew it out into the darkness. "Why do these things keep happening to me, Matt?"

His hand stroked her arm as it lay on his chest. "I've been thinking about this. I think it's a distraction thing. When your mind isn't totally focused on something you get clumsy, or you cause whoever is with you to get clumsy. It's not you. When you're concentrating, your grace is a thing of beauty."

She snuggled into him. "I feel really bad about Bob."

"I know." He kissed the top of her head. "He's fine. You heard the doc."

She felt her bottom lip tremble. "Are people really calling me Calamity?"

"Don't worry about it, they don't mean anything by it. It will pass."

"No, it won't. I'm a disaster."

"Don't say that."

"I am. What about the other dates I've had? Patrick with his broken toes…"

"He was the one who forgot to put the handbrake on. Which the moron might have noticed if he hadn't been so busy trying to get you up against his truck. It's not your fault it ran over his foot."

"What about Michael's dislocated shoulder?"

Matt barked out a laugh. "He fell off the path. You didn't push him. Maybe if he'd spent more time watching where he was going instead of trying to impress you with his knowledge of nature, he wouldn't have fallen. Plus he knows those trails like the back of his hand. There's no excuse for him."

"Graeme got concussion. I did push him. It was my fault." Matt's warmth was beginning to lull Jena to sleep.

"The guy is a wimp. He got a nosebleed tying his shoe last week. A playful push from a wee lassie shouldn't have toppled him."

"You're good for my self-esteem."

His shoulders shook as he chuckled. "You're not totally innocent, princess. There was the guy who fell in the loch when he took you for a boat ride. He got a fright when you screamed." He looked down at her. "Is it true you thought you saw Nessie?"

"No. That isn't true." She wasn't that dumb. She knew Nessie only hung out in Loch Ness. Hence the name. Duh. She'd screamed because she'd been Googling something on her phone and almost dropped it in the loch. But she damn well wasn't going to tell Matt that.

"How come Frank is still in one piece? You lived with him. No. Wait. Don't tell me. He has a thing for pain."

She smacked his abs, making her palm tingle. Without thinking about it, she soothed the sting by rubbing her hand on his warm skin. Matt nuzzled her hair. Oh, this was nice. Maybe too nice. She decided not to think about the fact she was in bed beside a very sexy half-naked man. After all, it was only Matt. It wasn't like she'd crawled in with a stranger. Matt was nothing more than a friend.

A little voice whispered in Jena's ear that she wasn't in the habit of cuddling up to her half-naked friends while they were in bed. She dismissed it.

"Frank?" he prompted, bringing her back to the present.

"We didn't really date. He'd turn up at the clubs where I danced to keep me company. Next thing I knew, I was living with him. I don't ever remember there being a date."

"Ha! So that's the key to an injury-free relationship with Jena Morgan—don't date her."

"Funny. Oh so funny. I'm cracking up here." She yawned loudly, ruining any impact her sarcasm might have had.

They lay in silence for a while, Matt gently stroking her shoulder as the shadows from the trees danced around the walls. Jena felt her eyelids droop.

"It wasn't supposed to be like this here," she whispered.

"Like what?"

"Hard."

She rubbed her cheek against his firm muscle. He tugged her closer. His hand gently stroked her arm.

"It's hard everywhere, princess."

"I just wanted a home." She closed her eyes tight. The confession robbing her last defence. "All I wanted was to belong. Somewhere."

"And you do, you crazy girl. You belong right where you are." He nuzzled her hair with his chin. "Go to sleep. It'll all be better tomorrow."

Slowly, Jena felt her eyelids grow heavy as his heat seeped into her.

Sleep pulled her under, cocooned in Matt's protective embrace.

CHAPTER 14

Grunt sat in a booth in the pub on Saturday morning listening to Frank whine. It was the last place he wanted to be. The first being wherever Claire was. He poked at his food with a fork. It wasn't bad, but it wasn't what he wanted. The only options on the menu were a fried breakfast or porridge. What he really wanted was a pile of warm beignets straight from New Orleans. He wanted them dusted in a liberal amount of powdered sugar and served with chicory coffee that was strong enough to melt a spoon. Yeah, that would be great. The only thing that could make it any better would be to eat it with Claire.

Instead, he was eating black pudding with Frank. Could the day get any worse?

"I called in reinforcements. You two ain't doing the job I'm paying you to do. We need help." Frank sneered at them, and Grunt realised the day could indeed get worse.

He could almost hear Joe's teeth clench. "Reinforcements?"

"Yeah." Frank sat back in his seat. He was only drinking

black coffee. Frank worried he'd get a gut if he ate decent food.

"Want to tell us what's going on, Frank?" Joe's tone was flat and deadly. Most men would run when they heard it. Not Frank. He was too stupid.

"I called the mother." Frank tugged at his cuffs. His smile was nasty. Grunt pushed his food away before it turned in his stomach. "Jena's mom was real interested to know her daughter is hanging out in the same town as Josh McInnes. She'll be here on the first flight she can get. She's a big fan. Convinced that McInnes will hear her songs and give her the break she's been chasing her whole life." He looked smug. "I promised her I'd get her some face time with Josh if she came and talked to Jena. I made it clear if she doesn't get Jena on a flight to the States, there'll be no Josh time."

Grunt eyed his fork. He wondered how it would look sticking out of Frank's throat.

Joe was not impressed. "I thought you wanted to talk to Jena, not make her go back with you. That's what you said when you hired us. We're here to show your woman what a big, important guy you are. Let her know what she's missing. Why the push to get her stateside?"

Frank leaned forward, arms on the table. "I don't need to tell you shit. You're hired meat. Performing monkeys. You don't need to know nothing." He pointed at Joe. "Your job is to do what you're told." He pushed out of the booth and sneered at them. "Waste of money. Amateurs. Be ready in fifteen. We're gonna try talking to Jena again."

With that he swept out of the room, like the president at a state dinner.

"I hate that guy," Grunt said.

Joe patted him on the back. "That's what I like about you, buddy. Straight to the point. No messing around." He looked at the door Frank had disappeared through. "He's an asshole."

No truer word was spoken. "Why you think he's got such a hard-on for this Jena chick?"

Joe shrugged, but it was tight. Forced. "Dunno. But I'm getting a bad feeling about it. I thought this would be an easy gig. Give the guy an ego boost. See Scotland. Now I'm getting a rash from taking his money."

No kidding. Grunt felt the need to shower every time he was around Frank.

"What do we do?" he said. "See this thing through or bail?"

Joe's lips tightened. "Got a bad feeling. Let's see how this plays for now."

"Watch the girl," Grunt said with a nod.

"Yeah, watch the girl. I think the moron may be planning more than we guessed. Definitely more than he told us. Wouldn't want to see Jena hurt."

No, Grunt thought grimly. There was no way they'd let that happen.

"WHAT'S with you and all these first dates, anyway?"

It was Saturday afternoon. Matt was busy prying nails from the old floorboards in her kitchen. Yet another job he'd taken on without consulting her. She'd also found paint samples on the table. She was beginning to suspect Matt had taken over her renovation.

She'd been a bit disorientated when she'd woken in her living room instead of her bedroom. She'd been alone in the bed, which was more of a relief than anything else. Part of her had been anxious about dealing with Matt, but he'd behaved as he normally did—lecturing her about her breakfast choices while providing coffee that was actually drinkable. There was no awkwardness and there was no mention of the night before. Jena knew she should be pleased that it wasn't a big deal, but part of her was seriously disappointed. She laughed at herself. What was she expecting? For him to be so turned on by her close proximity that he fell at her feet? No. She was glad things were back to normal. Over the moon about it, in fact.

"Jena, are you listening to me? What's with all the dates? Are you desperate for a man?"

"Yeah. That's exactly it," she drawled. "I'm desperate. I can't live without a man in my life. I'm incomplete. Woe is me."

Jena continued to fill the black garbage sack with the last of the discarded wallpaper. Who knew there was so much paper on the kitchen walls? The room wasn't big, yet the garage was full of bags waiting for rubbish pickup day.

"I'm being serious here."

"How about you tone down the male chauvinist attitude and I might answer your questions?"

He narrowed his eyes at her, making her squirm. It was amazingly easy to forget he was a cop.

"What's the deal with the dates?" he asked again.

With a heavy sigh, she turned towards him. He looked sexy in his butter-soft blue jeans and old grey shirt. Her mouth watered at the sight. He had a body to die for. After a night spent cuddled up next to him, she knew exactly how good that body could feel. She shook her head to clear it.

"I know how much courage it takes to ask someone out and I don't want to throw it back in their faces. I give everyone a chance at a first date. Then at least I can tell them honestly if we don't click. Without the date, a rejection is just plain mean. I don't like hurting people's feelings."

Matt started laughing. "Jena, honey, you might not hurt their feelings, but the dates you arrange turn out to be deadly. Trust me, Bob would have gotten over a rejection a helluva lot faster than he'll get over first-degree burns."

Brilliant. He was laughing at her again. She was completely over the fact everyone in Invertary got so much entertainment from her life. She ignored him and turned her attention to the black trash sack she was filling with debris from the floor.

"I would have thought, after meeting Frank, you'd be off guys for a while anyway." Of course he wouldn't let the subject drop.

With an irritated sigh, Jena stomped to the old stained sink and washed her hands. "Not that it's any of your business, but he wasn't always like this. He was charming at one point. And, unlike most guys, he knew his way around a woman's body. That's a pretty appealing trait in a boyfriend." She gave him a wry look. "Trust me. Most men have no idea how to please a woman. They wouldn't recognise an erogenous zone if it bit them in the ass." She felt her face burn. "Not that I have a lot of experience, but girlfriends talk."

Matt dusted his hands off on his jean-clad thighs. He grabbed a couple of bottles of water from the fridge and threw one at her. His gaze was thoughtful while he watched her drink. "You don't need to know where a woman's erogenous zones are to get the job done."

Jena pointed the bottle at him. "See, that's exactly what I'm talking about. Get the job done for whose benefit exactly? For the guy? Because without a little bit of knowledge and effort on the guy's part, he's the only one who's going to get anything out of sex."

"No." Matt's eyes darkened. "I mean, if a guy is doing the job right, *every* area on a woman's body is an erogenous zone. You obviously haven't been with any men who know what they're doing."

It took Jena a second to decide how to react. She settled on laughing. "Wow, that's original. Never heard that before." She deepened her voice. "Trust me, baby, I know what I'm doing. I'll give you pleasure like you've never known. You'll forget all the men who came before me."

His eyes sparkled. "That's not what I said. I said the whole body is an erogenous zone—if you know what you're doing."

She smirked at him. "Which implies you know what you're doing."

"Aye. I do."

"Yeah, right."

"I'm serious."

"Of course you are. You're also deluded. I haven't met a man yet who didn't think he knew what he was doing in bed."

"I'm different. I can make you hot without going near any of your more obvious erogenous zones. I am *that* skilled." His lips twitched as he fought a smile.

"Okay, Mr Sexpert. Why don't you prove it?" As soon as the words were out of her mouth, Jena knew they were a huge mistake.

A slow smile curved his lips. His eyes sparkled with mischief and intent. "Come over here and I will."

"Uh-nuh." She shook her head hard enough to make her feel dizzy. "I didn't mean it. I'm fine right here."

"Coward."

Her eyes snapped to his. He was laughing at her. "I am not. I don't need a demo. If you believe you're God's gift to the opposite sex, who am I to burst your bubble."

"I promise not to touch any X-rated zones. It wouldn't prove my point anyway. Any idiot can get a woman hot by going for the obvious."

She expected his eyes to drift to some of those X-rated areas, but they didn't. He held her gaze and waited. Six foot two inches of pure lazy confidence. She didn't know whether to hit him or strip him.

"Come on," he teased. "Don't be a chicken. I'm trying to

make a point here. Otherwise you'll think I'm all talk. I wouldn't want you to slander my reputation during one of your girly get-togethers."

She chewed her lip as she wavered. The words came out of her mouth before she had time to think on them properly. "No groping or grabbing. If I wouldn't walk around with it on show at church then you can't touch it." This is was huge mistake. Huge.

"Come on over here, Jena." His voice was pure seduction.

With a forced sigh to cover her nerves, Jena moved to stand in front of him. "Now what?"

"I want you to face the wall. Put your hands on it."

"Are you going to frisk me?"

"Everyone's a comedian," he muttered.

Once she was in position, Jena's bravado began to waver. "I'm ready." Although the words came out of her mouth, she wasn't sure they were true.

She stared at the wall for a few moments, waiting for Matt to get on with whatever he planned to do. Her anxiety level shot up fast. She was two seconds away from making a run for it when he spoke.

"I like this top you've got on."

She'd worn an old pink halter that tied behind her neck. It dipped low on her back but flared loosely around her hips and over the top of her cut-off jeans. The top was one she often wore to work around the house; hence it was paint-splattered and stained in spots. Not exactly the sexiest of outfits.

"Anyone ever told you that you have a sexy back?"

Jena licked her dry lips. "Nope, no one. Are you hoping that being corny will turn me on?"

She heard a chuckle and a thud. She looked over her shoulder to find him kneeling behind her, his focus on her back. His blue eyes had bled to black. A tiny, knowing smile tugged at the corner of his mouth.

"I wasn't being corny. I was being honest. Eyes front, Jena. I want you to concentrate on what you feel."

She made the effort to roll her eyes. "Whatever," she told him, but turned back to stare at the wall. Her heart was racing. She was an idiot to let him do this. Especially since the memory of being held in his arms the night before was so fresh in her mind. Yet here she was, going ahead with it anyway.

"Lots of men ignore the back." Matt's voice was a low rumble.

Jena jerked when she felt his finger trail down her spine. Her skin tingled in the wake of his gentle touch.

"You can tease and tantalise a woman by touching her back, exactly the same way you can any other spot."

Warm, soft lips pressed against the dip between Jena's shoulder blades. Her eyelids grew heavy. Two large hands rested on the curve of her hips. He trailed his nose across her skin between her shoulder blades. Jena sucked in a breath. She locked her knees in place. And her eyes closed against her will.

Another kiss lower down her spine. Gentle. Fleeting. Teasing.

"It helps to coax the woman into the moment if you talk to her about what you're doing." Another kiss in the middle of her back. She moved into him, chasing his touch, and heard a low chuckle. "It builds the anticipation for both of you."

She shivered. His hands slid under her top to clasp her hips. His thumbs caressed lazy circles on the bare skin above her cut-offs.

Jena's head suddenly became too heavy to hold up. She

rested her forehead on the wall in front of her. The cool plaster against her skin made Matt's touch sear.

"From this position, I can see every tiny vibration of your body." A soft press of lips to the small of her back. Without taking her top off, he couldn't go lower. For that, Jena was suddenly very grateful.

"Your blood is moving faster now. It's chasing my touch. My lips." She felt his soft, warm lips against her spine. "My tongue."

A small groan escaped her as the tip of his tongue followed the line of her spine back up to the knot of cloth at her neck. The knot that would unravel with one good tug. Jena's fingers curled against the wall but couldn't find purchase.

She heard Matt inhale deeply before a breath of cool air blew across her skin. It caught on the trail his tongue had left behind, making her skin vibrate with sensitivity. She arched away from the wall with a breathy moan.

"If he's smart." Matt pressed against her to whisper in her ear. She was intensely aware of their difference in size. He was huge. Strong. Capable of taking her desire and making it burn. She shuddered at the thought.

His lips teased the shell of her ear before he nipped the lobe. Her breath caught. Stuttered. "He'll vary his touch." The words whispered over her sensitised skin. "Soft. Hard. Slow. Fast. A gentle brush of his cheek against your skin, followed by the sharp nip of his teeth."

She felt him match action to words as his cheek caressed between her shoulder blades. His bite was sharp. A sting that morphed into heat. She couldn't hold back a shuddering gasp.

He nipped his way down her back, all the while massaging her with his thumbs. His hands never left her hips. His hold like an anchor. She was losing her sense of place and time.

"Now, if you didn't have this top on I'd work my way slowly lower. I'd make circles with my tongue in the small of your back as I smoothed my hands up and down your sides."

His wide hands spanned her back, sliding from her waist to her shoulders and back. His agonisingly slow movement make her knees tremble.

"Once I knew you were losing your mind under my touch, I'd turn my attention to your neck. I'd bite down on the curve where your shoulder meets your throat and I wouldn't be gentle. I'd want you to feel my touch right through your body, waking up nerves, catapulting you to a place where only sensation exists."

Yes. Yes. That was what she wanted. All of it.

"Please…" The word escaped in a gasp and a whisper.

His breath was back at her ear. "Would you like that, princess?"

"Please, Matt, please." She wasn't sure what she was begging for now. All she knew for certain was she needed more. And she needed it now.

"Damn, you're irresistible," he murmured against her shoulder.

His teeth captured the muscle that was desperate for his bite.

"Yes!"

She felt her top tug free. It fell away, leaving her bare from the waist up.

Matt's tongue soothed the bite he'd made as his hands inched around her body to her stomach. Her breasts became unbearably heavy with the desperation to be touched. She needed. Oh, how she needed.

"Please…" A whisper. A word that was barely a breath. "I need…"

"Tell me." His order sent ripples of desire careening through her.

She wanted to tell him. Wanted more than anything to explain her need, but the words wouldn't come. Her breasts ached. Her nipples hard and sore from neglect. His lips were a brand on her neck. His hands burning their way across her flesh.

"Please…"

"Ah, honey," he groaned as his hands captured her desperate flesh.

A wild moan escaped her as she arched and pressed her breasts into his palms. "Oh yeah." She rolled her forehead on the cool wall.

His fingers teased her nipples, circling them so lightly she strained to follow his touch. His palms held the weight of her. His broad chest pressed against her back.

"Matt." A murmur of need.

"I know, princess, I know."

She was turning. His lips on her throat. His hands left her breasts, and she moaned her complaint.

Her back pressed against the cool wall as he nipped at her jaw. His hands captured her breasts again. Thumbs flicked over sensitive nipples. She moaned. He absorbed the sound with his mouth and the world disappeared entirely.

He tasted of sunshine and wickedness. His lips were soft and firm. His touch knowing. He licked his way past her lips to fill her mouth. Teasing her into a sensual dance of tongues and lips. Her hands clung to his shoulders. Her nails digging into firm muscle. Muscle that made her want to touch. To bite. To lick. Oh, her head was spinning. He had her now. She was incapable of anything more than following his lead.

"Amazing," he said against her lips.

"More," Jena demanded. "Matt, I need more."

He leaned back to look at her. The wild darkness of his eyes was a promise.

One he didn't keep.

Jena felt a chill steal through her as she watched realisation register in his gaze. His shoulders stiffened under her touch. His jaw clenched as Jena felt her cheeks heat. Her brain fought its way out of the daze it'd been locked in.

It was a game. A bet. Not real.

Her hands dropped.

Not real.

Her skin felt chilled as Matt released her. Without taking his eyes from hers, he reached down and pulled up her top. Jena pressed a hand above her breasts to hold it in place. Without a word, he tied the straps behind her neck.

He stepped away from her. Leaving her cold. Bereft. Fighting the need to beg him to come back. His face was shuttered. No emotion. No hint at what he was thinking. Nothing.

Matt cleared his throat. "I think that proves my point." His voice was tight. Forced.

Okay. Okay. This is fine. I can cope with this. It was a game. He won. It's all good.

She took a deep breath. It had gone too far. They both knew it. Only Jena could salvage things between them. She knew exactly what to do.

On shaky legs, she walked over to him. She pasted a wide smile on her face and smacked him on the abs. "You were right. I was wrong. I can say it; I'm a big girl. It's clear all those other guys didn't have a freaking clue how to touch a woman. Maybe you should teach classes? Or make videos for YouTube? The men of the world need you, Matt. It's your duty to save women everywhere from a life of mediocre sex. You the man, buddy."

Matt's eyes shot to hers before a small smile curved his lips. "You the man?"

"Oh yeah." She nodded solemnly. "You the man."

He opened his mouth to speak. Jena knew there was an apology coming. She cut it off.

"I'm so impressed you made me beg." She kept a grin on her face. Her cheeks hurt, but she'd be damned if it slipped. "Thanks for giving me what I asked for. I know *you* didn't want to go that far, but when a girl gets a chance to have a sexy guy's hands on her body, she takes it. Much obliged." She waggled her eyebrows at him. "Very hot, Matt. Don't worry; next time there's girl talk, your reputation will be safe."

His shoulders relaxed. His eyes softened. He ran a hand through his hair. Relief. She was watching relief. It bit at her.

"Okay," Jena said. "Thanks to you, I need to go upstairs and have a nice, long cold shower. Have fun with the floor while I'm gone."

She gave him what she hoped was a cheeky wink before sauntering out of the room.

When all she really wanted to do was run.

MATT HAD TAKEN it too far. He knew the minute he'd put his hands on Jena, and still he couldn't stop. Her soft pleas undid him. His control had been shot. He looked at Jena's back as she made a run for it—because that was definitely what she was doing. He couldn't blame her. She'd been great about his loss of control, but it was still his fault. He was a cop. A cop working to protect a girl. He wasn't on a date. And even if he was, going by Jena's track record, he'd probably be in hospital by now.

He ran a hand over his face, working to keep his breathing steady. Jena had relationship stamped all over her.

She was looking for permanent. She'd said it herself in bed. She was looking for a home. Somewhere to belong.

And he was looking for another job far away from Invertary. One that didn't bore him to tears or involve any pet rescues. Things with Jena were slipping out of his control. Being around her 24/7 was blurring the line between professional and psychotically horny. It was time to step back and let someone else watch over her.

Lake had promised a replacement on Saturday. Well, Saturday was here and Matt was ready to be replaced. He was about to call Lake to see where the guy was, when a thump at the front door changed his plans. Hoping it was Lake's man, Matt rushed to answer.

It wasn't Lake's man.

"Not going to happen," Matt said as soon as he spotted Frank Di Marco standing on the front stoop.

Today's suit was a black pinstripe, perfectly cut and obviously expensive. If it wasn't for the matching black shirt and ever-present bling, he wouldn't have looked out of place in London's financial district. As usual, he was flanked by his flunkies.

"Officer." Frank's tone was ingratiating. "It's a free world. You can't stop me from spending time with Jena."

Matt folded his arms. "I can if she doesn't want to see you."

"Look, we had a misunderstanding. I should never have dipped my wick where I worked. I get that now. When you have a sweet piece like Jena at home, you need to make the effort to keep it in your pants." He spread his hands wide, as though he had nothing to hide. "I made a mistake. I succumbed to temptation. What guy wouldn't? I mean, if you had access to an all-you-can-eat buffet of willing women, you'd snack too, but that's all it was, a snack. Jena is the real deal."

Matt cast a glance at the men standing behind Frank. The looks of disgust on their faces said it all. Frank wasn't impressing anyone.

Frank took a step closer to Matt and lowered his voice, as though letting him into a confidence. "What we had was special. I want it back. I want her back." His eyes narrowed. "To achieve this aim, I have to talk with her. I have to tell her that I know I didn't appreciate her. I learned my lesson. No more work pussy."

Matt took a step back, shaking off the crawling sensation that ran over his skin. "Good for you. You're enlightened. You learned what most guys know from the get-go—don't cheat on your woman. Unfortunately for you, Jena isn't into giving second chances. She won't want your wick after it's been dipped in half the strippers in Atlantic City."

Joe smothered a laugh as Matt focused in on Frank. "I suggest, strongly, that you go back to America. Find someone else to impress with your newfound knowledge that a guy never screws around on his woman—no matter if he's starving and the buffet is begging him to eat."

A little blood vessel in Frank's temple throbbed violently. Matt thought it might burst.

"Be careful, officer. You don't know who you're messing with."

"No." Matt took a step back into the house. "I don't *care* who I'm messing with. There's a difference." He slammed the door shut on Frank Di Marco's angry face.

As soon as it closed, he changed his mind about calling Lake. Frank Di Marco was trouble. Unfortunately, he didn't trust anyone else with Jena's safety—no matter how well trained Lake's men were. Nope, it looked like Matt was it for the duration. It was time to start acting like the trained professional he was. It was time to dial back the contact with Jena. She was a job. Nothing more.

With a plan in place, Matt headed back to the kitchen. It would be good if he got the room finished before he had to leave. Kill two birds with one stone. Yeah, the plan was perfect. He liked the plan.

Now all he had to do was keep his hands off Jena while he executed it.

CHAPTER 15

The Donaldson women were known for their propensity to fall in love at first sight. It was a genetic failure passed down from generation to generation.

Claire's mother swore she knew within an hour of meeting Claire's father that he was the man for her. She'd only been seventeen at the time, and her father a more mature twenty-one. Against their parents' wishes, they'd ran off to Gretna Green three weeks after their first kiss and got married by a blacksmith. Thirty-five years later, her mother's face still lit up at the mention of her father's name. Great-Aunty Fiona met her husband while waiting in a line for bread during the Second World War. Three days later she was Mrs Johnson. And Granny Bell won the prize for spontaneous decisions. Her husband proposed to her twenty minutes into their first date—albeit a chaperoned one—and she said yes. That marriage lasted sixty-one years and produced eight children.

Now that Claire thought about it, maybe the genetic trait leaned more towards finding men with no patience rather than falling in love at first sight. Whatever it was, it was still the family curse. Or blessing. Depending how you looked at it. Right at that minute, Claire wasn't sure which it was.

She was also terrified it was happening to her.

Twenty-four hours after Grunt grabbed her outside The Scottie Dog pub and proclaimed her his, she was beginning to think he might be right.

Megan's hand landed on Claire's forehead, snapping her out of her daze. She shoved the hand away.

"What are you doing?" Claire frowned at Megan.

"Seeing if you've got a fever. I think you're ill. Maybe a brain tumour. It's the only explanation I have for the fact King Kong is sitting on our couch."

"Stop calling him that." She pulled an oversized glass bowl out of the kitchen cupboard and proceeded to fill it with Haggis-flavoured crisps. She wanted to give Samuel a wee taste of Scotland, and this was as close as she got, since she wasn't the sister who could cook.

"I can't believe you're eating this stuff. It's disgusting." Megan popped one in her mouth anyway.

"Well, I'd have given him a nice Scottish dinner, but you wouldn't cook and we had to make do with pizza."

"So sue me. You should have taken him out for your date instead of hanging out here."

Claire folded her arms over her fluffy white cowl-neck sweater. "Take him out where? The choice is the pub or a drive to Fort William, and Samuel says he has to stay in town."

"Did he say why?"

Claire shrugged. "Something about being close in case his friend needs him."

"You don't think that's suspicious? Why would Joe need him? This just proves my point. You don't know anything about this guy, other than he has caveman tendencies and a pierced penis."

Claire felt her cheeks heat. "Stop talking about his penis. You shouldn't know anything about it. It's private. It's my penis."

Megan threw up her hands in disgust. "Listen to yourself. His penis doesn't belong to you. He doesn't belong to you. You're not behaving normally." She let out a heavy sigh, running her hand through her long hair. They were dressed identically today: cream sweaters, blue jeans and brown leather boots. They never planned to look alike—half the time they didn't even go clothes shopping together, but it just seemed to happen.

"I think," Megan said, "you're clinging to Samuel in an attempt to deal with Dad's illness."

Claire set the glasses she'd retrieved on the countertop. "How can you say that? Dad has been ill for eight years and Samuel isn't the first boyfriend I've had."

"Listen to yourself—he isn't a boyfriend. He's a middle-aged guy with stalker tendencies. What else would make you put up with him other than the stress of Dad getting worse?"

"Look, I know this situation is a little odd, but it's not like he's bullying me into spending time with him. I *want* to get to know him. There's something about him." A shiver went down her spine. "When he looks at me, I feel like I'm his whole world. I've never felt like that before."

"See." Megan pointed a finger at her. "Stalker. Stalkers are obsessed with their prey. They're the whole world to the stalker. You've just proved my point."

Claire rolled her eyes. "You sound like Matt."

Megan shuddered and made the sign of the cross. "We made a pinkie swear *never* to say that. Matt does overprotective to the nth degree. I am nothing like Matt. I want you to have a boyfriend. I know you're old enough for sex. Matt still thinks we're ten. I'm not being unreasonable. You don't know this guy, and he's freaking terrifying."

"Fine." Claire lifted her chin. "Let's go get to know him."

She marched into the front room that used to be Magenta's bedroom when she lived with them, but was now a living room. Grunt was sitting on the sofa watching the BBC World News. His arm was draped over the back of the couch and his legs were stretched out in front of him. He gave Claire a wicked smile that made her insides melt. Yum. She licked her lips. No matter what Megan said, cavemen had always appealed to Claire. She liked a little possessive behaviour from her men. And there was nothing sexier than a man who had the confidence to know what he wanted. Yeah, she liked that a whole lot. If Megan and her suspicious nature weren't in the room, Claire would have crawled into Samuel's lap to see if he tasted as good as he looked. The soft blue shirt he wore over faded jeans rippled on his shoulders as he looked between them. His eyes turned assessing. He nodded.

"Interrogation time," he said. "Fire away."

With an irritated huff, Megan sat in one of the armchairs, leaving Claire with the option of sitting in the other chair or curling up beside Samuel. Tempting as it was, she figured she should resist the urge to rub herself all over him like a cat. She sat in the chair.

"Tell us about yourself," Megan ordered.

Grunt's lips quirked into a little smile. "I'm thirty-one, never been married. Never wanted to get married. No kids. No living family."

"Job?" Megan's eyes narrowed.

He didn't look away from her. "Security. Bodyguard stuff mainly. I was in the navy until two years ago. Got out, went travelling, hung around until Joe told me he was looking for a business partner. Been working with Joe for a couple of months."

Claire smiled at him. "You went travelling once you got

out the navy? Didn't you travel while you were in it? I would have thought you'd be fed up with seeing new places."

"Babe." Grunt gave her a panty-melting grin. "We went to war zones. Not a lot of tourist crap to do on your downtime."

"Oh, yeah." She blushed and tucked her hair behind her ear.

Megan snapped her fingers. "Focus, King Kong. Do you have any sexual diseases?"

"Megan!" Claire glared at her sister.

Megan shrugged. "What? It's a good question."

Although it was clear Grunt was trying not to laugh, Claire was still annoyed.

"No sexual diseases. No diseases at all. Clean bill of health."

Megan cocked an eyebrow. "Proof?"

Claire groaned and sank back into her chair. There was nothing she could do to stop Megan. She was the one-woman reincarnation of the entire Spanish Inquisition.

"I can get some," Grunt said.

"Good." Megan stuck her nose in the air. "I want to see documented proof before you go near my sister."

Claire unwrapped the cowl neck of her sweater and buried her face in it. *I'm not here. I'm somewhere else. This is all a bad dream.*

"Are you prone to violence?" Megan asked.

"Not unless it's needed."

"Would you ever hit a woman?"

Grunt growled. "I would never hit Claire."

"Have you ever hit a woman?"

"No." Yeah, now he sounded like a pissed-off gorilla.

"Would you ever force yourself on a woman?"

"No." The menace in that one word made both twins' eyes pop. "No real man forces himself on a woman. No means no."

Claire trembled at his answer. She looked at Megan, telling her by telepathy to let the questions drop. As usual, the telepathy thing didn't work. So much for that bloody mystical twin bond.

"Have you ever killed a man?" Megan said.

Claire made whimpering noises. This was worse than anything Matt would do. Way worse. She almost wished he was there.

"Yeah. Line of duty."

"Did you enjoy it?"

"Megan!" Claire looked up to see her sister squinting at Grunt. Her eyes were aflame. There was no bringing her back. She was set on this.

Meanwhile, every muscle on Grunt's body looked either poised to strike or flee. He held Megan's eyes. "You would need to be a sick son of a bitch to enjoy something like that. The answer is no. I didn't. I still see the faces and hear the screams of every guy I killed. I know it was necessary. I know it was my job, but if there had been another way, I would have found it." He sat forward, placing his forearms on his knees. "I trained as a marine. We have honour. We don't screw around."

Claire's eyes went wide. Marine? Weren't they like the superheroes of the American armed forces? She wasn't sure. She gnawed at her bottom lip and wondered if anyone would notice if she pulled out her phone and Googled the marines. She looked at the two hard faces. Mmm, maybe later.

Megan looked thoughtful. "Gold digger?"

"I have my own money. Savings. Investments."

"What if Claire disagrees with you on something?"

He shrugged, relaxing back into the sofa again. "Then she disagrees. We work it out. We either compromise or one of us gets our own way. That's how all relationships work."

"So she's allowed to disobey you," Megan said.

Grunt actually laughed. "Who said I was looking for obedience? If I wanted a dog I'd buy one. She's an adult. Got her own opinions. Makes her own choices. I'd be freaking bored if it was any different."

Megan seemed to relax a little. "What are your intentions towards my sister?"

Claire looked at the ceiling and let out a long, low groan. When she looked back, Megan was frowning at her and Grunt was grinning. A delightfully sexy, knowing grin.

"My intentions?" He cocked an eyebrow at Claire, daring her to interrupt. She suddenly found her tongue was glued to the roof of her mouth. "My intentions are to get to know her. To get her naked. To get her into my house. To get married to her. And to get her pregnant. That's what I intend. Whether Claire wants that, or whether she likes what she sees in me, is something else, but I know my intentions."

Claire sat frozen in Grunt's heated gaze. Megan cleared her throat.

"Well, that's very retro. As in 1950s mentality." Megan lowered her voice. "Get woman. Keep woman. Woman must be barefoot and pregnant."

Grunt's lips quirked into a smile, but his eyes stayed on Claire. She felt the heat of his gaze melt her reserve.

Megan turned towards her sister. Claire smiled at her, but her eyes strayed back to Grunt.

"Claire, please tell me this is not attractive to you," Megan said. Claire could practically hear her roll her eyes. "Does the word feminism mean anything to you? This is just like that movie *The Faculty*, where the teachers were possessed by aliens. There's an alien in your body. It's the only excuse for your loss of sanity over this guy."

Claire grinned widely. "What can I say, Megan? It's the muscles. I mean, look at those shoulders."

Grunt playfully flexed his biceps for her.

"I think I just vomited a little in my mouth," Megan said. "Fine, the interrogation is over. I don't think he's a serial killer, or a woman beater, but I can't say for certain he's sane."

Grunt winked at Claire. She grinned widely. Out of the corner of her eye, Claire watched Megan stand. She headed towards the door. "I'll leave you two alone, but I'll be right upstairs if you need me. And remember. Keep your penis in your pants until the doc gives you the all-clear."

Claire's eyes broke away from Grunt to glare at her sister. "Don't I get a say in whether he opens his pants or not? And will you stop saying penis? It gives me the heebie-jeebies."

"Bloody hell, Claire, the more you hang around pre-schoolers the more immature you become. I take it back. You both belong in the fifties. Enjoy your little time warp together. And for your information, penis is a perfectly normal word. If you don't stop complaining I'm going to start using all those other words that freak you out. Like vagina, vulva, cli…"

Claire wedged her fingers in her ears and sang nonsense at the top of her lungs. Megan rolled her eyes and left the room. When Claire looked back at Grunt, he was shaking his head at her as he laughed.

"Babe," he said. "Is it only the official words you have a problem with, or can you say…"

Na, na, na, na. Clair shut her eyes tight as her singing and fingers blocked out the words.

Strong arms wound around her waist, giving her a start. Grunt lifted her, sat in her armchair and settled her in his lap. His grin was still in place.

"Okay, I gotta know. What do you call your—" She smacked a hand over his mouth before he could finish that sentence.

Claire swallowed a grin as his shoulders shook with

laughter. "I call it 'down there'," she said in the most prim voice she could affect.

His laughter deepened. With a roll of her eyes, she removed her hand.

"Guess we should all be grateful you don't call it down under. That way if you ever have a problem, the doc won't think you mean in Australia." He nuzzled the spot behind her ear that made her stomach do flips. "Babe, if you can't use the words, how will you tell me what you want me to do to you?"

"Oh, but I can say the words. I can say lots of words. I just like winding my sister up."

His eyes glittered with mischief. "What kind of words are we talking about here? You got to tell me some, or I won't believe you."

Claire straightened her shoulders. "Willy, dick, club of the gods, joystick, Mr Winky, the one-eyed monster, the mighty—"

Grunt smacked a hand over her mouth as he laughed. She waggled her eyebrows at him.

"Enough," he said. "I take it back. Someone who looks like an angel shouldn't have a potty mouth."

"Potty mouth? Big, bad Grunt says potty mouth? Does Joe know you say stuff like this? I'm not sure that even your manliness can handle saying potty mouth. You've just lost at least ten points on the macho scale."

"You need to shut up now." His sparkling eyes ruined the threat.

Claire leaned into him, until their lips were almost touching. "Oh yeah, why don't you make me."

"With pleasure." The low rumble swept through her body.

His fingers grasped the back of her head. He paused, barely an inch between them, and inhaled as though breathing her in. Her eyes fluttered shut as his warm lips met hers. They were soft, teasing in their touch, and mind-numbingly delicious. He coaxed her lips, easing her mouth open until he was able to take his time tasting her. Her fingers curled into the fabric of his shirt. His woodland scent engulfed her. It was the most perfect kiss she'd ever had. Slowly, with tiny nips to her bottom lip, he moved away from her.

Claire felt more than a little stunned. She wanted to stay right where she was forever. Wrapped in his strong arms, engulfed in his scent, able to taste and feel him whenever she chose. It was bliss.

He flashed that wicked smile of his. "I need to hit the road. Don't want you missing church in the morning and getting a bad rep 'causa me. But save the afternoon for me. I need my Claire time."

Claire smiled at him as her heart stuttered. It took a moment for his words to really register, a delay that amused him.

"I have a family dinner in the afternoon, then we're going to visit my dad."

"What time will I pick you up?"

Her brain stalled. He couldn't mean…? She blinked at him. "You can't come to our family dinner." She cringed. That sounded really rude.

"Baby," he said slowly. "Your family's got to get to know me."

"Do they have to do it tomorrow, though?"

"Yeah." His grin said he thought she was cute. "Sooner we get this outta the way, the sooner we can focus on us."

Damn, why did that sound reasonable and terrifyingly stupid at the same time?

"What time am I picking you up?" His tone was low and teasing, and his eyes sparkled with mirth.

"One." She gave in with a sigh.

He leaned forward and tucked his nose in her neck below

her ear. She heard him let out a long breath. "Good," he whispered.

He chuckled at her mewls of complaint as he led her to the front door.

"Lock up after me," he ordered.

She shook her head with a sigh. Maybe there was a handbook somewhere on how to deal with a bossy alpha male? With one last toe-curling kiss, he turned towards the path. Leaving Claire to wonder if she had the skills needed to handle a man like Grunt.

CHAPTER 16

Jena thought Sunday lunch with Matt's family would be a relaxing affair. Maybe even a little dull. That was before Matt's mother, Heather, led one of Frank's goons into the kitchen.

"No," Jena shouted, grabbed her purse and made a run for the back door.

Matt snagged the back of her purple wraparound dress and held on tight.

"Stay," he snapped.

"Do I look like your freaking poodle?" Jena snapped back, giving him the words he'd used on Bob the butcher.

Matt ignored her. Instead he turned to Mr No-Neck Mob Hitman. "What are you doing here? If Frank wants to talk, he can come to the station. In the meantime, you can get out."

"Matt!" His mother looked like she was ready to smack him. "I didn't raise you to be rude."

The goon kept his eyes on Matt. "I'm not here for Frank Di Marco. This has nothing to do with him."

Jena tried to prise Matt's fingers from the neck of her dress. If there was going to be a fight, she wanted to be far,

far away—even if dinner did smell delicious and her stomach rumbled loud enough to be heard.

"Leave. Now. Before this becomes messy." Matt was coiled tight, ready to pounce.

"What's going on?" One of the twins said as she came into the room. Her arms were full of Tupperware boxes, filled with what looked like cookies. Jena's mouth watered at the sight.

"We have an unwanted guest, Claire." Matt's jaw clenched. Jena tried to appear invisible. "This isn't the place to talk about Jena. You need to leave, Grunt. Before I forget my manners."

"What manners?" Claire smacked the containers onto the countertop. "Samuel is my guest. Do you see me trying to kick Jena out? No. You don't."

Matt's gaze snapped to his sister, and Jena cringed. She was so glad he wasn't her brother. Claire looked fit to spit. His mother looked annoyed and about ten seconds away from putting a stop to the confrontation happening in her kitchen—by any means necessary.

"What do you mean he's your guest?" Matt's voice was a low, threatening rumble.

Claire's face flushed. "I mean he's with me. I invited him, kind of…"

There was a deathly silence. Jena wished Matt would forget about her and let go of her dress. Instead his grip tightened.

"You're dating him?"

Everything within Jena screamed for her to run. The air crackled with the warning. The red in Claire's cheeks deepened. She tucked her long blonde hair behind her ear. The goon frowned, his jaw hardened and he stepped closer to Claire. Positioning himself between Matt and his sister. His fists flexed as his posture loosened. She'd seen that stance before—he was getting ready to fight. No, not fight—defend Claire. Jena's eyebrows tried to crawl up her forehead. Poop in a bucket, the goon was crazy about Matt's sister. World War Three was about to start in Heather Donaldson's kitchen. And Jena was trapped in the middle of it.

She took a deep breath as her sense of self-preservation kicked into overdrive. "Okay, so this has nothing to do with me. This is obviously a family thing. Best if I go. Don't worry, I'll see myself home." She tugged at Matt's grip as she tried to walk towards the door.

"I don't think so." He yanked her back. "Well?" he demanded of Claire.

"Yes." She glared at her brother. "If you must know, which you really don't, I am dating Samuel."

Samuel the goon cocked an eyebrow at Claire. "It's more than dating. You know it."

Claire seemed to have trouble breathing for a minute as her gaze locked with his.

Heather gasped. "It's the family curse. I'll get my wedding dress dry-cleaned. You'll be needing it."

Matt shot his mother a look that said "what the hell, woman?" before returning his attention to Grunt. Jena didn't think the atmosphere in the room could get any tenser. But it did.

"What games are you playing?" Matt said. "I won't let you, or Frank, use my sister to get to Jena."

Claire's jaw dropped as she turned to the goon. "You know Jena? How do you know Jena?" Her face paled the minute realisation struck. "Are you one of those no-neck guys that's hunting Jena for the mob?" She sucked in a loud, dramatic breath. "You're with the mob. You lied to me."

The muscles in Samuel's shoulders clenched. "Baby, I am not, nor will I ever be, with the mob. I'm exactly what I told you I am. Ex-marine. Current security guy. Nothing more.

What you see is what you get. And you get all of it, babe. What we have together has nothing to do with Jena."

"Semantics." Matt pointed at Samuel. "Mob or not, you're here with Frank Di Marco. Jena's ex is with the mob."

"Frank is not mob. Frank *wants* to be mob. Big difference," Samuel informed Matt.

Matt released his grip on Jena's dress and took a step towards the goon. Instead of running, like any sane woman would have done, Jena wound her hand into his T-shirt in an attempt to hold him back. Matt vibrated with rage. "Keep away from my sister."

"Not going to happen."

Matt glared at Claire. "Keep away from him."

"Not going to happen," Grunt answered before Claire could open her mouth.

"I'm warning you," Matt said. He strode towards Grunt, dragging Jena behind him.

"Help me, somebody," Jena said as her heels slid over the kitchen floor.

"Hit him and I'll never talk to you again," Claire shouted as she tried to get out from behind Grunt.

"I'll handle this, baby," Grunt told her softly before growling at her brother. An honest to goodness growl. The kind rednecks and brown bears made.

"She's too young for you and she doesn't associate with criminals."

"Who says I'm a criminal?"

"If you sleep with a dog, you catch its fleas."

"Are you saying I had sex with Frank Di Marco?" Grunt looked ready to morph into the Hulk.

Three women shouted at the same time, "It's just a saying."

It would have been funny if the amount of testosterone in the room hadn't sucked all the joy out of the house.

A door banged, and a minute later a grinning Megan barrelled into the kitchen. "What did I miss?" she demanded.

Everyone glared at her. She nodded with a chuckle. "Clash of the Titans. I get it. Carry on." She turned to her mother. "Got any popcorn?"

Her mother looked between the two men. "I have chocolate cake."

"Great." Megan rubbed her hands together. "Dish it up. This is going to be better than watching wrestling. I bet a month's worth of dishwashing that King Kong pulverises Don Don." She grinned at everyone, her glee overflowing. "Any takers?"

"I'll get the cake." Heather sighed dramatically. "Might as well; looks like we won't get to the roast I slaved over until these two are done hitting each other about the head. Take the fight outside, boys—we'll watch through the window while we eat. We know how you men like to have an audience when you're proving who's got the biggest willy."

The siblings gasped.

"Mum!" Claire covered her mouth with her hand.

"What?" Her mother held up her hands. "This is my house. This is the lovely meal that I cooked for my children and their friends. If it's going to be ruined, I can say what I like. After all, it isn't as though I have a lot to look forward to these days. What's another ruined family afternoon? I guess it's a bit much to hope that two grown men would set aside their differences for a couple of hours so I could take my mind off your father in hospital. We might as well have cake and watch them pummel each other."

And just like that, the tension was sucked out of the room. Both men seemed torn between guilt and the need to hit something.

"That roast smells delicious," Grunt said, earning a beaming smile from Claire. "Wouldn't want to miss out."

Matt ran a hand through his hair as he let out a heavy sigh. He pointed at his mother. "You are a master manipulator." She curtsied. "Fine, we'll eat." He stared at Grunt. "We'll pick this up later."

Grunt grunted.

"Great, sit down in the dining room and we'll get the food. Jena, you can help."

Feeling slightly bewildered as to why she'd been singled out, Jena watched everyone else leave the kitchen.

"I've been married thirty-five years," Heather told her as she pulled the roast from the oven. "If you want a healthy relationship with my son, never forget three things. Food will always triumph over any other need. When confronted with a wall of testosterone, nod as though you agree, then do what you had planned anyway. And if all else fails, resort to guilt. The men in this family can't stand the thought of their women losing out, even if they're the cause of it."

"You know I'm not dating your son, right?"

Heather grinned knowingly. "I know. And given your track record, I'm hoping it will stay like that. In the meantime, you two share that nice little house of yours and see what happens. I would really like grandkids while I'm still young."

Jena shook her head as she took the dish of potatoes she was handed. They smelled heavenly. Part of her wanted to stay in the kitchen and snack. She wasn't sure she'd be able to eat with the tension-laden atmosphere in the dining room.

"Hurry up, Jena," Matt's mother shouted.

With a sigh, Jena took the food to the other room.

THE TENSION in the dining room was painful. It was almost enough to put Jena off her food. Almost. As a woman who was fast running out of money, she wasn't about to pass up a home-cooked meal—no matter how much indigestion she'd have to suffer afterwards. As she dug into her meat and mash, she eyed the family photos that filled the walls. There were hundreds of them, all in different frames. Some sitting a little lopsided on the wall. Seeing the evidence of a happy family life, proudly displayed, made Jena's heart ache. She was pretty sure her mother didn't even own one photo of her, let alone the hundreds the Donaldsons had.

"That's our old dog, Roger." Matt pointed to the photo she'd been staring at, breaking the deathly silence in the room. "He had a thing for Dad's shoes. Used to bury them all over the garden. Dad had to go to work in his slippers or gumboots a couple of times because we couldn't find his shoes."

"I remember that." Megan's eyes lit up. "He used to pay us to dig the garden for his shoes. Fifty pence a pair, wasn't it?"

"Aye." Matt's eyes twinkled. "We were robbed. You'd work all afternoon, find one pair of shoes and didn't even make enough money for a bag of crisps."

The twins laughed as Heather pointed to another photo. It showed her husband tied to a chair in the garden. He was gagged and blindfolded and surrounded by a group of boys all dressed as pirates.

"That was the time Matt, along with his cousins and their friends, decided to play pirates and 'kidnap' Bruce. When I called them in for lunch, they ran into the house and left him there, trussed up behind a bush at the bottom of the garden. By the time they'd finished eating, the game of pirates, along with their captive, was completely forgotten. It was hours before I noticed Bruce was missing and went looking for him."

The siblings were laughing hard now.

"That one"—Claire pointed at photo of her dad shouting and pointing on the sideline of a soccer game—"is the time dad got banned from the pitch after he objected to a foul against Flynn."

Matt grinned. "It wasn't so much the objection. It was the language he used when he shouted at the referee."

Megan laughed. "What did he call him? A wee, hairy, bowlegged Sassenach with more intelligence in his balls than in his brain?"

"Aye, only with a few more swear words thrown in for good measure," Heather said.

"Oh, remember that?" Megan pointed at another picture of their dad buried up to his neck on a sandy beach. She grinned at Jena. "That was taken just before we dug a hole beside his feet and tickled his toes until he promised to buy us all ice cream."

"And look." Claire smiled. "That's him dancing with me at my ballet recital. I was five, and my partner, a whiny wee boy, backed out at the last minute."

"Yeah," Megan said. "Mum wanted Matt to step in, but he refused. Locked himself in his bedroom shouting something about 'real men don't dance'. Dad was great, though. He made up the steps as he went along and we couldn't get him off the stage at the end."

"No," Claire said, looking wistful, "he liked the attention."

"Madman," Heather mumbled with a loving smile. "Always loved being the centre of things."

Silence fell over the group. Jena watched as Grunt stroked the back of Claire's hair as she tugged her sister into a hug. Without thinking too much about it, Jena reached under the table and squeezed Matt's knee. He gave her a grateful smile.

"So." Claire's mum took a deep breath. A signal she was about to change the subject. Claire's heart sank when her mother turned to her. "Tell us how you two met then," she said with a smile.

Claire felt panic skitter up her spine. She licked her suddenly dry lips. It had been too much to hope that she'd make it through the afternoon without a grilling. As usual, her mum's cooking was delicious and her sister was entertaining. She wished she could just spend the afternoon relaxing in the home she'd grown up in, looking at the family photos covering the dining room wall and slowly eating herself into a comatose state. Instead she had to deal with the third degree—and this was before she'd gotten to the chocolate cake.

"Well"—she glanced at Samuel—"we kind of ran into each other one night."

"More like *we* ran into *him*," Megan added helpfully.

Claire shot her a sharp frown. "That's what I said—*we* ran into *each other*. But we weren't able to talk much that night."

"Or at all," Megan muttered before stuffing her mouth full of mashed potato.

Claire glanced at Matt to see if he caught Megan's words, and breathed in relief when it seemed he hadn't.

"So." She took a deep breath. "The following night, we were at the pub when in walked Samuel. He made a beeline right for us."

Megan nodded. "You could say he swept her off her feet."

Claire's toe shot out and kicked her sister hard. Megan yelped before glaring at her. Claire ignored her and carried on talking.

"We got to chatting and discovered we had quite a bit in common." Like their desire for Matt to never, ever find out about the accident. "Samuel asked me out, and we had our first date yesterday."

She looked around the table gauging reactions to her story.

Samuel seemed highly amused. Her mother was smiling widely. Jena seemed more concerned with her dinner. And Matt, Matt looked suspicious. He stared between her and Megan for a minute. She could see his brain working. She swallowed hard, willing herself to appear innocent and hoping Megan was doing the same. She breathed a sigh of relief when he suddenly relaxed and sat back in his chair. His smile was genuine. He suspected nothing. She almost high-fived her sister with the relief.

"So," Matt said, "which one of you was driving when you accidentally ran over Grunt?"

"Megan," Claire said without thinking. She yelped and slapped a hand over her mouth. She made wide eyes of apology at Megan as Matt's jaw began to clench. He turned on Megan, who was frozen with a forkful of peas halfway to her open mouth.

"How did you know?" Megan looked horrified. "What gave it away? It was the 'we ran into him' comment, wasn't it? Should have kept my big mouth shut."

The muscle on the edge of Matt's jaw began to throb. A clear sign he'd run out of patience. "You were in an accident and didn't report it?" His words were carefully measured. A sure sign he was about to blow his top. He studied Grunt. "Were you injured?" He didn't give Grunt time to answer before turning back to Megan. "Did you injure a man and neglect to call for help?"

"We took him to the doctor," Claire said. By the look on Matt's face, she wasn't helping things. "He only had a little concussion. Didn't you, Samuel?"

Samuel grunted. It may have been in agreement, but she wasn't certain.

Matt let out a low growl in Megan's direction. "Do you have any idea how much trouble you are in right now?"

Megan went white. Her arm snapped out. She pointed a

finger about an inch from Claire's nose. "She saw his penis, and it's pierced."

Claire gasped. "You saw it too." She pointed back at her sister while she faced Matt. "She couldn't stop staring at it, the pervert."

Samuel groaned. Jena gasped. Matt turned slowly towards Claire's date. "You flashed your penis at my sisters? You son of a…"

That was when he launched himself over Sunday lunch and straight at Samuel's throat.

CHAPTER 17

They were driving to Fort William. Matt's mom was behind the wheel, fuming. Jena was riding shotgun and Matt was squeezed into the back seat of the tiny brown car. He held a bag of frozen peas to his swollen eye. His mom wouldn't let him drive, or sit up front. "Get in the back," were the only words Heather had spoken since she'd broken up the fight in her dining room, by tipping a bucket of water over Matt and Grunt.

Claire, Megan and an equally battered Grunt had decided to visit Matt's father another day. Jena thought that was a wise decision.

"I really could have stayed in Invertary," Jena said again. She still hoped they'd turn the car around and take her home. "I'm happy to stay with Lake and Kirsty while you visit with your dad."

"For the last time," Matt said. "Where I go, you go. I'm not convinced Grunt was there seeing Claire. I think he was trying to get to you. They're up to something. I don't like it, and until I figure it out, you get to stay by my side."

"Yay me," Jena said, and groaned.

"That boy was most certainly there for Claire," Heather snapped. "You would have noticed that if you'd paid attention to the way he looked at her. He's head over heels. You were just being an overbearing brother. I keep telling you, the girls have grown up—they need to be able to make their own choices. And you need to deal with them."

Matt snorted. "There has to be at least ten years between Claire and Grunt. Plus he's here with a mobster. You don't need to be a cop to have alarm bells going off over this. What kind of big brother would I be if I didn't look out for my little sisters?"

Heather let out a heavy sigh. "The point is, my darling, they aren't little anymore. They have a right to make their own mistakes, the same as you have a right to make yours."

"So we should sit back and do nothing while Claire makes the biggest mistake of her life?"

"I thought Samuel was a very nice boy," Heather said. "Not much of a conversationalist, but he obviously adores Claire. Until I have proof to the contrary, I plan on giving him the benefit of the doubt."

The car slowed and pulled over to the side of the road. Heather turned in her seat to face her son.

"Matt, honey, you have to deal with the fact the girls don't need you the way they used to." She put her hand on his knee and squeezed. "I know how much it hurts. I know it leaves you feeling like you've lost your job. It's horrible to think you're not needed anymore. But they do need you, honey, just in a different way. If you want the girls to come to you when they're in trouble, then you have to let them grow up."

Matt sniffed, gave his mother a tight smile and sat back in the seat. "I don't like it."

"No, no parent does. And that's essentially what you've been to them these past eight years. I don't know what I would have done without you. If you hadn't come back home when your dad was diagnosed, I would have been lost. But it's time for you to find your own life now, son. Well past time."

"That's why I'm applying for jobs in the cities. I can put my degree in criminology to good use and concentrate on my career. I'm wasting my education here. Especially now I'm not needed."

Heather let out a heavy sigh and muttered something that sounded very like, "Stupid men, they don't have a clue about anything."

Jena bit her lip, stared out the window at the landscape and pretended she didn't completely agree.

THE VISIT with his father went much as Matt had come to expect. Each day his dad drifted further away from them. Matt didn't need the doctors to tell him they were nearing the end. A fool could see it wouldn't be long. An even greater fool convinced himself a miracle would happen, that his father wouldn't leave them, that his mother wouldn't be alone. He scoffed. Yeah, he was that big of a fool.

"I'm sorry, Matt," Jena said softly beside him.

They were standing in the hallway, watching his parents through the crack in the door. His mother sat on the bed beside the prone figure of his father. She combed her fingers through his hair as she talked to him. Her voice was the same soft, melodic tone he remembered as a child. The voice that brought peace when he was ill, or soothed after nightmares.

"He's been here two years." He took a sip of his coffee and cringed. Man, it was terrible. "Mum comes every day. She gave up her job so she could do this. She still works, free-lance proofreading, and she does well. She says she's really grateful for a job that fits around her life. She means him. Fits around him. Her husband."

He jerked with surprise as Jena wound her arm through his. She rested her head on his shoulder, lending him her strength, giving him her comfort. It was too tempting to ignore, and Matt found himself leaning into her heat.

"He was a lawyer. I thought about following him into the field, but I needed something a bit more active." He shook his head. "All those hours behind a desk were my idea of hell. Now my idea of hell is getting called out three times a week to find Morag McKay's scabby cat."

Jena chuckled, and he felt it vibrate through him, loosening something inside of him. Making him want. He wasn't sure what he wanted, but it was there. A slow keening. A yearning. A need opening up and throbbing within him. He took another gulp of the awful coffee.

"He was the local football coach. Under-sixteen squad. He used to joke he discovered Flynn."

"Who's Flynn?" Jena's voice was reassuringly soft.

"My cousin, Harry's older brother. Not sure if you've met Harry. He's the computer genius who sometimes does work with Lake."

Jena nodded against him.

"Well, Flynn is a professional soccer player. He's with Arsenal right now. Top of his game. Dad would have been proud." He grinned at the memory. "Dad said Flynn learned everything he knows from him."

"Men," Jena gently scoffed. "Always taking credit for everything around them."

He could hear the smile in her voice. "We wanted my dad to be there for Flynn's final game in the European Championship, but he wasn't up to it. Flynn's team won."

"You know." Jena looked up at him. "Sometimes it isn't the things people miss that matter, but the things they take with them. Your dad might not have been there for the most important game of your cousin's career, but he got to carry the knowledge he played a part in it. He might not remember Flynn's career, but remembering is different from soul-deep knowing. I bet deep inside, where it can't be affected by his illness, I bet he knows all about Flynn's success."

Matt felt the world shift at her words. He peered into those mesmerising honey-coloured eyes and time stopped for a few seconds. All he was aware of was the wonder he felt. The wonder of Jena and the gift she'd just given him. The gift of understanding. Of trying to ease the pain he rarely acknowledged—even to himself.

"Okay." His mother's voice broke the spell and restarted time. "Let's go home."

He watched as she cast an agonising glance back over her shoulder to where his father stared into space.

"Better tomorrow," she said, as though trying to convince herself.

"It's been a rough day." Jena reached for his mother's hand. "When days get rough for me, do you know what I do?"

"No." His mother was making an effort to accept the comfort Jena offered. "What do you do, Jena?"

"Well"—Jena's eyes sparkled with mischief—"I put on my favourite music, grab a pint of Chunky Monkey ice cream and dance round the house naked until I'm exhausted."

Hell, what an image. Matt's brain overloaded. It took all of his self-control not to rush out and buy Jena ice cream then beg to watch. His mother threw back her head and laughed.

"I've never heard of Chunky Monkey ice cream, and I think I'd freak the family out if I started dancing naked."

Jena shrugged. "That leaves plan B." She grinned wickedly. "We gorge on the chocolate cake we didn't get for pudding and watch Katherine Hepburn movies until our eyes bleed. Before you say you don't have any, you don't have to worry, I have everything she ever made. Trust me, no one can feel maudlin when they're watching Katherine Hepburn and Cary Grant in *Bringing Up Baby*."

She linked her arm with his mother's and led her through the nursing home. All the while she chatted about her favourite screwball comedies and held his mother's hand tightly.

As they reached the car, she looked over her shoulder at Matt and winked. And that was when it happened. Matt Donaldson decided he wanted Jena Morgan. Possibly more than he'd wanted anything in a very, very long time.

Stunned by that knowledge, he drove his mother home, stopping on the way to pick up Jena's movie collection. And then he sat with them into the early morning laughing at Katherine Hepburn movies and watching Jena worm her way into his family's heart.

Into his heart.

CHAPTER 18

Jena spent Monday in the hardware store learning the ropes. She'd stayed up too late watching movies, then crashed in Heather's guest room. Now she was feeling a bit worse for wear. Although she also felt content. She'd never spent time hanging out with her own mom, so it had been a novel experience hanging out with Matt's. Novel and good. Being around the Donaldsons had shown her what it was like to have a real family. It was as wonderful as she'd imagined—even with the fight in the dining room and the achingly sad visit with his father.

"You really want to know this stuff, don't you?" Gordon's question snatched her from her thoughts. He scratched his thick grey beard as though she perplexed him.

"Of course I do. I have a whole house to fix. I *need* to know this stuff."

"Aye, there is that, though I'm thinking you enjoy it too. You act like you've caught the DIY bug, lass."

She grinned at him. "I don't just like DIY. I love it." She practically danced on the spot as she cleaned the shelf in front of her. A shelf that had been filled with assorted nails, all of which she now knew had a specific purpose. "You take something old and you make it new. Something unattractive becomes attractive. It becomes useful. I'm not sure I'd like to build something from scratch, but I like the thought that my house will be a home when I'm through renovating it. How cool is that?"

"Very cool indeed." Gordon chuckled. "Didn't you do work around the house with your dad when you were little?"

"Don't have a dad." Jena put the nails back on the shelf. "Not one I ever met, anyway. Far as I can tell, I'm the product of a one-night stand between my mom and a talent scout from a New York agency. Mom really wanted to be signed. Instead she got me."

A dark cloud gathered in his eyes. "Hell, lassie, that's some story."

"You don't miss something when you've never had it." She winced at the lie. She might never have had a father, or really a mother who gave a damn, but she'd sure spent a lot of time as a kid wishing for them.

"Not sure about your thinking there, Jena," Gordon said. "Brenda and I couldn't have any kids, and we still miss the gap they left. Otherwise it would be 'Stewart and Son' above the door." He looked wistful. "I imagined a wee boy with a tool belt and a penchant for hammering everything in sight."

Jena's throat closed. She blinked hard. "Guess you'll have to make do with teaching an American woman who owns a pink tool set and still struggles to hit things with a hammer."

His face paled. "Tell me you're lying. You don't really work with pink tools, do you?"

She shrugged. "Got them cheap through an Avon catalogue."

Gordon muttered a string of words in horror. Jena wondered if he was cursing in Gaelic.

"You finish the shelves. I'll sort out some proper tools for you." He pointed at her. "You're throwing out that pink crap."

Jena bit back a laugh. "How about I make Matt use them instead?"

"That works for me too." He considered her for a moment with a strange look in his eye that Jena feared may be pity. "Do you want me to show you how to tile a backsplash when you're done there?"

"Awesome!" She bounced on the spot before giving him a quick hug that left his face red.

"I'm thinking that's a yes."

Jena wasn't listening; she was already trying to figure out what colour of tiles she'd use in the kitchen. Since she'd been bullied into renovating the room, she may as well do it exactly the way she wanted.

"Do we sell tiles?" she asked. Her face flushed when she realised that she'd said we instead of you. "I mean—"

"Yes, we do," Gordon said. "Mostly we have them in a catalogue people can flick through, but there's a wee selection in the back room."

"The junk room?"

"That's not junk. It's overflow."

"Seriously? People are supposed to shop in there?"

"It's not that bad."

"Yes. It is." She put her hands on her hips. "I'll sort that room next."

As Jena turned her attention back to her work, she realised that, for the first time in a long time, she felt happy. Sure, her house was a dump, her bank account was teetering on empty, she'd had to sell her car to pay for new roof tiles and her cheating ex was hounding her. Yet despite the chaos that was her life, she felt good. She'd found something she loved doing, in a place she loved being. She was making friends, getting to be part of a family—if only for a little while. People were keen to get to know her past the persona who danced wildly on stage at night. It felt good. She felt good. Coming to Scotland was the best decision she'd ever made.

When the bell over the door rang, announcing a new customer, Jena turned towards them with a genuine smile.

It froze on her face as though she'd been doused with quick drying cement.

"Jena, honey!" The squeal was excited. The greeting enthusiastic. Pity Jena had nothing to do with either emotion.

She was suddenly engulfed in a cloud of cheap perfume and immobilised in a vice-like embrace.

"You were so smart moving to Josh's hometown. That's my girl. Always thinking of ways to help her mom's career."

With weary resignation, Jena patted her mother's back in a semblance of a hug.

"That's exactly why I did it, Mom, just for you." She knew her mom would completely miss the sarcastic tone.

"I know!" Her mother stepped back from her and clapped her hands in glee. "Now where is he? I have my guitar in the car. I'm ready to go."

MATT PICKED up lunch for Jena after a morning dealing with the insanity of Invertary. He'd split up a fight at the old folks' home over a dominoes game gone bad. That was followed by a call from Morag McKay insisting Betty had stolen her cat—again. Matt was beginning to hate Morag's cat. And quite possibly Morag as well. Lastly, he'd swung past the pub where Claire's new boyfriend was having coffee with his criminally insane boss. He hadn't spoken to Grunt; instead he'd spent half an hour staring at him. He was certain Grunt got the message. The one where Matt promised a painful death if he kept spending time with his sister.

After doing his brotherly duty, he'd stopped at the new café on the outskirts of town. It had won Matt over the first time he'd popped into the place. The woman who owned it knew how to cook. She also sold the best sandwiches on the planet. The bread was made in store, the ingredients were organic and the dressings were mind-blowing. He eyed the bag on the seat beside him and wondered if he should have bought a couple extra for later.

He let the peace of his hometown soothe the frustrations of his morning. The midday sun blinked through heavy grey clouds that promised afternoon rain. A lone boat bobbed on the loch, and even from the top of the high street Matt knew it was the Murdoch family out fishing. Part of him hated that he had to leave the place he loved to have a career—one that didn't involve filing reports on missing cats.

He pulled up in front of the hardware store to find Lake waiting for him.

"Trouble?" Matt grabbed the bag of sandwiches from the seat beside him.

"No, but I have news. Harry's in the shop." He nodded towards his security shop, Eye Spy.

Matt put the sandwiches back in his car. Taking food anywhere near his cousin was a mistake. Harry had hollow legs and a constantly growling stomach.

They pushed through the door into the security shop. The front of Lake's business was set up as a normal shop, selling things like alarm systems, webcams and window locks. The back and the converted apartment above the shop were used as offices and meeting rooms for his security business. He was fast gaining an international reputation for providing quality personal security, and for being able to solve situations that sat outside the normal interests of the

JANET ELIZABETH HENDERSON

law enforcement agencies. Things they didn't have time for, or were hampered by borders and conflicting national laws. There was a waiting list for his services, and he was taking on staff as fast as he could manage. It didn't hinder his reputation any that the UK's boy wonder of cybersecurity had set up shop in Invertary and seemed to like working with Lake. Matt's cousin Harry said it was as though he got to play James Bond for real.

"Hey." Harry looked up from his laptop long enough to acknowledge Matt had arrived. It was more than he usually did when there was a computer near him.

"What did you find?" Matt sat on the old armchair that belonged to Betty McLeod—the town's resident evil genius and Lake's octogenarian mascot. "Where's Betty?"

"Getting her hair done." Lake flashed a rare smile.

Matt froze before grinning. "The whole three strands of it?"

"She said she wants it to look nice under her hairnet."

They grinned at each other as Matt felt something prod into his backside. He fished around behind him and came out with a set of false teeth. With disgust he stood, threw them on the chair and marched to the sink to wash his hands.

"I think I'll sit at the table," he told a laughing Lake.

As Matt sat down, Harry looked up from his keyboard and seemed surprised to find his cousin in the room. "Hey," he said again.

Matt rolled his eyes. "What have you got?"

Harry turned his lean body away from the desk he was working at and faced the other men. "Frank Di Marco is in it up to his neck." He stretched his long, jean-clad legs out in front of him and crossed his arms over a *Big Bang Theory* T-shirt.

"Meaning?" Matt prompted before the laptop stole

Harry's attention again. Sometimes his genius cousin forgot the people around him couldn't read his mind.

"He might be telling people he owns the strip club, but he only owns about twenty percent of it. The other eighty is owned by the Rizzoni family. I found some mumbling about what Frank did for the Rizzonis to get their backing—no one gave details, but it looks like he was involved in a couple of things. The most serious being a bank heist and a money-laundering scheme. He's also been linked to the disappearance of a guy called Tony Markam." Harry ran his fingers through his overly long hair. "I think it's safe to say the disappearance is of the indefinite kind."

Matt felt the blood leave his face. "He killed a guy?"

Harry shrugged. It was Lake who spoke. "We don't know for sure. We don't think so. He's not known for being violent. All we know right now is he's involved."

"Very involved. As in up to his neck involved," Harry added.

Lake nodded. "It's possible he was dragged along as a witness to the act. It's a standard way to gain loyalty. And to intimidate. There's no doubt he's in deeper with the mob than we first thought."

Matt rubbed a hand over his face. He leaned forward and put his arms on the table.

"If he's in that deep with the New Jersey mob, what's he doing chasing down an ex-girlfriend in Scotland?"

Harry's eyes went hard. "The rumour is the Rizzonis aren't happy about the way Frank is running the club. Frank promised to turn the place around. Instead, after a year in charge, the club is losing more money than it was before Frank took over. He spent more time screwing the dancers than he did working. He's on a deadline. As far as I can see, they need the club to be a huge success—there are rumours of commitments from the family to launder money through the club for partners elsewhere. If Frank can't make it work, they'll find someone who will."

Lake cleared his throat. "If they don't have a use for Frank, then they don't need him around. He knows too much and he isn't a family member. He's a liability."

"We think this is a do-or-die situation," Harry said. "Literally."

Matt spread his hands wide in exasperation. "Again, what has this to do with Jena? Shouldn't Frank be in the States dealing with his problems?"

"He's dealing with them here. He needs Jena to save the club," Harry said. "If she dances, the crowds will come." He thought about it. "Hopefully not literally, because that's gross."

Matt felt his eyes go wide. "She's a stripper?" He knew she was a dancer of some sort, but hadn't given it much thought.

"Nope, she isn't stripper. She's a go-go dancer. She's famous in Atlantic City, a bit of an institution. She's known nationally too. But that's for her pole dancing. She's won lots of competitions." Harry blushed at the thought. "Not erotic pole dancing. I don't think they have competitions for that. Do they?" He looked to Lake, who shook his head slowly, as if questioning Harry's sanity.

Matt gave Lake a pleading look. "Help me out here. I'm missing something. I don't see a connection, unless Frank plans to hold dance competitions."

"Go-go dancers are hired by normal clubs to get the crowd going," Harry said. "They get really popular, like DJs. They have their own following. Some of the more popular ones have fans and websites. Jena was huge. She was in demand. Made a bomb. Which, as far as we can gather, she spent propping up Frank. Strip clubs have been after Jena for years. The demand to see her dance while stripping is high. Any venue that has Jena stripping would be sold out. It would save Frank's club to have her headline there. Probably save his life as well."

There was silence for a minute.

"He can't force her to leave with him," Matt said.

"Physically removing her from Scotland is nigh impossible. But we don't know what else he might try." Lake folded his arms. He stood army straight, taking up more space than he should reasonably take. "Threaten her. Blackmail. Intimidate. Seduce. If I were in his position, I'd use it all. He needs Jena. He's already told his partners he's bringing her back to save the business. His reputation is on the line. He's desperate. Desperate men are unpredictable."

"Plus the guy isn't known for his brain," Harry said. "This is probably the only plan he's come up with. All of his eggs are in one basket."

"Jena," Matt said on a sigh.

"Aye," Harry said. "Jena."

"We need to step up security at the hardware store." Matt looked at Lake. "Gordon's a great guy, but he's hitting retirement and I don't think he'd be much use against Frank and his two goons."

"I called a guy. He's on his way," Lake said.

"I'll stay with her until your guy gets here. I should probably tell her what Frank has in mind while I'm at it."

"Take chocolate," Harry said. "It always works with Magenta. Accidentally blow up the TV while making it more efficient—chocolate smooths it over. Back the car into the house while finishing a game of Angry Birds on your phone —chocolate takes the edge off. Seriously, there is nothing chocolate can't fix. Ask Lake, he's practically married." He turned to Lake. "Tell him. I'm right. I know it. I keep a supply on hand wherever I am. It always works."

Matt gaped at his cousin. "It's a miracle you're in a relationship."

Harry sighed in disgust. "Fine, don't take my advice, your loss." He turned back to his laptop and Matt was instantly forgotten.

With a last worried glance at Lake, Matt went to inform his charge that her ex needed her to strip to save his worthless life.

CHAPTER 19

Matt didn't get a chance to tell Jena anything. When he slipped through the back door of the hardware store, he found her face to face with a woman who looked like she'd stepped out of the pages of *Rolling Stone* magazine. She was dressed in tight black leather trousers, a black leather form-fitting vest—with nothing underneath—and high black stiletto-heeled boots. She had a silver bag slung over her shoulder, about a million silver bangles and thick black eyeliner. Her dyed blonde hair was long, wavy and tousled—and she was obviously Jena's mother.

The resemblance was startling—although the mother was a thinner, harder version of her daughter. Where Jena didn't have to make any effort to look sexy, this woman worked hard at it. Where Jena's eyes lit with kindness and mischief, her mother's eyes were dull and calculating. After about two seconds assessing the woman, Matt decided he knew everything he wanted to know about her. And he didn't like any of it.

"What do you mean you won't take me to see Josh McInnes?" Jena's mother was saying. "Isn't that the whole point of your move here? To get close to him so you could introduce me."

Matt clenched his teeth as he stood behind a shelf and watched.

"Mom." Jena spoke with the tone of a person who had already answered the question. "I didn't move here to meet Josh. I was joking earlier. I kind of moved here by accident. I was looking for houses on the web, somewhere far away from Atlantic City, and the name of this town stuck in my mind for some reason, so I ended up here."

Her mother rolled her eyes. "It was in your mind because I've been talking about Josh's move to Scotland for forever. When are you going to start paying attention, Jena? You didn't even tell me you'd moved country. If Frank hadn't called, I'd never have known."

Jena rubbed her arms as though comforting herself. Matt took a step towards her before he felt a hand on his shoulder. He looked up to find Gordon. The man shook his head. Matt didn't like anyone telling him how to deal with Jena, but tightness in Gordon's expression made Matt pause.

"I did tell you, Mom." Jena's voice brought Matt's attention back to her. "Several times—including when I came to see you the night before I left."

"Was that the night I played Caesars?"

"Yeah, that was the night I dropped by Caesars."

"Jena, that was the night there were scouts in the audience. Record companies. I told you about them when you arrived. You distracted me and made me miss my chance with them."

Jena winced as Matt stifled a growl.

"I'm sorry, Mom."

What the hell? Why was she apologising? He shared a look with Gordon, who seemed equally surprised. This wasn't the Jena he knew. Where was her smart mouth? Her sass?

"Yeah, well, you can make it up to me by taking me round to your friend Josh's house. I've got a demo on me, my guitar in the car and I have a new song that's perfect for him. Plus, I cleared my schedule for a few weeks before I left. I'm sure once he hears me, he'll want to book me for his tour. I'd like to be his support act, but I'd settle for backing singer to get a foot in the door."

"Mom." Jena took a deep breath. "I live here now. I'm getting to know these people. They value their privacy. They came here to get away from everything. They don't want to be pestered in their home."

"Are you saying I'm a pest? You know better. Just because I know how to take advantage of every opportunity that comes my way, doesn't mean I annoy people. I'm not one of those talentless wannabes you see on *American Idol*. I am gifted. All I need is a lucky break and I'd be as famous as Josh McInnes."

Jena seemed to shrink in on herself. Her normal spark snuffed out by the one woman in the world who should be nurturing it. It made no sense to Matt. Where was the bubbly, crazy woman he'd come to know?

"Where's Frank?" her mother said. "Frank said he'd introduce me to Josh. He knows the value of using your contacts. Of networking."

Jena didn't even look at her mother to reply. "We split up. I told you about that too."

"Jena." The disproval in that one word was massive. "What did you do? He's a great guy. Good looking, charming, working hard to get ahead. How could you throw away a relationship with a guy like that? He's going places."

"Yeah," Jena mumbled, "straight to jail."

Matt grinned, but her mother frowned. "You need to get

your act together, stop messing around over here and go back home with Frank."

Jena's head snapped up, and some of the fire in her eyes returned. "He asked you to talk me into going back with him, didn't he? What did he promise you in return? No. Don't answer. I know. He's going to connect you with Josh."

Her mother let out an exasperated sigh. "Why are you getting mad? This is win-win for everyone. You get to go home to a beautiful house and a man who loves you, and I get the break I need. Who suffers in this, Jena, huh?"

Jena put her hands on her hips as her cheeks flushed. "He cheated on me, Mom. A lot."

"Men do that." Her mom waved a hand dismissively, as though it was nothing. "You need to compromise in a relationship. You're lucky you caught his eye in the first place. You'll never get another man like Frank, one who'll help you with your career. Who'll make sure you never want for anything. Plus he's hot. What else is there? If you keep being selfish like this, you'll be alone forever."

Matt had heard more than enough. He left Gordon shaking his head in disgust as he stepped out into the store. Jena's mother's eyes shot straight to his, and to his disgust, they showed interest. She batted her lashes, fluffed her hair and pushed her boobs out. The sight made him want to vomit. When Jena spotted him, she took a step towards him before stopping herself. For some reason, her hesitance annoyed him. She was damn well within her rights to lean on him. If she needed to be rescued, he could do that. Hell, he was great at rescuing women. He had a lifetime of experience.

"Hey, princess," Matt said. "I brought lunch. Can't have you wasting away."

Her eyes widened at his tone, silently asking what he thought he was doing. Matt couldn't have answered even if he wanted to. All he knew for sure was that he didn't want her mother to think Jena was alone. She wasn't alone. She had him.

"Matt, look who's come to visit." Her smile was tight enough to crack a tooth. "It's my mom. Mom, this is Matt, my…"

"Boyfriend." Matt held out his hand as Jena looked like she was going to choke. "I was lucky enough to snap Jena up when she came to town. There have been guys queuing up to date her."

Her mother tried to hide her shock as she shook his hand. She held it a minute longer than was polite. He had the urge to rub his palm on his leg when she released him.

"You're a cop?" She lifted an eyebrow in Jena's direction. "You never told me you were dating a cop."

"You never asked," Jena muttered.

"They must grow them big in Scotland," Jena's mother told Matt, making him cringe. "Call me Mona." Her smile was sultry. Her laidback tone completely different to the one she'd been using with her daughter. She let out a throaty chuckle before he could say anything. "I know what you're going to say. I get it all the time. Folk are generally shocked I have a grown daughter. We look more like sisters." She cast a snide glance Jena's way. "Although if you keep dressing like that, honey, they'll think you're the mother." She laughed again. It was forced and nasty.

"No," Matt said. "I wasn't going to say that. You definitely look like her mother." He turned away from her shocked expression to look down at Jena. "Your mum has a great sense of humour." He wrapped an arm around her waist and pulled her into his side. "Nobody would take one look at you both and think you were older. Hell, you don't have the same wrinkles she does, for a start."

Mona gasped. "They said Scottish men were tactless."

Matt gave her a smile that often got him out of trouble as a teen. "Was I being tactless? I can never tell."

Jena was stiff as a board in his hold. Matt ignored it. He knew exactly how pliant she could become when he put in a little effort. The thought made his blood heat. Okay, so he hadn't thought through the whole being Jena's pretend boyfriend thing, but there was definitely an upside—he got to touch Jena again. Sure, he said he wouldn't do that. He'd been determined to remain at a professional distance. But this didn't count. It was all part of his duty to her—as a cop. Kind off. Maybe. Aw, to hell with it, he just wanted to hold her. Stuff being professional. There weren't any rules against dating the women you were protecting. Hell, it wasn't even an official job anyway. He nodded to himself. It was settled. There was nothing to stop him. He was dating Jena. He smiled at her as something settled within him. The anxiety of being around her and not touching her melted away. Yeah, he was definitely going to have a relationship with Jena. It was the right decision. Now he just had to tell her.

"You must be starving, princess," he said softly. "You didn't eat much for breakfast this morning."

"Oh, she'll be dieting," Mona said before Jena had the chance to speak. "I'm glad you took my advice," she said to Jena.

Matt felt the muscle in his jaw tick. "I really hope that's not the case. You don't need to diet. In fact, you lose one inch of that gorgeous body and I'll tie you to the bed and force-feed you cupcakes. No man wants a skinny woman in his bed, isn't that right, Gordon?"

The old man came up to stand on the other side of Jena. He folded his arms over his overalls. His face was shuttered and his eyes were hard. "Aye, that's right. All these women trying to get the body of an emaciated wee boy. What man in his right mind finds that attractive. Unless, of course, he's perverted and sick in the head. No, give me a woman with sexy curves any day of the week."

Jena gave him a grateful smile and relaxed slightly. "Don't let your wife hear you say that."

"Now why would I look at another woman, when I found the perfect one?" His eyes twinkled.

Mona had obviously had enough. "It was nice meeting you both, but Jena's taking me to see her other friends—Josh McInnes and his manager, Mitch. Mitch is here, right? I checked the web and it said he was here."

Matt shook his head. "Jena and I have plans for the afternoon. Maybe some other time."

"Jena." Mona stared at her daughter, her smile fixed in place. "I came all this way to see you. Surely you have time for your mom."

"Tell you what," Matt said. "Why don't we meet up for dinner later in the pub? That's where all the locals hang out. You can usually find Josh there in the evening. Isn't that right, Gordon?"

"Auch, aye, he loves the pub."

"Really?" Mona perked right up, her need to spend time with her daughter totally forgotten. "Why didn't you say so? That gives me the afternoon to get changed and organised. I came straight from the airport."

The way she spoke implied she was waiting for a compliment on how great she looked.

"Aye, you look like you could use a spruce-up," Matt said instead.

Jena coughed slightly and covered her mouth with her hand. From Matt's viewpoint, he could see her hiding a smile. It warmed his heart. He never wanted to see that beaten and dejected look on her face ever again.

Mona sneered at Jena. "Maybe you could spare a couple

of minutes of your precious time to show your mom how to get to your house."

Jena froze. "You want to stay with me?"

"Where else would I stay?"

"You never stay with me. I mean ever. I left home ten years ago and you've never even visited, let alone spent the night."

"You've never moved country before."

Jena shot Matt a look tinged with panic. "It's, I'm, the house…" She let out a sigh. "The house is a mess, Mom. It needs a lot of renovation. I don't have space to put you up."

"You're sleeping there, aren't you? I can sleep in your bed. You can take the couch."

"Now, that would put me out a tad, seeing as I'm in that bed too," Matt drawled.

Jena flicked him a look. She cleared her throat. "There are rooms above the pub. They're really pretty. You'd be much more comfortable there."

Her mother folded her arms and glared at Jena. Matt readied himself to intervene. "Why don't you stay at Matt's place and I'll stay at yours, if it's gonna be so horrible to share a house with me."

"Can't do that," Gordon said. "Everybody in town knows Matt has a rat problem. They even had a video of it on in the pub. He's stuck at Jena's until it's sorted."

Matt smothered a grin. What he had was about a hundred soft toy rats, courtesy of his sisters.

Mona put her hand on her hip, drawing attention to the star tattoo that encircled her belly button on her very flat stomach. "You're telling me I came all this way to spend money on a hotel room. What happened to family taking care of family?"

Matt almost choked. From the woman's behaviour, she had no idea what family taking care of family meant.

"You're totally right, of course," Gordon said with a gleam in his eye. "A daughter should put her mother up, even if it is an inconvenience. After all, Jena, she did come all this way, *just* to see you. Pity, though." He scratched his beard. "Those rooms in the pub are damn nice. Some of the guests for Josh's wedding stayed there—they even have a celebrity page set up on Facebook for the hotel. It's become *the* place to visit when you're in Scotland." He faked a hearty laugh. "The rooms are so good you can't get some people out of them. Mitch Harris moved into one when Caroline had the baby. He says the castle is too noisy now and he doesn't want to buy a house. He likes the food at the pub too much."

Mona perked to attention. "Josh's manager is living above the pub?"

Gordon shrugged, although his eyes held pure mischief. "Only when he's in town. Which seems to be all the time these days. Can't keep that boy away."

Mona turned to Jena with a gleeful smile. "Why didn't you tell me how great the pub is? If it's good enough for Hollywood, it's good enough for me. I mean, if Mitch Harris stays there, then that's a recommendation in itself. I wouldn't want to miss out on the chance to stay in a Scottish landmark." She flashed a wide smile. She was backing out of the shop as she spoke, in a hurry to get back to the pub now she knew Mitch was in residence. She faked a yawn. "That trip really took it out of me. I mean, who can sleep on a plane? It's a miracle I was able to drive from Glasgow without passing out. I'll just go book a room before they sell out. We'll meet tonight. What time do people eat around here?"

"Seven," Matt said. "We'll see you there at seven."

"Great. Big kiss," she said, then turned and practically ran from the shop.

As soon as the Wicked Witch of the West was out of the door, Jena pushed away from Matt. He instantly missed the soft warmth of her curvy body and scowled. She smacked him on the chest. It was like being swatted by a fly.

"Why did you let my mother think we were an item?" She spun on Gordon. "Why did you tell her Mitch was living at the pub? That's mean."

"Matt?" Gordon said.

"I'm on it." He took out his phone and held a finger up to make Jena wait. "We'll deal with the relationship thing in a minute." She scowled. It was cute. "Mitch," Matt said when he answered. "Jena's mum is in town. She's called Mona Sage. She's a singer looking for a break and she seriously doesn't deserve one. She's scented your blood at the hotel. I'd get out before the shark gets you."

Mitch thanked him for the heads-up and hung up. Matt turned to Jena, who had her arms folded and was tapping her toe in clear irritation. Now why didn't she behave like this with the witch?

"Explain," she demanded.

He let out a sigh. "She was horrible. I didn't like it. She said you couldn't get a decent man. I'm a decent man and I decided you could get me. Plus you need someone watching your back while she's here, and it may as well be me. I'm already doing the job where Frank is concerned. Might as well double up."

It sounded perfectly reasonable to him. Unfortunately, from the look on Jena's face, she didn't agree.

"The lad's right," Gordon said. "That woman is toxic. She'd walk over your broken body to get to Josh. You're better off with someone in your corner, lass, when you deal with her."

"What do you mean by 'get you', Matt?" She eyed him suspiciously.

Matt took a deep breath. Here goes. There was no point explaining the logic behind his decision. In his experience, male and female logic were two completely different beasts. Best to give her the final result of all his thinking. "I've decided to skip the whole dating thing and jump straight to the relationship. It's safer."

She blinked at him as Gordon laughed so loudly it echoed through the room.

"You're serious? You want to be involved with me? Romantically?"

Matt folded his arms. "Don't go getting all worked up about it. That leads to accidents. And I don't want to be set on fire. A plain thank you will do just fine." He stepped towards her. "We should really seal the deal on this new relationship with a kiss. Pucker up."

Jena let out a frustrated wail, made a fist and thumped him in the stomach. Thankfully, she punched like a girl and his stab vest blocked most of the blow.

"Your sense of humour is sick," she told him.

"Who says I'm joking. Close your eyes, Gordon, I'm going in." With a grin, he stepped towards Jena.

"Ignore the idiot," Gordon said through his laughter. "He's right about one thing though. You need all the help you can get dealing with that woman."

Jena threw up her hands. "I've been dealing with *that woman* my whole life. I don't need backup to cope with my mom." Hands on hips, she looked at the ceiling for a moment. Her pain was almost tangible. The sight of it made Matt ache, and from the look on Gordon's face, it had the same effect on him. Jena's head dropped back down. She looked so lost. "She's a really focused person. She's put a lot into her career. And she is good. Trust me. You'd want to hear her sing. All she needs is a little bit of luck to make it to the next level."

"Is that you talking or your mum?" Gordon said gently.

"She wants it really badly. It's all she can think about. She doesn't realise how she comes across." Jena wrapped her arms around herself again. She was breaking Matt's heart. "Once she gets where she wants to be, she'll calm down. She won't be so insensitive to people."

To her daughter, she meant. He could see it in her face. So earnest. So eager to believe the best of everyone, even as they walked right over her or treated her like muck on their shoes. He couldn't bear to see her standing so alone any longer.

"Come here." He pulled her into his arms.

"Matt, I'm over the joking."

"It's a friendly hug, nothing else." If that was what it took to get her to come to him, then he'd roll with it. For now. "You'd give me one if I needed it. So shut up and enjoy. And don't tell anyone or they'll all want one."

She laughed against his chest, but her arms threaded around his waist. She sank into him, and something within Matt settled. He had an overwhelming sense of being in the right place at the right time. Here, with this woman, lending her his strength when she needed it.

Gordon clasped his shoulder before taking off for the back of the shop, shaking his head in disgust as he did so.

Matt snuggled Jena closer, engulfing her with his heat. He stroked one hand over her hair while his other held her tight against him. If he had his way, nothing and no one would ever get close enough to hurt her again.

With that thought, Matt realised that his feelings for Jena ran a lot deeper than he'd suspected.

And he couldn't bring himself to worry about it.

Not when holding her felt so completely and utterly right.

CHAPTER 20

We're not in a relationship," Jena said.

They were in Matt's cop car, on the way to see Abby. Jena's friend had called asking Matt to stop by, which had Jena worried. Matt was currently ignoring Jena as he drove out of town.

"One kiss does not make a relationship," Jena said.

"It was more than a kiss." His smug grin made Jena want to smack him. She restrained herself.

"It wasn't even a real kiss. You only kissed me to prove a point."

He cocked an arrogant eyebrow in her direction. Like he knew better.

"I'm not dating you." She folded her arms and glared at him.

"Thank the Lord for that. Men only date you if they have a death wish."

Jena wished his uniform came with a gun. She would have used it to shoot him.

"I'm not kissing you again, either. It's not a relationship if I won't kiss you."

She squealed as the car suddenly lurched off the road. Matt turned to her, a sexy grin on his face.

"How about I kiss you, then? No pressure. Don't feel the need to participate."

Before she could get an objection out of her mouth, he'd leaned over, clasped the back of her neck and was pulling her towards him. Jena was embarrassed to say she didn't put up any resistance. She'd liked the last kiss. She wasn't above taking another one.

The little smile he gave her before his lips met hers made her think he might be able to read her mind on the matter. And then she wasn't thinking at all. His lips were soft and firm. His touch was confident. He tasted like chocolate lemon Pop-Tarts—something he would probably take offence at if she told him. She made a note to tell him later.

As his tongue slipped past her lips, she let out a little sigh of delight. She was losing herself in him. And she loved it. Her fingers curled into the stiff material of his uniform. She pressed forward, seeking the heat of his body, the bone-melting awareness of his size and strength. The seatbelt tugged her back, making her groan in frustration.

All too soon, the kiss ended. Matt nipped her lower lip before caressing her cheek. Jena felt herself swaying into him.

"Don't worry," he whispered over her lips, "I'm okay with this not being a relationship."

With a grin, he put the car in gear and swerved back into the road. Jena glared at him. She wasn't sure what was going on—and she definitely wasn't sure she wanted it to stop. She decided the best course of action was to ignore him and this thing that was happening between them.

Denial was good. She liked denial. As a life choice, it worked great.

Jena's friend stayed in an old Victorian house in the hills

outside of town. Only a small field separated her house from Jena's. Abby owned the local mushroom farm, which sat in a section of the old abandoned mine—part of which ran under the field towards Jena's house. Abby said the old Victorian house she lived in used to be the home of the mine manager, back in the day when the old mine was at its height. Being the home of the most important person in Invertary at that time, it had been built with status in mind.

The grey stone had been shipped in from Inverness; the long drive had been planted with poplars along each side to make it feel like you were driving through a regal tunnel to get to the house. The house itself was three stories high, with large bay windows and a grand entrance.

Fortunately, successive owners had taken the time to keep the house in a decent condition, and Abby had added her touches to it, to make it homely and welcoming. Abby was standing at the door when Matt's car drove up. The dark circles under her eyes were getting worse, and Jena was worried about her.

"Aunty Jena's here," she called when Jena got out of the car.

There was a squeal from inside the house, and a few seconds later Katy barrelled out. She was dressed as a princess in a pink merengue gown and sparkling plastic tiara.

"Aunty Jena! Uncle Mattie!" She flew down the steps, launching herself at Jena, who gave her a tight cuddle before she wriggled away to throw herself at Matt.

Jena shook her head with a grin. No matter how muggy the day, Katy was a breath of fresh air. You had to have something seriously wrong with you not to smile when that little girl was near.

"We need to get you one of those dresses, princess," Matt said as he led her to the house with his hand on the small of

Jena's back. Even his slight touch made her feel gloriously boneless. *Ignore it. Deny it. It isn't happening.*

Yeah, maybe this denial thing was a bit broken.

Abby noticed his move and raised an eyebrow. Jena felt heat flush her cheeks.

"I've made tea and scones." Abby gave Jena a hug, and she found herself clinging more tightly to Abby than usual. "Tough day, petal?"

"Mom's here."

"Well cluck in a bucket, I should have made chocolate cake."

"Cluck in a bucket?" Matt said.

"Should I use foul language around my daughter?" Abby stood straight, her head high and not a stitch out of place.

"Instead you use *fowl* language?" Matt said.

"Funny guy," Abby muttered.

"Do you even know how to swear, Abby? If you don't, I can whisper some words in your ear for later." Matt grinned.

Abby wagged a finger at him. "You're a rascal, Matt Donaldson."

"Aye, so I've been told. Now where are the scones? And what do you need me for?"

"It isn't important." Abby chewed her bottom lip, something she never did—it went against her very proper upbringing. "I wanted your advice on something. It can wait until we've had tea."

"Happy to be of service. Especially when I'm being fed at the same time."

Abby led the way through the grand hallway to the kitchen at the back of the house. Katy held her hands up to Matt, who picked her up without missing a beat and carried her to the food. He made impressed noises when the baby girl showed off the new nail polish she'd painted her fingers with—not just her nails, her *whole* fingers. And if Jena wasn't mistaken, she'd also put lipstick on her eyebrows again.

The kitchen was huge, like the rest of the house. The Victorians loved their grand proportions. A large oak table took up a chunk of the floor space. The matching chairs had a selection of patchwork cushions in warm colours. It was peaceful, pretty and welcoming. Jena sank into a chair as Matt put Katy down in her play corner. Jena expected him to come sit beside them, but instead he sat on the rug beside the four-year-old and listened to her tell him all about Minnie Mouse and Donald getting into trouble for having a disco in the bathroom.

"Mum says Minnie's not allowed to play with water anymore," she said before looking at her mum. When she was convinced Abby wasn't listening, she leaned towards Matt and cupped a hand over her mouth. "Don't tell her, but it wasn't Minnie who made the mess." She giggled as she stage-whispered. "It was Donald."

Matt tickled her. "And who helped Donald, you little monster?"

"I don't know, Uncle Mattie." Her eyes were wide with faux-innocence.

"Your mum's in town, then?" Abby said as she handed Jena a cup of tea. In a pretty blue porcelain cup and saucer. Jena wasn't even sure Abby owned a mug. "When did she get here?"

"Oh, I'd guess about thirty-six hours after Frank called and told her I was living in the same town as Josh McInnes."

Abby grimaced. "I can't say the words I'm thinking, but they're bad ones."

"Not bad enough," Jena said.

"We should call Caroline and warn her that your mother is here to pester her husband."

"I'll do that." Matt stood. "I need to make some calls anyway."

He nabbed a plate, loaded it with scones and jam and headed out of the back door. He stayed close to the house but far enough away so he had the privacy he needed to talk. As soon as he was out of earshot, Abby turned to Jena.

"What's going on with Matt? You two look cosy." She waggled her eyebrows. It looked silly on a woman who was the walking definition of elegance.

Jena laughed. It felt good. "Nothing's going on. He's only sticking by me until Frank leaves town."

"Uh, huh, and I'm the Queen of England. Pleased to meet you."

"Are you really, Mum?" Katy sounded hopeful. Jena hid her chuckle behind her cup.

"No, sweetie," Abby said. "The Queen is just a cousin."

Jena spat her tea. "You're related to the Queen? The real one? The one in Buckingham Palace?"

Abby waved the questions away as though they were nothing but hot air. "Distant cousin. It's not like we pop down for holidays. It's no big deal. The Queen is related to half of England."

Jena wasn't convinced. If she was related to the Queen, however distantly, she'd get a T-shirt printed so everyone knew. Maybe even invest in a tiara. "You know, Abby McKenzie, you are really good at keeping secrets."

"Isn't that good for you, because if I wasn't I'd tell everyone you and Matt were getting it on."

"We are not!" Well, not really.

"Why not? He's gorgeous. Single. Honest. Fairly intelligent—when he's not being a sexist fool. Although I've often thought that most of the offensive things he says are deliberately spoken to get a reaction. He does love to wind people up. Especially the twins."

Jena reached for another scone as Abby topped up her teacup. The memory of Matt's kiss derailed her thought process. She could still feel him on her lips. Still taste him. Thinking about the kiss made her think about the way he'd held her in the hardware store. Which led to a full-colour replay of their time in the kitchen. She shivered. The man oozed sex appeal. It flowed from him like a waterfall. It was impossible to get close to him and not get a little wet.

"I'm not dating Matt. You can ask him. He'd tell you." She had no idea what she was doing with Matt, but it definitely wasn't dating. "We're not talking about this," she told Abby.

Abby huffed. "We never talk about the good stuff."

"Yeah, that's because there isn't any. You don't have a love life and I am a serial first dater."

"True." Abby smiled, her eyes gentle with compassion. "What are you going to do about your mum?"

"I'm thinking of hiding from her until she goes back to America. That's the tactic I'm using with Frank. It's a one-size-fits-all plan."

Matt saved her from Abby's lecture by sauntering into the room. "Josh has been duly warned. I told him your mother isn't hard to miss—she looks like a blonde version of Chrissie Hynde. What's with all that eyeliner, anyway?"

Jena ignored him. Not that he was expecting an answer. Her mother was forgotten now he had the rest of the scones in front of him.

"What do you need my input on, then?" he asked Abby as he filled his plate.

Abby looked at Katy nervously. The little girl was busy making a picture with crayons and glitter. She didn't care what the grown-ups were talking about.

"I think someone's been messing with things around the property."

Matt was instantly alert. The food was forgotten. "Messed with in what way?"

Abby shrugged, but it was clearly forced. "It's probably nothing. Things aren't where I put them. Some things have gone completely missing." She picked at a speck on the table-cloth. "I hear noises in the back of the mine, behind the mushroom farm. It was closed up when we moved in here—there shouldn't be anything in there to make a noise."

"When you say things are being moved, what do you mean?" Matt studied her intently.

Abby waved a hand as she gave a little laugh. "Katy's bike was outside the back door, and then I found it down by the stream. The boxes I put out for recycling disappeared. I can't find them anywhere. Things like that. Silly things." Her brown eyes blinked at Matt. "I'm worried I'm moving things and can't remember. I get tired. Although I can't figure out why I'd take Katy's bike down to the stream. I feel like I'm losing my mind."

Matt's eyes were sharp. "Do you have an alarm for this place?"

Abby nodded. "David had one put in shortly before his illness."

"I'll get Lake out to check on it. It wouldn't hurt to have him look over your house. Make sure everything's being done to make it secure."

"I'm probably making a fuss about nothing. I mean, why would anyone move Katy's bike?" She nodded as though coming to a decision. "I'm sorry I called you, Matt. I'm sure this is just my imagination and bad memory."

"Better safe than sorry, Abby. Trust me, talking to you about your worries beats dealing with Morag's missing cat." He smiled at her. Jena knew it was supposed to be reassuring, but his eyes showed concern. "What about your employees? Would any of them play around like this?"

Abby shook her head. "You know the people who work for me. I have three retirement-age workers who come in part-time to help with the mushrooms. I don't see them moving my things. They're more interested in gossiping and swapping mushroom recipes."

"I'll have a chat with them anyway. We'll get Magenta in to look at the mine as well."

"Didn't you do that already?" Jena said.

Abby gave her a sheepish look. "I meant to. I forgot."

More like she didn't want to bother Magenta with her worries.

"Now," Matt said, "enough of this. We'll sort it out. You got any more scones? Or is this it? I'll just make a call to Lake while you're getting the food. Coffee would be great too. I don't do tea in fancy wee cups." He disappeared outside the back door again.

"I dare you to give him coffee in a fancy wee cup," Jena said as she watched him go.

"You are bad, Jena Morgan." Abby reached into the cupboard. "I have just the thing, though." She held up a tiny espresso cup and matching saucer. It was delicate, pale purple and covered in daisies. Abby gave her an innocent look. "It is an actual coffee cup, after all."

"I like how you think." Jena laughed. "But don't put the pot within his reach. He'll take one look at the cup and just drink from the pot."

Abby was laughing when she turned back to the counter.

CHAPTER 21

It said a lot about Jena's relationship with her mother that she spent more than an hour trying to pick the perfect clothes to wear to dinner. It was a wasted effort. She knew no matter what she wore, her mom would find fault with it. She threw her latest outfit onto the pile of all the other ones that didn't make the cut. With a groan, Jena fell back onto her bed. It was all getting a bit too much. She felt like her head would burst with all the worries crammed into it. There was only so much one person could take.

"Wear the bronze dress you had on the other night."

Jena used what little energy she had left to lift her head and look at Matt. He was leaning in her bedroom doorway, hands in his pockets, ankles crossed. Dressed in a dark blue tee and faded jeans, he was effortlessly sexy. Typical. Men had it so easy. All they needed was a pair of jeans that cupped their ass and a tee that stretched across their shoulders and they were good to go.

"I set fire to a man in that dress. It has bad memories." She might never wear it again. Not without seeing a hysterical Bob rolled in a rug.

Matt grinned, and it melted her organs, turning them to mush inside her body.

"Aye, but it has good memories for me. You set Bob the butcher on fire in that dress, then I got to hold you while he whined like a baby. Good times." His eyes darkened. "Wear the dress, princess, and I'll give you some good memories to replace the bad."

She resisted the urge to fan herself at the heat in his eyes. "I doubt an evening with my mom will improve the mojo of the dress."

"She won't be with us all evening. Wear the dress. Do it for me."

Her mouth went dry. "If I wear it for you, what will you do for me?"

"If I tell you that now, princess, we won't make it to dinner with your mother."

Jena let her head fall back onto the thick duvet as she laughed. The tension eased from her body. Man, she needed that.

"I forgot about you thinking you're a sexpert." She wiped her eyes. "Thanks, Matt, I needed a laugh."

"Happy to be of service. Anytime. Anywhere. In any way."

She could hear the humour in his voice. Jena let out a heavy breath. "Dinner is going to be horrible."

"Hate to break it to you, but I already figured that out." She felt the bed dip as he sat beside her. He stroked her cheek. "Don't worry about it. We'll get through whatever this evening brings. Together."

Her heart clenched at the word. Together. Like she belonged. She wondered if he knew how much she longed to belong to someone. To be part of a family. To be wanted instead of used.

"You're really lucky with your family, Matt." Even Jena was aware how wistful she sounded.

"I know. They drive me nuts, but I hate being away from them. It's one of the reasons I've stayed around Invertary this long. That and Dad. Mum needs support right now."

What was unsaid was heavy in the air between them. His mum wouldn't need him forever, because his dad wouldn't be around forever.

"You're a good man, Matt."

"Not that good, Jena. Right now I'm undressing you in my head and wondering if I can get you to stay in bed instead of going to the pub."

Jena laughed at his frustrated expression.

"You don't have a hope. I keep telling you—we're not in a relationship. We're not even dating."

"And yet you want me." He waggled his eyebrows at her, making her giggle.

"Right now, I *want you* to get out of here so I can get dressed."

"I can do that. If you wear the bronze dress."

She rolled her eyes at him. "Fine. You win. I'll wear the damn dress."

"I win. I like that. Keep it in mind. Persistence usually pays off, and I'm very persistent." He grabbed her hand and pulled her to sitting. "One more thing before you get ready."

Before she could ask what he was talking about, his lips were on hers. His fingers wove into the hair at the back of her head. His other arm wrapped around her waist, pulling her tight against him. She offered no resistance. She wasn't an idiot. The guy made her toes curl just from a kiss. What woman in her right mind would pass up on that?

The kiss finished all too soon for Jena's liking. It took a minute to calm her pulse and focus her eyes on his face.

"Better get ready, princess. I want to get there, get this over with and get home as fast as we can. I have plans for you and your dress." With a sexy little smile, he kissed the tip of her nose, then sauntered from the room.

Leaving Jena dazed, horny and seriously confused.

THE PUB WAS PACKED, more so than usual for a Monday night. As Matt led Jena into the restaurant area, he got the impression people were there for more than the food. Word had spread round Invertary at warp speed. The curious were out to watch Jena and her mum. Matt wasn't surprised; the locals treated everybody else's business as the equivalent of a live reality TV show. There was an air of expectation in the room, a buzz of anticipation. He didn't like it one bit.

As soon as Dougal spotted them, he rushed over. Another bad sign. If the town's unofficial mayor and pub owner was tense, there was usually a reason for it. One Matt knew he wouldn't like.

"Hi, Jena." Dougal gave her a tight little smile. He grimaced at Matt. "Jena's mother is in the booth round the corner of the bar." He paused as he gave Jena a sympathetic look. "She has company."

Matt was instantly on alert. "Don't tell me she managed to get hold of Josh and Mitch. I gave them a heads-up that she was on the prowl."

"No, lad, it's not the boys. She's with Frank."

Jena froze beside him. He rubbed the small of her back through the silky material of his favourite dress to reassure her, and to remind her she wasn't alone. Anyone wanting to mess with her had to get through him first.

"Your mum has been telling everyone you're going back home with Frank. She also told anyone who would listen that you were"—he cleared his throat—"only sowing your wild oats with Matt, that your relationship isn't serious."

Jena hung her head. Matt felt her heart pound under his

hand. "Everyone thinks we're dating." She looked up at him, her honey-coloured eyes wide and panicked at the thought. Matt wasn't sure whether to be insulted or amused.

"No they don't, princess. Remember, I'm still in one piece."

She elbowed him in the ribs. At least she didn't look so desolate anymore. "Be serious for one minute. This is a mess. We're not dating. Tell him we're not dating." She pointed at Dougal.

Matt did as he was told. "We're not dating." He even managed to keep his face straight while he said it.

Dougal's eyes flickered with amusement. "So what are you doing, lad?"

"I'm living with her."

Jena gasped before glaring at him.

"I thought it was best to skip the dating stage," he told Dougal.

"Wise decision." Dougal nodded. His lip twitching as he hid a smile.

"Matt, it's one thing to let my mom and Frank think we're an item, but you can't let it spread through town. Once Frank and my mom go home, people will still think we're together."

"You're right," he said. Really? What else was there to say? They were together. Jena would eventually catch on.

"Anything else we should know?" he asked Dougal.

"Nothing concrete. Although I have a bad feeling. Those two are after something, and I get the impression they're not above using our Jena to get it."

"That's not going to happen."

Dougal nodded as though he hadn't expected anything less. He made his excuses and headed back to the bar. Matt pulled Jena closer to his side as they wound their way around the tables. People gawked and whispered. Matt ignored it. He'd been living in Invertary practically his whole life, so he was used to it. Jena wasn't. He felt her stiffen beside him. If she didn't relax, she'd never make it through dinner with her mother and ex-boyfriend.

"Princess." He pulled her to a stop beside the bar. He held her hand in his as she looked up at him. He hated the anxiety in her eyes. "You look gorgeous." Her eyes softened slightly. He cupped her cheek with his hand. "You take my breath away."

"Matt," she admonished. The pretty pink flush that coloured her cheeks made him wish they were alone.

He leaned into her. Her scent engulfed him, making everything else fade away. "You are definitely the sexiest woman in town," he whispered, pleased when she shivered. "I can't wait to get my hands on you."

He placed a light kiss on her luscious lips. Man, she was beautiful. He heard the murmurs behind him and didn't care. He was well aware he'd made his claim on Jena as public as possible. It was a nice side benefit of getting her mind off their evening. Hopefully now the men of Invertary would stop asking his woman out. Because she was his woman. She just didn't know it yet.

JENA'S first thought when she saw her mom sitting, heads together, with the man who broke her heart, was that she hadn't moved far enough away. She should have followed up on the little house she'd seen in New Zealand. Maybe it wasn't too late to move. Surely someone out there was dumb enough to buy her house.

It was clear the minute her mom and Frank spotted her. Her mother looked annoyed and Frank looked angry, then just as quickly they both covered their reactions with charming smiles. Wow. It hit Jena hard—she'd somehow managed to date the male version of her mom. How twisted was that? And now she'd realised it, she'd need therapy to get over it. Lots and lots of therapy.

"Jena, honey, isn't it wonderful? Frank was free for dinner, so I invited him to join us. I knew you wouldn't mind."

Matt pulled out a chair for Jena and settled her into it. He ran a hand over her bare shoulder as he nabbed the seat beside her. Frank and her mom studied every move Matt made, with pursed lips and angry eyes.

Jena bit back her ire. Was there any point in arguing with her mother's decision to invite Frank? All Jena wanted was to get this over and go home. With Matt. "No, I don't mind at all. Do you, Matt?"

"Nope." He wrapped an arm around the back of her chair and caressed her shoulder.

He appeared to be so laidback, he came across as bored. Not to mention he looked particularly hot in his grey v-neck shirt, black blazer and dark blue jeans. Casual but smart, laidback but sexy. His black hair was tousled as though he didn't care enough to style it, and still it looked cool. To make it perfect, the blazer was cut to show off the strength of his shoulders. The sight of him made her mouth water.

Frank leaned across the table towards Jena, breaking into her consideration of Matt's many charms.

"I want to talk about things between us," Frank said. His earnest look was back, and Jena found it irritating.

He was dressed in his uniform of black suit and black shirt. Compared to Matt, Frank looked like he was trying too hard.

"There's nothing to talk about, Frank. There's nothing between us."

Her mother's smile was shark-like. "It wouldn't hurt to listen to the man, would it? He came all this way to talk to you. You could make the effort to give him five minutes of your time. I'm sure Matt wouldn't mind waiting at the bar while you have dinner with your family."

"Frank isn't family," Jena pointed out.

"You know what I mean. It would be nice to spend some time alone with my daughter."

"In that case, Frank can sit at the bar with Matt."

"You're not being reasonable," her mother snapped.

"Probably not, but if Frank stays, Matt stays."

"I'm hungry and I'm staying," Matt said. "Plus, Jena is wearing my favourite dress. There's no way I'm letting her out of my sight when she looks this hot."

Jena rolled her eyes at him, but she was smiling while she did it.

"I can understand that." Frank's voice made Jena feel slightly nauseated. She found it hard to believe she'd once thought herself in love with the man. She'd been blind. Blind and stupid. He smiled that greasy smile again. "A man would be insane to let a woman like Jena out of sight. A man would be insane to let a woman like her get away."

"Aye." Matt's smile was ice cold. "Good job I'm not insane."

"I need to go to the ladies' room," her mother suddenly announced, and stood. "Jena, come with me. We'll do the chick thing and go together."

Yeah, like they'd ever done that before. It seemed strangely fitting that Jena's girl time with her mother would take place in a toilet.

"Order for me?" she asked Matt.

"No problem. Make sure you're back fast, or I'll eat it."

He would, too. In the time Matt had been camped at her house, she'd discovered nothing got between him and his food. Jena stood to follow her mom, who was dressed in a skintight black leather mini dress. For a second Jena felt a familiar burst of inadequacy, but it passed. She stepped away from the table.

Before she could second-guess herself, she leaned over and kissed Matt. His eyes flared with heat. "I'll hurry," she said against his lips.

"You'd better."

The spell he cast over her was broken when her mom cleared her throat. Jena pushed back her shoulders and followed her mom.

"You doing Jena, then?" As soon as the women had disappeared from sight, the question Matt had been expecting popped out of Frank's mouth.

Matt stared him down for a beat before answering. Frank Di Marco was the living definition of revolting. "She isn't going back with you." Matt decided to cut to the chase. The tick beside Frank's eye telegraphed his displeasure at Matt's words. "You can give up on your plan to talk her in to stripping at your club. Jena doesn't strip. Especially for you."

Frank's surprise oozed through a crack in his easygoing façade. "You've been doing some investigating, *officer*." Frank spat the last word out like it was an insult.

Matt shrugged. Like he cared what Frank Di Marco thought about anything. "I've done some digging. You're in trouble with the club. Your investors have given you an ultimatum to turn things around. You think Jena is your ticket out of trouble." Matt leaned forward. "Let's be clear about something. Jena isn't your ticket to anything. Jena isn't your anything at all. You blew your chance with her. She's done. It's time for you to go home. Find another way to save your sorry hide."

Frank clenched his fists on top of the table. "You don't get to tell me nothing. You're insignificant. Jena and me got history. One mistake don't wipe that out. You have no idea what you're dealing with here, cop. Back off before you regret it."

Matt's eyes went hard. "Are you threatening me, Frank?"

The easygoing smile was back. He spread his hands wide. "Now what makes you think that, officer? I'm just giving you a friendly heads-up that Jena is fair game. Unless you got a ring on her finger, you ain't got a claim to her. If her feelings for me should persuade her she'd have a better life back in the States, then so be it. You can't do nothing to stop her going home with me." He laughed. It was small and pathetic, but it still made Matt want to break his nose.

"You're delusional if you think she has feelings for you. You're also delusional if you think I don't have a claim."

"We'll see." The smug smile on Frank's face acted like a target for Matt's rage.

"Be very careful," Matt said. "I don't play games with the people who belong to me."

"Good she doesn't belong to you, then." Frank leaned forward and sneered inches from Matt's face. "You got her on loan, cop. Jena belongs to me until I say otherwise. And I ain't ready to let her go. Not while I still have use for her."

"You son of a…" Matt pulled his fist back, ready to let it fly.

A hand clasped his arm and held him back. Matt looked up to find Grunt staring down at him. His muscles were clenched with the effort it took to hold Matt back. His face was blank.

"Don't," was all he said.

Matt felt everything within him still. If he had to go through Grunt to get to Frank, so be it. In fact, it would be Matt's pleasure.

"This is not the time," Grunt rumbled.

Matt clenched his teeth as the room came into focus.

Every eye was on him. He never lost control. He never forgot he was a cop. Never. Not until Jena. He couldn't cope with a threat to Jena. All he could think was that he had to eliminate the threat—now.

Grunt leaned over to talk in Matt's ear. "Your girl's coming back. She needs you."

Matt's eyes shot to the bathroom doors. Grunt released his hold on Matt and stepped back. Jena stepped into the room. She walked stiffly as though injured. Her face was pale, and her eyes were glassy with tears. Matt's eyes shot to Jena's mom, who seemed pleased with herself. Now Matt had two people to kill. He wondered if Lake would help him hide the bodies. With effort, he swallowed his anger. Jena needed him.

Jena stopped beside him. "I want to leave. I don't feel well." She kept her eyes on the floor.

"I think it's all the rubbish she eats," her mother said with barely concealed glee. "Carrying extra weight can make you feel real bad."

Jena's head lifted slightly and big, sad eyes beseeched him. "Please," she whispered.

"You know we can," Matt said softly.

He stood, wrapped his arm around Jena and, without a word to Frank or Mona, he led her out of the pub. Shielding her from the Invertary gossips as he did so.

CHAPTER 22

Jena walked straight into her house without a word to Matt. She couldn't talk to him even if she wanted to—the voices in her head were too loud to talk over. All she could see, and hear, was a continuous replay of her time in the restroom with her mother.

She stalked up the stairs, stripped out of her bad-luck dress and pulled on her favourite PJs. Once her feet were clad in fuzzy bunny slippers instead of her usual wedges, she rummaged around in the back of her closet for the box she knew was there. Once she'd pulled it out, she strode back downstairs to the front door.

"Jena, princess, what are you doing?" Matt appeared from the living room. She'd forgotten he was there. He'd taken off his jacket, and Jena was momentarily distracted by how good he looked in the soft grey v-neck he wore.

"It's okay," Jena told him. "You can go to bed. I have something I need to do."

"Jena, it's only nine o'clock. Even my mum doesn't go to bed this early." He eyed the box. "Want to tell me what you're up to?"

She pasted on her best smile. Sure, it might have looked a little manic, but she could live with that. "Nothing for you to worry about," she said.

She put the box on the floor beside the door before she turned and strode into the kitchen. She lifted the can of paint stripper she'd brought home from work and a box of matches.

Matt eyed the paint stripper. "You're beginning to worry me."

She smiled serenely, picked up her box and headed out the door. Without checking to see if he was following, she marched to the shell of the burned-out car and threw the box inside. A minute later she'd doused it with paint stripper and set it alight.

As she watched the blaze dance, she felt Matt come up behind her. To her surprise, he wrapped his arms around her shoulders and pulled her into him, her back to his stomach. He rested his chin on top of her head. Jena felt quite toasty with the fire in front of her and Matt's heat behind her.

Jena sank into him as she stared at the flames, but she wasn't seeing them. Inside her head was a Technicolor replay of her time with her mother.

Her mother.

Not mom. Not anymore. Just mother. Jena shuddered at the memory, and Matt pulled her closer. With his support, Jena closed her eyes and let the memory come.

Her mother stood in front of the mirror in the ladies' room of the pub. She fluffed her hair as she eyed Jena.

"I want you to go home with Frank," she said.

"What?" For a second Jena thought she'd misheard.

"He has plans for you." Her mother nodded firmly. "He's a good man. Got a head on his shoulders. Knows what he's aiming for, and he'll get there. You need to give up this." She waved her hand to signal she meant Invertary, or perhaps Jena's life. "You need to go home."

"Mom, he cheated on me."

Her mother shrugged. "There isn't a man alive who can keep it in his pants. You'd best get that through your thick head. So what if he takes a bit on the side." She looked Jena up and down, her displeasure clear. "Not every man wants a chunky girl in his bed every night." She turned, perched her bony hip on the edge of the sink and folded her arms over her fake breasts. "You need to grow up. Be realistic. Frank came all this way to take you home. You're being petty making the man jump through hoops like this. He's said he's sorry. He'll be more discreet from now on. You should think yourself lucky he wants you back."

Jena gaped at her mother. "Mom, he cheated. He spent years using my money to finance his schemes. Now he's working with the mob. He isn't a catch. Why are you pretending like he is?"

Her mother shook her head. A mocking smile in place. "You are so naïve. The world is a dirty place, and you do what you can to get ahead. I thought I taught you that. After all, you were a product of my trying to get ahead." She let out a longsuffering sigh. "Jena, I've carried you for years. I would have been famous by now if I hadn't had to deal with being a single mom. You've held me back long enough, and yet here you are, trying to do it again. You won't introduce me to Josh or Mitch, even though you deliberately moved to the same town, and after everything I've done for you."

Words Jena wanted to say, words she *should* say, stuck in her throat. All she could do was stare at her mom's spiteful smile and feel the cut of each word as it struck her.

"Frank's offered to introduce me to Josh and Mitch. Turns out he knows them from way back. All he wants in return is to take you home and spoil you rotten. I think that's a fair trade, don't you? After all, what have you got here? I hear your house is a dump and you're running out of money." Her mother laughed. It was nasty. "Did you know they call you Calamity Jena? They take bets on you behind your back. They have a board set up beside the bar where they take odds on some guy getting injured dating you. You're the laughing stock of Invertary, probably Scotland, and you didn't even know." She sneered. "I'm ashamed of you, Jena. You're over here chasing any man who'll look at you twice, when you have a great guy like Frank begging you to come home. Do us all a favour. Grow up. Stop playing games. Take your man back. Then we'll all be happy." She turned towards the door, smiling over her shoulder at Jena. "After you, honey. Your small-town cop is waiting. I wonder how much he bet on getting lucky with you tonight?"

In a daze, Jena walked stiffly past her mother and out into the pub. Frank was leering at her. His smile said he thought he'd won. He'd played his ace. He'd always known how her mother could cut her down to nothing with a few well-placed words. Her gaze swung past him to Matt. He was being held in place by Grunt. Every muscle in his body screamed with rage, but all Jena saw was the worry in his eyes. Worry for her.

Without a glance at anyone else, she headed straight for him. Matt wouldn't bet on her, she knew it. Her mother was making up more vile lies.

"I want to go home," she told him. "I don't feel well."

As she knew he would, he whisked her out of there and straight home.

The scene played over and over in her head. Each time her mother looked more malicious. Frank more smugly calculating.

Matt broke into the memory by kissing her neck. Warmth

slid through her, melting the ice her mother had left behind. The flames in front of her came into focus once again.

"Feeling better now?" he said against her skin.

"I thought you'd stop me," she said to Matt.

"Wasn't worth the effort to stop you." She felt Matt shrug. "This seemed like something you needed to do. What was in the box?"

"Mementoes. Things I thought meant something, but didn't really."

"From Frank?" He nuzzled against her hair.

"And my mother." Jena smiled as she watched the flames dance. "I figured something out tonight."

"Going to share?"

She nodded as she sank back into him. "I figured out that I'm a big fat coward."

He laughed. "There's nothing big or fat about you, princess."

"I noticed you didn't take issue with the coward comment."

"What makes you think you're a coward?" He stroked her bare arm with his big hand. It was soothing.

"I've let my mother and Frank walk over me, all because I was scared to say no. Scared they wouldn't love me if I stood up to them." She snorted. "They don't love me anyway." She noticed he didn't disagree. "I'm tired of being walked over, Matt. I'm tired of agreeing so someone will love me. I'm tired of being scared of what will happen if I stand up for myself. See? Coward."

"Not cowardly. Sounds to me like you were taught that love is a reward for compliance. It isn't. It's freely given, even when the other person pisses you off." He nuzzled her head at her temple, placing a kiss there. It felt like the most natural thing in the world. To be in Matt's arms, to be taking comfort from him.

"I need to be more courageous. More honest."

"I love it when you're honest with me, and I don't mind a bit of conflict." He pulled her even closer. "I hear angry sex is mind-blowing. I'm keen to give it a try. Want to be my guinea pig? I'll say some annoying stuff, you can tell me off, we'll build up a tonne of adrenalin then go upstairs and work it off."

Jena chuckled, but her body vibrated with agreement. It was a very good plan indeed. They stood in silence for a few minutes, watching the flames burn out. Who knew having a burned-out car in your yard would be so useful?

"My mother wants me to go home with Frank. She made a deal with him where she forces me to go back with him and he introduces her to Josh. Part of me isn't surprised she'd do something like that. It says a lot about our relationship, huh?"

"Aye, it says she shouldn't be a mother."

Jena snorted. "I don't know why Frank wants me back so badly. It's out of character for him. He's a guy who gives up easily."

Matt stiffened behind her.

"You know something," she said. "Don't protect me. Tell me." The insane macho man would probably make her wear bubble wrap if he could.

"I was going to tell you, but other things got in the way. Lake did some digging. Frank is in trouble with his business partners, the Rizzonis. He's been too busy sleeping with strippers to make the club a success, and they want him to turn it around fast or they'll make an example of him." He paused, but he didn't need to say anything else. Jena knew what kind of example he'd turn into. The kind that sank to the bottom of the ocean.

"He wants me to go back and strip in the club, doesn't he?"

"Aye."

Jena wasn't even surprised at Frank's plan. He'd watched her politely turn down offers to strip for years. He knew how she felt about it. She thought he'd understood. Obviously understanding only went so far when it got in the way of something he wanted.

"They only want me for what I can do for them." It wasn't a question. It wasn't even a realisation. Deep down, Jena had known this for a very long time.

"Not everybody is like that. You need to learn how to tell the difference. You need to stand up for what *you* want instead of doing whatever everyone else wants you to do. You can start by saying no to all these bloody men who ask you out."

Jena laughed hard. It felt good. It felt freeing. She turned in Matt's arms and slid her hands up to rest on his pecs. She felt his heart beat under her fingertips. Slowly, she looked up to find him studying her. His eyes dark with promise.

"I need to stand up for what I want. That's what you said. Right?"

His blue eyes darkened with desire and amusement. "Aye, that's what I said."

"I know what I want," Jena whispered. "I'm standing up for it right now."

"Tell me," he whispered back.

"I want you."

Matt's eyes turned as black as the night sky above them. His hands flexed on the small of her back. His lips quirked into a mischievous smile that made her stomach clench.

"I'm really hoping you mean in a sweaty, naked way and not in a supportive friend sort of way."

Jena smiled up at him. "Is that what we are, Matt? Friends?"

"No, we're not friends. I keep telling you, we're in a relationship. A sweaty, dirty, sex-filled relationship."

Jena couldn't resist an eye roll. "Yeah, that sounds delightful. Not."

"Don't worry. I'll show you exactly how delightful it can be."

"Promises, promises. You asked what I want and I told you. Are you going to give it to me?"

"Always, princess. Always. You only have to ask."

With a sexy little smile, his lips descended on hers.

His kiss dominated her. His passion inflamed her. His very touch demanded she meet him halfway, that she fight to participate. This was no claiming. It was a dance of equals. A beautiful, passionate dance.

She wound her fingers into his hair and clutched him closer to her. Rising on tiptoe to get nearer, to gain dominance. Exhilaration zapped through her body. She'd never experienced anything like this before. It was supercharged. Mind-blowing in its intensity.

"I'm not stopping," he whispered breathlessly against her lips.

"If you do, I'll hurt you. I have pink power tools and I know how to use them."

He laughed against her lips, making her knees weaken. "No, you really don't," he said.

Strong arms scooped her up, and she found herself cradled against hot man flesh. He strode through the house and up the stairs to her bedroom as Jena spent her time kissing, nipping, licking her way up his throat to his jaw. The sound of him kicking her door open did nothing to distract her.

The cool, soft cotton of her bedding hit her back as Matt placed her on the bed. A second later he was stretched out at her side, up on his elbow, her face cupped in his hand, his mouth on hers. He didn't tease. He devoured.

Jena clung onto his shoulders, her nails digging in to firm muscle. She threw a leg over his hip and pressed up into him.

"Speed up," she demanded when she came up for breath.

"In a hurry?" He cocked an eyebrow with a grin.

Jena trailed her fingertip over his kiss-swollen lips. "Yes."

He growled as he captured her mouth again. A large hand slipped under the back of her top. Her skin burned at his touch. She groaned her approval as her hands ran down over the muscle on his back. She wanted to flip him onto his stomach and torture him the same way he'd tortured her in the kitchen. She wanted to lick and kiss every inch of him. She wanted to trail her nails over sensitive skin and bite shoulder muscle that was so thick it wouldn't budge. She wanted it all. She wanted all of him. And she wanted it now.

"More." The forcefulness of the demand surprised her, even through her daze of need.

She felt her pyjama pants slide over her hips. She kicked them off. Fingers snuck under the seam of her panties and they ripped away. A deep rumble came from his chest and worked its way through her body.

He wasn't going fast enough. She needed him. She needed him now.

With strength she didn't know she possessed, Jena toppled Matt and climbed on top of him. She ran her tongue down his neck to the shoulder muscle she wanted between her teeth.

"Hell, Jena, I'm burning here." His voice was a deep rasp of need.

He pulled her shirt over her head and threw it to the floor. A second later, his hands engulfed her breasts. Jena pushed into him with a moan, her tongue never leaving his skin. He tasted of salt and musk. Of crisp summer rain on her tongue. It was addictive. Her lips trailed to his nipple and she nipped at him. He cursed, his fingers flexing on her nipples in retaliation. A surge of heat rushed through her body. She felt lightheaded, but it hardly registered, because overwhelming everything else was a desperate need to feel him. To have him inside of her. To have all of him.

She pushed his pants over his hips as she swirled her tongue around his belly button.

"Jena." She wasn't sure if her name was a protest or a plea.

She didn't care. She had what she wanted in the palm of her hand. On one smooth move she arched up over him and slid him into place. His hips came up off the bed as he thrust up into her.

"Yes. That's it. Don't stop." She threw her head back as his hands moved to her hips.

Jena was lost in a whirl of sensation. She couldn't think. All she could do was feel. Need. Desperately need.

"Fast. Hard." Her voice wasn't her own. It was hoarse, demanding, desperate.

Matt gave her what she needed as her nails dug into the flesh on his stomach. He propelled her upwards, out of her body, far away, riding on a wave of sensation and need. Riding the crest of overwhelming desire. All at once the wave broke. She screamed as she fell. Overwhelmed. Lost in him. She only knew his touch, his taste, his scent. There was nothing else. She felt him groan beneath her as she collapsed onto his chest.

Slowly, oh so slowly, she came back to herself. Matt's hand stroked her back as his breathing evened out beneath her. She felt his heartbeat slow as she trailed her fingers through the smattering of hair on his chest. His hand worked its way up to the back of her head, where he clutched her hair. He angled her head to look in her eyes.

As soon as Jena's eyes met his, her breath caught. No one had ever looked at her like that before. Like she was everything they wanted. Her heart stuttered at the sight. He pulled her up to his lips and gave her a lazy kiss.

"I changed my mind," he told her with that panty-melting grin of his. "Next time you want me, don't ask, just take. Taking works great. Taking is good. You can take anytime."

With a chuckle, Jena rested her cheek back on his chest and closed her eyes.

Taking was indeed good. Cocooned in his warmth and strength, she felt her eyelids grow heavy. A moment later, she was asleep.

CHAPTER 23

"I need to get Jena alone." Frank Di Marco was pacing his hotel room. Agitation poured from him. Grunt noticed the trembling hands his temporary boss tried to hide. He was terrified. Things weren't going as planned. Time was running out and he was getting desperate. "That Keystone Cop is with her all the time. You need to do something about him." He pointed at Joe. "I ain't paying you to sit around. This is no vacation."

Joe's jaw clenched. His biceps flexed. Grunt knew the signs. He was holding on to his self-control by a thread.

"What do you want us to do, *boss?*" Joe spat the word.

"What do I want?" Frank shouted. "I want you to do the job I'm paying you to do. I need access to Jena. And I need it now. How am I supposed to convince her to come with me if I can't even talk to her? That cop won't let her out of his sight. I need him gone. I need her alone. And it needs to happen now. Her mom isn't pulling her weight. Jena isn't listening to her." Frank poked another finger in Joe's direction. Joe looked about ten seconds away from breaking the finger off and feeding it to the man. "I need you two gorillas to pick Jena up. There's an old factory outside town. I want you to take her there." He cracked his knuckles. "I'm done screwing around. She's gonna listen to what I have to say and I need a real quiet place where she can hear me properly." His grin was equal parts stupid and malicious. Not a good combination. "Got it?" he yelled.

"Got it," Grunt said to distract Joe from violence.

Frank threw up his hands. "The ape talks!"

Now it was Grunt's turn to imagine all the ways he could pop the guy's head like an overripe grape.

Frank waved a hand in disgust, oblivious to the fact he was skirting close to death. "Get out of here. Do the job you're being paid for. If this hadn't been last minute I woulda had time to hire a decent crew. Guys who knew what they were doing. We're on the clock. No more excuses. Get me the girl." With a flick of his hand, they were dismissed.

Without a word, Joe and Grunt left Frank to his pacing. Once outside Frank's room, Joe's demeanour turned murderous.

"I would seriously love to pour some concrete around that little shit's ankles and drop him into the loch."

Grunt couldn't disagree. They went into Joe's room, where Grunt sat in the only armchair and stretched his legs out. Joe handed him a beer from the mini-fridge. Grunt grunted his thanks. Joe seemed to deflate as he plopped down on the edge of the bed.

"This is falling apart around our ears," Joe said. "This guy is losing control. If we're not careful, we'll go down with him." He ran a hand over his military-short hair. "I thought this job would be a breeze. Instead we're likely to get locked up in a foreign jail because we're taking orders from a moron. We should walk. While we still can."

Grunt took a large swallow of cold beer. "What about Jena? Frank's losing it big time. We can't trust him with her."

"If we see this through. It means kidnapping her for Frank. You ready to face kidnapping charges if this goes south?"

"I like to think of it as borrowing."

"Borrowing?"

"Yeah." He finished his beer and put the empty bottle on the table beside him. "We take her. We put her back. Borrowing. Not kidnapping."

Joe scratched his belly. "I got a bad feeling about this." He let out a sigh. "I also don't think we have a choice."

"We could tell the cop. Give him a heads-up."

"What will he do? He's already powerless against Frank. Until Frank breaks the law, the cop's hands are tied. All he can do is stand between Frank and Jena, looking mean. If we tell him, we tip our hand with Frank, then this gig really is over. Who'll look out for Jena if Frank decides to persuade her with his fists? No. We can't risk telling anyone."

They stared into nothing for a while, each with their own thoughts.

"Guess we're borrowing Jena, then," Grunt said.

"Yeah, years in the marines have come down to this—aiding and abetting an asshole."

"So we have a plan?"

"We have a plan. We're going to kidnap a cop's girlfriend for a guy who's in thick with the New Jersey mob. It's a great plan. Not dumb at all."

"Borrow a cop's girlfriend," Grunt amended.

Joe rolled his eyes before fetching more beer. "Hope your woman is the understanding sort. Last time I checked, women frowned upon their men kidnapping other women. Especially the women that belong to their brothers."

"She'll never find out."

Grunt finished his beer to the sound of Joe's laughter.

. . .

MATT WOKE to find himself pinned by a snoring Jena. She was sprawled over him, her head tucked under his chin, one hand in his hair, the other curved around his body. She had one knee cocked over him, the other leg snuggled at his side. Matt ran his hand down the curve of her back to her glorious backside. She let out a loud snort and Matt shook with laughter as he fought not to make any noise.

"Lie still," she grumbled, her voice hoarse with sleep. "Go back to sleep. Let me go back to sleep too."

"I would, princess, but I can't sleep through your snoring."

Her head came up and sleepy golden eyes tried to glare at him. "I don't snore."

He couldn't stop the laugh that escaped. "You sound like a pig snuffling out truffles."

She moved her hand and pinched his side. He jerked, almost toppling her. "I'm not a pig, Matthew Donaldson, and I don't snore."

He opened his mouth to speak, but she narrowed her eyes at him. Man, she was cute.

"If you ever want to get lucky again, you'll think about what you're going to say before you open your mouth."

He grinned widely. "My mistake. You definitely don't snore."

"Darn tootin'." She let her head fall back against his chest as she snuggled against him.

"You know," Matt said, "threatening to cut me off isn't going to work. You were the one who jumped me. I'm irresistible."

She grunted. "Not so much. Let's see how long that cocky attitude lasts when you have to wait until I'm in the mood."

He looked down at her. The smile on her face made his chest swell. "How often are you in the mood?"

Her eyes twinkled as she looked up at him. "I could be in the mood very soon if you made me breakfast in bed."

"This is your house. I'm the guest. Shouldn't you be feeding me?"

She stuck her cute little nose in the air, sniffed, then dismissed him with a haughty look. "Guess I'll have to get in the mood another time, then."

"Minx." Matt's stomach betrayed him. He'd woken it up with all the talk of food. It let out a loud, betraying rumble that made Jena giggle.

"Give me a kiss and I'll fetch food." He faked a longsuffering sigh.

"Sheesh, is nothing free?" She lifted her head, shut her eyes and puckered her lips.

Matt chuckled at the lack of effort before flipping her onto her back and claiming her mouth. His desire was amped by the way she melted into him. He captured a delicious little moan of need before his belly protested again.

Jena broke the kiss. "Feed me. Feed your stomach." She pushed him away.

"Fine, but you're showering with me after we eat. I'm fed up braving that ice water of yours all on my own." He waggled his eyebrows at her. "I can think of a few ways we can heat it up."

"Go away," she mumbled as she snuggled down under the duvet. "Sleeping here."

With a shake of his head, Matt pulled on his jeans and T-shirt before heading to the kitchen.

As he passed the living room, he heard his phone ringing where he'd left it beside the pull-out bed. It was his mum.

"There's been an accident. Your dad fell out of bed and broke his hip. They're taking him to the hospital." The worry and fear in his mother's voice brought out all of Matt's instinct to protect.

"We'll be right there. I'll get the twins. Don't worry, Mum. He's tough. He'll be okay."

"Aye." She didn't sound convinced. "See you soon, son."

Matt hung up the phone and dialled his sisters, and told them he'd swing by to pick them up. He then ran up the stairs to tell Jena breakfast was postponed.

She was sprawled across the bed on her stomach, her head under a pillow. He lifted the pillow.

"Go away," she grumbled. "I don't smell coffee or food. Come back when you have both."

"Breakfast will have to wait, princess. I got a call. Dad's in hospital. He fell out of bed and broke his hip."

She sat up, rubbed her eyes and blinked up at him. "What can I do?"

His chest unclenched. He ran a finger down her cheek. "Nothing you can do. I'm going to Fort William to see what's happening. I need to drop you off at Abby's house. Is that okay?"

"Sure thing." She clambered over the bed. "I'll get ready fast."

"That's my girl." He grabbed hold of her for a quick kiss as she headed to the bathroom.

CHAPTER 24

Jena felt bad that she couldn't keep the smile off her face. She tried to, she really did, but it was like it was stuck there with superglue.

"You're making me nauseous," Abby grumbled.

After a day of helping Abby around the mushroom farm and looking after her delightful, but hyperactive, four-year-old, Jena was in need of a relaxed evening. Matt was still at the hospital with his family. His father's broken hip was being operated on to replace the shattered bone. They would be gone for hours yet. Jena wished she was at the hospital with them, although she knew she would be of little use.

Still, she was pleased to be able to spend time with Abby now that Katy was in bed. They relaxed at her kitchen table for a sumptuous Sunday night feast—complete with wine and chocolate cheesecake. Katy was fast asleep. Pete, the guard Lake had provided while Matt was gone, was standing by the window. Far enough away to allow the women privacy but close enough so he could keep an eye on them and on the driveway leading up to the house.

"If you feel nauseous, does that mean I get to eat all of the cheesecake?"

"No. It means *I* get all of the cake, because you are so obviously getting something else."

Jena blushed even though she made a conscious effort not to. Abby pointed a fork at her.

"I'm hating you right now. You could be a bit less obvious about the fact you spent a night in Matt's bed."

"Technically, it was my bed." She shovelled more cake into her mouth.

"I miss having a man," Abby said on a sigh. She put her elbows on the table in front of her and perched her chin on her hands.

Jena eyed the bottle of wine and mentally calculated how much Abby had drunk—enough to loosen her lips.

"Are we talking about having in the biblical sense, or having as in 'he'd be useful around the house'?"

"Both." Abby reached for the wine and topped up her glass. "I've been thinking lately that I might be ready to start dating again." She gave Jena a cautious glance to catch her reaction.

"That's great, honey." Jena patted her hand. "Remember, you don't need to rush it. Take your time. Don't push yourself."

"Ha! Says the woman who's had more dates in the past four months than I've had in a lifetime."

"You should listen to me. I know what I'm talking about. I'm an expert on dating without becoming attached." She took the hair tie off her wrist and wrapped her hair up in a messy knot on the top of her head. "I don't want a relationship. Not after the disastrous one I had with Frank. Nope, one-date wonder is a great way to be."

Abby laughed so hard, Jena was worried about her falling off the chair.

"Jena, you dolt. You're *in* a relationship right now." Abby put her hand on Jena's arm. "Matt is living with you. He's sleeping with you. You do your grocery shopping together. He's renovating your house. He's made it clear to anyone who asks that you're an item. You need to shake that dippy little head of yours and wake up. You have a boyfriend."

"No, I don't." Jena folded her arms over her Snoopy sweatshirt and frowned. "As soon as Frank leaves, Matt will go back to his own house. We aren't living together. We're just—convenient."

"I bet ten pounds you're married to him before you even realise it's happening."

"That's the bet going at the pub," Pete piped up.

Jena glared at him. "You said you couldn't hear anything from over there."

"I lied." He grinned. "I put twenty pounds on the wedding happening within the next two months. Dougal bet Matt would have you married without even proposing."

"This town has got to stop betting on me."

"At least they're not betting on when Matt will get injured," Abby said with a smile. "I haven't heard anyone call you Calamity in ages—well, at least two days, anyway."

Jena threw up her hands. "Oh well, then, I'll consider myself blessed. Has anyone even asked if I *want* to marry Matt?"

"Sweetie," Abby said, "everyone knows you're gun-shy after what happened with Frank. The general consensus is you won't admit to being in love, or to wanting a permanent relationship—that's why he has to slip in under your radar."

"I'm not in a relationship and I'm definitely not in love!"

"See?" Abby said to Pete.

"Aye, they were right," Pete said.

"That's it. Time to change the topic, before I kill my best friend. Did Magenta check the mine for you?"

"Yes. She didn't find any sign of anyone having been in there. She did find some old explosives, which she removed. So it wasn't a wasted venture. She's calling in a crew to go through all of the tunnels with a fine-tooth comb, just in case there are more explosives tucked away in there. Apart from that, she thinks I may have heard some rats fighting, but she could have been saying that because Harry was with her. He still goes grey at the mention of a rat."

"What about the missing stuff? Anything moved mysteriously recently?"

Abby shook her head. "I think it was my imagination. I haven't slept at all well since David died."

"No," Jena said, "I don't imagine you have."

"It's getting better," Abby said softly, as though speaking to herself.

Jena reached over and squeezed her friend's hand.

"Someone's coming up the drive," Pete called from his post by the window. "I don't recognise the car. Are you expecting someone, Abby?"

She shook her head.

"I'll answer the door," Pete said. "If it's Frank or his goons, I'll get rid of them."

Jena sat back in her chair with a sigh. "I don't know why they think I need to be protected from Frank. What's he going to do? Beg me to death? Whine me into submission? There isn't a lot the guy can do over here. I have my own life and he has no power or influence over it. This is insane."

"No, it's Matt being Matt. He's almost Neanderthal in his need to protect."

"He's nuts. This is nuts."

They turned towards the door as Pete appeared. "It's your mother, Jena. I let her in."

Before Jena could even process those words, her mother

pushed past Pete and into the kitchen. She cocked her head towards Abby.

"So this is another one of your friends you won't introduce me to."

Jena took a deep breath and reminded herself she was brave and didn't care about consequences. She faced her mother. "Mom, you can't just barge in here. This isn't my house."

"It's fine." Abby ruined the reprimand with her ingrained polite behaviour. "Nice to meet you, Mrs Morgan. Please have a seat and I'll get you a cup of tea."

"It's *Ms* Mona Sage, and I'd rather have some of that wine." Jena's mother hooked her black suede bag on the back of a kitchen chair. "I never married Jena's father. It was a one-night stand." She sat down and crossed her leather-covered legs. This time her trousers were white, and she'd matched them with an off-the-shoulder black and white striped sweater. The kind of sweater Jena could only dream of being able to afford. "Actually," her mother said, "it was a one-afternoon stand. I gave it up on his office couch for the promise of a recording career. Instead of fame and fortune, I got Jena."

"Mom!" Jena felt humiliation burn her cheeks.

"What?" her mother said. "It's no secret."

"It's the way you tell the story, as though you regret having me."

Her mother's silence spoke volumes. Jena fought not to let it sting. She was over letting her mother get to her. She'd made a dramatic bonfire to prove it.

"What are you wearing, Jena? Children wear Snoopy sweaters. That shape adds at least ten pounds to your frame. Pounds you can't afford to add."

"If you're here to be rude, Mom, you can turn around and go back to town. I like this sweater. It's cute. I may not look like an emaciated waif, but I'm nowhere near fat."

"I couldn't agree more." Abby placed a glass in front of Mona and topped it up with wine.

Jena's mother scowled. "What's gotten into you? You're never usually this confrontational."

"I'm not trying to be confrontational," Jena said. "I'm trying to be honest."

Her mother laughed coldly. "Good luck with that."

"Why are you here, Mom? Is there a reason you tracked me down to Abby's home?"

"Yeah, there's a reason. I flew across an ocean to see my daughter, and she's never around. I'm beginning to think you're avoiding me."

Jena shook her head as she smiled. "You didn't fly across the ocean to see me. You came to see Josh."

Her mother spread her arms wide. "Am I wrong to want to take advantage of every opportunity that comes my way?"

Jena massaged her temples. The tension of dealing with her mother was morphing into a full-blown headache. Without a word, Abby got up, fetched a bottle of aspirin from the cupboard and placed it on the table in front of Jena. With a smile of thanks, she swallowed two. Jena leaned forward, placing her hands on the table.

"We've been over this. I'm not introducing you to Josh and Mitch, Mom. This is their home. They don't like strangers accosting them. They want to live here like normal people. Anyway, I thought Frank was helping you. Isn't that what last night's chat was all about?"

"Listen to yourself. So selfish." Her mother sneered. "What kind of daughter did I raise?"

Jena took a deep breath. "You didn't raise me at all, Mom. I did it myself while you were touring, or playing gigs, or hanging out with your latest boyfriend."

Mona narrowed her eyes as Jena's heart raced. She couldn't ever remember a time when she'd talked to her mom like this. Usually at the first sign of confrontation she agreed or ran, desperate not to jeopardise what little love she was given. Standing her ground was hard. Hard and painful.

"You're right. I don't need you to introduce me to Josh. Frank will do it. Dougal has been helping as well. He texts me when there's been a Josh sighting so I can get there in time. See, this is what we've come to. My own flesh and blood won't help me, so I have to rely on strangers."

Jena glanced at Abby and saw she was fighting a grin. It took all of Jena's self-control not to laugh. Dougal was brilliant. She bet he was having a blast sending her mother on a wild goose chase throughout Invertary.

"I'm glad you've got it sorted without me," she said.

"I didn't come here to talk about Josh anyway," her mom said. "I know you don't care enough to help me with him. You've made it perfectly clear. I came to tell you to get your ass in gear and patch things up with Frank. That man has the patience of a saint, but he isn't going to wait forever for you to make up your mind whether you want him or not."

"He doesn't have to wait one more minute. I don't want him. I want Matt."

"The cop?" Her mother scoffed. "Yeah, like he can help your career. Frank is willing to let you headline his club. You would be the star attraction." Her eyes glittered with envy. "Imagine the publicity, the attention. You'd be famous not only in Atlantic City but throughout the country. He's got the power to make you a star. Don't turn your back on that."

"He wants me to strip."

Abby sucked in a breath and bugged her eyes at Jena. "The man wants you to become a stripper? At his club? The same club where he slept with his other strippers?"

"Yeah," Jena drawled. "Frank is classy like that."

Her mother ignored the comment. "You'll be famous. You'll have money. What else is there?" She clearly could not understand Jena's refusal to go with Frank.

"Uh, how about self-respect, dignity, a life without men drooling over you and making lewd gestures they think will turn you on? I'm pretty sure all of that is better than fame and money."

Her mother stood. Disgust clear on her face. She grabbed her bag and slung it over her shoulder. "Don't be a fool. You're a dancer and Frank is offering you the perfect opportunity to do what you love. He'll take care of you. You'll want for nothing. If you pass this opportunity up, you're an idiot."

With one last look of disgust, her mother turned on her four-inch heels and stalked out of the house.

"She's charming," Abby said sweetly. "Positively delightful."

Jena chuckled dryly. There was nothing funny about her mother. "I'm sorry about that," she said.

"Don't worry about it. It's forgotten. You did brilliantly. You didn't let her walk over you even once. I'm seriously impressed."

"I was shaking in my shoes," Jena confessed.

"You couldn't tell, and that's the main thing. Now, don't go ruining this new and improved you by chasing after her and apologising for everything you said to her."

"I won't. I feel no urge to hunt her down. Trust me."

"Good." Abby nodded firmly. "Keep it that way. If you feel the urge to screw things up, call me and I'll talk you down."

As Jena reached for the cheesecake, her eyes flicked to the door her mother had disappeared through. In her mind she knew she'd done the right thing. The way her mother treated her wasn't love. Still, it was all she'd ever known, from the only family she'd ever had. And it hurt to be unwanted, to be used, to feel alone.

As if reading her mind, Abby covered Jena's hand with hers. She gave Jena a sympathetic smile.

"Let's talk about the non-relationship you have with Matt," Abby said.

Jena rolled her eyes, but she smiled. Abby's tactic worked. Her attention was no longer on the pain her mother left in her wake, but on the sexy cop who thought he lived with her. As she grinned at her best friend, she changed her opinion. She wasn't alone. Not anymore. She had Abby. And she had Matt.

For now.

CHAPTER 25

"I've changed my mind," Grunt told Joe on Monday morning. "I don't like this plan."

"It was your plan."

"Yeah. I was wrong. This is a bad plan. We need to abort the plan."

Joe sighed as he turned in his seat to face Grunt. They were sitting in the front of an inconspicuous white van Joe had rented that morning in Fort William. The van was parked in the alley behind the high street shops. All that stood between them and the back door to the hardware store was an old yellow Dumpster. If it wasn't for the fact Grunt had spotted a white van making deliveries in the same alley three days in a row, they would have stood out like a sore thumb.

"We're committed. We told Frank. He's expecting us. If we don't turn up now, if we don't carry out the plan, Frank will dump us and go it alone. That would be bad for Jena." It was clear Joe was losing patience. With Grunt. With Frank. With everything. "If you didn't like this plan, you should have kept it to yourself. You're the one who saw Jena take out the trash. You're the one who spotted the white van that would get us into this alley. And you're the one who said we should 'borrow' her long enough for Frank to chat with her."

Grunt was about ten seconds away from turning green and roaring in rage.

"Don't Hulk out on me," Joe said. "You know we don't have any other options. Jena's a sensible woman. I'm sure she'll understand."

"Claire won't."

Joe sighed. "This isn't the time to worry about what your latest toy thinks."

Grunt could feel his muscles start to swell with the urge to hit. To pummel. "She's not a toy. She's mine."

"Yeah, yeah, yeah. You might have mentioned that a time or two, subtle like."

Grunt leaned in towards his oldest friend until he was in the guy's face. Joe didn't back off. Joe never backed off. The idiot had more guts than sense. "She's mine. As in, she's the one. This is my last job. I'm moving here. Gonna talk to the security guy, Benson, about a job. I don't want to screw things up with her family. Her cop brother isn't going to understand this. She's close with him."

Joe threw up his hands in clear exasperation. "Great. No problem. You win. We don't want to damage your precious relationship. What were we thinking?" Grunt growled at the sarcasm, but stilled when Joe pulled out his phone. "I'll call Frank and tell him it's off." His disgust was clear, but at least he was making the call.

He slid his finger over the screen of his phone then held it to his ear, all the while glaring at Grunt.

"Boss," Joe said when Frank answered. "We're abandoning the plan. We'll find another way for you to talk to Jena."

There was shouting, but Grunt couldn't make out the

words. He watched as Joe's jaw clenched tight. Not a good sign.

"We think this is a sure way to get the cop on your ass," Joe said.

A pause.

"I know you don't care about the cop, but you might change your mind when you're locked up tight in a Scottish jail." Another pause. Joe's grip on the steering wheel tightened until his knuckles were white. "I don't think that's a good idea," he told Frank. From the look on his face, it was *far* from a good idea. "Give me a minute."

He hit mute and turned to Grunt. Grunt knew he wasn't going to like what Joe had to say.

"He's going to lift her himself. He says he's fed up with this shit. He's going to tie her up, toss her in the trunk of his car and drive her to the continent. He says if she resists, he's gonna show her who's boss."

Grunt felt everything within him still. "Tell him we'll be there soon."

Joe nodded grimly. He tapped the phone. "It's on. We'll text when we're on our way." He hung up on Frank shouting.

"That guy is on borrowed time," Grunt said.

"Yeah, but while he is, we're stuck dealing with his crap." Joe gave Grunt a grim look. "Guess we're taking Jena for a ride after all."

Grunt didn't say anything, because there was nothing to say.

They sat in a heavy silence staring down the alley. Twenty minutes later, the back door of the hardware store opened and Jena stepped out. She was carrying a bag of trash. She shouted something over her shoulder and shook her head with a grin. Grunt's heart sank like the *Titanic*.

"Showtime." Joe opened the van door.

With a grunt, Grunt followed him. There was no going

back. They were committed. What was that saying—better to ask forgiveness than permission? He hoped Claire knew that one. And he hoped she was just as forgiving as he thought she was. Because he was seconds away from kidnapping her brother's girlfriend.

THE ALLEY behind Invertary high street didn't smell like any of the alleys Jena had been in around Atlantic City. Gone were the scents of rotting garbage, stale urine and sweaty bodies. Instead it smelled of dry earth, crisp air and cardboard. Jena inhaled deeply and smiled. Her eyes were drawn to the green hills that cradled the town. Being able to see them was like taking a breath. She wondered if she would ever take the beauty for granted. The closest she'd come to it in the States was when she'd walked along Atlantic City's famous boardwalk with her attention on the waves. For a girl who grew up surrounded by concrete and neon, the peace that came with nature was a welcome surprise.

With a bounce and a grin, she threw open the heavy black lid to the Dumpster and lobbed the trash bag inside.

A hand covered her mouth. Jena's heart nearly burst through her chest. Her brain froze.

Another arm wrapped around her waist. She gasped for air in staccato pants. Spots appeared in the corners of her vision. She was losing consciousness. She fought to slow her breathing. To calm herself.

Her feet left the ground.

She screamed, but the sound was muffled.

She was moving. Fast. Through the air. A solid wall of muscle at her back. Her brain started to work again. Kidnapped. She was being taken.

She sucked in air through her nose. The spicy scent of male flesh filled her mind.

She kicked.

She jerked.

She fought.

It made no difference. The arm around her waist was a clamp. Tight. Immovable. Strong. Someone huge came into view in front of her.

"Calm down." It was an order. "No one will hurt you. Frank only wants to talk."

It took a minute for Jena's eyes to focus on the huge beast of a man. Her eyes went wide. *Grunt?*

"What the hell do you think you're doing, you imbecile?" she shouted at him. Unfortunately, there was a hand over her mouth, so all he heard was "Urg umph da umph u arumph." Still, she hoped her fury was clear.

Grunt winced slightly and actually looked ashamed. She frowned at him. Hard. She tried to communicate with her eyes that he was totally dead once this was over.

"We need you to talk to Frank. Once that happens, we'll bring you back. I promise you won't get hurt."

Like she'd believe the word of her kidnapper.

"Enough explaining," the guy holding her said. She assumed it was the other half of the goon duo. "Let's get this over with."

Jena felt rage vibrate through every tense muscle in her body. He may as well have been transporting a marble statue, she was that stiff with indignation.

Her captor climbed into the back of a van, taking her with him. Grunt sat in the driver's seat. He looked over his shoulder at her.

"I promise, you're safe with us. We won't let the idiot harm you in any way, and we'll bring you back here as soon as he's done talking. You won't be gone long." He gave her a sheepish smile. "You think, maybe, you could avoid telling Claire about this?"

She bugged her eyes at him. Seriously? He was worried what his girlfriend thought of him kidnapping someone.

"Can we not make this about your weird relationship?" Joe said lazily while his grip on her remained vice-like. "Get this van moving. Sooner we're out of here, sooner this is over."

"You two are so dead," Jena shouted into the hand. Again, her threat was lost in translation.

The van moved. She'd expected a screech. Instead they drove slowly.

Jena sat wrapped in a coil of muscle, unable to move or call for help. The reality of the situation began to sink in past her fear and anger.

She'd been kidnapped.

She'd been taken.

Where the hell was Liam Neeson when you needed him?

Her eyes narrowed. Frank wanted to talk, did he? Well, she could talk. Oh yeah, she would make sure Frank heard her loud and clear. Then she planned to talk her head off to Matt and Claire. She was going to talk so much she'd run out of words before she was through. Nothing on this planet would keep her quiet. The goon duo, Dumb and Dumber, were in for a truckload of trouble. And Frank, well, she had a whole lot of things to say to him. Things she should have said before she left the States. Things she planned to get off her chest now she had the opportunity.

And when she finished having her say, she intended to kick Frank Di Marco's slutty, cheating balls hard enough to make them fly out his lying, kidnapping mouth.

CHAPTER 26

Matt was exhausted. He'd spent a good chunk of the night in the hospital, making sure his mother held it together. His father had a plate and pin inserted in his hip. The doctor said it was a heavy operation, but they had to do it or the pain would have been too much for him to handle. He also told Matt things would be touch and go for a while. The seriousness of the fall, added to his father's already greatly deteriorated state, meant they were in a "wait and see" situation. His mother was staying by his father's side in the hospital, and Matt and the twins were taking turns keeping her company. There was nothing else any of them could do—so it was back to Jena duty for Matt.

Matt pushed open the door to the hardware store, spotted Gordon behind the counter and nodded at him.

"How's your dad?" Gordon said.

"Still unconscious. The operation went well, though. We'll need to see how he does from here."

"Aye, it's a rough time for everyone, that's for sure. Tell your mother we were asking after her. If there's anything we can do to help, just shout out."

"Thanks, Gordon." Matt looked around the empty store. "Where's Calamity?" He held up the bag. "I brought lunch."

"Got enough for me?" Gordon licked his lips as he eyed the brown paper bag.

"Ha! No way. It's not like you'll starve. Your wife will be here in about ten minutes with a nice cooked meal. You're spoiled, old man. Spoiled rotten. So where is she?"

Gordon cocked his head towards the back of the shop with a chuckle. "Taking the rubbish out back."

"Alone?" Matt frowned. "Where's the minder Lake sent?"

"We told him to go get some lunch."

Matt pursed his lips. He didn't like that one bit. "He's supposed to stay with her, Gordon. Someone else could have fetched the food."

"She's fine. You worry too much." Gordon rolled his eyes.

"It's my job to worry," Matt grumbled.

Matt made sure to hold the bag away from the threat of Gordon's sticky fingers as he headed through the shop. It wasn't until he pushed the door open that the hairs on his arms stood to attention. Without questioning his instinct, he put the bag down beside the door and cautiously stepped out into the alley. Nothing. He studied the space in front of him. No Jena. No sign of a struggle. Nothing at all.

Matt felt anxiety take hold of his stomach as his appetite fled. He pushed the door open again and called for Gordon. "She isn't here. Did you send her somewhere else?" The words were bitten out. This was wrong. She wouldn't wander off. She wasn't stupid.

"Do I look like an idiot, son?" Gordon came up beside him with a frown. "I remember what you told me. Jena does too. If she isn't here, there's a problem."

Matt swallowed his fear. He took out his phone and dialled Lake. "Jena's missing. She went out back with the rubbish and she's gone."

"On my way," Lake said, then the phone went dead.

Gordon's whole head had turned red. "I'm sorry, son. This is my fault. I shouldn't have let her come out here alone."

"We don't know if it's anyone's fault. She may have just wandered off." Although Matt didn't think Jena was stupid enough to do something like that.

And from the look on Gordon's face, neither did he.

A minute later Lake appeared in the alley, leaving the back entrance to his shop open behind him.

"Tyre tracks." Lake pointed to the dirt-covered ground.

"There are vans and trucks making deliveries here all the time," Gordon pointed out.

One by one the back doors of the shops along the alleyway opened and the shopkeepers stepped out.

"I had Harry call everyone," Lake said.

"You take that end." Matt pointed down the alley. "I'll start at the other end. Somebody had to have seen something. This town is full of people who can't mind their own business."

They separated and jogged off towards the worried townsfolk. All the while, Matt forced himself to concentrate on the task in hand and not on the panic making its way through his gut.

THEY HAD BEEN on the road for about ten minutes when Joe removed his hand from Jena's mouth. She knew there was no point screaming; she was pretty sure they'd cleared the edge of town anyway. There was no one to hear a cry for help other than the two idiots who held her captive.

"You two have got to be the most stupid criminals alive. You've kidnapped a cop's girlfriend." She turned to Grunt. "A cop who just so happens to be your girlfriend's brother. I really don't see how you're going to get out of this with all your limbs intact. Not to mention you can kiss goodbye to Claire's bed. Once she hears about this, you'll never get to touch her again."

Grunt grunted. It sounded like a painful grunt. One where he acknowledged his gross stupidity. Jena scoffed. It was way too late for remorse.

"You said you didn't work for Vince Rizzoni," Jena said to Grunt. "So why are you doing this? I hope Frank is paying you enough money to face a kidnapping charge. I don't think they're as lenient with felons in Scotland as they are in the States. You want to do the time for Frank? A guy who doesn't know the meaning of loyalty. If you think he's going to stick by you when the shit hits the fan, you are seriously mistaken."

Joe let out a heavy sigh. "When we said we were taking you to make you talk, we didn't mean to us. How about you zip it until you have Frank's attention?"

Jena barked out an angry laugh. "Yeah, I'll get right on that. After all, you did kidnap me, therefore I should do everything you tell me to do. You two must be new to this criminal thing. I've got to tell you, I'm far from impressed. Used to be there was a better class of criminal in Atlantic City. There were professional standards. You're falling short, boys."

Joe sighed heavily. "We aren't criminals. This is a job. One we regret taking. Trust me, we want Frank to head back to the States as much as you do. Now how about you cooperate and we'll get this over with?"

She twisted in his hold and glared up at him. "You've never been in a serious relationship, have you? I bet the only women you're used to are the ones you pay to do as they're told. Well listen up, buster, you're about to learn something important. Real women, normal women, don't get paid by the hour to follow orders."

Joe frowned at her while there was a bark of laughter from the front of the van.

Jena's head snapped towards Grunt. "I don't know why you're laughing. Do you think your innocent little school teacher will want you now you've kidnapped her brother's girlfriend?"

"Mine," Grunt practically roared.

Joe winced. "Ignore him. He does that. He's got a possessive streak a mile wide when it comes to Claire." He lowered his voice, until Jena was sure she was the only one who could hear him. "Unless you want him beating his chest and climbing the nearest tall building with a roar, it'd be good idea not to yank his chain."

Yeah, like she was going to listen to that advice. She rolled her eyes at the idiot holding her. "Hey, Animal Man," she called to Grunt. "First thing I'm doing when I'm free is have a very long, and detailed, chat with your girlfriend. Even if she still wants to see you after that, you'll need to get past her brother and half of Scotland's police force to do it."

The noise that echoed through the van was a mixture of angry gorilla and disgruntled Hulk.

She flashed an evil grin at the back of Grunt's head. "How about you turn this van around and I won't talk to Claire? This can be our secret. Right now all you've done is take me for a little ride. That's all. I bet we can get back to the shop before anyone even notices I'm missing. You can still save your relationship with Claire. You want that, don't you, Grunt?"

Grunt shot a look at Joe. She could see the indecision in his eyes, and for a moment she thought she had him.

"Don't even think about it," Joe snapped. "You know the

alternative. I'll help you do damage control with Claire. She'll understand. Eventually. Keep this van heading forward."

With a frustrated grunt, the big man turned his attention back to the road.

"I don't see how you can fix this," Jena told them both. "I'm a woman—trust me, kidnapping another woman isn't something you get over."

A beefy hand covered her mouth.

"I like you better when you can't talk," Joe said.

Jena let out a muffled wail. There was nothing she could do now but stew until they reached their destination.

CHAPTER 27

Matt, Lake and two of his men piled into their cars and headed north out of Invertary. Witnesses had seen a white van loitering in the alley. They'd assumed it was delivering to the post office, but that didn't check out. Someone else described Grunt as the driver. A woman said she glimpsed Joe, Grunt and Jena in the alley at the time Jena was taking out the trash. It was more than enough evidence to convince Matt that the men had taken Jena. Harry worked his magic online and found a van had been rented to Joe Barone in Fort William that morning. He then hacked into the speed camera network and managed to get a general direction for them to follow. Matt knew Harry would hijack a satellite if it would help them find Jena.

"They turned off the highway onto Robertson Road." Harry's voice came over loud and clear in the earpiece Lake had given Matt.

"They're probably heading to the old mill," Lake said over the shared line.

Lake was following Matt in his SUV, along with two of his men, Jason and Rusty.

Matt tamped down the feral rage that fought to overtake him. "I don't get this. Why take her like this? What can they hope to accomplish?"

"We know Frank is desperate to talk her into going back with him, and this move smacks of desperation," Lake said.

"At least this gives you the legal reason you need to kick him out of Scotland." Jason's voice joined the conversation.

"If I don't kill him first and bury his body in the hills," Matt mumbled.

There was laughter in his ear.

"Your mic is live, cuz," Harry said. "If you're plotting murder, you might not want to confess publically beforehand."

Matt scowled. He wasn't plotting murder. He was finding it hard to think straight, never mind plot. All he wanted was to bring Jena home and hurt Frank. Was that asking too much?

"I'm not going to kill him," Matt said tightly. "But if my fist slips a few times in the direction of his face, that would be fine."

"You do have that strange muscular tic," Harry said with humour in his voice. "I've often seen your arm fly out without conscious effort. Wouldn't be your fault if it happened around Frank. It is a stress-related condition, and this is stressful."

There was more laughter. Matt let out a tight sigh. "Unless she's in physical danger, we don't strike out. Let's do this by the book."

Sometimes it sucked to be a cop.

"What book?" Lake said. "You're the only cop here. My book is different from yours."

"Yeah," Jason said. "Lake's book is way more fun. It's thinner and has fewer rules."

Matt gritted his teeth. It took all of his self-control not to set the men loose. "My book," he said. "We follow my book."

"Killjoy," Jason muttered as they turned into Robertson Road.

In the distance, Matt could see the roof of the old mill. "You're sure they went this way?" he said, knowing Harry could hear him.

"One hundred percent certain," his cousin said. "The only thing down that road is the mill, Robertson Gully and Braden Stream. People tend to pick buildings to conduct nefarious business. I don't know why. I would go somewhere more intimidating. Like Glencoe. Glencoe scares the crap out of me."

"Harry," Matt said tersely.

Harry cleared his throat. "Probably they need a safe place to keep her for a while and think it would be harder for her to escape from a building, so Glencoe wouldn't work for them."

They better not be planning to keep Jena. Matt's blood boiled at the thought.

"Stop at the tree line." Lake's voice broke into his rage. "We'll go in on foot. Don't want to spook anyone into doing something foolish."

"Something more foolish than kidnapping Matt's girl-friend?" Harry said.

THEY'D TAKEN her to an old abandoned building in the middle of nowhere. The whole setup screamed cliché, and made Jena wonder if they'd learned how to be mobsters by watching HBO specials. Joe didn't bother making her walk; he carried her through the doors and into a room full of rusting machinery. Frank was leaning against the doorjamb of what looked like the old office. He was dressed in a black suit, white shirt, polished shoes and gold bling. Jena felt like she was looking at a stranger. The Frank she'd met had worn jeans and T-shirts all the time. But then, he'd also kept his pecker in his pants and didn't act like he had a role in *The Godfather*.

"Jena." He oozed fake sincerity. "I'm sorry it had to come to this. I need to talk to you, baby, and you're not making it easy."

Jena shrugged off her abductors. "There's a reason for that, Frank. The reason being I don't want to talk to you. Not now. Not ever. How about you jump on a plane back home and leave me in peace."

He placed a hand flat on his chest, where his heart would have been if he had one. His smile was the one that used to make her feel weak at the knees. Now it made her feel nauseated.

"You wound me, baby," he said. "I came all this way to get you back and you won't even hear me out. I need to tell you I'm sorry. I love you, baby. Come back home with me. We'll start over. Things will be better."

She narrowed her eyes at him. "You don't screw around on people you love, Frank."

"It was an accident." He worked at being sincere. If she didn't know him so well, she would have believed him. "An error in judgment. Surely you can't hold one mistake against me after years together?"

Jena pretended to think about it while anger built like steam ready to blow. "Ah, yes, I can hold it against you."

"I wasn't thinking." He moved towards her. She'd seen this before too. The lazy sexual walk, the heated look in his eye, the small smile promising sensual delight. She almost laughed. How had she never noticed his acting ability in all the time she was living with him? There was only one reason for her ignorance. She'd wanted to believe him. How pathetic was that?

"Baby, I want you back." He stroked the curve of her jaw. "Tell me what I need to do to get you back and I'll do it. We were meant to be together. I can't function without you."

Great, now his dialogue was being written by Hallmark. She narrowed her eyes.

"You want me back? Really? You'd do anything to get me in your life again?"

"You know it. I'm nothing without you. I screwed up, but I can change. Forgive me and we'll start over. Tell me what to do to make it happen."

"That's easy, Frank. All you need to do is give up your club and move to Invertary to be with me."

She watched as a whole slew of emotions rushed across his face. Fear, panic, anger. Then just as quickly as his control had slipped, it was back again, and his features were schooled into a look of regret and longing. A look that made Jena want to kick her own ass for ever believing Frank Di Marco cared more about her than he did for himself.

"I can't do that." He sounded regretful; heartbroken, even —and if she believed him, she was ready to buy a bridge. He ran his hands over her arms until he held her hands. The touch of his skin against hers made her feel revulsion.

"I can't pull out of my business arrangement with the Rizzoni family. I'm contractually obligated to do my part. I need to make sure the club is a success." He looked earnest. "I got at least a year's worth of commitment to them. Come back with me, baby, and once the club is going strong, we can move back here." He licked his lips as calculation briefly flashed in his eyes. "We could maybe even get back sooner if you helped with the business. And"—he looked sheepish —"you could keep an eye on me at the same time."

Obviously Frank didn't know she was well aware of what

her part in the business would be. Yet, for some reason, she had to hear him say it. She had to hear him tell her he only wanted her so she could strip for him.

"I don't know, Frank." She worked at sounding as though she was being swayed. She could act too. "I don't know what I could do at the club. I don't have any experience with business."

His eyes flashed with victory. He believed she was hooked. "Baby, you can dance. You know the city's been desperate to see you dance. You'd be a headliner at the club. You'd have it all—your own dressing room, name in lights. People queuing to watch you perform. It's your dream."

No. It wasn't. It had never been her dream. She'd performed and danced because she couldn't do anything else. But it wasn't her dream. Especially not the kind of dancing Frank was offering.

"You think people would flock to see a go-go dancer?" She batted her eyelashes at him.

He clenched his jaw as a flash of frustration escaped. "Baby, we're a strip club. You know we're classy, but we don't need a go-go dancer." He stepped closer to her and lowered his voice until it was pure honey. "We need a headline stripper. We need you. With your skills and reputation, you could put on a real class act. We'd be together, baby. Working side by side. Building something good together."

Jena hid her anger to give him the same faux-innocent look that Katy used. "I don't know if I can work day in and out with all the women you've screwed, Frank."

His grip tightened on her hands, and for a second she saw a flash of brutality in his eyes. What would he do to get what he wanted? How far would he go? Jena realised in that moment she'd never really known him. She'd been living with a figment of her imagination.

"I'm staying here, Frank. I have a house here. A home. Find another woman. Find another dancer."

She tried to move away from him, but he held her tight.

"No. I need you." His lips tightened. "You don't have a house. You have a dump. I don't know why you're desperate to hold on to it. It's nothing. You're coming back with me. You're going to dance in the club and we're going to start again."

"I'm not stripping for you."

"What's the big deal? You dance in the clubs wearing barely anything. Everyone can see your tits anyway. So what if you take your clothes off? Is it too much to ask to save our future?"

"Our future? *We* have no future. You threw it away when you screwed your staff."

"Grow up. It wasn't a big deal. It was only sex. You're my woman. You have your place. You don't need to feel threatened by a bit of pussy. Just ignore it. That's what the other women do."

Jena stilled. "The other women? What other women?"

Frank let out an aggravated grunt. "The Rizzoni women. They know their place and the benefits of staying in it."

"Listen to yourself. You honestly believe that's okay. That a woman should turn a blind eye to her man screwing around."

"I have needs you weren't meeting, baby. If you'd stepped up and kept your man happy, we wouldn't be in this situation."

Jena gasped. "You did not just say that."

"I'm done with this shit." Frank sneered. "We're going home. Now. You're gonna strip and you're gonna shut your mouth about my extracurricular activities. I shoulda put my foot down with you when Vince told me to. Instead I had to be gentle with you, and now look where we are: you're throwing a tantrum and running halfway round the world to make your point. And I'm chasing you like some dumbass loser. I'm through playing nice. You need to learn your place in the scheme of things. Your job is to listen, do as you're told, please your man and look sexy. And if you do a good job, you'll get to buy pretty things and hang out gossiping with the girls. It's an offer of a lifetime. What else you got going for you? Nothing. You ain't got no skills, no money, no family. Nothing but that crap house. You're going to do what you're told. Or, so help me, I'll make you." He took a step towards her. "Plus you owe me for the car you stole and sold. Don't think I forgot about it, baby. That's fifty grand worth of dancing before I even consider calling us even."

"In that case, you can give me back the money you *borrowed* over the years."

His mask fell away. His face was cold and hard. The slap came out of nowhere as he backhanded her across her cheekbone. For a minute Jena couldn't feel the pain over the shock of him hitting her. Grunt roared as he lunged towards Frank. Jena got there first. Her knee came up hard. Frank went down with a howl, clutching his most prized possessions as he did so.

"Grunt, deal with that asshole. We're done with him," Joe ordered as he followed Jena towards the exit.

Her face throbbed, but all she felt was shock.

"My pleasure," Grunt said.

Jena heard a thump and looked over her shoulder in time to see Grunt knock his fist into Frank's face. The force sent Frank flying through the air. He hit his head on some rusted piece of crap and slumped to the floor.

"Don't run," Joe told her. "We'll take you back. We're done here."

"Consider that our resignation," Grunt said.

He strode towards her as the doors flew open. Men rushed in. Jena spotted Matt a second before his fist hit Joe's jaw.

And then all hell broke loose.

CHAPTER 28

Matt stepped back from Invertary police station's one and only jail cell. With all the trouble happening in town, he needed more space to lock people up. Right now, he was stuck with one tiny room. He slid the viewing window open and glared at Frank. He sat on the plastic-covered foam pad that lay on the concrete shelf used as a bed. His expensive suit was ripped. His lip was bleeding and his eye was swollen.

"You're gonna regret this," Frank spat. "I want a lawyer."

"And I want to go six months without someone coming into my town to piss me off. Guess we're both out of luck." Matt snapped the tiny door shut.

Let's see how accommodating Frank becomes once he's spent a night in the cell. The white-tiled room, with its tiny window and metal toilet in the corner, had a way of softening a man up.

With a hard smile, Matt strode towards his office, where Grunt and Joe were currently handcuffed to chairs and being watched over by Lake and his men. Not only did Matt need more cells, he needed more personnel. He almost laughed at the memory of him calling his job boring.

Jena was currently sitting on a high stool at the front desk. She had a blanket over her shoulders and was nursing a mug of hot chocolate. Matt nodded to her minder, Pete, to tell him he could go. Matt needed a minute with his woman.

Once the door closed behind Pete, Matt went around the counter. He took the mug out of Jena's hands, wedged himself between her knees and wrapped his arms around her. He loved the way she snuggled into him, rubbing her cheek on his chest, as though she was trying to get as close as humanly possible.

"I've called Abby to come sit with you. I'd let you go home, but I can't stand you being out of my sight right now."

She pushed back to look up at him. Matt felt his whole body tense at the sight of her bruised cheek. He gently stroked the mark. She should never have been hurt. This was his fault. He should have been with her.

"I'm fine, Matt. Really."

"They abducted you." He had to force the words out of his mouth.

The fear he'd felt when Jena had been taken still lingered, and it was enough to overwhelm him if he let it loose.

"Go easy on Grunt and Joe, will you? It wasn't their fault. It was Frank. He made them do it. They were trying to protect me."

Matt's eye twitched. She was too damn nice. Everyone got the benefit of the doubt with his Jena.

"Those two idiots were the ones who took you." He tried to keep his tone gentle. It was hard.

"They wanted me to talk to Frank. Sure, they could have gone about it differently, but they had no intention of letting me get harmed. Grunt was more worried about upsetting Claire than anything else. When Frank became rude and abusive, Grunt knocked hell out of him." She grinned up at Matt. "You should have seen it. It was like something out of a superhero movie. With one punch, Frank flew through the air and hit the wall."

Matt didn't smile. Nothing about this was entertaining. "Grunt will not be seeing Claire again." If Matt had his way, the only thing the two goons would see for a very long time was the inside of a prison.

The door swung open and Abby rushed in. "I left Katy with Caroline at the castle," she said. "Are you okay?"

She rushed around the counter, pulled Jena from Matt's hold and hugged her friend.

"As I keep telling this guy, I'm fine. Just a little bruise. In fact, I got to clear some stuff up with Frank. You would have been proud of me, Abby—I told him to go to hell then kicked his balls into next week."

"Go, girlfriend!" Abby high-fived her while Matt clenched his teeth.

Why were they acting like this was a fun day out? Nothing about this was entertaining. Nothing.

"The doctor has checked her out," he told Abby. "If you could sit with her while I talk to these idiots, that'd be great. I'm worried she'll go into shock."

Jena rolled her eyes. He ignored her. She obviously didn't realise how serious the situation was.

"I'll leave Pete on the door," Matt said to Abby. "He'll deal with anyone who turns up. No one else will get in here today. This could take a while. Are you okay with that?"

Abby nodded. "Katy loves it at the castle. She gets to pretend the baby is a doll, and she treats Josh like another kid she can play with. When I left they were building a fort in the grand room and demanding Caroline bake cookies."

Matt nodded. His mind already on the two men he intended to interrogate. He cupped Jena's cheek as she smiled up at him. "I'll fix this," he promised.

"I know you will, but please go easy on Grunt and Joe. They really weren't that bad."

Matt shook his head. Sure, he'd go easy. If going easy meant throwing them in jail and forgetting where he put the key. They messed with Jena. His Jena. He stared at her. He wasn't sure she knew she belonged to him. He'd need to make that clear. Later. Right now he had goons to deal with and a story to unravel.

Not caring that Abby was watching, he pulled Jena off her seat and kissed her hard.

"Be good," he ordered.

She looked a little dazed, which made him feel chuffed.

"Can we send Pete to pick up some food?" she said. "I'm starving. I missed lunch."

"No. No more sending Lake's men to fetch food. Pete is here to guard you."

"Matt." She put her hands on her hips. "Everyone I know who's out to get me is in here. Please. I need to eat." She batted her eyelashes. Like that would work.

"Fine." He let out a sigh. "Pete stays here, but you can call the pub and get them to deliver something."

She pouted. "The pub doesn't deliver. Well, not to anyone but you."

"Tell them it's for me, then. Once they hear where you are, someone will be over in record time just to get the gossip."

With a shake of his head, he left the women to sort out food as he strode towards his office. His heart pounded painfully at the thought of what could have happened. He could have lost Jena. He didn't know how he would cope if he lost her. Especially seeing as he'd just found her. He stopped dead at the door as realisation sucker-punched him. He loved her. He looked back at her. She was laughing with Abby, her head thrown back, her cheeks flushed and her eyes sparkling. She was so damn beautiful it hurt to look at her. *To hell with this.* He spun around and strode back to her. He saw the minute she spotted the look on his face, because her eyes went wide and her mouth made a startled little O shape.

He clasped the back of her neck and stared her in the eyes. "Just so we're clear," he said. "I love you and I'm keeping you." The look of shock almost made him smile. Instead he kissed her until they were both breathless.

As Jena swayed gently on her perch, looking stunned and more than a little turned on, Matt said to Abby, "Take good care of her."

"Don't worry, I'm on it."

He ignored Abby's wide grin and headed back to his office.

As THE DOOR slammed shut behind Matt, Jena turned to her friend. "He loves me?" She stared at the closed door. "He did say that, right?"

"Oh, he absolutely said that." Abby's eyes sparkled with delight.

Jena pressed her fingertips to her swollen lips. She could still taste him, and it was an addictive taste, one she definitely wanted more of. "He's keeping me?"

"You are *so* in a relationship." Abby laughed hard.

Pete joined in the laughter. Great, she was entertainment for the mindless masses.

"When Dougal comes over," Pete said, "I'm going to change my bet. I think the wedding will happen within the month."

As Jena's head began to clear, she frowned at them. "This isn't funny and it isn't a game. That man"—she pointed at the door—"seems to think he owns me."

"Ah, but he loves you as well," Abby said with a grin. "Don't forget the love."

Jena climbed off the stool and started to pace. "He can't keep me. I'm a person, not a piece of property. Aren't you supposed to ask a person if they want to be with you before you declare you're keeping them? Who the hell says things like that, anyway? Men with too much testosterone, that's who. And love? How can he love me? We haven't even been out on a date. He's only staying in my house to protect me from Frank. This doesn't make sense."

She stood still long enough to face Abby. "We can't be in a relationship. I would have noticed." She started pacing again. "So what if we slept together? People do that all the time. Men do it all the time and they don't *keep* the women they sleep with. This is insane. He can't drop a bomb like that and wander off. Can he?"

She shook her head. No, he couldn't. Where the hell was he? She needed to clear a few things up. She took a step towards his door.

"Bad idea," Pete said.

For once, she agreed. She'd have to wait until he was finished yelling at Grunt.

"I'm not looking for a permanent man." Jena resumed her pacing. "I only date because I can't say no. I *never* go on a second date, because I don't want a relationship. I just got out of a relationship. It was awful. I don't need another one." She stopped dead, bent over double and groaned. "I live in a dump that will take a century to fix. I'm fast running out of money and my only option for making more is to hold illegal dance classes. My ex-boyfriend abducted me from beside a Dumpster to tell me he wants me to strip in his club and that he won't take no for an answer. My mother has come to visit for the first time ever and she isn't even here to see me—no, she's chasing Josh sightings all over Scotland, and when she has free time she stops off to tell me Frank is the man for me because I'm too fat to get another one. I'm so freaking accident-prone the town calls me Calamity Jena and runs a betting pool on what my next accident will be." Her head was spinning. She took a deep breath. "And the local cop wants to keep me!"

She felt a hand on her back, rubbing soothing circles. "Okay, sweetie," Abby said in her mom voice. "It's time to calm down now. You've had a lot to deal with today. How about some nice hot chocolate? I can get Dougal to bring some. Doesn't that sound lovely? Pete can call, can't you, Pete?"

Jena groaned loudly. She was still standing in the middle of the room, bent double, facing the floor and wondering how her life had managed to implode without her even noticing.

"Tell Dougal to bring chocolate cake and ice cream," Abby told Pete. "Lots of ice cream."

Abby grabbed Jena's arm and pulled her towards the wall. "Let's sit on the floor. We'll have a little picnic when the food comes, won't that be nice?"

Jena slid down the wall to sit on the floor. She wasn't sure her legs could hold her up much longer anyway.

"My life is a mess," she told Abby.

"Everything will be okay," Abby said. She seemed perfectly calm, but there was a hint of panic in her eyes.

"Yeah, right," Jena scoffed.

They sat side by side against the wall. Jena stared into nothing. Her life wasn't just a mess. It was a disaster zone. The best solution was probably to wipe it clean and start again.

"Do you love him?" Abby said softly.

Jena looked at her friend. "I don't know," she whispered.

"There's so much going on. My brain is overloaded. I don't know how I feel about him."

Abby wrapped an arm around Jena and tugged her so that she rested her head against Abby's shoulder.

"Don't worry," Abby said. "It will all work out."

Jena appreciated the sentiment, but she wasn't so sure. In her experience, when things went to the dogs, the only thing that happened was you got bit in the ass. And she felt like she was standing with her ass hanging out, waiting for that agonising chomp.

CHAPTER 29

"Start talking," Matt said as he entered his office. "Don't stop until I tell you."

The men were cuffed with their hands behind their backs. They sat on metal-framed chairs in the centre of the room. Lake, Jason and Rusty stood at different points around the room, their focus on the Americans.

"We're happy to cooperate," Joe said.

"Aye, I got that from the way you abducted my woman."

"There was no other choice. We're trying to work with you here."

"Don't know if you noticed, but we aren't partners in this. You're the one in cuffs."

Joe sat lazily in his chair. He smiled. It was deadly. "That wouldn't have stopped us if we wanted out of here. We're here through choice."

Matt was about to roll his eyes when Joe went from lazy to deadly in the blink of an eye. One second the cuffs were behind his back, the next they were in front of him and he was brandishing a chair. Every man in the room, except for

Grunt, who was still stretched out in his chair, took a step back.

Joe cocked his eyebrow at Matt. "Did I make my point?"

"Sit your arse back down, Rambo." Matt pointed at the chair.

With a grin, Joe did as he was told. Making it clear with his relaxed acquiescence that he had chosen to comply instead of doing as he was ordered.

"We know all about your time in the service." Matt perched on the edge of his desk and folded his arms over his stab vest. "What we don't know is why two ex-marines are working for the New Jersey mob."

"We're not working for the mob. We're working for Frank Di Marco. He wanted two guys to come with him to Scotland. As far as we were aware, it was nothing more than a show of strength. Intimidate by presence. He wanted to look like the big man for his ex-girlfriend."

"I'm still not picking up why you took the job," Matt said.

"Money. A free trip to Scotland." Joe sat forward and placed his elbows on his knees. "Sure, it wasn't the smartest decision we've made, but we didn't know Frank would go postal when he got here. We thought he was a blowhard. Thought we'd spend a little time here enjoying the sights while he puffed hot air and tried to talk Jena into stripping for him. Nothing more. The guy is an asshole. You know that. Hell, everybody knows that. I thought the hardest part of this job would be putting up with the crap coming out of his mouth. Instead we're running around doing damage control."

"By kidnapping Jena?" Matt's fists clenched as he fought the urge to hit first and ask questions later.

Joe noticed the action and let out a heavy sigh. "Frank made it clear if we didn't pick Jena up, he would. He planned to lock her in his trunk and drag her to the continent, where he'd *persuade* her to get on a flight to the States. He would use whatever means necessary to get her to do what he wanted." He gave Matt an apologetic look. "He was going to hurt her. We couldn't let that happen. The only way to stop it was to pick up Jena and stick close to her." He rubbed his chin awkwardly with his cuffed hand. "As soon as things started to go south, we bailed. Grunt stood between Jena and Frank. If we'd known he was gonna smack her, we would have stopped him." Joe's eyes turned deadly. "Trust me when I say I'm not pleased about being too slow to catch him before he hit her."

Matt pinched the bridge of his nose. "Neither am I. You idiots let my woman get hurt. Your reasoning sucks. Why didn't you come to me? Tell me what Frank was planning?"

Joe barked out a mirthless laugh. "And you'd have done what? Arrested him for talking crap? Locked Jena away for the foreseeable future? We both know there's nothing you could have done. We controlled the situation. Trust me, the last thing you want is for Frank to go off doing things on his own. The guy is unstable. And he's an idiot. Those two qualities do not go well together. At least with us doing his dirty work, he was being contained."

Matt caught Lake's eye and saw his agreement. He hated to say it, but Joe was right. He couldn't have done anything except issue empty threats and try to hide Jena until Frank left the country. Knowing there was nothing he could have done made him feel sick. Helpless and sick. It wasn't a pleasant feeling.

"What now?" Joe asked.

"Now, we send you lot back home where you belong. I could charge you, but I'm guessing Jena wouldn't want that. She'll probably just want Frank gone. I'd feel a whole lot better with all your arses back in the States."

Grunt sat up straight. His eyes narrowed. "I'm staying here."

Joe groaned as Matt frowned at Grunt.

"You kidnapped my girlfriend—think yourself lucky I'm just sending you home."

"This is home now," Grunt said. "I'm sticking with Claire."

Matt shot to his feet. Maybe he'd get to hit someone after all. Lake took a step towards Grunt—whether to protect the American or help Matt pummel him wasn't clear.

"You're leaving on the first plane out of here. This thing you have with my sister is over."

Grunt rose slowly. He faced Matt, somehow managing to look formidable, even though his hands were cuffed behind his back. Matt had no doubt his restrained arms would in no way hinder him in a fight.

"Claire is mine." His voice was a deep rumble of menace.

"Not this again," Joe said, groaning.

Matt faced off with Grunt. "Claire is *my* sister. You're only a passing interest. One she'll forget about easy enough. She does *not* belong to you." He took a step closer to the snarling man. "You're going home to Atlantic City, or you're going to jail. Your choice, but your time with Claire is over."

Grunt roared. His head shot back before crashing forward into Matt's forehead. Matt rocked backwards. It was like being hit by a wrecking ball. His fist shot out, catching the mountain in the jaw. Grunt grunted. His head went down, then he growled and charged. Straight at Matt, taking him off his feet and ramming him into the wall. Shelves crashed to the floor. Chairs toppled. Men tried to pull Grunt off Matt. It took four of them. Matt shot to his feet, rammed his shoulder into Grunt's stomach and jabbed at his kidneys.

"Cut this crap out," someone shouted.

Matt didn't care. He kept his hold on Grunt as he hit at him. Feeling the satisfying thud of flesh on flesh.

"Claire is mine," Grunt roared.

Grunt kicked Matt's legs, and they shot out from under him. He landed with a thud on his back.

"Grab him before he flattens Matt," Joe shouted.

Matt fought to get to his feet. Lake's arms clamped around him, dragging him away from Grunt. Matt was disgusted to see it took three guys to hold Grunt back and only Lake to stop him. The men struggled to get to each other. Snarling like beasts. The debris of what used to be his office was scattered around their feet.

"What the hell is going on?" Jena's voice cut through Matt's rage.

As one, the men turned to the open doorway, where Abby, Jena and Claire were gaping at them.

Claire focused on Grunt. "You kidnapped Jena?"

Outrage emanated from Matt's little sister, but there was hurt in her eyes. She really did care for the big guy, maybe even loved him. Damn. The wind went out of Matt. His sister was falling for Grunt. And there was nothing Matt could do to stop her.

Grunt took a step towards Claire, but was halted by the three men who held him. He growled at them before turning back to her. He almost looked contrite.

"Baby," he said.

Claire pursed her lips as she glared at him. "Don't you 'baby' me, Samuel Dayton. You grabbed Jena off the street and now you're beating on my brother. I don't know you at all, do I?" She turned her back on him, then looked over her shoulder. "Go back to America. We're finished with each other."

"No!" Grunt roared as Claire walked away.

Matt wiped the back of his hand over his bloody mouth as he watched the big man lose his mind. He almost dragged three huge guys in his wake to get to Claire. And the look in his eyes was sheer agony. Double damn. His mum was right. The monster loved his sister.

"I hope you're pleased with yourself," Jena said to Matt. "You got to hit someone. Well done, you. I'm going home. If you lot are going to act like possessive little boys fighting over their toys, then there's no point in hanging around here. Idiots."

She linked her arm with Abby's and the two of them followed Claire out of the station.

"Wow," Joe said with a grin. "Looks like you two aren't getting any tonight."

Matt's fist shot out in the direction of Joe's eye.

"What the hell?" Joe shouted as he covered the rapidly swelling eye.

Grunt ignored his friend as he quietly faced Matt. "Let's get something clear. I'm here to stay. Claire will come around. I'm going to marry her, have a family with her and make her happy for the rest of her life. If you have a problem with that, then stay away. Either way, I don't give a crap. Now, get these cuffs off of me. I've got to do some damage control with my woman."

Matt took a deep breath. "Not until we clear a couple of things up." Grunt growled. Matt took that as agreement. "Consider yourself on probation," Matt said. "I don't have a problem stepping between you and my sister. You hurt her and you'll pay. Are we clear?"

"I won't hurt her."

Matt ran a hand through his hair and nodded at Lake, who produced a set of keys.

"I'm watching you," Matt told Grunt. "One wrong move and they won't find the body."

"I heard you the first time, *brother*," Grunt said. "You'd better get used to me. You're about to have a Yank in the family."

He strode out of the door and after Claire.

Matt righted his office chair and plopped down into it.

"What about the idiot in the cell?" Jason said. "You going to arrest him?"

"No." Matt let out a sigh. "I'll give him a warning and an escort to the airport. I want him gone. Any volunteers?"

Pete shrugged. "I could use a trip to Glasgow."

"You're it, then."

Pete nodded in Joe's direction. "What about those two?"

"*Those two*," Joe said, "are staying in town for the foreseeable future. Grunt's the only family I've got. Where he goes. I go." He grinned at Lake. "Got any vacancies? I can offer you two well-trained marines."

"You have got to be kidding me," Matt said. "After grabbing Jena, you want Lake to hire you?"

"Come by the office. We'll talk," Lake said.

"Seriously?" Matt said. "You're really considering this?"

Lake gave him a cool look. "They're well trained. They did the right thing in a bad situation. And it looks like Grunt is sticking around. I would hire him for his right hook alone. Did you see what he did to Frank? There was a hole in the wall where Frank hit it."

"That's it. I'm done. Everybody out." Matt pointed to the door.

"He's a grumpy ass, isn't he?" Joe said, and Jason laughed.

Matt stretched out in his chair and closed his eyes. As the men left, he opened one eye and called to Lake. The Englishman turned back to him.

"Thanks," Matt said.

"Anytime." And then Lake was gone.

Leaving Matt alone with his bruises.

CHAPTER 30

"Men are stupid," Claire said.

"Dumber than dirt." Jena lifted her almost empty wine glass to toast Claire's sentiment.

"Hey!" Harry called from the bar, where he was perched with his laptop open in front of him. "I'm a man."

"Yes, you are." Magenta patted him on the head before heading back to the table full of women, armed with more bottles of wine.

Harry shrugged and went back to whatever he was doing.

The women had pushed two small round tables together in the middle of the bar area of the pub. Jena, Abby, the twins and their best friend Magenta sat around the tables. In the corner, a couple of old men were playing dominoes. It was a quiet Monday night for the pub part of Dougal's business, but from the hum of noise coming from the restaurant area, he was still having a good night.

"Samuel told me he was different." Claire topped up everyone's glasses.

"They all say that," Abby said. "Even David. I still remember his earnest declaration that he was a better man."

"Better than what?" Megan said.

"That was always the questions," Abby said wistfully.

"It's caveman thinking," Jena said. "Matt's all 'grr', 'aarrr'. He's only happy when he's hitting something or flexing his muscles. When he's not in protector mode he's in possessive moron mode. He told me he's keeping me. Like I'm a piece of lost property no one claimed."

Harry let out a bark of laughter, and the women scowled at him.

"This is ladies' night," Claire told her cousin. "Stop listening or leave."

"My mistake," Harry said. "I won't listen anymore."

For a second that seemed reasonable to Jena, and she vaguely wondered how much wine she'd drunk.

"I don't belong to anybody," Jena declared. "I'm my own person. I'm responsible for me."

"Hear, hear," Claire said. "Samuel told me he's moving here. He keeps telling me I'm his and he'll stick around as long as it takes for me to agree. That is *not* normal behaviour. It should have set off alarm bells, but I was too distracted by the muscles and the penis piercing to pay attention." She sighed. "Sometimes I think the only word he knows is 'mine'. It's like those seagulls in *Finding Nemo*—'mine, mine, mine, mine…' I'm nobody's freaking fish."

"You've got to stop using the movies you watch in kindy as your social reference point," Megan said. "Last week you were quoting Mickey Mouse. That is not cool."

"Wait a minute." Abby leaned across the table and pointed in Claire's face. "Go back a step. He has a penis piercing?" Her eyes went wide.

"Yep, he has a ring. It's called a Prince Albert piercing. I don't know why."

As one, the women around the table leaned towards Claire.

"How does it feel? For you, I mean. You know, when you, you know?" Abby stage-whispered.

Harry coughed loudly. Jena frowned at him. Was he listening again? He seemed focused on his computer screen, so she turned her attention back to Claire, who was blushing bright red.

"We haven't done that yet."

"Can you call us once you have," Magenta said. "I'd like to know how it goes." She gave Harry a thoughtful look. "Maybe it's something we can try."

Harry choked on a mouthful of coffee. Yep, he was definitely listening. Jena frowned over at him, but he kept his eyes on the screen.

"Is it a normal ring, or a vibrating ring?" Abby said.

The women stared at her.

"What?" She held up her hands. "It's a perfectly reasonable question."

"Can you even get vibrating rings?" Megan asked. "Is that just your imagination talking?"

Nobody knew the answer. Jena whipped out her cell phone and consulted the oracle Google.

"Holy crap," she said. "You can get loads of vibrating rings for all different parts of the body." She gave her friends a look of wonder. "There's vibrating tongue jewellery."

Abby spun on Claire. "Does he have his tongue pierced?"

"No." Claire looked disappointed before she remembered she planned to have nothing more to do with the man. "This is a moot discussion. I've broken up with Samuel. He isn't the man I thought he was." She pointed at Jena in outrage. "He kidnapped my friend!"

"Good point," Abby said. "But do you think he would get his tongue pierced if you asked him to?"

"How much wine have you had?" Jena said, confiscating Abby's glass.

"Enough to know I'm horny and fascinated by vibrating male body parts. You should be applauding me. It's only taken three years, but my sex drive has finally woken up."

Jena returned Abby's wine glass, then gave her a hug. "You're right. Ask all the questions you want to ask."

"You know," Megan said, "I've often thought men's body parts *should* vibrate. And not just their penises either. Vibrating fingers would come in really handy. Get it? Handy!"

The women descended into giggles.

MATT STOOD in the doorway of the police station's only cell. Frank Di Marco sat on the bed smiling smugly up at him.

"You're being escorted to Glasgow Airport. You'll be put on the first flight out of here. If you show your face in town again, you'll be arrested for kidnapping and assault. This is a one-time deal. I would take it seriously if I were you. I'm more than happy to lock you up and throw away the key."

Frank sneered at him. "This isn't over."

"It is for you. Find another way to save your club and your sorry arse. Jena is a dead end. Am I clear?"

"Oh yeah, you're clear." The hard, flat look in Frank's eyes was murderous.

Matt didn't care. He just wanted him gone. He closed the door. Pete waited in the reception area.

"Get his stuff from the hotel, take the SUV and get him out of here."

"You want him cuffed?"

"Absolutely. Take no chances. Keep him immobile until he's on that plane. Then he's somebody else's problem."

"Gotcha." Pete headed to the door.

"I'll call ahead, make all the arrangements for him. I'll

have someone waiting for you at the airport. This isn't official. There's no court order for his removal, but we'll make it look good. Just get him on the plane. I've had enough of him."

"Haven't we all?" Pete said as he pushed the door.

Matt headed back to the office, passing the tiny kitchen, where Joe was making coffee. He cocked an eyebrow at the man. "Why are you still here?"

Joe shrugged. "Thought I'd hang around in case you needed another pair of hands. Plus I might get the opportunity to hit Frank."

Shaking his head at the guy, Matt left him to it and went to make the calls. The sooner Frank was gone, the better.

GIRLS' night out had descended into chaos. Sometime after the great penis debate, the women of Knit or Die had come in from the restaurant and joined the party. The half-dozen or so middle-aged women bought more wine and commiserated over stories about stupid macho men who thought they owned their women.

Somewhere along the way, the conversation turned to Jena's many problems. At the news of how much work she had yet to do in her house, the women organised a work party for the following weekend. The older women insisted she raid their garages and attics for anything she could put to use in her house. There were hugs all around—and more bottles of wine.

It was after Jena had lost track of how much wine she'd drunk that the conversation turned to earning money. Jena informed everyone that her only marketable skill was dancing, but Matt had forbidden her to run classes in her garage. There was outrage. Which pleased her immensely.

"What kind of dancing do you do?" Kirsty's mom,

Margaret Campbell, asked. "Do you twerk? We learned to twerk for Caroline's wedding."

Shona nodded. "Twerking is hard on the hips."

"I was a go-go dancer, so I did all types of dancing," Jena said.

"What's a go-go dancer?" someone asked.

"It's a dancer who revs up the crowd, gets everyone excited about being there, makes sure there's a good party atmosphere. She gives people something to watch."

"Is there stripping involved?" Margaret asked.

Jena frowned at her. Why did people always think she was a stripper? Did she look like a stripper? She eyed her feet. Maybe it was the shoes. "A go-go dancer is *not* a stripper. Sure, you wear sexy club gear, but you don't take it off. You don't work a stage and you don't dance to make the men horny. Mainly you get a tiny area high above the crowds." She eyed the table in front of her. "About the size of this table. And you dance like a demon in it. The idea is to get the party going. We're like club cheerleaders."

"I like the sound of that," Megan said. "I'd be good at it."

"You would be amazing," Jena agreed, even though she didn't know if Megan could dance or not.

"Did you train as a dancer?" Magenta asked.

"Kind of." Jena shrugged. "I had classes when I could afford them, but mainly I learned from the dancers around the clubs where my mom sang. I spent a lot of time with them and they'd teach me things and let me practice with them."

"That sounds cool," Megan said.

Or lonely, Jena thought.

"Okay." Shona pointed at Jena. "Get up on the table and show us what you've got."

"Aye." Margaret nodded. "If you're offering to teach us to dance, we need to see if you have the skills or not."

Jena laughed. "I can't dance to this." The pub was playing folk music.

"You've got tunes in that huge bag of yours," Abby said. "Dig them out."

Jena felt her excitement build as she did as she was told. She handed her iPod to Megan. "The playlist labelled 'dance' is the one I need."

"On it." Megan turned to the bar, where the new bar staff was hiding.

Early in the evening the twins had discovered the woman was called Mindy. They'd greeted her with "Na-Nu Na-Nu" every time they went to the bar, and swore an oath to help her find her Mork. The woman didn't know whether to scream or laugh.

"Dougal won't let me change the music," Mindy whined.

"Dougal isn't here," Megan pointed out. "He's at the council meeting. They go on for ages. What's the harm in playing some better music for a wee while?"

"I don't know…"

"I'll set it all up. You don't need to do anything." Megan let herself behind the bar. "That way, if Dougal is angry, he can be angry with me." She gave Mindy a bright smile.

The woman backed away from Megan. It was clear to Jena that Mindy wasn't cut out for pub work. Megan disappeared through a door behind the bar, and a moment later will.i.am's latest hit blasted through the room.

The old guys playing dominoes shouted their protest. The women whooped with joy. Chairs were pushed back to make a dance floor. The table in front of Jena was cleared. A second later she was standing on top of it, letting loose. It felt great.

"You're really good," Shona shouted above the music. "She's really good," she told anyone who would listen.

Jena tuned them out. She was in the zone. The door to the

restaurant opened and curious townsfolk flooded in. The lights dimmed. The laughter grew. And the dancing started in earnest.

It was club night at The Scottie Dog.

CHAPTER 31

Matt answered his phone with a growl. Frank was on his way to Glasgow. He'd just gotten rid of one problem, and he didn't need another one. If this was Morag calling about her bloody cat, he was going to lose the plot entirely.

"You need to get down to the pub," Harry said in his ear. He sounded like he was grinning. "Your woman is drunk and dancing on a table."

"What the hell? I can hardly hear you over the music. Talk louder."

There was a pause. "We're in the pub. Jena's dancing on a table. So are the twins. And Kirsty's mum. Yep. That's the whole Knit or Die crew up on tables now too. I'm fairly certain only half of them are drunk."

Matt pinched the bridge of his nose. "I'm on my way."

"Yeah, you don't want to miss this. Your Jena's got moves that shouldn't be seen in public. She's gathering an audience. I reckon you're about five minutes away from Jena being propositioned by half the men in here. Wow, I didn't know a body could do that. I really need to get Jena to teach Magenta how to dance. Magenta dances like a five-year-old at a school disco."

With a growl, Matt hung up.

"Need help?" Joe was still hanging around the station. Why, Matt didn't know.

He let out a sigh. "Another set of hands would probably be good. The women are drunk and dancing on the tables at the pub."

With a wide grin, Joe dug out his phone. "Your woman's at the pub," was all he said.

"Grunt's coming too then," Matt said with resignation.

Joe rubbed his hands together. "This should be fun."

"Aye. Fun," Matt said grimly.

He left his stab vest hanging on the back of his chair. He was pretty sure he wouldn't need it to deal with the women. On second thoughts… He strapped the vest back on.

"Coward," Joe mocked.

"Let's see if you're still saying that at the end of this thing." Matt locked up the station behind them. It was a five-minute walk to the pub, but he pointed to his car. He'd need it with him to get Jena home.

"I like this town. I'm gonna get a kick out of living here." Joe grinned as they headed to the pub.

A DJ REMIX of popular UK bands of the eighties was blasting through the pub. Jena was in her happy place. The music had taken over. Her body was flowing to the rhythm. The troubles of the past few months faded away. There was just the movement of her body and the vibrations of the beat as it thrummed through her. It reminded her of the parts of her life she missed. The overwhelming noise of the clubs that managed to drive out all other thoughts and somehow gave her brain space to rest. The darkness and coloured lights that made her feel like she was transported somewhere else, somewhere far away from her everyday mundane life. It was like a secret world where she could take a time out from life. And it was wonderful to have a version of it back, even for a little while.

The music snapped off. "What the bloody hell is going on here?" a voice boomed through the silence.

The lights came on full. The glare hurt Jena's eyes and made her groan. Along with about a dozen other women.

"Dougal, put the music back on right now," someone ordered.

"Don't you tell me what to do, Margaret Campbell. This is my pub. Not yours."

It took Jena a minute to focus on the rotund, red-faced Dougal. He didn't look pleased. His red cheeks clashed with his pink shirt. Not a good look.

"Get off the tables right now," he ordered.

"No." Margaret put her hands on her hips. "We're having fun. You're just being an old fuddy-duddy."

Jena started to giggle. *Fuddy-duddy.* She caught Abby's eyes and noticed she was smothering a giggle too. Abby stood on the table nearest Jena. With her long brown hair and very proper grey dress, she made it look like Kate Middleton was table dancing. It made Jena giggle harder.

The door opened and Jena's giggle stopped dead. Matt, Joe and Grunt strode into the room. Only Joe was grinning.

"Oh hell no," Claire shouted. "You have no reason to be here, Samuel Grunt Dayton. I officially broke up with you. Go back to America. Or your cave. I don't care where you go, as long as it's away from me."

Grunt growled and took a step towards Claire before Matt's arm shot out to stop him.

"Get down off the tables. Now," Matt ordered.

Jena folded her arms. She noticed none of the other women rushed to do as they were told either.

"We"—Jena pointed at Claire—"have decided we don't like your attitudes. You treat us like property. We're people. You can't claim people. You can't say you're keeping them. And you can't boss them around. This is the twenty-first century. Isn't it?" She looked at Abby, who nodded. "Yes," Jena continued. "This is the twenty-first century. Slavery has been abolished. We won't stand for your caveman attitude anymore."

"Exactly," Claire shouted. "I'm nobody's fish!"

"It's time you changed your attitudes," Jena said.

"And stop kidnapping people," Claire added.

"Yeah." Jena made a fist sign at Claire. "No more kidnapping. Kidnapping is wrong. Unless you're in a Liam Neeson movie, then it's okay. But that's the only place it's okay."

Her arms shot out to steady herself as she wobbled on the table. Matt took a step towards her, but stopped dead when he saw she was fine. Jena wondered vaguely if she was maybe a little tipsy.

"Baby," Grunt said, his low voice echoing through the silent room. People were holding their breaths, afraid to make a noise in case they missed something. "I kidnapped Jena for her own good."

Yeah, that was not the thing to say. The screams of outrage from the women were so loud that Jena had to cover her ears.

Claire put her hands on her hips. Her eyes blazing. "There is no excuse for kidnapping and abduction, Samuel Grunt Dayton. You've been bad. Very bad."

"Claire, you're embarrassing me," Megan told her sister as people laughed. "Are you going to send him to the naughty corner?"

"Okay, okay." Claire held a hand up to stop her sister

from saying anything else. She glared at Grunt. "You've still been bad, and I'm not dating you anymore."

"Baby," Grunt said. "We weren't dating. We were starting a life together."

There were some very soppy *aw* sounds from the peanut gallery. Jena glared around the room. "No 'aw'. That's not an 'aw' thing. It's an 'oh hell no' thing. Did you two talk about a lifetime commitment?" she asked Claire.

"No. We did not." Claire folded her arms and glared down at Grunt.

"See?" Jena glared at Matt. "This is exactly what we're talking about. You guys have got it all wrong. You think you're the dictator of your own little relationship country. And we won't stand for it anymore." Jena stamped her foot to a cheer of approval.

The table shuddered. The leg gave way. She screamed as she fell. Out of the corner of her eye she could see Matt running. Her table hit the table beside her. Abby squealed as her table tipped. And just like that, Jena watched as all the women fell off their tables one after the other. There were screams. Crashes. Thuds. It was like some bizarre domino-toppling event.

"Are you okay?" Matt's hands ran up her limbs, checking for injuries. "Did you hit your head?"

"I'm fine. I think. I landed on my ass. There's gonna be a bruise."

"You were lucky," he said grimly.

Oh, oh, she recognised that look. She was in trouble. She eyed the door.

"Don't even think about running," Matt said. "I'm going to check out the rest of these crazy women. You stay put. Don't touch anything. Don't move an inch." He strode into the chaos.

"Abby?" Jena shouted. "Are you okay?"

"I ripped my dress," came the reply. Abby appeared beside her. She watched Matt nervously. "I think I'll go home before Matt starts shouting."

"No way," Matt called across the room. "Abby, you're staying put. Men," he shouted, "no drunk women are allowed to leave. We'll divvy them up later. Make sure they get home safe, once we've checked them out."

There was a chorus of agreement.

Abby plonked down on the floor beside Jena. "Looks like we're stuck here."

"Let go of me right now!" Claire's voice rose above the rabble.

Jena's jaw dropped as Grunt stalked past with Claire slung over his shoulder. "Put me down." She beat at his back. He didn't seem to notice. "Matt! Matt! I'm being kidnapped. He's at it again. Matt, help me!"

Matt looked over at Grunt. They shared a look Jena couldn't decipher before Matt nodded.

"Check in when she calms down," Matt said.

Grunt grunted and carried on out of the pub.

"Donald Matthew Donaldson," Claire screeched. "I am so telling Mum about this."

"Don't let him talk you into anything without negotiating," Megan shouted. "Hold out for vibrating piercings. You can do it! I have faith in you."

And then the door slammed behind them.

"Doc's on the way," Dougal shouted across the bar.

Jena and Abby shared a worried look. "Doctor?" Abby said.

"It's okay," Margaret Campbell called back. "I only broke my wrist."

"Damn, Maggie," Shona said. "How are you going to knit?"

Jena groaned as she wrapped her arms around her shins

and hit her head on her knees. "I've injured someone else," she said.

Abby patted her back. "At least it wasn't a date this time."

"Aye," Dougal said. "She's branching out. Now we have to be worried about more than the town's single men. Not to mention the state of my pub." He shook a finger at Jena. "We're going to have a long talk about damages in the morning, my girl."

Great, more bills to pay.

"Don't worry," Abby whispered. "We'll all chip in. Plus, you can run dance classes in my old barn. You'll be earning money in no time at all. Everything will be fine."

Jena caught sight of Matt's frown from across the room.

"Can I stay at your place tonight?" she asked Abby.

Abby opened her mouth, but the voice came from Matt. "No way in hell, princess. You're going home with me."

"It's too late to run, isn't it?" Jena whispered to Abby.

Her friend nodded with a sympathetic smile.

CHAPTER 32

"Put me down, right now." Claire thumped Grunt's back. She was getting nowhere. "I'm getting sick of this Hong Kong attitude. Megan's right; you can't pick me up and cart me around like this. Put me back in the pub."

"No." His shoulders shook, making her even dizzier. "And you mean King Kong. You're blitzed, babe."

Hong Kong, King Kong—who the hell cared? He was missing the point. That he was abducting someone. Again. That crap was not on. She puffed her hair out of her eyes. Being upside down was beginning to make her feel nauseated.

"Put me down or I'm going to vomit all over your back. I'm serious. I feel sick."

He swung her up and put her on her feet in front of him. Claire felt the world spin. She sank down to sit on the pavement, legs folding under her. Her hands held her head on tight. The cold concrete seeped right through her jeans and into her bones, but at least the nausea passed.

Grunt crouched down beside her. He tucked her hair behind her ear.

"Go away. We're not dating. I don't want to be around you."

"Sure you do. You're mine," he said.

Claire groaned. Too much wine. She never drank wine. She wasn't much of a drinker at all. Sure, she'd tried pretty much everything as soon as she'd become legal at eighteen, but she didn't like any of it. Now and then she'd have a cold beer, but that was about it. Her head ached; her stomach swirled. She definitely shouldn't have touched the wine. It was Grunt's fault. All his fault.

"I'm not yours," she said.

"Baby, we're gonna talk this through when you've sobered up. If you hear me out and still want me to go, I'll go. Until then, you're still mine."

"No I'm not." She looked up at him, fury coursing through her. "You kidnapped Jena. Snatched her from outside her work. Scared her. Terrified Matt. What kind of man are you? What happened to the honour of a marine? This wasn't honourable, *Grunt*, it was despicable. I was right when I said we don't know each other. You might tell me who you are but your actions speak louder than anything you have to say. An honourable person doesn't snatch people off the street. A good man wouldn't have kidnapped my brother's girlfriend. You said you'd never hurt a woman and then you did. What does that make you? How can I trust you? Take yourself back to America. This thing between us is over."

Grunt ran his hand over his face. "I had to take Jena, otherwise Frank would have done something without me and Joe there to watch him. The only thing standing between Jena and Frank going nuts was us."

"What about telling my brother? You know, the cop? Maybe he would have come up with a smarter plan."

"What could he have done? Nothing. Frank would just have hidden and taken Jena anyway. Trust me, you don't want Frank around Jena without someone watching her back."

"Trust you?" Claire glared at him. "Did you just say trust you? Are you insane? Megan warned me about this. She warned me about you. She said you had stalker tendencies, that you would hurt me, that you couldn't be trusted. She was right. You work for the mob."

"I don't work for the mob. I told you this already. I took one job with Frank Di Marco. He isn't even full mob."

"No, he's just a criminal who wants to hurt Jena." Claire struggled to her feet. "I'm finished with this talk. I'm going home. Alone."

She turned to stalk away from him, but the ground was moving and she wobbled on her heels. Grunt's arm wound around her waist.

"You're gonna get hurt. Let me take you home."

"No."

"Don't be stubborn. I'm only taking you home. We'll talk more tomorrow."

"No. We really won't."

Grunt grunted and picked Claire up, as though she weighed no more than the preschoolers she taught.

"Put me down."

"No."

Fine, she fumed. Let him go all He-Man. She didn't care. She sat stiffly in his arms as he carried her the short distance up the high street to her house. Exhaustion overcame Claire and she found she was rapidly past caring about his manhandling of her. Slowly, her muscles eased as his warmth overwhelmed her senses. It was his damn scent that undermined her anger. It made her want to curl into him and sleep.

She rested her cheek on his shoulder, tucking her face into his neck, and did what she needed to do. She went to sleep.

. . .

THE DOC ARRIVED at the pub, took one look at the room and burst out laughing. Soon after he left in an ambulance with Kirsty's mom. As they wheeled her away, Margaret was still reassuring everyone present that the break wouldn't interfere with her knitting. Kirsty had been called and went to the hospital with her mom. Lake stuck around to ferry the other women home. Abby went to the castle to spend the night. She wanted to be near Katy and was in no state to take her daughter home. That left Jena, a room full of damaged furniture, a disgruntled business owner and the town's only cop.

Dougal's frown looked wrong on his face. It was like seeing Santa grumpy. It didn't work. "Come in tomorrow; we'll have a wee chat," he told Jena.

Yeah, that was going to be a blast. She nodded solemnly and let Matt pull her to her feet. He wrapped a hand around her upper arm and led her to the door. People gave her cheery waves and called out, telling her they'd enjoyed her dancing. She smiled and waved back.

"Get in, princess." Matt opened the passenger door of his car.

Jena did as she was told, mainly because she wanted to go home and this was the easiest way.

"Abby said I can teach dance classes in her barn," she told Matt with a grin when he climbed in beside her.

He mumbled something that sounded suspiciously like, "God help us all."

"The women are coming round to help clear out the house this week." She bounced around on the spot at the thought of all that help. "Margaret said she has some furniture she doesn't need. Shona's got a fridge-freezer she doesn't use. And Magenta's mum has a cooker I can have. They're all in good condition and way more modern than the stuff I've got." She poked him in the arm as she grinned widely at him. "And they don't want any money for them. How cool is that?"

"Very cool." Matt's lipped twitched, as though he didn't know whether to smile or not.

"It's amazing, Matt. People are treating me like I belong here."

His eyes softened as he smiled at her. "You do belong here, princess."

She relaxed back in her seat with a huge sigh. "Everything might just turn out okay. If I can teach dance in Abby's barn then I can make some money. I'm already working for the materials to fix the house, so that's covered. With you and the Knit or Die crew helping with the renovation, I should have somewhere decent to live in no time at all. What's that saying? Everything's coming up roses?" She thought about it. "You plant roses in manure, right? Because if that's what it means, it's dead on."

Matt chuckled. His fingers wound through hers and he rested their joined hands on his thigh. "No more dancing on tables, though, okay?"

"Naw, the tables can't handle it."

It was warm in the car, and Jena felt her eyes begin to droop. "What's happening with Frank?"

Matt squeezed her hand. "He's gone, princess. He's being escorted to Glasgow Airport as we speak."

"Freaking roses all round," Jena said.

And she fell asleep listening to Matt's chuckle.

CLAIRE WOKE up to find Grunt sitting in the armchair in the corner of her bedroom watching her. Well, that wasn't creepy at all. She sat up, pulling the pink blanket up to her neck as she did so. Grunt just watched her. His expression serious. His eyes dark. Claire's stomach flipped, but she put it down to having a hangover.

"Aspirin and water." He pointed to the white table beside her bed.

"Why are you here, Grunt?" She didn't move to fetch the aspirin. Although she probably should have. She felt like someone had taken her brain out of her head and played basketball with it before returning it.

Grunt cocked an eyebrow at her using his nickname instead of calling him Samuel. He ran a hand over his short hair and sighed heavily.

"I screwed this up."

Claire felt the air in the room thicken. He trapped her in place with his gaze.

"I shoulda asked you out like a normal guy. Took you for a meal. Told you how pretty you are. Let you get to know me slow like." He leaned forward until he rested his forearms on his knees. "See, it's like this, Claire. I'm nowhere near normal. When I saw you, it hit me like a freight train. All I could think was I had to have you and I had to be fast about it, before someone else beat me to it."

Blood pounded through Claire's veins, making her head hurt even more.

"You're right," Grunt said. "We don't know each other. Your experience of me isn't how I am, usually. I don't grab women off the streets shouting 'mine' like an idiot. I don't kidnap women for guys who are skirting the law. I haven't done anything normal since I met you." His beautiful eyes were so sad. It made Claire ache. "Here's the thing. I don't know how to fix this without doing more of the same. I want to pick you up, run away with you and keep you locked up until you admit you're mine." He scoffed. "And yeah, I know a psychiatrist would have a field day with that."

He stood up, filling the room with his presence. Making

her pink and white décor seem childish. Making her feel like she didn't belong.

"I can't give up on you." He gave her a little smile. It broke her heart. "I can't walk away. I know we'd be great together. I don't know how I know this, but I do. I'm gonna work hard at not throwing myself at you, but I am sticking around. I want there to be an us. I want you. Only you." He stepped towards the door. "Call if you need me. The ball's in your court."

Claire couldn't take her eyes from him. The beautiful, overwhelming man. In another time, another age, he would have been a warrior. A man who *did* grab women from the street and hide them in his castle. A man who would take because he didn't know how to ask. But they weren't living in that time. And Claire didn't know if she had the strength to deal with a man like that. A man who could swallow a person whole with the force of his will.

"I can change. For you, I can change." His words were a whisper.

He opened the door, stepped out and closed it quietly behind him. Leaving Claire achingly alone in her childish room.

CHAPTER 33

The phone call Matt had spent eight years dreading came the following morning as he was making Jena breakfast in bed. She'd been so wiped out the night before she'd slept through Matt carrying her to bed. She'd been out cold since then. After a night holding her tight and listening to her snore, Matt had plans for breakfast, and a shower with Jena before he headed to work. Instead, he answered his phone and his life changed forever.

"Hey, Mum," Matt said. He was standing shirtless in the kitchen, frying bacon and making toast.

"Matt, sweetheart." There were tears in her voice. "I'm at the hospital. I need you to come get me. I have bad news, son."

Matt turned off the cooker without another thought for breakfast. Everything within him stilled. He knew what she had to say. He knew she didn't want to tell him over the phone, but it was too late. He knew. His throat tightened.

"It's happened, hasn't it?"

"Aye." Her sob broke free, the sound ripping through his

soul. "He got a post-op infection." She couldn't say any more, but the words were there—his dad hadn't recovered from it.

"Have you called the twins?"

"Not yet." Her voice broke. Matt felt tears well in his eyes. He blinked them away. There were things to do. He didn't have time to get upset. He had to be practical.

"I'll do it. I'll get them. We'll be there soon. Hold tight, okay?"

He hung up and stood in the middle of the room unable to move. It had happened. The day he'd known was coming for eight years. And yet it was still a shock. How was that possible? Part of him wished for one more day, while another part of him knew it was long overdue. So fast. It had been so fast in the end. A broken bone. An infection his body didn't have the strength to fight. Matt didn't think it would happen like this. He scrunched his eyes tight against the pain. There was a lot to do. He had to remember there was a lot to do. His family needed him to be strong. To stand for them. To help them get through. There would be time for feelings later. Much later—if he could face them.

"Matt?" Jena's soft, hesitant voice made him open his eyes.

She looked at him questioningly as she walked towards him. He'd put her into bed naked, but she was dressed in her yellow pyjamas now. Her hair was a sexy, tousled mess and there were dark circles under her eyes. She ran her hand up his chest.

"I heard the phone." She wrapped her arms around him.

He fought to get the words past his throat. The words part of him didn't even believe. Words he would have to say to his sisters. His breath hitched at the thought. *It's fine. It's all fine.*

"I need to go to Fort William," he said at last.

"Okay, honey."

He became aware he was clenching his phone tight

enough to break it. He let it fall to the kitchen table as he wrapped his arms around Jena. He could take a minute before he spoke to the twins. He just needed a minute. A second for the news to sink in. For his brain to reboot.

He buried his face in Jena's hair and breathed deeply. "Dad died." The words barely made it out of his mouth.

"I figured."

She kept holding him as the shock of it eased. It had happened. The man who defined him was gone. Matt felt a numbness creep over him.

Jena stroked his back in an easy rhythm. The feel of it comforting him. She was so much stronger than she thought she was. So much more courageous than she knew. And he needed that strength now.

He needed her.

But he couldn't put her through the hospital visit. His mum would want privacy. He knew Jena would understand. "I'll go on my own, but when I get back…"

"I'll be here. Whatever you need. Don't worry about it, okay?"

"Okay." He held her tight.

And in that moment, he knew he never wanted to let her go.

THE TWINS CLUNG to each other and sobbed all the way to Fort William. They found their mother waiting in the family room off the intensive care unit. She was sitting in the corner, staring into space. She had a stunned, lost appearance. A tiny woman, alone not only physically in the large, bright room, but now emotionally too. The twins ran to her, almost crushing her in their embrace, and the three of them cried together.

Their sobs tore at Matt. He swallowed hard at the sight,

turned on his heels and went to speak to the staff. It didn't take long to pick up his father's meagre belongings and a copy of the death certificate. For a long time he stood in the hallway outside the family room, staring at the piece of paper that told him his dad was gone. It didn't seem real. None of it seemed real. Before he even realised what he was doing, he pulled out his phone and dialled Jena.

"Hey, honey, how you holding up?" she said as soon as she answered.

The sound of her voice made something settle deep inside Matt. This was a new thing for him—to have someone in his corner. Someone who gave him their strength and support. "I'm doing okay. I just picked up the death certificate." He took a deep breath. "They asked if we wanted to see him—he's been taken down to the morgue—but I said no. We'd talked about it in the car and none of us need to do that."

"There's nothing wrong with that. You do what is best for you, not what other people think you should do."

Her words cut right to the heart of his guilt. He'd been wondering what it said about him that he didn't want to see his father's body. But it was only a body now, right? His soul was gone. He was gone. He pinched the bridge of his nose.

"I wish I'd brought you with me," he said.

"Oh, honey."

Matt cleared his throat and stood straight. "I need to go. The twins and Mum are distraught. I need to get them home."

"Yeah, you do. Call me when you get back. I'll come over with food. Although I don't expect anyone feels like eating."

"I need to call the cousins too. Mum hasn't told anyone but us."

"How about I call Magenta and get her to deal with it? She can tell Harry and he can tell everyone else."

He felt his shoulders sag with relief. "That would be great." He'd told plenty of people over the years when their loved ones had died. This was different. Harder. He wasn't ashamed to admit he needed the help.

"He'll understand. We all understand," Jena said.

He closed his eyes as tears threatened. He needed this. Touching base with Jena. Keeping himself sane. He needed her.

"I meant what I said, princess," he said. "I love you and I'm keeping you."

"Yeah, we'll talk about that later, you Neanderthal." There was a smile in her voice, though. It gave him hope.

They said their goodbyes as he pushed the door open to the family room. His eyes hit Claire and he knew he had to say something. He knew it was time to let her go. To let them go. His mum was right. He'd been holding on to his role as their pseudo-parent for far too long. He felt his chest clench as he crouched down in front of Claire. He put his hand on her cheek and almost felt overwhelmed by the love he had for his sisters. Claire gave him a questioning look.

"Grunt." Matt swallowed hard. "If he's the one, don't let him go. He's a decent guy. He meant well. He's crazy about you. Give him another chance."

Her bottom lip trembled as she threw herself into his arms. He hugged her hard as his mother smiled at him through her tears.

"I'll still kill him if he hurts you," he told Claire.

"I know," she whispered. "I'm glad."

"Always, kiddo—I'll always be there for you and Megan."

His other sister tackled him with a hug. Matt fought to hold back his tears. At least one of them had to be in a fit state to drive, and by the looks of it, the job fell on him.

Not that he'd have it any other way.

CHAPTER 34

The sad news about Matt's dad made Jena think about her mom. There was something she needed to do, something she'd been putting off, and the time to do it was now. Jena dressed in her favourite jeans and Snoopy sweatshirt, and cycled to town on the old bike she'd bought second hand. She stopped off to speak to Dougal first, apologised profusely and promised payment for damages. To her surprise, Dougal refused the offer of money.

"You've got enough on your plate, lassie," he said. "How about we just agree you won't go dancing on any more of my furniture?"

"I promise." Jena held a hand over her chest to prove how much she meant it.

Dougal seemed suitably impressed by her sincerity.

"And how about you don't bring any more dates into the pub? It's costing me a fortune."

Her face flushed as she tucked her wild hair behind her ear. "I promised Matt I wouldn't date for a while." She shuffled her red embroidered wedges on the carpet. "He seems to think we're in a relationship and doesn't want me to say yes to any more men."

Dougal barked out a loud laugh. "You make sure you call as soon as there's even a hint at a wedding. I've got a whole betting pool running on this."

She narrowed her eyes at him. "Come on, Dougal, you've got to stop people betting on me. It's not on."

He shook his head as he folded his arms over his yellow shirt and green tartan waistcoat. "Now go, Jena love. I'll absorb the costs of your misadventures, but I'm keeping the betting going. It brings in business."

She frowned at him, but she couldn't very well argue the point. She'd seen the state of the bar—there was a lot of damaged furniture, and she had no money to repair, or replace, any of it.

"Fine, keep betting, but if you're running a pool on my wedding, I want to put ten pounds on never."

"No problem. I'll get right on that." Dougal walked away from her, still laughing and muttering about her making a fool's bet.

Jena growled in his direction before stomping up the stairs to the hotel rooms above the pub. The stairs were carpeted in red tartan and the walls painted a deep green. It should have been gaudy, but it wasn't. It was warm and expensive looking.

Jena knocked on her mother's door and waited. She could hear her banging around inside. Her stomach clenched, her palms tingled and her heart raced—all over talking to her mom. She shook her head. If that didn't say something about their relationship, she didn't know what did.

The heavy wooden door swung open and her mother scowled at her. "Well, well, you decided to spend time with your mom. Took you long enough."

Jena followed her into the room. It was lovely. Decorated

in creams with a red tartan accent. Classy as well as comfortable.

Before Jena could say anything, her mom was off on a new tirade. "I can't get a hold of Josh at all and Frank has disappeared off the face of the planet. He's checked out, his room is empty and no one knows where he's gone." She faced Jena with her hands on the hips of her skinny jeans. Her white vest clung to her enhanced breasts. Her neck and wrists were decorated with copious amounts of silver and her eyes were outlined in her trademark black. "I hope you're here to take me to the castle. I can't stay in Scotland forever. I need to get this song to Josh and find out if he wants me to tour with him in the next few months. I have arrangements to make."

When her mother took a breath, Jena jumped in. "Frank was arrested for trying to kidnap me. He's been sent back to the States."

Her mother blinked a couple of times before licking her lips. "I guess that means you're it where Josh and Mitch are concerned. Let me get my jacket and you can take me to him. They won't even let me past the gate to the castle."

The news of the kidnapping had about as much impact on her mother as a speck of dust would have colliding with the moon. Her mother turned away to nab the black leather jacket that was lying on the bed. Jena put her hand on her mom's arm to stop her. She looked irritated when she turned back to Jena. She tapped her toe impatiently on the thick cream-coloured carpet.

"What is it, Jena? I want to get out of here."

Jena took a deep breath. "I didn't come here to introduce you to Josh. I came to ask you to go home."

Her mother sucked in a loud, dramatic breath. Her hand flattened against her chest. "You're kicking me out of your town?"

Jena swallowed hard. "No. I'm asking you to leave. I'm not going to introduce you to Josh or Mitch. No one is. Dougal has been sending you off on a wild goose chase, making up Josh sightings to keep you out of the way. No one in this town wants you to hassle Josh or Mitch. They belong here. They're protected here."

"From crazy opportunists or fans. Not from serious musicians like me." Her mother dismissed her with a wave and turned back to get her jacket.

"Mom." Jena clenched her hands tight in front of her. "You fall into the crazy opportunist camp. You've come all this way to force Josh to listen to your songs. You're hunting him down like a stalker, making deals with people to get to him. It's not going to happen. You need to go home."

Nastiness shone from her mother's face. "What if I want to stay here to visit with my daughter?"

Jena shook her head. "Yeah, we both know you don't want to visit with me. You've never visited me. I left home at sixteen and you've never come to see me, not once. I visit you. Usually in whatever club you're singing in. I call you, you never call me—unless you want something." She looked up at her mother. "Let's stop pretending. You don't want to be around me. I think you should go home."

Her mother sneered. "Of course I don't want to be around you. You're a loser, Jena. If you didn't have my eyes, I'd wonder where you came from. Look at you. You've wasted every opportunity you've been given, you've thrown away good men, let your career die and now you're hiding in this backwater. And for what? A house that's falling apart and a small-town cop. It's pathetic."

Jena stared at her mother for a moment. All the years she'd tried to earn her love flashed before her eyes. They were wasted years. It had been a wasted effort. This woman, her mother, didn't love anyone but herself. In fact, Jena wasn't even sure she could see anything outside of herself and her needs. Jena knew, without a doubt, she was all but invisible to the woman.

"Okay," Jena said at last. "I've said what I came here to say. Don't come round the house, Mom. You won't be welcome."

She left her mother standing with her mouth hanging open. She closed the door gently behind her and left the way she'd come in. Feeling both lighter and heavier at the same time. Deep in her heart she knew she'd never belonged to her mother. She'd never belonged anywhere. A smile started slowly until it was so wide she was grinning. She'd never belonged anywhere until now. Now she belonged in Invertary.

Matt was waiting for her outside the pub. He was leaning against his SUV, looking worn out.

"I just got back," he said. "I dropped everyone at my mum's house. The rest of the family were already there. I told them I had to come get you."

Jena walked right into his arms without a second's hesitation. "Let's pick up some food on the way. People need to eat."

Matt nodded, but he didn't stop holding her. People passed them, calling their hellos. Matt didn't respond. He just kept his arms wrapped around Jena, in the middle of the high street on a sunny Tuesday afternoon. And it felt perfect.

GRUNT ARRIVED at Claire's family home exactly ten minutes after Claire had rung him asking him to come. He didn't know why he was there. She still thought he was a criminal and a kidnapper. He couldn't allow himself to hope that something had changed. That she was giving him a chance to prove how much he cared about her.

He ran a nervous hand over his head before he knocked

on the front door of her mother's house. It was a nice place, well kept. A typical example of the grey stone buildings that dotted the town—the windows were large, the ceilings high and the roofs tiled with slate. It looked like a good family home. A place where Claire would have been happy. He was pleased about that.

The door swung open and Claire was standing there. Her eyes were red and swollen. She chewed on her bottom lip as she looked up at him with big, sad eyes. It took all of his well-trained self-control not to grab her and hold on tight.

"Baby, what's wrong?" He felt his rage ignite under his skin. All she needed to do was point him in the right direction and he would take care of it.

"Dad." The tears streamed down her face as her throat closed on the words.

She didn't need to say anything else. He knew. He felt her pain. All of it.

"He's gone, baby?"

She nodded, a sob erupting from her mouth. She wiped her eyes with the palms of her hands. Grunt was desperate to touch her. Desperate. Torture would have been better than suffering the distance between them when Claire needed him.

"I…" She looked away.

Grunt swallowed a growl. How as he supposed to act? What was he supposed to say? He was about ten seconds away from falling to his knees and begging her to let him love her. To let him take care of her, in any way she'd allow. Her eyes swung back up to his, glassy with tears.

"I need you, Samuel," she whispered, her lips trembling with each word.

Grunt closed the distance between them in record time. He lifted her right off her feet and cradled her to his chest. "You've got me, baby. You've always got me."

He held her while she sobbed. Never in his life had he felt as grateful as he did in that moment. Grateful for the chance to be Claire's rock. To hold her hand. To dry her tears. To keep her close.

"It's going to be okay, baby. I promise."

Over her shoulder he spotted Matt coming up the path, holding Jena's hand. Grunt's muscles tensed in readiness for whatever was coming. Matt stared at them for a minute, then gave Grunt a tight-lipped nod, clearly signalling approval. Grunt was still reeling when Matt closed the door behind them.

"I'll explain everything when you want me to. You only have to ask," Grunt said against Claire's soft blonde hair.

She shook her head. "Matt told me everything already."

Well, hell. He lowered himself to sitting. And right there, on the Donaldson doorstep, in the bright Scottish sun, he held his woman and gave her a safe place to grieve.

CHAPTER 35

The funeral took place three days later on a warm Friday morning.

The Presbyterian church was filled to capacity as people came from all over to attend. Jena could have sworn the whole town was there to support the Donaldsons. The old building had been decorated with bunches of blue and white flowers. Someone played soft piano music. People were quiet.

Heather sat in the front row, flanked by the twins. Grunt sat beside Claire, sombre in his black form-fitting suit. Jena sat beside Megan, holding her hand while Matt walked to the front of the church. He was so handsome in his black suit, pristine white shirt and black tie. It made Jena's heart ache to see the sadness in his eyes.

Matt nodded to the minister, took his place at the carved wooden lectern and looked out over the crowd. Jena gave him a tremulous little smile and watched his eyes soften.

"Dad was a great believer in accepting circumstance and doing the best you could with it." His voice was strong. Jena wrapped an arm around Megan's shoulders as she sobbed quietly beside her. Matt had wanted Jena seated with the family. He wanted her with him. And Jena was happy to give him what he wanted.

"He was also famous for his dodgy sense of humour, which often came out in the face of adversity. When he was diagnosed with Alzheimer's he had these T-shirts made," Matt said with a sad smile. There were titters of laughter throughout the church. People who obviously knew what he was talking about. "The one he had made for me said: 'I'm with stupid.' The one he wore said: 'Who the hell are you?'" There was more laughter. "He followed that up with a shirt quoting Popeye on the front—'I am what I am.' And on the back it said: 'Who was that again?'" More laughter.

Matt looked down for a minute before he carried on. Jena felt her throat tighten as she fought the tears that threatened. Heather sat in the seat along from her, tears streaming down her cheeks, but a wide smile on her face. Proud of her son. Devastated by her loss. Overwhelmed by all of it.

"I was lucky." Matt smiled at his mother. "I *am* lucky. I grew up knowing some things for certain. I knew my family loved me. I knew they loved each other. And I knew my mum and dad were devoted to each other."

Claire made a strangled little noise and Grunt wrapped her in his arms. She buried her face in his chest as her shoulders shook with silent tears.

"My dad was my example in all areas. He taught me how to be a man. He taught me that life wasn't always easy or fair, but you accepted it and lived it as best as you could. He taught me that forgiveness was more important than revenge. Facing your fears more important than courage. And loving a good woman, having a family and helping your community were goals worth living for. He led a full life. He loved hard. Laughed hard. Played hard. Worked hard. He said if it was worth doing it was worth doing right. And he did it *all* the right way. Even his illness and now his death. He died the right way because he didn't leave his family alone now he's gone. We have the love for each other that he helped us build, we have the friendships he helped forge and we have a lifetime full of memories to make us smile while we wait to see him again. My father, my dad, will not be missed. Because he will always be with us."

Matt strode from the lectern and took his place beside Jena on the pew. She wound her fingers through his and held on tight—thanking God, and Bruce Donaldson for the man his son had become.

Most of the mourners went from the graveyard to Heather's house. Claire clung to Grunt, who looked like he wanted to punch someone for hurting her. His helplessness at her distress was a painfully beautiful thing. Megan busied herself playing hostess so her mother wouldn't have to, although she stopped frequently to hug Matt. It was as though she was topping up her reserves of strength by taking from him. Each time he held her tight, kissed her hair and said something to make her smile.

Matt's cousins, Harry and his soccer-playing brother Flynn, took turns checking on the twins and Heather. They patted Matt on the back when they passed and made sure no one was alone in grief. His aunt and uncle sat with Heather, one on each side, lending their support. It was a family united in grief. A family loving each other and holding each other up. It was the kind of family Jena had longed for.

As the house emptied, Jena helped clear up. Grunt had taken the twins home and Heather had refused her relatives' offers to stay with her. She wanted to be alone with her memories, she'd said.

With the house clean and nothing else to do, Jena went in search of Matt. She knew it would be hard for him to leave his mum, and she was prepared should he demand they spend the night in Heather's house. She found him standing in the hallway outside his mother's bedroom. The door was ajar and Jena could hear voices. Quietly she walked up to him, wrapped an arm around his waist and rested her cheek on his chest. She could almost taste the pain and weariness emanating from his body. She'd hardly seen him since his father's death, and knew the grief had taken its toll.

He swallowed hard as he wrapped his arms tightly around her.

"She's watching his videos," he said quietly.

Jena turned her head to see what he was talking about. His mom was sitting in a huge armchair with her back to the door. On the TV in front of her, a younger version of the man Jena had seen in the hospital was talking.

"So," Bruce was saying, "I've been told I'm going to lose my mind." He laughed. "It's a miracle there's any of it left after dealing with my wild wife and children all these years." He cleared his throat as emotion robbed his speech for a moment. "I'm making these movies for you, my love. I know in the days, months, years to come that times will be harder for you than they will be for me. I won't suffer looking at your face and knowing the pain of not being recognised, of not knowing I'm loved. But you will be loved. I can promise you that." He sniffed and sat up straighter. "I have a lot to say to you before this disease robs me of my mind and memories, but I wanted to start with the most important stuff first." He leaned towards the screen. His handsome face a hint at what Matt would look like in the years to come. His eyes softened with the love that poured from him. Tears gathered in Jena's eyes and her throat clenched in pain.

"Heather, my darling," Bruce said, "I might not remember you, or recognise you, but I want you to be certain of one thing. In my soul, I will *always* know you. My soul will always recognise yours. It might not be obvious, but don't you ever doubt it. The love I have for you is soul deep, darling. It will never change, or fade, or disappear. It only grows with each passing year that you return my love. You have made my life perfect in every way—even when you made me mad." He gave a sad little smile as he reached out. His fingers touched the screen as though he was trying to reach his wife. "Soul mates, my darling. We're soul mates. It may get to the stage where I don't know you in this life, but I'll know you in the next. When our souls are reunited, you will never doubt that I always loved you. That I kept you hidden in the parts of me this disease couldn't steal. So when things get tough, remember that. Remember I still recognise you in my soul. I still love you with all of me. Nothing can take you from me. Not this disease. Not death. Nothing at all."

Jena turned her face into Matt's shirt as sobs escaped her lips. He held her tight as he pulled the door shut on his parents.

"Let's go home," he whispered against her hair.

Jena nodded. She wasn't sure if he meant her house or his, and she didn't care. Home had become wherever Matt happened to be.

She wiped her eyes as he led her down the stairs and from the house.

CHAPTER 36

Matt took Jena to his house. Not because it was home, but because he needed to see her there. Without her presence, the rooms were empty and sterile. And that was something he couldn't bear any longer. He wanted to be surrounded by life, not by pristine organisation. He wanted the place to be full of colour and music. He wanted it to be full of Jena.

She didn't say anything when he led her into his home. Although he was sure the characterless box the police force had provided for him made her lips curl in distaste. He could almost hear her thoughts. She would replace the ugly orange dimpled glass in the windows for sure. Then she'd get rid of anything even remotely beige. She'd fill his neat, lifeless rooms with colourful cushions and potted plants.

She'd make it a home.

Matt found himself longing for a home. A home with Jena in it.

As soon as the door closed behind them, Matt turned to Jena, backing her into the wall. Her wide eyes looked up at him, but she didn't protest. He gripped her hips through the plain black dress she wore and buried his face in the curve of her throat. Jena. She smelled of springtime, of new beginnings, of hope. He breathed her in as her gentle hands stroked his back.

"I need you." The words came out as a growl against her skin.

She tightened her hold on him. "Then I'm yours."

The rightness of that sentence made him want to roar. He wrapped his hand tight in the hair at the back of her head, angled her face up towards him and took her mouth. It wasn't a kiss. It was more. Part of him wanted to absorb her into him. Make her a part of him in a way that would never change.

She moaned into his mouth, making his blood heat. He used his weight and size to overwhelm her. He wanted her to feel all of him. To *know* all of him. Her breathing turned to panting as she yanked his jacket from his shoulders. He released his hold on her long enough to let it fall to the floor.

With desperation, he plundered her mouth. Drinking in her desire. Stealing her sanity. Possessing her need. She tasted vaguely of honey. Warm, delicious honey. Her slender hands fumbled over his tie and shirt. She growled with impatience and then tugged. Hard. Buttons popped. She sucked in a deep breath.

"I'll buy you another one," she muttered against his lips.

He didn't care. All he cared about was the fact Jena's hot hands were now running over his skin. A growl of possession escaped him as his hand found the zip at the back of her dress. He yanked it down, then unclasped her bra while he was there. He pushed the dress and bra to the floor before hooking his thumb into the side of her panties. He tugged. They ripped and fell away, joining the dress on the floor.

"We're even now," she said.

Her words barely registered. Matt's need was driving him. His rational mind had given way to pure instinct and lust. He couldn't get close enough. Couldn't eliminate the distance between them.

Hands on her hips, he lifted her. Her legs automatically wrapped around his waist, as her arms wrapped around his shoulders. Sharp little nails bit into his scalp as her fingers grabbed hold of his hair. Matt reached between them, unzipped his trousers, pushed them and his underwear over his hips, and found her entrance. With one smooth thrust, he was inside her.

He swallowed her groan as her legs clenched around him. Their kiss was relentless. Wild and desperate. Matt felt the restlessness within him settle. At last the distance was gone. There was only Jena.

He moved against her in a slow rhythm at odds with the frenzy of their lovemaking. He wanted to know every inch of her. He wanted to possess her. To be possessed by her. To have them merge into one.

Gasps. Sighs. A pant. A moan. Muscles strained. Fingers clenched. Tongues tasted. He was in a spiralling freefall. Clinging to Jena as though she could save his life, his heart.

With a shuddering cry, Jena arched into him. Her head against the wall, her eyes closed. In the dim light from the window, Matt revelled in her flushed cheeks and swollen lips.

"Matt." His name was a gasp. "Matt."

He kept moving. He wanted more. He wanted all of her. He felt it. The force of her climax as it crashed through her and into him. With a growl, Matt followed. The two of them tumbling together, into bliss.

Jena was limp in his arms. Her breathing heavy, her heart pounding hard against Matt's chest. He felt a smile curve his lips as he watched her. Holding her tight lest she slide to the floor.

Soul mate.

The words reverberated through him.

Slowly, languorously, her eyes opened. She licked her lips as she looked up at him, dazed and sated.

Yeah. She was his soul mate. And he was never letting her go.

"This is *definitely* a relationship," he told her. He was firm. Serious. He wanted there to be no doubt.

Jena smiled widely as she blinked up at him. Her chest began to shake, and with a giggle she snuggled into him. With a shake of his head, Matt carried his giddy woman up the stairs. Tomorrow, he'd explain that he was never letting her leave him. But first, he really wanted to get her in a shower that had hot water. With a slow, wicked grin, Matt kicked open the bathroom door. The heaviness he'd been carrying around for years was gone. He'd found the purpose he was looking for. He'd found it in Jena.

He'd found it in his soul mate.

CHAPTER 37

"So I take it you're not looking for a job in the city anymore?" Josh said to Matt. There was a wicked gleam in his eye.

It'd been a week since the funeral and life was back to normal in Invertary. Well, as normal as it ever got. November had hit and the temperature had plummeted. Even the stoic Scots who wore their shorts at the first sign of sun had packed them away for the winter. Matt had slipped into an easy rhythm with Jena. One where he picked her up every day after his shift finished and took her back to his place. He wasn't sure if she'd noticed they were living together, and he didn't want to ruin the peace by bringing it up. Apart from a lingering sadness from the loss of his dad, all was good with the world.

Josh elbowed him in the ribs to get his attention. "So you're staying put in Invertary, then?"

"Aye, I'm staying put." All Matt wanted to do was have a nice, quiet breakfast with his mates. Unfortunately, he'd forgotten those mates came with their dodgy senses of humour.

"Guess there's plenty of excitement in Invertary for you after all," Josh said.

Matt glared at him as Mitch, Harry and Lake started to chuckle.

"Okay, Josh, spit it out, what are you getting at?" Matt sat back and folded his arms.

Josh grinned with glee. "Seems like your life has taken an unexpected turn. One you weren't exactly keen on. What did you say again? Harry, help me out here."

"I think his exact words were: 'I'm not looking for a woman; I have enough trouble without one.'"

Mitch cleared his throat before he grinned. "Yeah, weren't you the first to laugh when Lake got engaged to Kirsty?"

"That's a good point." Matt turned to Lake. "When are you getting married, anyway? Is it ever going to happen?"

"Don't change the subject," Josh said. "You can't get away with this. You're the one who told us we were nuts letting women walk all over us. You laughed at the L word. You mocked my wedding ceremonies."

"To be fair," Matt said. "You did have two."

"Not the point." Josh folded his arms over his *Breakfast Club* T-shirt. "The point is you've fallen and you're in just as deep as the rest of us."

"You're desperate to sing na-na-na-na-na, like a little girl, aren't you?" Matt said.

"What do you mean, rest of us?" Mitch said. "I haven't succumbed to this mating frenzy you guys are in. I don't plan to, either. There's no way I'm giving up my single life. While you guys are here, cosying up to your one and only woman, I'll be going out with a different one every night." Mitch grinned widely. "Idiots."

As one, the men laughed at Mitch.

"What?" he demanded. "What's so funny? I'm not the one wrapped around somebody's finger."

Harry pointed at him. "You insist on jinxing yourself, man." He shouted at Dougal, "Start a new board. Put Mitch's name on it. I bet one hundred pounds he falls hard before the year is out."

Dougal grinned as he turned the chalkboard over, wiping off the heading of Calamity Jena. "Any other takers?"

Mitch smirked as the bets were made. "You know what they say, a fool and his money are easily parted. Well, say goodbye to your money, suckers, because I'm too smart to tie myself to one woman."

There was more laughter.

That was when the earth shook. A huge blast vibrated through Invertary. A minute later, it was followed by a much larger one.

"What the hell?" Matt was on his feet and running towards the door.

The men were close on his heels as they ran into the street. In the distance, on the edge of town by the hills and the old mine, was a massive plume of black smoke.

"Jena," Matt said.

"Damn," Josh said. "Has she blown something up?"

Matt snapped, "Everyone to their cars." He looked at Dougal. "Call the doc. Get fire and medical out here too."

"On it," Dougal said as he bustled off.

The men ran to their cars.

"Take this." Lake thrust an earpiece into Matt's hand. "Stay connected. I've got my men coming in."

The men kicked their cars into gear and headed towards the source of the explosions. Matt gripped the steering wheel until his knuckles were white. He prayed Jena was okay. She had to be okay. She had to.

MATT HAD DROPPED Jena off at her house early, telling her he had a breakfast meeting with the men. She'd grinned—gossip session, more like. She'd kissed him goodbye, leaving herself breathless and regretting his absence, then she'd hiked up her stereo volume and blasted Taylor Swift as she finished tiling the kitchen.

With Matt's help, the room was coming together nicely. The walls were a lovely, soft eggshell blue, and the tiles were bright white with a navy accent. The counters had been ripped out and the floors sanded. All that was left in the room was an old white butler's sink she'd salvaged and bleached, and her ancient fridge. Even her oven was in the dump as she waited for the new one Magenta was dropping off later in the week. Gordon had sourced a set of kitchen cupboards for her at cost price. They were cheaper than usual, as they were factory seconds. The small areas of damage on the white wooden doors were negligible, but it still brought the price way down. And the best part about the deal was her working the costs off in the shop. Gordon had also volunteered to show her how to install the units. Life was good.

She grinned around the room. Her kitchen was going to be gorgeous. Just like a real kitchen, in a real home. If she let herself, she could imagine a family here. Her family, maybe with tiny boys running around, all with Matt's blue eyes and black hair. She shook her dream off as she concentrated on aligning the tiles. She worried her bottom lip, not wanting to make a mistake.

That was when the doorbell rang. With a grump about being interrupted, Jena went to answer it. She wiped her hands on her faded jeans and tugged at her vintage Backstreet Boys T-shirt. Her hair was in a messy knot on top of her head and her feet were bare. Whoever was at the door would have to take her as they found her.

Her smile disappeared as soon as the door swung open. Frank was smirking at her.

"Thought you'd get rid of me that easy?"

Jena jerked back as she tried to slam the door. Frank was too fast for her. He pushed the door back and grabbed her arm.

"You're coming with me," he spat at her. "You're going to come back to Atlantic City and do as you're told. Or you'll regret it."

"I already regret knowing you."

He lifted her, holding her tight against his body as he marched towards his car. Jena struggled, clawing at Frank. Yelling for help. It was useless. He just propelled her towards his car.

She noticed two other cars beside his. The men leaning against them were hard, scarred and terrifying. Jena stiffened with fear, making Frank laugh.

"I picked up some friends of mine on the way through Glasgow. What you and that asshole cop keep forgetting is I got connections. You don't mess with me and get away with it." He wrapped his hands tight in Jena's hair to stop her from struggling. "Boys, get it done."

One of the men nodded. He leered at Jena as he pulled his car door open. "Do we get to play with her on the way back?"

"If you don't do any damage. I need her in one piece to dance at the club."

Jena felt her head spin with his words. Her breakfast fought to come up her throat.

"We can do that," the guy said before he climbed into his car.

To her horror, he revved the engine and aimed for her house. The car crashed through the living room window, hitting the house at an angle so the passenger side took the brunt of the damage.

Jena screamed. Frank laughed. The maniac in the car climbed out and sauntered over as though he drove into houses every day of the week.

"See," Frank said against her ear, "it's like this. When we're through, there'll be nothing to keep you in Scotland. This piece of shit house is about to be demolished. You'll have nothing left. No house. No money. Nothing. You're out of options, Jena. Time to do as you're told and work off the money you owe me."

"No," Jena wailed. Tears streamed down her face. Her house. The home she was making. The work she'd put in. "No!"

Frank laughed. "Two minutes enough, boys?"

"More than."

Frank threw Jena into the back seat of his car. She scrambled to get out. He leaned in and smacked her across the face. "Kid locks. You ain't going nowhere."

Jena cradled her face as he climbed into the driver's seat.

"Better buckle up, baby—this is gonna get real." He backed down the road at full speed, making Jena scream. He screeched to a halt at the side of the road, coming alongside the other car. He nodded at the men. Someone held something up, gave her a sick smile and pressed a button.

And the whole world exploded.

"Hell yeah," Frank shouted. "Shut up or I'll smack you again."

It took Jena a minute to notice she was screaming. She bit her lip and whimpered as she fought to keep silent. Tears streamed down her face as she looked at the site where her house used to stand. The car had been rigged. It had taken the house with it when it blew. There was nothing left except rubble and smouldering ashes.

The men were laughing when the second explosion rocked them. Frank's car slid off the side of the road into the ditch. Jena screamed as she tumbled inside it. Her head struck something. Pain shot through her. She blinked hard to get her bearings. Frank was up on the road. He'd been thrown away from the car. The driver's door was still open. Jena scrambled for it.

"What the hell was that?" someone shouted.

"I only rigged one explosion," the other guy yelled.

Jena ran. Fast. Hard. Stones and sticks bit into the soles of her feet. She had to get away. She had to get help. Frank shouted. Jena cast a quick glance over her shoulder. He was chasing her, but she still had some distance on him. She ran across the field. She saw Abby standing on her front stoop. Abby shouted. Jena didn't hear the words. Her lungs burst as she pushed herself to go faster. She could make it. She had to make it.

The earth trembled. It began to disappear under her feet. Jena screamed as she fell. The mine beneath her collapsed. Darkness overwhelmed her.

She was underground.

CHAPTER 38

The desolation that confronted Matt almost brought him to his knees. The house was levelled. There was no sign of Jena.

"Keep it together," Harry ordered him. As though Matt had any other choice.

"Over here," Lake yelled. "Two guys. Both injured. One unconscious."

Matt ran to where Lake was standing beside the road. A car had been thrown off the tarmac into the bushes. A guy lay out cold beside it, blood on his head. The other one was propped against a tree, cradling his arm. Matt recognised the type—Glasgow thugs.

Matt strode over to the one who was conscious. "Jena. The woman. Was she in the house?"

The thug ran his tongue over dirty lips. "Naw. She was in Frank's car."

Matt looked around. He didn't see a car. "Where?"

"Up the road a wee bit."

"Lake?"

"I'm on it."

Matt took a step towards the guy. His body vibrated with barely contained rage. "Is she hurt? Did you hurt her?"

The hard Glaswegian thug licked his lips again nervously. "We didnea touch her."

He was leaving something out. Deliberately. "Did Frank touch her?"

"Just a slap."

The rage inside Matt turned cold. Frank Di Marco was a dead man.

"Matt." Lake's voice was eerily calm as it came through Matt's earpiece. "Get over here. We have a problem."

Matt felt fear battle anger. "If anything has happened to her..."

He watched the man pale before he turned and ran towards Lake. He barked an order over his shoulder at Jason, telling him to watch the men.

Lake was standing at the edge of what used to be a field. Now it was a series of ravines. The earth had collapsed into the old mine shafts. Matt could hardly process what he was seeing. Before the explosions there had been a grassy expanse between Jena's and Abby's houses. Now there was dust, rubble and holes in the earth. Beyond the field he could see Abby standing on the doorstep of her house, Katy in her arms. Matt pulled out his phone and dialled her number. He watched as she reached into her pocket and retrieved her phone.

"She was running over the field and just disappeared." Abby's voice shook.

Matt stilled. "Jena?"

"She fell into the mine." It was a whisper.

Matt's heart actually stopped as he stared at the mess in front of him. She was under this?

"Lake." Matt looked at this friend. "Jena's under here."

Lake's jaw clenched. "We need silence." He pressed his ear

and gave the order. Matt relayed the word to Abby. The whole area went deadly silent.

That was when they heard it. The best sound Matt could ever have heard.

"Help, somebody help me."

Jena.

JENA WAS PRETTY SURE her ankle was broken. From the pain she had when she took a breath, she would guess there were a couple of cracked ribs as well. She used the light feature on her still intact cell phone to look around her. She'd slid down with some earth and landed in an old tunnel. The whole area between her house and Abby's was a warren of tunnels and shafts. Some of them quite close to the surface. From the time it'd taken her to fall, Jena guessed she wasn't buried very deep. She looked up at the earth packed above her and swallowed hard. Okay, deep was relative—she was still pretty far underground.

The earth had collapsed on either side of her, leaving her in what looked like a small room. There was no way out. All she could do was hope the support beams holding up the dirt over her head would stay where they were. One of the collapsed dirt walls had an old pipe sticking out of it. A wide, rusting metal pipe that had come down with the explosion. Jena waved her hand in front of it—there was air coming through it. A slightly cooler breeze.

Her heart raced. If there was air, then the other end of the pipe had to be above the surface. She dragged her broken leg closer to the pipe, breaking out in a sweat as she did so. The pain made her sob. She clenched her teeth as a wave of dizziness swept over her. She couldn't pass out. She *wouldn't* pass out.

She checked again to make sure it wasn't possible to ring

for help, but, unsurprisingly, there was no cell reception underground. Taking a deep breath, she pressed her mouth to the pipe and shouted for help.

Someone had to hear her.

The alternative was too horrific to contemplate.

"THERE." Lake pointed to a dip in the ground with an old broken pipe sticking out of it.

They ran to it. Matt sank to his knees. The pipe was wide, large enough for him to fit a hand inside. Jena's voice came out through it. She sounded strained and terrified. Without hesitating, Matt put his mouth to the pipe.

"Jena, we're here. We're going to get you out."

He heard faint, relieved sobbing.

"It's okay, princess. It's going to be okay." Damn, he hoped he was telling the truth. She had to be okay. There was no other option.

"I'm in a bit of the tunnel that's still standing. There's a collapse on either side of me," Jena shouted.

Matt looked around him and knew exactly where she was. There were two large sinkholes with an island of grass between them. One of several islands in a sea of ravines and potholes. His heart raced. She'd been lucky. She could have easily been buried with one of the sinkholes instead of being pushed into a cavern.

"I think my ankle is broken and my ribs are cracked."

He closed his eyes. "We're going to get you out. I promise."

"I'm scared, Matt."

"I know, princess. It won't be long. Just hold on tight."

"Is that her?" Magenta and Harry came running up to stand beside him.

"I picked Magenta up," Harry said. "She'll know what's down there."

Magenta took in the alien landscape in front of her. "She's at a junction. Those have extra reinforcement." She pointed over the field. "See the pattern? Every grassy bit is a junction."

Now she'd pointed it out, Matt could see the pattern. The junctions were grass islands in a sea of dirt.

"That's good, right?" He didn't want to sound desperate, but he couldn't help it.

Magenta nodded. "Really good. If they haven't collapsed by now, they probably won't. She's safe." She bit her lip and cast a worried look at Harry.

"What?" Matt demanded. "What else?"

"She's safe unless there's another explosion."

Matt's stomach clenched. "Is there likely to be another explosion?"

"I don't think so." Magenta looked at Harry, and there was uncertainty in her eyes. "I found some explosives in the mine when I checked it for Abby. I cleared them out and called in some munitions experts to check the rest of it. They're due out this week." She looked devastated. "I didn't think there was a need to rush. I'd cut off that whole section of the mine."

"The second explosion." Matt rubbed his face. "That was explosives in the mine?"

"Yeah," Magenta said. "The good news is, if there are more explosives, they should have gone off with the first lot. Chain reaction sort of thing."

"Okay." Matt clenched his jaw. "Let's assume everything that could explode already has. How do we get her out?"

Magenta looked around. "We need to dig through the most stable area, otherwise we'll bring more dirt down on her. There." Magenta pointed to the middle of the grass area. "Dig in the centre. Keep it small. You shouldn't have to go down too far. You might even be lucky and hit an old air shaft, and speed things up. This area is covered in them."

Matt looked at the gaping hole between him and the island of grass. "How the hell do we get a digger over there?"

"We can do it," said a voice. It was Grunt.

Matt looked up to find Grunt, Joe and Lake standing there, looking like members of the A-Team.

"We did stuff like this all the time in the marines," Joe said.

Matt looked at Lake, who nodded confidently. Matt took a shaky breath. "You got what you need?"

"I'll get it," Lake said.

The men set off at a run as Matt turned back to the pipe. "We're coming to get you. Magenta is here and she knows where you are exactly. Lake, Grunt and Joe are getting the equipment we need to dig you out."

Magenta tapped his shoulder. "Can I talk to her?"

Reluctantly, Matt moved out of the way.

"Jena," Magenta shouted into the pipe. "I need you to find a corner under a beam. Can you see down there?"

"I have a flashlight app on my phone."

"Good. Get to a corner under a beam. Stay there. We're going to dig through the middle of the ceiling above you. The rubble trapping you shouldn't get too disturbed, but you might get some dust. Do you have something you can use to cover your mouth and nose?"

"Yeah," came the trembling reply.

Matt clenched his fists. This was the last time he was ever going to let her out of his sight. Every time she was unsupervised she got injured. The woman was a magnet for accidents and mishaps. He hung his head as he tried to calm his breathing. He'd wrap her in freaking cotton wool if he had to.

"If the air gets too stuffy, breathe at this pipe," Magenta

shouted. "You aren't that far down. It shouldn't take long to get to you. Try to stay calm."

Magenta signalled for him to come to the pipe. "Talk to her. Keep her calm. Make sure she's okay. This shouldn't take long once the equipment is here. Look, you can tell how deep she is by how much the earth has fallen on either side of her. This part of the mine is near the surface. She was lucky." She gave him a quick hug. "I'll go get my climbing gear. Don't worry, Matt, we know what we're doing."

She ran for her car. Harry patted Matt on his shoulder. "You stay here. Talk to your woman. I'll coordinate with the emergency crews. They should be here any minute. We'll get the area checked out and cordon the dangerous bits off. I already sent someone over to check on Abby. She's shaken up but fine. The mine doesn't run under her house, so that's good, but the mushroom farm was taken out in the blast. There's no way to salvage her business."

Matt ran a hand over his face.

"Frank?" he asked Harry.

"In the wind. I've put out the word to keep an eye out for him. His car's still here. He can't have gotten far."

"How the hell did he get back here so fast? He must have just jumped another flight as soon as he got back to the States."

"I'll find out what happened." Harry's tone was grim. He nodded to the ground. "Let's get Jena sorted first, then we'll deal with that moron."

"Aye." Matt nodded.

"Matt?" Jena's slightly panicked voice drifted up to him.

He knelt beside the pipe. "It's okay, princess, I'm here."

CHAPTER 39

Jena wedged herself into the corner closest to the pipe. It wasn't directly in front of her, but she could lean forward to shout through it. She could hear Matt, which was the most important thing. Without his voice she would be all alone in the darkness. She felt like she'd been stuck underground for hours, but it couldn't have been that long. Could it? Matt had been talking to her, telling her tales of life with the twins and his cousins. Telling her all about the trouble they got into as kids. His voice was the only thing stopping her from having a complete and utter meltdown.

Her broken leg was stretched out in front of her and throbbed with pain that made her want to wail. She dug her fingers into the dirt beside her every time it became too much. Her ribs didn't ache as much as her ankle, but moving and breathing were uncomfortable. She was pretty sure she was covered in cuts and bruises. Her head still ached from the tumble in the car, and she didn't even want to think what bugs were nested in her hair.

Sounds echoed down through the pipe. People shouting. Orders given. An engine revved. Something heavy hit the ground with a thud, making some loose dirt shake down onto her. She shuddered.

"Matt? What's going on?"

"They're laying down a couple of wooden beams for the hobby digger to roll across." His voice sounded tight with tension. "You're under a kind of an island; there have been cave-ins all around you. We're trying to get the equipment to the right spot without causing any more damage."

She rested her head back against the wall behind her as a shiver of fear went through her. He meant they were trying to avoid burying her alive. Yeah. It would be real good if they did everything they could to avoid that. A spasm of pain hit her, making her groan through clenched teeth. She was shivering and sweating at the same time. Adrenalin reaction. Nothing she could do about it except distract herself.

"Frank—did you get him?"

"Not yet." The promise of pain was clear in those two words.

"I don't understand why he's still in town. Didn't you send him away?"

"Harry checked. Frank didn't make the connecting flight in London. No one thought to tell me."

Jena closed her eyes. The thought of seeing Frank again made her shudder.

"You'll get him, right?"

"I promise." There was absolute confidence in those words.

Jena let out a relieved sigh then winced at the pain it caused. The room was closing in on her. The air becoming increasingly stuffy. She had to get her mind off it—before she went insane.

"You're sure Abby's okay? And Katy? Was their house damaged?"

"They're fine, princess. The only person who was hurt was you."

She barked out a tight laugh, jerking her ankle and making it throb. "They're going to start calling me Calamity again, aren't they?"

"They never stopped, princess." His voice was soft. His worry clear. He was trying to distract her. She appreciated it. With her eyes closed, she could almost imagine she wasn't trapped underground. That she was cuddled in the dark with Matt.

"They're moving the digger across now. You'll feel some rumbling, and some dust will fall once it starts, but don't worry about it. Magenta says you're safe, and she knows what she's talking about. She's dug up some old plans of the mine and there's definitely an air shaft above you somewhere —that will help us to get to you. We have a drill attachment for the digger. You'll be out in no time."

"Will it make a hole big enough for me to climb out?"

"Of course it will." To Jena's anxious ears that sounded an awful lot like a "probably not".

"The doc wants to know if you're allergic to anything," Matt said.

Jena half laughed, half growled. "Dark underground spaces."

"Funny."

"No, nothing. I'm not on any medication. Except the pill. Which is probably something we should have talked about before we had sex without using condoms."

There was silence, then lots of muffled laughter.

"Jena, there are a lot of people around here and they can hear you."

She wiped a hand over her eyes. She didn't care about eavesdroppers. Invertary was full of them anyway. You couldn't sneeze without someone knowing about it. She blinked back a bout of sleepiness. How was it possible to be in pain, yet so incredibly tired at the same time? She wanted Matt. She wanted his arms around her. She wanted his strength and comfort. She wanted his deep brogue whispering in her ear. If she had anything left in life, she'd give it all to have him with her. Touching her. Soothing her.

"Tell me you love me again," she said. *Please don't be the last time I hear it. Please.*

"You're trying to embarrass me, aren't you?" He didn't sound like he minded.

Jena smiled through a sudden sharp pain. "No, I just want to hear it."

"I love you, Jena. And I'm keeping you."

She laughed, but it sounded strained. "You had to add that last bit, didn't you?"

"Because it's true. I can't wait to get you out of there, princess. I'm never going to let you out of my sight again."

For once, Jena wanted nothing more. All she wanted was Matt. The man she needed. The man she loved. A sigh left her at the acknowledgment of something she'd known for weeks.

"Now, can we stop talking about personal stuff in the middle of a crowded field?" Matt said. "Or is this payback for Magenta's turn in the mine with Harry? It wasn't my fault the whole town turned out to listen to them make out."

Jena had no idea what he was talking about, but made a mental note to ask Magenta when she got out of the mine. *If* she got out of the mine. She wiped her damp forehead. She couldn't decide if she was hot or cold. Weird.

"I need to tell you something else." She took a deep breath, forgetting that her ribs were damaged. The pain robbed her of breath, making her action pointless. "I love you, Matt," she said.

There was a whoop. Then a growl.

"You say that *now*? Princess, your timing stinks."

She swallowed hard. "You're not wrong there. I wanted you to know now. In case…" Her eyes welled up. The tears fell. She hiccupped back a sob.

"Don't you dare say anything else. We're getting you out of there. You're going to be fine and you're damn well going to say those words to my face." He sounded angry and desperate.

"They destroyed my house, Matt." She wiped her tears away.

"I saw. You can stay with me. I want you to stay with me."

"Your house is butt ugly, Matt."

There was laughter.

"Well, you can fix it up and we'll look for a new house together."

Together. She liked that, but it made her wonder. Why did he want her? She had absolutely nothing to offer. She was homeless. Penniless. Now she couldn't even work. Being a dance teacher with a broken leg was tricky.

"I can't contribute anything right away, Matt, I can't even teach dancing for a while."

"That's okay, princess. I don't care. I only want you. Don't worry about anything. I'll contact immigration and get you an extension on your visa. They'll understand under the circumstances that you can't work straight away."

Jena's head was woozy. She wasn't sure what Matt was talking about. "What visa?"

"Jena." Matt sounded like he was trying really hard to be patient. "What kind of visa do you have?"

She shrugged, then groaned when her ribs protested. "I don't know. They stamped my passport at the airport when I arrived."

"You're here on a visitor's visa?" His voice was unattractively high-pitched. "The standard visa only lasts twelve weeks. You've been living here illegally since it ran out, Jena."

"Oh. I assumed it would be fine. After all, I bought a house. Doesn't that make me a resident?"

"No. Crap, it really doesn't. We need to fix this or you'll get deported. I'm going to have to marry you."

There was howling laughter and cheers. Jena was dizzy. The pain was making her see double. She'd never been good with pain. Some people had really high tolerance for it. She wasn't one of them.

"Did you just propose?" Jena found it hard to focus.

"No. I told you we're getting married. Probably this week. Otherwise you'll get kicked out of the country."

"I think that's a bit extreme," Jena told him. The noise above her head was getting louder. "Nobody knows I don't have a visa, so who's going to kick me out?"

"Jena, try to remember for five bloody minutes that I'm a cop."

"Oh, yeah." Were the earth walls spinning, or was it in her head? "What if I don't want to marry you?"

"I didn't ask. We're doing it."

Part of her knew she should be mad at him. Instead she just felt strange. "Matt, I don't feel so good."

"What is it? What do you feel? Are you bleeding from anywhere?"

"No, I just feel weird. Is the ground moving?"

"Jena, take deep breaths. You're going to be okay." He sounded panicked and very far away. Jena swayed in place. Her ribs made her groan. Her ankle jerked and she whined with pain.

"Jena, listen to me, hold on. We're nearly there."

"Love you, Matt," Jena said softly.

And then she lost consciousness.

. . .

"Jena? Jena?" Matt looked at the men around him in panic. "She's not answering."

"She's probably passed out," the doc said.

"What if there's gas down there? Lack of air? Magenta, what do you know?"

Magenta tossed her bobbed black hair and peered at him, her eyes rimmed with thick black eyeliner. "There's air. There's no gas. Trust me. I know. This mine isn't anywhere near a gas seam. Especially this close to the surface. They didn't use gas of any sort in the mine."

"Right, okay."

Harry patted him on the back. It didn't help. Punching Frank a time or twenty might have eased him a little, but right now the only thing that could make a dent in his stress level was getting Jena out of that hole.

"We're through," Grunt shouted.

There was a cheer. Matt made a move to rush across the beams to the grassy island. Magenta put her hand on his arm. "We've got this. You'll get in the way."

Matt wanted to roar. Instead he nodded. He put his hands on his hips and bowed his head. It was the worst feeling in the world to stand back and do nothing when others were saving the woman he loved. He took a deep breath as he watched his friends work.

The digger had been removed. The drill-bit attachment they'd been using to get deeper was gone. The two large wooden beams stayed in place. A frame rested across them. Attached to the frame was a swing-like construction, with a harness. It hung over the newly drilled hole. The idea was for Jena to sit on the swing and be strapped into it. Then the men would winch her up. Gordon had put most of the contraption together while they waited for the hole to be dug. Magenta was the one to source the harnesses and safety rigging from her caving business.

Magenta strapped on a safety harness and a hard hat. "Okay, I'm going in." She winked at Harry and jumped into the hole, abseiling down to Jena.

"She's an expert," Harry reminded him. "She's also the smallest here. None of those ex-forces guys would get through the hole."

"Magenta wouldn't let them anyway," Matt said.

"True." Harry chuckled. It sounded tense.

The wait was endless. At last the signal was given. Grunt and Lake hoisted Jena up. Matt held his breath until he saw her honey-coloured hair appear in daylight. There was a cheer. Matt ran across the beam to get to her. No one and nothing would have stopped him. The men were laying her on the grass beside the doctor.

"Is she…" Matt fell to his knees beside her.

"She's passed out. Probably too much pain."

As the doc examined her, Matt did the same. Magenta had immobilised her ankle with an inflatable boot. She'd placed a brace around her neck for the ride out of the mine, to stop her head lolling and to prevent any neck injury. Her arms were strapped to her waist to reinforce her ribs. It was a good job. As Magenta climbed out of the mine, he gave her a grateful smile.

"She did good, Matt," Magenta said as she unstrapped her safety hat. "She was in the right spot. The room was pretty stable too. There was plenty of air down there. She would have been fine for a while yet. I think her ankle got to her. It looks bad."

Matt clenched one of Jena's hands in his while stroking her hair with his other hand. "Will she be able to dance?" he asked the doc.

"I hope so," he said. "Let's get her to hospital and find out."

Matt leaned forward and kissed her grubby, tear-stained cheek. "It's going to be okay, princess. I promise."

He stood aside to let the paramedics load her onto a stretcher. Matt followed them over the makeshift bridge to find his family waiting.

"We'll go to the hospital with her," his mum said.

The twins nodded.

"Grunt will take us," Claire said.

Grunt wrapped an arm around Claire's shoulders and she leaned into him. "I'll make sure they're safe. I'll check in with you every half an hour."

"Every fifteen minutes," Matt said.

Grunt grunted. Matt ran a hand through his hair. He wanted to be the one to go with her.

"You can't," his mum said, as though reading his mind. "You need to arrest the bastard who did this."

His eyes shot open as the twins told his mum off for swearing. His mum gave him a quick hug. "Don't worry, son —we'll take good care of her. After all, she's about to become family." And with the first smile he'd seen on her face since her husband died, she followed Grunt to his car.

Matt watched the ambulance until it disappeared. When he looked away from it, it was to find half the men in Invertary watching him, waiting for orders. He nodded his thanks.

"There's been a sighting," Harry said. "The domino boys saw Frank near the loch. They're keeping an eye out."

Matt took a deep breath. "Jason, Rusty, you follow the Glasgow boys to the hospital and hand them over to the local cops."

The men nodded and left.

"Pete, Dougal, you two rope this area off. I don't want anyone near it."

"No problem," Dougal said as he rolled up the sleeves of his surprisingly white shirt. Although he had teamed it with bright red tartan trousers, so he was still Dougal.

"The rest of you are with me," Matt said. "Time for this to end."

Grimly, the men climbed into their vehicles.

CHAPTER 40

The men of Invertary and the women of Knit or Die, who weren't ones to be left out, lined up along the shore of the loch. They watched in stunned bemusement as the most stupid visitor ever to come to the Highlands tried to escape by boat.

"Does he know this is a loch?" Josh watched Frank power away on the tiny motorboat.

Frank flashed a one-fingered salute to the watching crowd.

"There isn't even a road over the other side," Harry said. "There are only bushes, badass cows and old Gilbert's hunting lodge."

"He said he's going to Glasgow." Archie, one of the domino boys, took off his cap and scratched his head in wonder.

"Did anyone tell him a loch is basically a big puddle?" Harry said. "There is no exit. The idiot is landlocked. If he's trying to get to Glasgow, it's going to take him a while."

Archie shrugged. "Might as well go get a bite to eat, then."

The ancient domino boys headed for the pub.

"This is disappointing," Matt said. "I really wanted to hit him."

"You can still hit him," Lake said. "You just need to wait until he figures out he can't do anything but go round in circles. He'll come back to town when he gets hungry."

"Do you think the idiot will come back or try to walk through the gorse on the other side of the loch?" Josh said.

"Frank isn't known for his brain, but he likes his shoes," Joe said. "Kept telling me they cost more than my life was worth. He won't damage his shoes."

The men stood watching the boat in awe.

"I feel a bit lost now," Matt said. "I was all worked up to hit the guy. It's a bit of a letdown."

Mitch patted him on the back. "If it helps, I'll lend you Josh later on. He can wind you up until you're ready to strike out again."

"Happy to oblige," Josh said.

Matt sighed and looked at Lake. "I'm going to the hospital. Can you deal with this?" He pointed in the direction of the idiot on the water.

"I'll call when he runs out of petrol for the motor." Lake's lip twitched.

"The bomb site is under control," Matt said. "The fire crew are there, but I'll tell them to call you if they need anything."

Lake nodded.

"I need more cops," Matt said. "Ever since you foreigners came to town, I've been run off my feet."

"You would be in a boredom coma without us," Josh said.

"Good point." Matt turned to his SUV. "Call if anything turns up."

The men nodded then went back to watching Frank drive his stolen boat.

"What we need," Josh said, "is some fries and a beer. Mitch, run over to the pub and get some takeaway."

"Get it yourself," Mitch said.

Matt shook his head with a grin as he climbed into his car. It was time to see his woman. As he drove, a plan began to form in his mind. He smiled wickedly as he flicked on the hands-free set for his phone. A couple of calls and it would all be in place.

"WHERE'S MATT?" Jena said when she came to.

Her head hurt. Her mouth felt like it had been washed out with sand and her eyeballs were scraped raw every time she blinked. It felt a lot like a hangover.

"He had to stay in Invertary and arrest Frank." Heather, Matt's mom, came into focus. She was smiling down at Jena.

Jena blinked, wincing at the scraping sensation. "Where am I?"

"Hospital. Fort William," one of the twins said as she grinned from the other side of the bed. "You broke a couple of bones when you were sucked underground by the explosion."

The words made the memory rush back at Jena. She closed her eyes and groaned.

There was a smacking sound. "Good job, freakoid, you've upset her." That had to be the other twin.

"Girls." Heather used her mom voice, which was strangely reassuring. "One of you give Jena a drink of water and the other one fetch the nurse."

A cup with a straw appeared in front of her face. She accepted it gratefully.

"Samuel, raise the bed," Heather ordered.

The bed was promptly raised. Jena looked out of the corner of her eye to find Grunt grinning at her.

"Glad you're alive," he said.

"Thanks." Jena shifted on her pillows, groaning at the ache in her side.

She looked down her body and took stock of the damage. Her ribs were strapped beneath the hospital-issue gown she was wearing. Her lower leg was in a bright pink fibreglass cast and her left hand was bandaged. She held up the hand. She didn't remember that one.

"Nasty cut," Heather said. "Same as your head."

Jena reached up with her right hand and, sure enough, there was a dressing attached to her temple.

"Did they have to cut my hair?" Why she was concerned about her hair and not her broken bones she wasn't sure, but it seemed the most important worry.

"No, dear, your hair is fine." Heather patted her hand, and for a moment Jena felt as though she was being mothered. It was nice. Strange, but nice. It brought tears to her eyes. She worked hard to blink them away.

"It was nice of you to come," she told them. "But you don't need to stay. I'm sure Matt will be here when he's finished knocking Frank into next week."

"We're staying," Claire said. Jena knew it was Claire because she was sitting in Grunt's lap.

"You're a member of the family now," Heather said.

Jena felt her bottom lip tremble. She felt stupid. Twenty-six years old and the thought of having a family made her insides turn to custard.

"I'm not. Matt and I aren't even dating." Her words came out all pathetic and trembling.

"Oh, sweetheart," Heather said. "We're the Donaldsons. We don't date. We tend to get married and worry about the other stuff later. Matt proposed to you while you were trapped. So it's a done deal. No getting out of it now."

"He didn't propose, he ordered me."

"Same difference." Heather seemed unconcerned.

"Doesn't it bother you that your son wants to marry me?" Jena demanded. "I'm a mess. My house is rubble. I have four-teen dollars, I mean pounds, in the bank. I don't have a proper job and I can't teach dance like this. My mother can't stand me. My ex-boyfriend tried to kidnap me and turn me into his pet stripper." Her bottom lip wobbled. "I just found out I'm living here illegally. All of my belongings are now under a house. I don't even know where my clothes are. I know I was wearing some when I was rescued. On top of that, everything I touch breaks. And everyone around me gets hurt at some point. I'm the last person you should want your son to marry."

The tears came. She couldn't stop them. She was a joke. A useless waste of space. No good for anything.

"No." At Matt's voice, Jena's head snapped to the door. "You're not the last person I should marry. You're the *only* person I should marry. You're the only woman I *want* to marry."

He stepped into the room. His eyes only for her. Jena chewed her bottom lip as tears fell. She was so relieved to see him. At the same time she knew he should run far, far away from her. "You're only saying that because you feel sorry for me."

Matt burst out laughing. "Silly girl." He stepped up to the bed, sat on the edge and put his palm on her cheek. His thumb brushed away her tears. "You make me laugh. You make me take things less seriously. Your enthusiasm and sense of adventure means every day around you is fun. You're hard-working. You're kind. You're so optimistic you make the sun shine just by being you. You look out for every-one." He leaned forward to press a kiss to her forehead. "You are incredibly sexy. You're unpredictable. Eager to learn. Slightly mad and seriously accident-prone."

Jena gave a sad little laugh.

Matt's beautiful blue eyes held hers. She saw in them the truth of every word. She saw the depth of feeling he had for her. It was all there. Raw and open for her to read.

"Don't send me away, princess," he whispered. His voice husky with emotion. "I need you. Without you I'll become one of those sad, uptight old men who only cares about rules, regulations and how neat his house is. I need you to drive me crazy every day of my life and remind me what I'm living for." He kissed her lips ever so gently. "I'm living for you, princess. You're my soul mate. Don't take that from me."

"I love you so much," Jena whispered. "But I don't deserve you."

He smiled at her, making her heart melt further. She was defenceless against him. "I'll remind you of those words frequently."

She shook her head at him. Matt looked over his shoulder towards the door. "Come on in," he called.

From the looks on his family's faces, they were none the wiser about who he was talking to either. The door opened and the vicar of Invertary Presbyterian Church walked in. Jena shot a confused look at Matt. He held her uninjured hand tight and pinned her with his gaze.

"We're getting married. Now. Here. Don't argue. It's a done deal. Just accept it," he said.

"What?" Jena gaped at the vicar. "Shouldn't I agree to this first?"

"Generally, yes," the vicar said, but didn't seem at all bothered that she hadn't.

Meanwhile, Matt's mum burst into tears as she hugged Matt. "This is wonderful. I love it. Your dad would have loved it. It's exactly the kind of thing he would have done."

She wiped a tear from her eye before giving Jena an

equally enthusiastic hug. Jena winced, and Matt's hand shot out to pull his mom back. "Remember her ribs are cracked."

"Oh, sorry, Jena." His mother fussed over her, and it was kind of nice.

"Right, let's get this over with," Reverend Morrison said.

"Hey," Matt said. "Attitude."

The old man rolled his eyes. "I've got the paperwork. There aren't any rings. So all we need to do is say the vows, sign the certificate and you're done here."

Matt scowled at him before smiling at Jena. "We can have another wedding when you feel better. A proper one. We can go shopping for rings together."

Jena blinked at him. "Is this really happening?"

Heather and the twins laughed as Matt smiled at her. "Oh yes," he said.

"Does she have concussion?" the minister said. "Is she in her right mind? I can't marry her off to you if she doesn't know what she's agreeing to."

"Jena, tell the man you want to marry me," Matt ordered.

She stared at him for a long couple of minutes while everyone in the room seemed to hold their breaths. "Yes, I absolutely want to marry this idiot," she said.

The women squealed with delight. The vicar sighed heavily and Matt winked at her. "Good decision. Well done. But how about less of the idiot stuff?"

Before she could answer, the vicar cleared his throat. "Dearly beloved," he started, and Jena didn't hear anything else.

All she could see, all she was aware of, was Matt's smiling face and his eyes full of love.

Love for her.

Jena Morgan had found a home at last.

EPILOGUE

SIX MONTHS LATER

The frame for their new house was going up, and Jena couldn't wait to see it happen.

"Get up." She bounced on the bed beside Matt.

He groaned and shoved his head under the pillow. "Go away. This is my first day off in months."

"Liar. You were off last weekend."

"I was on call last weekend. There's a difference."

She grabbed the pillow and lobbed it over the room. "You need to get dressed. We have to get to the building site. I want to see the house go up."

Matt rolled onto his back, momentarily distracting her with his pecs. Yum. She shook her head. No. Not yum. There was no time for yum. His eyes sparkled as he guessed what she was thinking.

"Why don't we stay here for a while instead?" He reached for her, but she jumped out of his way.

"I don't want to miss this. Get up and get dressed right now."

He groaned. "Explain to me why I have to be there so you can see it. You can see it perfectly well without me."

"Matthew Donaldson, this is our first home. Probably our last home. We've been planning it for months. This is important. It's something we need to share together."

"Fine, I'll get up, but you owe me."

She clapped her hands and bounced some more as he hauled himself out of bed. "You shower, I'll get your clothes. Hurry." She shooed him in the direction of the bathroom.

Apart from the fact it was exciting to see their house being built, she was also excited that there was an end in sight to living in Matt's horrible police-issue house. No matter how much colour and mess she threw at it, it still seemed sterile. Not to mention the orange glass windows made her want to vomit. She did a little twirl as she waited for Matt to finish in the bathroom. Normally she would have climbed into the shower with him, but she actually wanted to leave the house sometime before lunch.

She could never have guessed how fabulously things had turned out. Her old house had building insurance. It wasn't enough to cover building a new home, but it had been damn close. Then the government had gotten in touch. It turned out they planned to pay damages for the fact her property sat on an unsafe mine. It meant Jena and Matt had more than enough to build the house of their dreams. Not that Matt was bothered. He kept telling her that his savings were now her savings. Which was great, kind, generous, all of those things. She still felt better sharing his savings when she had something for them to share too.

An arm wrapped around her waist and Matt buried his face in the crook of her neck.

"Delicious," he rumbled against her skin. He kissed her shoulder before nuzzling the spot behind her ear that made her go weak at the knees.

She stepped away, thrusting his clothes at him. "No distracting me."

He laughed, the devil. "Are Gordon and Brenda coming?"

Jena nodded. "They're meeting us there."

"I hope they're bringing food."

Jena ignored him. Everything revolved around food for Matt. She was pleased Gordon would be there for the start of their house. He'd really taken her under his wing at the hardware store. She'd learned so much the past few months, and after her house had blown up, Gordon started paying her in money rather than materials. She loved it. She loved everything DIY, and Gordon was talking about her becoming a partner in the business. He said he wanted to change the sign above the door to "Stewart and Daughter". It made her cry— much to Matt's amusement.

"Hurry up," she told him.

"I'd go faster with coffee," he grumbled.

She held up the to-go cup she'd put on the dresser. His eyes lit up.

"Have I told you I love you?" He reached for the coffee.

"Once or twice." She laughed.

At last they managed to get down the stairs and out of the house. Jena wriggled in her seat all the way through a town that looked pretty empty for the time of the morning. Highland folk tended to start their days early, yet there was no one in sight.

"Just think," Jena said, "in a few short months the house will be finished and decorated and we can move in." She grinned wickedly. "Then, of course, we'll have to christen every room."

"Evil woman," he said.

They drove up the quiet country lane towards her land, and Jena could see the field the council had been working in. They were filling the holes the mine made. By the time they finished, the area would be stable and safe. It was slow work, but at some point the field would be covered in grass once again. As they turned the corner to their new build, Jena's jaw dropped. The road was filled with people. It seemed like the whole town was there.

Jena turned to Matt. "Did you know about this?"

"Nope, but are you really surprised?"

Surprised didn't cover it. She was shocked as hell. They squeezed into a parking spot and climbed out to cheers. People were milling around drinking coffee from flasks and chatting.

The Donaldsons descended on the pair. Jena was engulfed in a hug from Heather, who insisted Jena call her Mum. Something Jena loved to do.

"Isn't it exciting?" Heather said.

"Aye, so exciting that Jena hardly slept last night. I'm knackered from all her bouncing around."

"I don't want to hear about what you two do in bed, son," Heather said with a twinkle in her eye.

Claire took her turn to hug them, and Jena grabbed the opportunity to have another look at her ring. Grunt had gone all out on a diamond and sapphire combination. "It is so beautiful." Jena sighed.

Claire looked up at Grunt with adoration. "I love it too. I couldn't have done what you two did. It was romantic, the rush wedding in the hospital, but I'm glad we're going the more traditional route. I'm having a great time planning the wedding, and I wouldn't have wanted to miss out on the ring."

Matt stiffened beside her. "I can get you an engagement ring if you want one."

Jena rolled her eyes. "It's a bit late for that, He-Man."

"I don't want you to feel you missed out."

"I don't." She grinned up at him. "Still, if you want to make it up to me, I saw a real cute ankle bracelet the other day. It would go a long way towards fixing any hurt feelings that may be hiding deep inside."

"Minx." He kissed the tip of her nose.

"When's the wedding?" Jena asked Claire.

"Next May. That gives us the year to plan. Plus, I want a spring wedding."

"Let me know if I can help."

"You're kidding, right?" Claire gaped at her. "You're one of the bridesmaids. I thought you knew."

Jena blinked at her. "You didn't tell me."

"You're family." Claire shrugged. "I assumed you'd figure it out."

Jena was about ten seconds away from smacking her insane sister-in-law. "I've never had a family. How am I supposed to know these things?"

"My bad." Claire winced. "In future I won't assume."

"Good," Jena said. Then pulled Claire in for another hug.

"Any word on the court case?" Grunt asked.

"It'll be another few months yet," Matt said grimly.

The men shared a look that made clear exactly how much they wished they'd dealt with the Frank problem themselves rather than handing it over to the courts. The stupid, dangerous man had eventually figured out the loch didn't lead to Glasgow. He then abandoned the boat as far away from Invertary as he could and tried to walk over a gorse-filled hill. He'd been chased by a herd of Highland cattle. Lake's men waited until he'd tired of running from the cows, and then they'd transported him to Fort William's jail. He was being charged with a whole slew of things, including kidnapping, acts of terrorism and attempted murder. Neither Matt nor Grunt had seen him when he'd been caught, and both of them were still holding a grudge over it. Jena was just pleased it was Frank in jail and not her husband for killing her ex-boyfriend. Last she'd heard, Frank had tried to get the New Jersey mob to help him. They'd disowned him. The strip club he'd "managed" had gone bust. And Candy the stripper was working at McDonald's. Jena grinned at the thought.

"Can I have everyone's attention?" Dougal boomed over the noise. The crowd went quiet. "We're here to christen Matt and Jena's new home."

Jena blushed, and Matt threw an arm around her shoulder. "Not the way you mean," he whispered in her ear.

"As you all know," Dougal carried on, "we weren't invited to the shotgun wedding they had in the hospital." There were good-natured boos. "So we thought we'd turn this into the wedding reception you never had. Even if it is at an ungodly hour of the morning." The crowd parted to reveal a long table covered in food and drink. There was a banner above it saying "Welcome home, Jena and Matt".

Jena felt her throat tighten as tears threatened.

"Please join me in raising your glasses to the happy couple." Glasses, mugs and cups were held high. "Here's to Matt and Jena. May you have a long and happy life together. And here's to your new home in Invertary—may it never blow up." There was laughter.

"To Matt and Jena," peopled shouted.

"Welcome home, princess," Matt said as Jena grinned so wide her face began to hurt.

As she looked around her friends and family, she realised she'd found in Scotland the thing she'd longed for most.

She'd found her family.

She was home at last.

EXCERPT FROM BAD BOY

"I'm going to make a prediction—it could go either way."
Ron Atkinson, former England soccer player and manager

"What are they doing, Muma?"

Five-year-old Katy's nose was pressed up against the kitchen window. Her attention firmly focused on the raucous crowd gathered on the plot of land Flynn Boyle had bought from Abby. The gorgeous flat land that ran between Abby's Victorian house and the stream. The same land that would soon hold his no doubt monstrous house and block her view of the water.

Abby took a deep breath. No one had put a gun to her head and told her to sell to the bad boy of European soccer. Nope. That particularly stupid decision was all on her. She'd been swayed by his movie-star good looks and the fact her bank account was deep in the red.

Clenching her teeth, Abby tried to think beyond the noise. The *incessant* noise. When Flynn turned up with his grotesque RV, her peaceful life had shattered. Squealing giggling girl-women, loud, thrumming music, men shouting at sports on TV and revving engines now filled her days. The noise was never-ending. Day in, day out. Night and day. For two long, long months. She was losing her mind from it.

Abby put down the paring knife she'd been using to slice a carrot and rubbed her temple. It made no difference. The tension headache was still there, taking over her personality, driving her insane.

"Muma." There was a tug at the sleeve of her cream-coloured silk blouse. Her daughter frowned up at her. "What's he doing? Is it another party? Why didn't he invite us? How come he never invites us?"

Katy folded her arms over her blue Elsa princess dress, which she'd teamed with luminous orange gumboots and a yellow woolly hat with a Minion face on it. She had purple eye shadow on her eyebrows and at least twenty strings of sparkling multicoloured beads around her neck. It other words, it was a normal day in the world of Katy fashion.

"It's rude not to invite us to his party." She pouted. "I would invite him to mine. Everybody knows you need to ask the people who live beside you. It's a rule."

Abby ran a hand over Katy's chestnut-coloured hair. There were moments when love for her daughter assaulted her. The depth of it stopped time itself leaving Abby breath-less in wonder. This little, perfect person was hers. Time started again and she smiled at her grumpy little girl.

"It's an adult party, baby. Little girls don't go to adult parties."

Katy waved her arms dramatically. "That isn't fair. It isn't even my bedtime yet. Adult parties are supposed to happen when I'm asleep."

Abby couldn't argue with her logic, although she'd rather the party didn't happen at all. The thought of lying awake for yet another night listening to her inconsiderate neighbour was really too much to bear. "Why don't you play with your Lego? Dinner won't be long."

Katy gave her a look of disgust, one clearly implying her mother wasn't doing enough to get her into the party, and then she stomped off. Abby picked up the paring knife. The vibrations from the thumping bass of Flynn's music worked their way through her body, leaving tense muscles in their wake. She was exhausted. Wound tight enough to snap. And she was so incredibly fed up with cleaning up after the mess Flynn Boyle left in his wake. From dealing with hysterical women banging on her door at midnight, demanding Abby find them a taxi, to mending the fences mown down by his drunken friends after they'd joyridden through her paddocks —Abby was up to her ears in the fallout from selling land to Mr Boyle.

She glared out the window at her hateful neighbour, and froze. Katy was stomping across the field towards the RV, a look of grim determination on her face. Without a second thought, Abby ran to intercept her daughter.

Forgetting she still held the paring knife in her tightly clenched fist.

* * *

Flynn kept a grin pasted to his face and thanked God his sunglasses hid the fact the smile never made it to his eyes. The Ball Babes were in the inflatable pool, whooping it up for the watching men. Their tiny bikinis barely covered their pricey assets, which he appreciated. Although he found himself wondering when plastic had become a valid substitute for the real thing. Sometimes he got to second base with a woman and felt like he had his hands on a waterbed. And what was with all the white-blonde hair? Was there a rule all soccer groupies had to bleach their hair? And why the hell did it bother him when they did?

Some genius had thought to empty a bottle of bubble bath into the pool. It was now filled with foam and frolicking women. He looked around at the leering faces of his former teammates and felt disconnected. This was boring. *He* was bored. And didn't that sum up his mental state. There were near-naked women playing around for his benefit and he'd rather they went home. He wanted to be alone. Alone with his broken leg and broken dreams. He scoffed at himself. Now even his pity party was too pathetic to tolerate.

"Whoa. Grumpy princess alert." Michael, Arsenal's best defender and a legend in the making, pointed his beer bottle in the direction of Abby's house.

Flynn swallowed a groan. Abby McKenzie was a wet dream walking—unfortunately, she had ice in her veins and a deep desire to kill all his joy. She was the fly in his ointment. He thought about it for a minute. Who the hell gave a crap about ointment? She was the fly in his beer. Yeah, much better. She was the rain on his parade. The hair in his soup. The bug up his...

A tiny figure appeared in front of him. Oh hell, it wasn't the ice queen, it was her mini-me. Flynn sat up straight. Where was her owner? Shouldn't she be in a pen, locked up tight with lots of plastic dolls? He flicked his gaze to the women in the pool at the thought of plastic dolls. It was official. He was losing his mind.

The girl folded her arms. Frowned with purple eyebrows and pursed her lips. "It's rude to have a party and not invite me."

"Oh, she is so cute," one of the Ball Babes squealed.

Aye, cute like a piranha.

Flynn blinked at the kid. How the hell was he supposed to deal with this? He had a minimum age limit for dealing with the female species—nineteen. His maximum was twenty-two. Anything younger was alien to him. Anything older wasn't worth his effort.

She tapped the toe of her orange gumboot and waited for his answer. "Well? Why didn't you invite me?"

Flynn rubbed his jaw, absently noting he hadn't shaved in...a while? Hell, he couldn't remember the last time he'd bothered. It didn't seem worth the effort. Very little did anymore.

"I didn't invite you because I didn't want you here, kid."

She narrowed her eyes at him. "That's rude. Are you always this mean? Muma says you're proof pretty isn't the same as nice or smart."

There was laughter. The guys were getting a kick out of his mini-tormentor.

"I don't need to be smart. Your mum is smart enough for all of us." Pretty too, but he wasn't sharing that thought with the kid. "Don't you have to go to bed or something?"

"It isn't even dinnertime. I don't go to bed for hours." She put her fists on her hips. "Don't think I'm going to invite you to my party." She said it like it was a threat.

"I'll live."

She opened her mouth to say something else, but stopped when a loud whoop came from the pool. One of the Ball Babes decided she wasn't getting enough attention and took off her bikini top. She swung it above her head as she jumped up and down in the water, ensuring everybody present got an eyeful of her foam-covered tits—including the kid.

Flynn groaned as the mini-terrorist's eyes went wide. Her jaw dropped. She pointed at the girl and shouted. "I can see her boobs!"

"You have got to be kidding me." Abby's clipped upper-class tones cut through the laughter.

He didn't need to look at her to know she was oozing

343

disapproval. Where he was concerned, Abby always oozed disapproval. Flynn's chin dropped to his chest. He could not get a break. He took a deep breath, let out a sigh and turned his head to the ice queen.

And stopped dead.

Flynn's easy charm faltered and his heart stuttered. The sight was not what he had expected. Abby had transformed. Gone was the calm, controlled demeanour he was used to dealing with. In its place was a wild woman. Her hair was flying, her cheeks were flushed and her eyes sparkled with fury. The ice queen had melted. Flynn felt his shorts tighten with raw hunger at the sight of her replacement. For the first time in months he got a glimpse of the passionate woman he'd spotted at his uncle's funeral. He'd known she was in there somewhere. The sight made him want to grab her and hold on tight.

At least it did until he spotted the knife in her hand.

Flynn struggled to his feet, holding his weight on his good leg. He held out his hands in a placating gesture. Behind him the voices were deadly silent.

"Now, Abby, don't do anything rash."

Her eyes flashed at him before scanning the scene in front of his motorhome. Picnic tables were covered in empty beer bottles and discarded food. The grass was littered with trash. The giant inflatable pool overflowed with bubbles as three Playboy Bunny wannabes stared wide-eyed at the wild woman. Aye, so it didn't look good. It wasn't his fault. He had too much on his mind to keep the place tidy. As for the women…he shook his head. Okay. There was no excuse for them.

The tiny terrorist's arm shot out. She pointed straight at Flynn. "He said he didn't want me at his party."

"Tattletale," Flynn grumbled at her, and she stuck out her tongue.

With an irate wail, Abby stormed into his RV. There was a loud crash and the music stopped dead. Well hell, that wasn't good. A moment later she appeared looking even crazier than seconds before.

Her lips thinned, her gaze focused on the pool and she strode purposely towards it. Flynn rushed to get into her path, but tripped over his weak leg. Michael's hand shot out to grab him before he hit the dirt. The defender thrust Flynn's walking stick into his hand. Flynn looked at it in disgust before turning his attention back to Abby. He was too late to stop her. He could only watch in shocked awe as she repeatedly stabbed the inflatable pool.

The Babes screamed, high-pitched and girly. The noise made him wince. They scrambled out of the side of the pool furthest away from the mad woman. As the pool deflated and water flooded the field, Abby whirled towards Flynn.

"Now, don't do anything you'll regret." Flynn's eyes were on the knife.

She let out a seriously scary screech as she caught sight of the topless woman sneaking towards the RV. "You!" She pointed at the half-naked Babe. "Get dressed. Get some self-respect. Stop flashing yourself at mindless men. Do something with your life."

The Babe gasped before running into the RV. She'd wisely decided to do what the woman with the knife ordered.

Abby spun to him. "You!" She closed her eyes for a second while she worked to control her breathing.

Flynn watched her closely as he willed her success. Control would be good. Really good.

"You," she said again, "will stop playing loud music." She took a step towards him. Her whole body vibrated with fury, making him notice the curves under her prim, yet seriously sexy, dress. "You won't shout in the middle of the night. And neither will your friends. You won't rev engines. Or scream.

Or bang around. You will remember that normal people sleep at night and remain respectfully silent." She took another step, making Flynn's eyes drop to her feet. She was wearing drop-dead sexy heels. They were nude coloured, with a peep-toe that flashed her pale pink nails. He shook his head. What the hell? There was a crazy woman with a knife and he was admiring her feet. He needed to cut back on his pain meds.

She pointed at him. With. The. Knife. "You will stop messing the place up. You will stop throwing orgies in plain view of the neighbours. You will be mindful of the child living next door to you."

Said child gave him a smug smile. He rolled his eyes at her.

Abby stepped closer until he could see the gold flecks in her blazing hazel eyes. "You will stop being an inconsiderate, immature, misogynist moron and grow up. You will do this right now. This minute." Her eyes narrowed. "And if I hear one more peep out of you, or your friends, you won't be pleased with my reaction. Do you understand me?"

For the first time since the tackle that'd destroyed his career, Flynn felt his interest in life spark. No. His interest in *Abby* sparked. A slow smile curved his lips as his hand snapped out to curl around her wrist. She jerked with shock. He held the hand clenching the knife as he leaned in to whisper in her ear.

"You are seriously sexy when you're mad."

Her back went ramrod straight. "This isn't a game, Mr Boyle. My patience with your childish antics, and inconsiderate behaviour, has reached its limit. I won't tolerate it anymore."

"I know." He squeezed her wrist, making her drop the knife.

He could almost feel his teammates' shoulders slump with

relief. Flynn ignored them as he held Abby's gaze with his. They stared at each other for a millennium, as Flynn wallowed in the passion and heat glittering in her eyes.

"Mr Boyle..." she started, but he noticed a waver in her voice, born of the awareness sparking between them.

"Call me Flynn." He slid his hold down her hand and over her fingers before releasing her.

Want flashed in her eyes before she took a wary step away from him.

"Let's go." She held out a hand to the kid.

With one last unreadable look at Flynn, Abby grasped her daughter's hand and stalked back to her house. The kid turned back to him and stuck out her tongue. Flynn couldn't stop a laugh from erupting.

As he watched Abby's curvy behind sway, Michael came up beside him.

"That's a helluva neighbour you've got there. You never mentioned she was so freaking wild. Hot too. Kate Middleton hot. Classy. I like that in a woman."

Flynn noted the lust-filled interest in his teammate's voice and scowled. "She's off limits."

Michael raised an eyebrow at him. "Are you sure?"

"I am now." Flynn watched Abby shut the door quietly behind her. As though the stately Victorian house was too refined for slamming doors.

"Did you get that?" An excited voice snapped his attention back to the people who invaded his space. "Please tell me you got it. That woman just propelled this documentary into the stratosphere. This is BAFTA material."

Flynn let out a disgruntled sigh. He'd forgotten about the damn camera crew. He turned to the producer.

"You can't use the footage."

The slimy weasel grinned. "You signed a waiver. Full access to your life for the duration of the shoot. The only stipulation you made was that we had to stay in this one-horse town. Everything else is fair game." He cast a lecherous glance towards Abby's house. "Looks like this shoot is going to be more interesting than I thought."

"My neighbour didn't sign a waiver. She isn't part of your show."

"She was on your property. Attacking your belongings. Shouting at you." The weasel laughed. "Seeing as this programme is about your life, she's just become part of the show." He turned to his mousy assistant. "Find out all you can about the neighbour. We need to come up with a way to give her more airtime." The terrified girl nodded, but her eyes darted nervously to Flynn.

"This documentary is about my life after injury. It isn't about my neighbour." Flynn kept his tone even. Cold. It was the voice he used to scare the crap out of opponents.

The weasel was too far gone with thoughts of BAFTA Awards to care. "You said it—your life. And she's in it." He turned his back on Flynn. "I want highlights on the web within the hour. Contact the news. Maybe we can get it picked up in time for the ten o'clock slot. People are going to see this teaser and wet themselves with excitement." He rubbed his hands together.

Flynn clenched his fists and took a step towards the man. A firm palm hit his chest to halt him.

"Not worth it," Michael said. "Call your lawyer. Agent. Whatever. Get the suits to sort it out."

"My agent got me in this mess in the first place." And wasn't Flynn the prize fool for letting it happen.

Michael shook his head. "I told you at the time you needed to spend some energy on vetting a new agent instead of screwing around. I told you about the rumours. Barney had some dodgy deals going on. The guy is only interested in money."

"Thanks for the I-told-you-so. It's always really helpful when I get them." Flynn rubbed a hand over his face. "You're right, though. I shouldn't have signed with the first agent who sucked up after Gerry retired."

"Barney saw a cash cow and went for it." Michael's nod was knowing. "The guy can be convincing."

"Aye, but I made it easy for him. I wasn't exactly paying attention." His memories of the months before his old agent retired were a little hazy. He remembered a buxom brunette, a vintage Corvette, too much Italian wine and a speeding ticket outside Milan. But he didn't remember much about screening new agents.

"He probably set this show up because he's pissed you cut off his cash supply."

"My heart bleeds for him, how he must have suffered when I got injured out of the game." He glared at Brian. The look of glee on the guy's face made Flynn's fingers twitch. "I want to hit him."

Michael's eyes were hard as he stared at the producer. This wasn't the first time the team had dealt with the man. "We all do. Call your people. Just don't hit the guy on air. No matter how tempting it is."

Flynn took a deep breath. His old teammate was right. Flynn losing his cool would just make better TV. He needed to end this. Not help it along. With a grunt of frustration, he grabbed his phone and made the call.

Get Bad Boy now to keep reading!

ABOUT THE AUTHOR

I'm a Scot, living in New Zealand and married to a Dutch man. I write contemporary romance with a humorous bent – this is mainly due to the fact I have an odd sense of humour and can't keep it out of anything I do! If I wasn't a writer, I'd like to be Buffy the Vampire Slayer, or Indiana Jones. Unfortunately, both these roles have already been filled. Which may be a good thing as I have no fighting skills, wouldn't know a precious relic if it hit me in the face and have an aversion to blood. When I'm not living in my head, I'm a mother to two kids, several pet sheep, one dog, four cats, three alpacas, two miniature horses, eight guinea pigs and an escape artist chicken.

Printed in August 2019
by Rotomail Italia S.p.A., Vignate (MI) - Italy